and a

Half Motives

A Rose Gardner Mystery

Books by Denise Grover Swank

Rose Gardner Mysteries
Twenty-Eight and a Half Wishes
Twenty-Nine and a Half Reasons
Thirty and a Half Excuses
Falling to Pieces (novella)
Thirty-One and a Half Regrets
Thirty-Two and a Half Complications
Picking Up the Pieces (novella)
Thirty-Three and a Half Shenanigans
Rose and Helena Save Christmas (novella)
Ripple of Secrets (novella)
Thirty-Four and a Half Predicaments
Thirty-Four and a Half Predicaments Bonus Chapters (ebook only)
Thirty-Five and a Half Conspiracies
Thirty-Six and a Half Motives

Rose Gardner Investigations
Family Jewels (November 2016)

Magnolia Steele Mystery
Center Stage
Act Two (September 2016)

The Wedding Pact Series
The Substitute
The Player
The Gambler
The Valentine (short story)

Bachelor Brotherhood Series
Only You
Until You (spring 2017)

Thirty-Six

and a

Half Motives

A Rose Gardner Mystery

Denise Grover Swank

Chapter One

Sometimes life gives you what you want, but it comes at a price you didn't want to pay. Five days had passed since I'd spoken to my almost-fiancé Mason, and I was sure I'd lost five pounds.

"Did you starting writing up the Westfield proposal?" Neely Kate asked from her office chair. My best friend hadn't been working very long at my landscaping office, but she was catching on quickly. I'd already taught her how to write up estimates.

I leaned my shoulder into the frame of one of the large windows at the front of the office, keeping my gaze on the courthouse. Mason was probably inside, filling in for the Fenton County District Attorney, who had been arrested and removed from his office two days earlier. While Mason hadn't yet decided if he planned to stay in Fenton County, Neely Kate had heard that he'd been moved up to his old boss's position.

I wanted to tell him congratulations. I wanted to know how he felt not only about the D.A.'s arrest, but also about the arrest and arraignment of J.R. Simmons—the man whose shadow had loomed over us for months. But I couldn't ask. Mason now knew that I was the infamous Lady in Black, and he was taking some time to work through my betrayal.

While he hadn't called, he had sent me a text asking if I was okay.

I had wanted to text back: *No. Nothing is okay without you.*

Of course, he knew that already. He knew my heart was broken, and in all fairness, his was broken, too. But I wouldn't lie to him—not anymore—so I'd said the only truthful thing I could come up with that didn't sound desperate or whiny.

I'm here.

Neely Kate's voice snapped me out of my thoughts. "*Rose.*"

I slowly turned my head to look over my shoulder at her. "What?"

She stood and grabbed our coats off the coat tree, then stooped to grab my purse off the floor. "We're getting out of here."

I turned away from the window. "No, you're right. I need to finish that estimate."

"I can see how determined you are to get to it," she said dryly, "while trying to sprout X-ray vision to catch a glimpse of Mason in the courthouse."

I considered protesting, but what would be the point? She knew me too well. Besides, anyone with half a brain knew there was no arguing with Neely Kate.

She handed me my coat. "Come on."

I took it from her and slipped my arms into the sleeves. "Where are we going?"

"You'll find out when we get there. You're driving."

"Like that's a surprise," I grumbled. "Your car's still broken down."

As soon as the words left my mouth, I regretted them. Neely Kate's husband was a mechanic, and her car was a piece of junk he'd babied way past its expiration date. But he'd left her a little over a week ago, and as far as I knew, she'd only heard from him a couple of times. She refused to discuss it.

"Neely Kate . . . I know you don't want to talk about Ronnie, but since Mick Gentry is dead . . . Ronnie's free of him. Why is he still in hiding?"

I'd been shocked to learn that my best friend's husband had sworn his loyalty to a criminal who was trying to take over the Fenton County crime world. It was yet another thing Neely Kate refused to talk about. "He says everything in the underworld is still shaken up."

Was it? I hadn't talked to Skeeter Malcolm, the Fenton County crime lord, since we'd pulled off the sting that had ended in J.R. Simmons's arrest. There should have been numerous charges, but so far the only ones filed were murder in the second degree and assault. The murder charge would be hard to evade, considering multiple witnesses had seen J.R. stab Skeeter's rival, Mick Gentry. The assault charge came from J.R. slashing my arm with a knife and holding the knife to my throat. Joe Simmons, J.R.'s son and my former boyfriend, but more importantly the current Fenton County Chief Deputy Sheriff, had assured me more charges were coming. The murder charge would hold him until they could build a more solid case against him.

But while Skeeter had faced his old mentor and won, I was certain he considered his win a disgrace. Rather than face J.R. head on, like he would have preferred, he'd let me try to trick J.R. into admitting to a few of his many crimes, including concocting false evidence to suggest that I'd hired someone to kill my mother. The significance of what Skeeter had done for me had finally started to sink in over the past few days. He'd overlooked his own pride—and risked his reputation—to save me.

And I had given him nothing in return.

One more thing to toss onto my enormous pile of guilt.

Nevertheless, I had figured his position in the crime world would be safe now that his chief rival was dead—but apparently I'd been wrong about that, too.

"Do you want me to talk to Jed?" I asked Neely Kate. "I can get him to talk to Skeeter about Ronnie."

"No." Her tone was blunt.

"Don't you want to have this all settled?"

She gave me an emotionless stare. "I've filed for divorce."

"You did *what*?"

Neely Kate shook her head and opened the door, flipping the sign in the window to *Closed*. "I don't want to talk about it."

"But . . . how . . . ?" I stammered, completely flabbergasted. "When? You didn't even tell me."

"I talked to Carter on Monday."

"*Carter Hale?* But he's a defense attorney." He was *my* defense attorney. Or at least he had been before the charges against me were dropped.

She gave me an irritated shrug. "He says it's a simple enough case. Plus, he's going to give me a discount."

My eyes narrowed. "What kind of discount?"

"Never you mind about that," she grumbled as I followed her out onto the sidewalk before locking the door behind me.

I turned to face her and took her hand in mine. "Neely Kate. Don't rush into anything. You need to let this sit for a bit. You've been through so much the last few weeks—your miscarriage, Ronnie leaving . . . Just take a breather before you make a decision like this."

Her face hardened. "Why? Are you tired of me living with you?"

"What kind of nonsense is that? I love having you there, but it seems selfish. I'm lonely for Mason . . ." My voice trailed off as my thoughts once again shifted to Mason. We weren't married, but we'd been living together. Had he already decided to leave me for good? Was he just waiting for the dust to settle before he gave me the news and came to get his stuff?

Tears stung my eyes, but I reminded myself that this wasn't about me. This was about my best friend. "Neely Kate, I love you. You know that. You can live with me until you're a hundred and two. I'm just suggesting that you take your time, because I don't want you to have any regrets. I'll support you no matter what you do."

Her face softened. "I'm sorry. It's just that Ronnie's family is giving me fits, and Ronnie hasn't even been served the papers yet. The investigator Carter hired can't find him."

"Then how does his family know?"

"Because my fool cousin told his friend, who told his friend, who knows Ronnie's brother."

I frowned. "Shouldn't his family be more concerned that he's been working for a crime lord?"

"They don't know."

I sighed. "What a mess."

Neely Kate straightened her back and plastered a smile on her face. "Come on. We have somewhere to be."

"And where exactly is that?"

"A surprise," she said, leading the way to my truck parked at the curb.

"You *do* know you have to tell me at some point since I'm driving."

She laughed. "And *you* know that I'll always tell you where to go."

"That's what I'm worried about," I grumbled in a teasing tone as I climbed into the truck cab. Once we were buckled in, I cast a glance at Carter Hale's office across the street. I'd been meaning to pay him a visit anyway, but now I had a really good excuse.

I intended to find out why he was helping my friend. I had a feeling there was more to it than his obvious crush.

Chapter Two

Neely Kate told me to pull into the parking lot of Magpie's, a new restaurant close to the landscaping nursery I owned with my sister Violet and Joe. I'd noticed the renovation on the old service station over the past few weeks, but I hadn't realized it had opened.

I gave her a questioning look, but she shrugged. "I know we usually eat at Merilee's, but I thought we'd try something new."

Was she trying to protect me? Mason and I had gone to Merilee's together more often than I could count. I suspected he was too busy to get away, so there was little chance of running into him there.

That thought spiraled into a worry, like most of my thoughts tended to do lately. Who was making sure he ate? Over the last three months, I had been the one who had always brought him lunch when he got busy. Had his assistant taken over that task?

"No thinking about Mason," Neely Kate said in a firm voice.

"Who said I was?"

"Well . . ." she drawled. "Other than the fact that you think about him pretty much nonstop, the goofy look on your face confirmed it." Then she made an exaggerated dreamy face.

I laughed. "I do not look like that."

"I'm going to start taking photos and posting them on Facebook."

"You wouldn't."

She gave me a taunting grin. "Try it again and see what happens. I'm starving. Let's eat."

With that, she got out of the truck and headed toward the restaurant. Instead of going in, she whipped open the door with a flourish and held it for me.

Shaking my head, I followed her. But when I walked into Magpie's, I was shocked to see it was full of guests—and I knew most of them. Jonah and his girlfriend Jessica were there along with Bruce Wayne, Mason's mother Maeve, Deputy Randy Miller, and my sister Violet.

I stopped short inside the doorway. "What's going on?"

As she pushed me inside, Neely Kate whispered into my ear, "I thought you needed a reminder that you're not alone."

Leave it to Neely Kate to set aside her own problems to do something like this for me. I spun around and wrapped my arms around her. "But I knew I wasn't alone, Neely Kate. I have you."

She pulled back and smiled at me with teary eyes.

"Hey, now. I want a hug, too!" Maeve said, wrapping me up in her arms. I rested my cheek on her shoulder as I squeezed, reassured that even if Mason remained lost to me, I still had his mother—the closest thing to a loving mother I'd ever had.

I moved down a receiving line of friends, their smiles and embraces restoring more and more of me to myself. Violet held me a little longer than the rest, rubbing my back in soft circles, just like when we were little. It reminded me of how she'd always protected me from Momma, who'd made both of our lives hell.

I looked deep into her eyes. "I miss you, Vi."

"I miss you, too," she said with a trembling smile. "I don't know what I'd do without you." She looked as exhausted as I felt. There were dark circles under her eyes, and now that I was studying her, she looked like she'd lost ten pounds.

"Vi, are you okay?"

"I'm fine," she said dismissively, taking a step back. "But I'm starving. Let's order."

We all sat down, except for Jonah, the pastor of the New Living Hope Revival Church. He stood behind his chair, resting his hands on the back. The bright, unnaturally white smile that had made his sermons a TV sensation lit up his face. "Now Rose, I'm sure you think this is just an ordinary lunch, but it's a celebration of your charges being dropped. Every single one of us would have moved heaven and earth to help you. It seemed only fitting to celebrate, even if it's several days after the fact."

"Thank you, Jonah," I said, but part of me was sad. There were people missing—Mason, Skeeter, and Jed. Even Joe, although it would have been strange for the person who'd arrested me in the first place to come to my exoneration party. Of course, Joe claimed it had been part of his plan to help me, but he'd never deigned to include me in the details. "I don't know what I'd do without all of you."

I glanced at Bruce Wayne, my landscaping business partner, who'd helped me get mixed up with Skeeter Malcolm in the first place. We'd had a fight before my kidnapping, and things hadn't felt right between us since.

He squirmed in his seat. "Let's eat. I'm starving," he said, but he lifted his gaze to catch my eye, and the smile he flashed told me all was forgiven.

We spent the next hour eating and laughing, and I realized how lucky I was to have this group of people in my life. Even if Mason didn't change his mind and come back to me, I would get through this. I would be devastated, but life would go on. My breakup with Joe had taught me that.

When we finished, everyone hugged me goodbye, but Violet stayed behind, casting an anxious glance to Neely Kate. "Do you think I could steal Rose for a bit? I can drop her off at your office."

My best friend, fully aware of the turmoil in my relationship with my sister, gave me a questioning look.

I nodded, then dug the truck keys out of my purse. "You head on back to the office. I'll be there in a bit."

"Okay." She looked reluctant but took the keys and left.

"Do you want to talk here?" I asked, scanning the mostly empty restaurant.

"Actually . . ." Violet glanced down at the floor for a moment before meeting my eyes. "I'd like to go somewhere else, if you don't mind. Somewhere more private."

That surprised me. "Okay."

I followed her to her car, the booster seat and toddler car seat in the back reminding me that I hadn't seen my niece and nephew in weeks. "How are Ashley and Mikey?"

A soft smile covered her face as she started the car. "They're great." She paused. "They miss you."

"I miss them, too. I'm sorry I've been too busy to stop by. Are you going out this weekend? I could babysit."

She slowly shook her head. "No. Me and Brody are done."

"I won't judge you, Violet." Not after committing so many sins of my own. My sister had carried on an affair with the mayor of Henryetta for months before breaking up with my brother-in-law—only, she'd pretended the relationship had started *after* she and Mike split. Brody had gone back to his wife, but for a while, he and my sister had continued their affair, putting them both under fire from the citizens of Henryetta.

"I appreciate that," she said softly. "I do deserve better, I think . . . despite everything I've done."

"Me too. But maybe you just want to go out by yourself . . . or with your friends."

"Thanks, but I want to spend as much time with the kids as I can." She gave me a quick smile, then turned her gaze back to the road.

Violet had always been a doting mother, but something about the way she spoke about her children now set me on edge. It was clear she wanted to tell me something, and I was starting to dread the conversation. I looked at the road and realized that she was taking us to the Henryetta Park.

Not long after, she pulled into a parking space in the nearly vacant parking lot, then turned off the car and got out, leaving me to follow. Once I joined her, she led the way toward the splash area.

A lump filled my throat. Last June, I'd let go of my inhibitions by playing in the water with my then-four-year-old niece—and I'd dragged Violet in with me. That seemed like ages ago now. Far longer than eight months.

She didn't stop until we reached the benches on the opposite side, overlooking the play area. It looked sad and desolate with the dry spigots sticking out of the concrete and twisted metal poles.

We sat down, and my heart beat like a scared rabbit's while I waited for Violet to speak.

She took a deep breath, then turned to me with a sad smile. "I'm sick."

Fear crept down my spine and spread through my limbs. "Okay," I said, forcing a matter-of-fact tone. "Have you seen the doctor?"

"Several." She looked down for several seconds before glancing up and staring across the play area. "I have something called lymphoma, and the doctors say I need to go to Texas for treatment."

I struggled to keep my composure. I'd known about the doctor's appointments, but I wasn't prepared for this. "Why can't you have your treatment done here? Or in Little Rock?"

"They say it's too advanced. That my best chance is at MD Anderson." She clasped her hands together, squeezing so tightly I worried she would break her fingers. "But I need to ask a favor."

"Anything," I said, choking a little on the lump in my throat. "Do you want me to come? Do you want me to take the kids? Just tell me."

She finally turned and looked at me, a soft smile on her face. "I love you, Rose. Even if you say no."

"Why would I say no?" I protested. "You haven't even asked me yet."

She pushed out a sigh, then shifted her gaze back to the fountains. "Remember when we came here last summer? And you dragged me out to play in the water with you and the kids?" She paused. "I was so scared. Aunt Bessie had just told us that Momma wasn't your mother, and I was sure I was going to lose you."

"I know we've had our differences, Vi. But we're sisters." My laugh sounded small and scared to my own ears. "We're supposed to fight. We're stuck with each other. That's the beauty of family."

"But you found your own life after that, and I was so happy for you, even if I was jealous." Her admission was no surprise. She'd confessed the same thing months ago.

She shifted on the bench, turning to face me. "You were still a girl when Momma died, but you've grown into a beautiful woman, inside and out. I'm so proud of the woman you've become. Strong and independent. I hope Ashley grows up to be just like you. Will you make sure that happens?"

The blood rushed from my head. "Violet, you're scaring me. What did the doctors say?"

"Lymphoma is cancer, Rose. And it's bad. It's in my bone marrow. I have to have chemo and a bone marrow transplant, and even then . . . well, it might not work out."

I stuffed down my rising hysteria. Violet needed me to be strong. "But there's a chance, right? That's why you're going there?"

"Yeah, but I have to find a bone marrow match."

"Oh." The realization of what she was about to ask hit me, followed closely by a new terror.

"The chance of you being a match isn't the greatest since Dora was your mother, but . . ."

"Violet, there's something I need to tell you."

She grabbed my hands. "Don't tell me no yet. Please? I didn't want to ask, but the chance of finding a match in the national donor list is so small." For the first time, she started to cry. "Ashley and Mikey . . . they need their mother."

"Violet," I choked out, tears stinging my eyes. "Stop. Of course I'll be tested." I squeezed her hand back as hard as I could. "But there's something you need to know. Something I haven't had a chance to tell you yet."

"Okay," she said, nodding and looking so hopeful my heart hurt.

"Over the last few weeks, I've done a lot of digging into Dora's life."

"I know," she said. "Mason told us. That's why J.R. had you arrested. Because Dora had evidence you could use against him. A journal Joe took from you."

"But Mason didn't tell you everything." I took a deep breath. "Dora had an affair with Paul Buchanan, the son of the factory owner. He was married, but he planned to leave his wife and marry Dora."

"*What?*"

"Paul was killed in a car accident. Only, it wasn't an accident. His sister cut his brake lines. Just like what happened to Dora."

She sat back, her eyes wide. "What are you saying?"

I held on tight to her hand. "Dora had an affair with Daddy, but then she had one with Paul. Somewhere in that time period, she got pregnant with me. Her best friend Hattie thinks Paul was my father, but it could also be Daddy. I think Beverly thought so, too, and she killed Dora to keep her quiet. Then Daddy and Momma ended up raising me, of course."

"Oh, my God." Her face became so pale and her voice so quiet I worried she was about to pass out. "You're not my real sister."

"Violet," I said, trying to remain calm. "I still might be. Beverly and Hattie were sure I was Paul's daughter, but why would I have the gift of sight if Daddy's mother wasn't my blood relative?"

She shook her head, her eyes wide. "I have no one."

My back tensed, and I squeezed her hand tight. "You stop that right now, Violet Mae Beauregard," I said in a firm tone. "After the whole Momma mess, I thought we'd already established that we were sisters even if we had different mothers. Family isn't blood, Vi. Family is being there no matter what. And I'm *your sister* no matter what, even if I find out I was spawned in a cabbage patch. I'm here. I will do whatever you need." I shook her hand. "You will fight this, and you will beat it—do you understand me?"

She nodded, her eyes full of unshed tears.

"How soon until you leave?"

She sniffed. "They want me there in a couple of days. I leave the day after tomorrow."

That soon? My mind struggled to keep up. "Do you need me to watch the kids?"

"No, Mike's going to take them. His parents are going to help."

"Where do I need to go to be tested?"

"Um . . ." She hiccupped, fighting tears. "The Henryetta Medical Clinic." She tried to open her purse, but her hands were shaking too much to work the clasp.

"Violet." I grabbed her arms and pulled her into a hug, stroking the back of her head. "It's going to be okay."

A dam of tears burst loose, and she cried against my shoulder, heavy sobs that shook her entire body, and I clung to her, trying to assure her that I was the one who would be her anchor in this storm. She'd carried me through more tribulations than I could count.

I couldn't help but think back to that summer afternoon, how we'd lain under the full trees on a blanket after splashing around in the water park. How Violet and I had held hands and cried over the revelation that we were half-sisters. And how Violet had confessed her fear of losing me.

But now I was the one afraid of losing her.

"I love you," I said softly. "You're my sister, and I will love you forever, no matter if we're angry with each other or not. Don't you ever forget it, okay?"

She nodded and leaned back. "We need to talk about the nursery and the house."

I shook my head. "No, Violet. Not now."

"Yes, Rose. *We do.* We have to be practical about this. I could be gone for weeks or months. I have to make sure everything's in place."

"Months?"

She held my gaze. "I don't know how long I'll be gone. We have to plan for the worst."

The worst. I'd experienced too much of *the worst* in my life. I didn't want to think that way now, not when my sister's life hung in the balance. "Our daddy is my father. I'll be a match."

She gave me a patient smile. "Even if he is, there's only a slim chance you'll be a match."

Part of me wanted to offer to have a vision, but I was terrified of what I'd see. I wasn't sure I could handle seeing my sister's death, let alone blurting out that the trip might be hopeless. Some things weren't meant to be known. "Let me get tested. Then we'll deal with the rest. You have to think positive, Violet."

She cracked a grin and nodded. "Yes, ma'am. But we still have to talk about the nursery." She paused to make sure I was listening. "Anna is still so new, but she's learned a lot. I think she can handle most of the day-to-day operations, and Maeve has agreed to help out."

"Maeve? She knows?"

"She guessed something was up. And I've already told her and Anna that I'll be gone for awhile. Just not the full details. I wanted to tell you first."

"What about Hilary's baby nursery plans? I thought you were going to decorate her baby's room."

"I gave her some ideas and left her to do the rest. I've been too tired."

"I've known you weren't feeling well for weeks, but I was too self-absorbed—"

"Rose, stop." Pinching her lips, she shook her head. "This isn't your fault. And if you'd asked, I would have lied and told you everything was fine. But now it's time to come clean. I need you to help me."

I nodded, biting my lower lip to keep it from quivering. "Okay. If you think Anna's capable, I'll let her run the nursery. I can have Joe check in on her since she seems to hate me."

"What are you talking about?" she asked in surprise. "Why would she hate you?"

I shook my head, refusing to confess my paranoia. This wasn't about me. "Never mind, just a weird feeling. But since Joe's part owner, he'll need to step up. Have you told him yet?"

"No." She swallowed. "Like I said, I wanted to tell you first."

I pushed out a breath. "Okay. Then tell him that I'll only step in if he thinks I'm needed. Otherwise, I'll leave it to Anna and Maeve." It made me feel better to know Maeve would help oversee everything. But then a new thought struck me. "Oh, my word. You're going there alone! I can come—"

"No," she said softly, "Aunt Bessie's coming with me." She grimaced. "I only told her before you because I asked for her help."

"Oh." I searched her face. "Are you sure you don't want me to come?"

"For weeks?" She shook her head. "No. You have your own problems to sort out. I still can't believe Mason left you like that. Especially right after you were kidnapped. What is that man thinking?"

"You can't blame him, Violet. I did something that hurt him terribly. He has every right to be upset with me." I swallowed my tears. "I only hope he finds it in his heart to forgive me."

"What could you have possibly done?" Violet asked in disbelief.

I shook my head. "This is about *you*, not me. Will you take me to get tested? I want to get it done right away."

"Of course. Thank you."

"Is there anything else I can do for you?"

She studied me for several seconds and then stood. "No, you're already doing it."

I got to my feet and took her hand in mine. "Okay, but I want to come visit you in Texas, all right?"

She squeezed back. "I'm counting on it."

Chapter Three

Violet sat with me while I had my blood drawn in the clinic, then dropped me off in front of my office downtown. I gave her a long hug, pushing my worries aside as best as I could. When it came down to it, she had to be okay. I couldn't imagine my life without her.

I stood on the sidewalk, waving goodbye as she drove away. When I turned to go inside, I saw Neely Kate through the window, focused on her computer screen. Something made me stop before going in. I couldn't do anything else to help Violet, but maybe I could still make things better for Neely Kate.

It was time to pay Carter Hale a visit.

Besides, I didn't just want to grill him about what he was up to with my best friend. I wasn't happy with the slow wheels of justice in J.R. Simmons's case, and since Mason and I weren't on speaking terms right now, and since Joe's answers were always carefully worded to placate me, I needed to talk to someone else who might know something.

Greta, Carter's receptionist, looked up from her desk when I walked through the door.

"Hi, Rose. What are you doing here? Carter said your legal troubles were all cleared up."

"They are . . . kind of. I was wondering if he was in. I need to talk to him about some follow-up issues."

"Sure, just let me buzz him," she said, picking up the phone. I half expected him to tell her no, but to my surprise, she gave me a warm smile. "He says to go on back."

His door was ajar when I got to the end of the short hall. I pushed it open and found him sitting at his desk, his feet kicked up, his grin stretching from ear to ear. "Why, Rose Gardner, to what do I owe the honor of this visit?"

"I thought I'd stop by to chat," I said, stepping through the doorway.

His eyes lost some of his sparkle, but his grin remained in place. "I'm not able to discuss Ms. Colson's case with you, no matter how close the two of you are. She's asked me to keep it strictly confidential."

That would have surprised me if I hadn't known Neely Kate's cousins' penchant for nosiness. I wouldn't put it past them to needle Carter for information. But now I couldn't very well ask him any questions about the divorce papers. I'd have to swing the conversation back later. "Well, I'm not here to ask about her, so I guess you're in the clear."

He sat up, swinging his feet to the floor. "If that's the case, then why don't you close the door behind you and take a seat?" He motioned to the chairs in front of his desk.

I shut the door and perched on the same chair I'd sat in a week ago, back when I was still facing murder charges. Which got me thinking—we still didn't know a thing about the man who'd bailed me out of jail. "I wanted to see if you know what's going on with J.R.'s case, and if you found out anything about Glenn Stout."

He laughed. "You don't beat around the bush, do you?"

"Did Glenn Stout pick up the million dollars he posted as my bail?"

"Nope."

"So the money's still sitting there?"

"Yep."

"Who leaves one million dollars sitting around?" I asked in disbelief.

He winked. "*That* is the million dollar question."

I shot him a glare. "Very funny."

He sat back in his chair. "In all seriousness, I suspect he's waiting until things die down, hoping he can pick it up without someone noticing."

"Is that likely to happen?"

"Not a snowball's chance in hell. Although, frankly, other than your boyfriend, no one's paying much attention."

I sat up. "Mason's watching?"

"Yeah, he's given strict orders to the court clerks to call him the moment someone shows up to pick up the money."

I wasn't prepared for the hope that warmed my chest. Mason still cared.

"But we're watching, too," Carter said in a slow drawl.

"And why do you care?" I asked.

"Because it's a true mystery, Lady. And any mystery man with that much cash is bound to be bad news."

"But why do *you* care? I'm not your client anymore."

"You really believe that?" He released a short chuckle. "I'm still *very much* your attorney."

"Why?"

"More like who. Skeeter Malcolm doesn't buy the story that J.R. Simmons orchestrated your kidnapping. He believed the bastard when he denied it. If that's true, whoever did it is still on the loose. Not to mention that J.R. definitely has it out for you now, if he didn't before."

"He's worried about J.R. coming after him?"

"No. More like he's worried about J.R. coming after *you*."

"But J.R.'s in jail—or at least he's about to be." At least that's what I told myself when I got worried. That J.R. was no threat to me now. Joe had told me that he was being transferred from the Henryetta Hospital to the Fenton County Jail that very day. The doctors had declared him ready to be moved out of the hospital even though he was still recovering from the gunshot wound to his thigh—courtesy of me.

"We all know he hasn't been neutered yet. J.R. Simmons's reach hasn't been eliminated just because he has a sheriff's deputy watching him."

Was Mason worried about me, too? He hadn't said, and Joe sure didn't seem concerned. But I'd been the one to take down J.R. It made sense he'd seek some kind of retribution.

"Don't you be worryin', Lady," Carter said in a patronizing tone. "You're under a watchful eye."

"What? Who?" But I instantly knew. "Why didn't Jed tell me he was watching over me?"

"They didn't say. I suspect Deveraux wouldn't appreciate the interference, but Skeeter and Jed have refused to let you go unprotected. Jed and Merv have been taking turns watching you 24/7." He winked. "But you didn't hear that from me."

I hadn't even suspected, but I hadn't been looking, either. After everything I'd been through, that was pretty stupid of me.

"But back to Glenn Stout . . ." Carter drawled. "It's in Skeeter's best interest to draw him out. You can bet he won't let this drop until he's unmasked him."

"And the courier? Sam Teagen? What about him?"

Carter held his hands out at his sides. "Disappeared into thin air."

I bit my lip, deciding to share something I'd previously dismissed. "Last Friday—the day after J.R.'s arrest—I thought I saw someone suspicious across the street from my office, around the courthouse. I'm pretty sure he was watching me. I went to confront him, but I lost sight of him somewhere around the antique store."

Carter sat up in his chair, releasing a grunt. "Why are you only telling me about this now? What did Deveraux say? Did he look into it?"

I shrugged, trying to play it off. "I didn't tell Mason."

"Why the Sam Hill not?" he asked. Then he glared at me. "Because he left you?"

I gaped at him. He looked annoyed.

"What? It wasn't that hard to figure out. Skeeter's known since Friday night. Neely Kate confirmed it when she came to see me on Monday."

I lifted my eyebrows, getting irritated. Did everyone know my private business? "I had no idea that Skeeter was a gossipmonger."

Carter laughed. "He always has his ear to the ground. You should know that by now."

I could have argued that Skeeter kept his finger on the pulse of the county's underworld, not the *Henryetta Gazette*'s gossip column. But we both knew that for me, he would make an exception.

"Skeeter knows you've been on your own, and like I said, he's made sure you're protected."

I hated to admit it, but it did make me feel better to know Jed and Merv were looking out for me. "I don't understand why you're still my attorney." I paused, deciding now was as good a time as any to swing our discussion back around to Neely Kate. "And I had *no idea* that you were now an expert on divorce law."

A slow grin spread across his face as he sat back in his seat. "And there it is."

"What?" I asked defensively.

"I knew you were here about Neely Kate."

"I came to see my attorney for an update on my ongoing troubles." I lifted my chin. "But yes, Neely Kate's my best friend, and it's my duty to make sure you have her best interests in mind."

"Ms. Gardner," he drawled, "Ms. Colson came to me seeking representation. I'm providing a service."

"Cut the crap, Carter. Anyone can see you like her."

He smirked. "You know, I actually used to like you until you became a thorn in my ass."

"You know what I'm talking about."

He pushed out a huge sigh. "Rose, I assure you that I'm not up to something devious or underhanded. I encouraged Neely Kate not to act rashly, but she insisted on drawing up the papers. My only other option was to tell her no and have her go to someone else." He cocked his head. "Now, I shouldn't have told you that much, but I want you to understand I'm doing the best I can for her."

I studied him to determine his sincerity. Call me a fool, but I was buying it. "She's been through so much these last few weeks."

"I know. Which is why I strongly suggested she wait, but she wants it done. She says they both misrepresented who they were when they got married."

That didn't surprise me. Neely Kate hadn't known about Ronnie's strong criminal ties, and she'd hinted that she'd hidden parts of herself from her husband. Despite everything, I liked Ronnie. I couldn't help but think they could work it out.

"Cheer up," Carter said, getting to his feet. "Neely Kate has the three-month waiting period to change her mind, and her husband still hasn't been served, so the clock hasn't started ticking."

I stood and placed my hand on my hip. "Is your guy looking very hard?"

"My usual guy is tied up, so I've hired someone else to help out. Floyd's like an old mule—slow and steady, sure, but he wouldn't speed up even if his ass was on fire."

Turned out I'd underestimated my attorney.

"But if you tell Neely Kate I've confided any of this to you, I'll destroy you myself, Skeeter be damned," he teased with a grin, although I could see a glint of truth in his eyes.

"No worries. She'd kill me if she knew I was asking. Since I now know we both have her best interests in mind, I'll back off."

"Yeah, right," he choked out.

"Okay, I'll *try* to back off," I conceded. "Thanks for looking out for Neely Kate."

"Always." But the warmth in the single word had me questioning his motives all over again.

Chapter Four

I stepped through Carter's office door onto the sidewalk and couldn't help but turn toward the courthouse, which loomed to my left. The knowledge that Mason was so close—that I only had to go in there to see him—tortured me. I'd promised to give him space to work things out, but I had legitimate questions that Carter really hadn't answered. Wasn't that reason enough to see him?

I dropped into Merilee's and ordered pork chops, a salad, and a slice of apple pie to go. The waitress behind the counter gave me a smile as she handed me the bag. "We haven't seen you and Mr. Deveraux in lately."

I forced a smile of my own. "He's been pretty busy."

"We heard about the shake-up in the courthouse. Mr. Deveraux is exactly what this county needs."

"Thanks," I said, taking a step backward. "I think so, too." I only hoped that he stuck around to help fix the county . . . and that he decided to stay with me, too.

I was confident in my plan up until I reached the outer door to his office, at which point I came to the conclusion that it was a terrible idea. He was going to think I was rushing him. I was about to turn and run—literally—when the door opened and Mason's assistant, Kaylee, stepped out.

"Rose! I haven't seen you in a couple of weeks." She glanced down at the bag in my hand. "Oh, looks like you brought Mr. Deveraux lunch."

"Yeah . . ." I glanced down at the bag. "He's probably already eaten."

"Actually, he hasn't. I was about to go pick up something for him. He's in his office if you want to go on in."

"I don't want to bother him if he's in the middle of something important."

"Don't be silly." She laughed, turning around and walking back into the office reception area. "He always wants to see you."

That used to be true. I wasn't so sure about this time. "Okay . . ."

I followed her inside, walked over to his partially open office door and stopped at the threshold. He sat at his desk, bent over his computer, a legal pad and a pen next to him, forehead furrowed with concentration. I watched him for several seconds, my heart in my throat, worrying about how he would react to my sudden appearance.

His gaze lifted, and his eyes widened in surprise when he saw me. "Rose."

"I'm sorry I didn't call ahead or make an appointment." It felt weird saying that. Never in the entire time I'd known him had I made an appointment with his assistant.

He closed the lid to his laptop and got to his feet. "Don't be silly. You don't have to call ahead."

"I . . . uh . . ." I lifted the bag of food, still standing in the doorway. "I brought you lunch. I heard how busy you've been, and I figured you probably weren't feeding yourself." Way to sound like a stalker.

A soft smile spread across his face. "You've always kept me well fed."

I swallowed the lump in my throat. "Somebody has to take care of you."

But truth be told, taking care of him was what had gotten me into this situation in the first place. Well, it had kept me in it anyway.

"Come in," he said, but there was a stiffness in his voice, a formality I wasn't used to hearing. At least not when he was talking to me.

"I actually had a purpose for coming." I walked into the room and held out the food. "But I figured I'd bring you food, too."

He set the bag on his desk and removed the large container.

"Pork chops and a salad . . . and a slice of apple pie."

He glanced at me, his expression guarded. "My favorites."

"Yeah."

"Thank you, Rose."

"You're welcome."

He walked over to me, and for a moment I held my breath, hoping he would take me in his arms and kiss me. Wishing he would tell me that he couldn't live without me and that he wanted to try again. But instead, he shut the door, then gestured to the chairs in front of his desk. "Do you want to take a seat?"

I nodded, the lump rising in my throat again. "Yeah."

I sat in the chair closest to the window. The blind slats were tilted so Mason could see out but anyone in the building across the street couldn't see inside. I couldn't blame him. Neely Kate and I had discovered that Joe's sister, Kate, had rented the apartment across the street to spy on Mason's office. The apartment had been all but empty except for a few piles of junk, a pair of binoculars, a wealth of files about Mason, and the kind of gun that means business.

He sat next to me, but I saw him cast a quick glance at the container he'd placed on his desk.

"Mason, I'm not here to talk about you and me. I'm here with legal questions. So if you want to eat while we talk, please feel free."

He grimaced. "You don't mind?"

"No. You should eat it while it's hot."

He fished the utensils out of the bag and dug into the salad. "Legal questions. Are you in some kind of trouble?"

"No more than usual," I said with a wry grin.

He looked like he wanted to say something, but instead he took a bite.

"I'm here to see if you have an update on Glenn Stout or on what's going on with J.R."

Guilt filled his eyes as he lowered his fork. "I should have called you to fill you in."

"It's okay. I understand."

"No," he said softly. "I'm not sure you do." He paused. "I wanted to call you with an update, but I wasn't sure what to say. I'm still sorting things out."

"I understand."

He looked into my eyes. "But you're still a citizen of the county, not to mention the victim of a crime. It was my job to fill you in on the proceedings."

My heart sunk, but I had no one to blame but myself.

"Have you found out anything about Glenn Stout?" I asked.

"No. I've notified the clerks to call me directly if anyone shows up to pick up the money, but there's been no sign of him."

I nodded. "Carter thinks he'll wait until things die down and then try to collect it unnoticed."

His jaw tightened. "You've been talking to Carter Hale?"

"He was my attorney, Mason," I said, trying not to get irritated. "I had no idea what was going on, and I needed to ask someone."

"Joe hasn't told you?"

"It's Joe. What do you think he tells me? The information I get from him is the equivalent of him telling me not to worry my pretty little head."

"You're right. I'm sorry." He stood and moved to the back of his room, running a hand over his head. "I should have called you."

"No, you shouldn't have," I said, suddenly pissed. "If you didn't want to talk to me, then you shouldn't have called." I got to my feet. "This was a mistake."

He spun around to face me, but his expression was still guarded.

"Last week I begged you to stay with me, Mason. Well, I won't do that again. You know I'm sorry. You know I regret deceiving you. I know I have to earn your trust back, but the fact remains that what I did saved both of our lives. More than once."

Anger sparked in his eyes. "I'm not having this conversation now."

"Yes, you are," I said, marching toward him. "Now is the perfect time to have this conversation." I stopped in front of him, my hands on my hips. "You clearly have something to say to me, so say it."

He took in a breath and pushed it out, his chest heaving. "Anything I have to say would be redundant. I said it all last week."

"It's clearly not out of your system," I said, waving my hand at him. "You're still ticked off at me."

"I'm at work, Rose. This isn't the time!"

"When did you come in this morning? Seven? Earlier?"

The scowl that wrinkled his forehead told me I'd guessed correctly.

"And how late did you stay last night? Eight? Nine?"

"What does my work schedule have to do with anything? Does this interrogation have a point?" he asked, irritation bleeding through his words.

"The *point* is that your work hours crowd into your personal life, so you can afford to take ten minutes in the middle of the day to talk to me."

"You think this will only take ten minutes?" he asked in disbelief.

"I don't know, Mason," I challenged. "You tell me. I have no idea what you need to say."

Fury filled his eyes. "I trusted you, Rose! I trusted you to confide in me."

"I know," I said, my own anger fading in the face of his.

"And I never suspected for a *single moment* that you would betray me by helping the very man I was trying to put behind bars. Do you have any idea how badly my reputation would be damaged if word got out?"

"I do."

"You ran off and did God knows what with him and those . . . those criminals, lying to me about where you were and what you were doing while I was oblivious to it all. I feel like a fool, Rose. An utter fool."

"I know. I'm sorry. But you're not a fool, Mason. No one would ever accuse you of that."

"I don't know if I can forgive you." He shook his head, releasing a derisive laugh. "But I love you. Despite it all, I still love you. And that makes me not trust myself."

I understood. I'd spent the past five nights in my empty bed, trying to imagine myself in his shoes. Truth be told, I wouldn't have believed him if he'd accepted my duplicity as if it meant nothing. But this still hurt like hades.

And I still needed answers.

"Do you think that J.R. will try to hurt me for what I did?"

He gave a tiny shudder, trying to switch gears. "I'm sure Joe told you this much, but he's being transferred to the county jail today."

"And you know that doesn't mean squat."

He nodded, looking down at his feet.

"So I'm at risk?"

"Yes."

"You left me alone at the farmhouse knowing someone could come for me at any time?" I asked in disbelief.

"You haven't been alone, Rose." His gaze lifted to meet mine, and the regret and sadness there stole my breath. "You've had someone watching you since the moment we left the farmhouse last Friday morning."

"Joe never told me."

"Joe doesn't know."

"Jed?" The blood rushed from my head when he didn't respond. "I didn't know, Mason. I swear. I only found out from Carter right before I came over here."

"You haven't seen him?"

"No." I paused. "How did *you* know?"

"I called Malcolm."

My mouth dropped. "You did *what*?"

"Joe couldn't get the sheriff's department to spare a deputy to keep an eye on you. And I don't trust J.R. Simmons for a minute. Jed was the one who saved you when you were kidnapped. I knew he'd be the best person to watch over you."

"But you hate Skeeter Malcolm."

"If I learned one thing last week, it's that Malcolm will go to great lengths to protect you." When I started to protest, he said, "Even if I was still out at the farmhouse, I wouldn't be able to watch over you 24/7, so this is the next best thing."

"Why would you protect me?"

"I might not be with you right now, but I still love you. Even though I'm angry as hell. Even though I feel utterly betrayed." He groaned and rubbed his forehead with the back of his hand. "It's killing me to not be with you, Rose. But I don't trust you. And without trust, we have nothing."

I nodded. "I know. And I hope to make it up to you somehow. I want to earn back your trust."

I wasn't sure what to do. Leave him alone to wrestle with the pain I'd caused him? Or stay and savor every moment I got with him? But maybe he was right. Maybe this wasn't the time to force a decision about our future.

"What happens after J.R. gets moved to the county jail?" I asked, purposefully changing the subject.

"The state may move him to their own facility—they're working on their own case—but for now he'll stay in the county jail, unless his attorney can get the judge to reconsider granting him bail."

"Will he?"

Mason sighed. "It's not outside the realm of possibility."

The thought sent a shiver down my spine. "Do you think he'll get out of this?"

"It'll be hard for him to shake the charges. But stranger things have happened, and there's no denying J.R. Simmons has a way of making situations turn in his favor."

"What about Kate and all the files she had on you?"

He paced to the window and lifted one of the wooden slats of the blinds to look across the street. "Joe says he found nothing. I can have you and Neely Kate give statements on what you saw, but I'm not sure that's in your best interest. Your presence there was legally questionable to say the least, and Kate has moved whatever she had there. We have no way of figuring out where she moved it. It's a dead end."

"She knows something, Mason."

"I agree, but when I went to question her, she denied it all."

"You went to her?"

He hesitated before turning back to face me. "Yes."

I wanted to tell him that he should have told me, but I wasn't so sure that was true. He had always kept county secrets from me—it was a part of the job—and I suspected this fell into the same category.

"Anything else I need to know?" I asked, standing next to the chair.

He studied me for a moment, his gaze softening. "Don't give up on me, Rose."

I wanted to ask how long my exile would last, but I didn't have the courage. Maybe he was just trying to let me down easy. After hearing Violet's news, I wasn't sure I could handle more heartbreak.

I made my way to the door and grabbed the knob, but before I could leave, Mason stepped up behind me, his chest pressed to my back, and wrapped his hand over mine.

"Wait," he said, his voice rough.

I pushed out a breath and closed my eyes, preparing myself for the worst. I considered forcing a vision to find a way out of this agonizing limbo, but I couldn't make myself do it. I wasn't ready to face the answer.

"I miss you so much it hurts," he said, pulling my hand away from the door.

"I miss you, too," I forced past the lump in my throat.

His hand slid slowly up my arm, then moved down to my waist, lightly skimming my abdomen as he lowered his face to the nape of my neck.

I froze, afraid to move and break the spell.

He slowly turned me around, his eyes full of pain, and it killed me to know I'd been the one to hurt him. That I had been the one to destroy us.

But despite how much I regretted this distance between us, I wasn't sure I would have done anything differently if given the chance. My Lady in Black alter ego had not only saved our lives, it had also gotten J.R. arrested. How could I regret *that*?

Mason's hand pressed against the small of my back, and I lifted my hand to his shoulder, waiting to see where this would go, not daring to hope that he'd changed his mind.

He lifted his hand to the back of my head, and his face lowered to mine. His mouth was soft and tender, and part of me wondered if it was a kiss goodbye.

"You asked me to not give up on you," I whispered. "Are you giving up on me?"

He gave me another gentle kiss and then lifted his head. "No. I want this to work out, but I still need time. That's not a line to placate you."

I nodded, looking down. "I just want to be prepared."

He was silent for several seconds, and then he lifted my chin and his eyes searched mine. "Have dinner with me tonight."

My eyes widened. "Really?"

"We can talk things over."

"Oh." That sounded ominous.

"How to fix *us*."

Hope blossomed in my chest. "Okay."

"Can you do a late dinner? I'm pretty busy here."

"Yeah," I said, still looking into his eyes. "Do you want to come out to the farm?"

Indecision flickered in his eyes. "No. Let's go out." He glanced at his desk, then back to me. "How about we drive up to Magnolia and eat someplace there? Can you meet me here at the courthouse steps at 7:30?"

"Yeah."

He leaned down and gave me another kiss, his thumb softly brushing my cheek. "I love you, Rose."

"I love you, too."

He dropped his hold on me, then reached around to open the door. Before I could slip through it, he leaned toward my ear and whispered, "Call Jed and tell him not to follow you when you're with me. He can pick up tailing you when you get back."

I glanced over my shoulder at him, taking in his grim expression.

"It's all right," he said. "Remember? I arranged it."

I gave him a nod, then walked out, grateful that Kaylee was on the phone.

Mason had told me to call Jed, but that meant he still had his thumb in the underworld, which would only drive a wedge deeper between us. But I had no idea how to resolve it—or if it could be resolved.

Chapter Five

C louds had rolled in while I was inside the courthouse, bringing a chilly wind. But I couldn't have this conversation in my office with Neely Kate around, so I sat on a bench on the main square and pressed the speed dial button on my phone.

"Is everything okay?" Jed answered, sounding worried.

"You're watching me right now, aren't you?" I asked, sounding more accusatory than I'd meant to.

"Deveraux told you?"

"No, *Carter* did. And then Mason told me that he'd called Skeeter. Why is everyone still treating me like some fragile glass sculpture?"

"Deveraux asked Skeeter not to tell you, Rose. If you have a beef with anyone, it should be your boyfriend."

I groaned. Jed was right, but I understood why Mason had done it. I would have refused Jed's protection in an effort to prove that my days as the Lady were over. "Mason is taking me to dinner up in Magnolia tonight. I'm meeting him here at 7:30. He's asked me to tell you that you don't need to watch me while I'm with him."

"Unfortunately for Deveraux," Jed spat out, "I don't take my orders from him."

My mouth dropped open.

"Don't look so shocked. He may have called Skeeter, but you *had* to know that Skeeter was already on it. He's no fool. He knows you're still a target."

"You really don't like Mason, do you?" I used the pause in our conversation to scan the square for him. It was like a real-life game of *Where's Waldo*, except Jed's outfit wasn't nearly as obvious. I finally spotted him in the window of Merilee's café, a coffee cup in his hand.

He lowered his cup when he realized he'd been spotted. "No, I don't. Putting aside the fact that he and I are on different sides of the law, I don't like how he's treated you. He's either with you, or he's not. You deserve better than that."

I looked away and nodded. While I understood why Mason needed time, I could see Jed's point, too.

"So while Mr. High and Mighty thinks he can give me the night off, I don't give a shit what he wants. I take my orders from one man."

Which meant it was time for me to reach out to Skeeter. "Fine. Wait for a call from your boss," I said as I stood and headed toward the landscaping office. "I'm about to get your orders changed."

He was about to say something, but I hung up. A new wave of anger washed through me. Once again, the men in my life were orchestrating plans and schemes behind my back, keeping me on a shelf, acting as if I couldn't handle the truth. I understood why Mason had kept this from me, but Skeeter had no excuse.

I stepped into the office and shut the door behind me. Neely Kate looked up from her screen, and Bruce Wayne—who had returned from dumping a load of mulch—took one look at me and then glanced back down at the paperwork on his desk.

"You were gone a long time," Neely Kate said. "It's nearly three o'clock."

"I went to see Carter—and Mason, too."

"Mason?"

I nodded. "We're going out to dinner tonight in Magnolia."

Her eyes lit up. "That's a good thing, isn't it?"

"Yeah," I said, feeling more subdued than I would have liked. I hated that Jed's comment had gotten to me. "He says he wants to talk about fixing us. But I have to run an errand."

"Oh!" she said in excitement. "Are you dropping by Beulah's Nip and Clip for a mani-pedi? I'm almost done with this proposal. I can come with you."

"No. I have to go see . . . someone."

The gravity in my voice wiped the smile off her face. "Who?" When I didn't answer her, she asked. "Skeeter? *Why?*"

Bruce Wayne's gaze jerked up, but he remained silent.

"Because it's time. And Mason set something in motion that I need to address."

"What?"

"I've been under twenty-four-hour surveillance, and no one bothered to tell me."

Her eyes widened. "Joe set it up? I haven't seen any sheriff's deputies."

"No. Skeeter. At Mason's request."

Bruce Wayne's eyes widened.

"I understand why Mason kept it secret," I said, my irritation growing. "He knew I'd try to refuse to prove myself to him. But I expected more from Skeeter. And I'm going to tell him so."

Bruce Wayne finally spoke up. "Do you really think that's a good idea?"

I put my hand on my hip. "I'm not afraid of Skeeter Malcolm." No, I was more worried about hurting him, especially now that I knew he was probably in love with me.

Bruce Wayne grimaced. "I know you're not afraid of him, and I've given up worrying that he'll hurt you. But you know he's under close watch now."

"People know that he played a role in bringing down J.R. I can make it look like I'm just thanking him for saving me."

That was the official story. Considering J.R. Simmons's high profile, the whole country was watching, not just the state. There was no hiding that Skeeter and Jed had been part of his takedown. But Mason had put his own spin on it, saying that Jed had saved me after I was kidnapped (true) and taken me to Skeeter (also true), and that I had convinced him to let me use the Lady in Black persona to trick J.R. into confessing.

People bought it, if only because no one believed that the Lady in Black—a sophisticated businesswoman from Shreveport—could be little Rose Anne Gardner. While I was partially offended, I was also relieved. And now the public record stated that Skeeter Malcolm and his employee had saved my life. I was certain I could get by with seeing Skeeter at least once.

Neely Kate watched me for a few seconds, then nodded. "Do you want me to stay at Maeve's tonight?"

I shook my head. "No. You can stay with me at the farmhouse, but I think I should have Jed or Merv watching the house while I'm gone."

To my surprise, she didn't protest.

My stomach was a jittery mess while I drove to the pool hall. Jed called me twice and sent three texts urging me to answer my phone, but I wasn't about to be dissuaded.

My phone rang again as I pulled into the lot. Figuring it was Jed, I reached for it, about to turn the ringer off, but the number wasn't one I recognized.

Worried it might be about Violet or my blood tests, I answered.

"What should I call you?" J.R. Simmons's voice filled my ear. "Rose or Lady?"

I sank back in the driver's seat, feeling like I'd just had the wind knocked out of me. But that had to be what J.R. was hoping for. After a second-long pause, I answered him, putting more force into my voice than I felt. "Rose will do."

"You think you're a sneaky bitch, don't you?"

The venom in his tone made me cringe, but I forced myself to keep my voice light. "I don't usually think of myself as a bitch."

"I'm coming for you, Rose Gardner. And I'm coming for your boyfriend, too. I wanted you to hear it from me."

"That'll be a little hard to do behind bars, J.R., which is where I hear you're headed this very afternoon."

"This backward Podunk county can't keep me locked up. I'll get out—and when I do, you're the first one I'm coming for. I think I'll make your boyfriend watch."

"Good luck getting Mason. He's well-protected." At least I hoped so.

J.R. laughed, a bitter sound that sent fear skating down my back. "Not the D.A." He paused. "Malcolm. Although I'm going for Deveraux, too."

I sucked in a breath. I considered denying that allegation, but I barely had enough energy left to finish the call. "I might be scared if I thought it was a possibility," I lied, proud that my voice didn't crack. "But if you come after me, I'll shoot you in your non-existent heart this time."

I waited for his response before realizing he'd hung up. Where had he called me from? The hospital? One of his henchmen's phones? He still had his mysterious Twelve men out there, waiting to do his bidding. Was I a sitting duck?

Jed rapped on the driver's window, making me jump and release a shriek. I pushed the door open, but he blocked my path.

"He doesn't want to see you."

"After the phone conversation I just had, I think he will."

That stunned him long enough for me to slip past him. I made it through the front door of the pool hall before he caught up to me, grabbing my arm and pulling me to a halt.

"Rose. Stop. Who called you?"

I gave him an ornery smile. "I think I'll keep that to myself for now." Pulling my arm loose, I marched toward the back of the pool hall. The bartender, whom I recognized from the day Neely Kate and I had hustled Dirk Picklebee, watched slack-jawed as Jed tried to block my path.

"Rose, you don't know what he's like when he's like this."

"Like what?"

He leaned closer, speaking loud enough for only me to hear. "He's hurt, Rose, and just like a wounded animal, he's lashing out at everyone and everything."

Oh. "You're afraid he'll hurt me."

"Not physically—he'd never touch a hair on your head—but he's bound to rip you to shreds if you go back there."

My eyebrows rose in a challenge. "I can give as good as I get, Jed."

He moved aside, but he didn't look very happy about it. I stalked toward Skeeter's office, trying not to lose my nerve. What could Skeeter possibly say to hurt me?

Plenty.

But I also knew he'd want to know about J.R. He *deserved* to know.

I came to a stop outside his office, hesitating before I rapped on his door with more force than I would ordinarily use. But there could be no timid knocks for Skeeter Malcolm. He knew me as strong and brave.

Truth be told, he'd helped make me that way.

"Come in," he grunted from behind the door.

I sucked in a deep breath and pushed open the door. He was sitting at his desk, reading something on his computer screen. He cast a cursory glance in my direction, then froze. His expression hardened, and he sat up straighter in his chair.

"Well, well, well. Look who's decided to go slummin'."

I shut the door behind me, my back prickling with irritation. "You stop that right now, Skeeter Malcolm. I never once thought of associating you with slummin'."

He eyed me, his expression carefully guarded. "You don't usually use the front door, now do you?"

"That was something we both agreed on in the very beginning, and you doggone know it."

He circled his desk and came to a stop in front of me, looking down at me. I knew he was trying to intimidate me. It worked with everyone else—even Jed—but not with me. Not after the first time I'd come to him.

His eyes narrowed. As if reading my mind, he said, "You didn't think much of me the first time we met."

"The first time we met, you nearly choked me to death and then proceeded to blackmail me. You really need to work on your first impressions if you want to make more friends."

The corners of his mouth twitched before he got them back under control. "What are you doin' here?"

I decided to keep the call from J.R. for last. If I led with that, we likely wouldn't talk about anything else. "I just saw Mason."

"Yeah," he said, sounding bored. "I know."

Damn Jed. "He told me that he asked you to have someone watch over me."

He sat on the edge of his desk, crossing his arms, and shrugged.

"Skeeter!"

He dropped his arms to his sides as he stood again, looking agitated. "What the hell do you want me to say?"

"Why didn't you tell me?"

"Deveraux asked me not to."

"Since when do you obey requests from members of the Fenton County legal system?"

His face reddened, and he balled his fists. "I don't take orders from the damned district attorney."

"Then why the big secret?"

"I was going to have you tailed anyway, so it didn't matter to me if Deveraux asked me to do it or not."

"So why keep it from me?" I shook my head, feeling like a fool. The answer had suddenly occurred to me as plain as day. It was the same reason Mason hadn't told me. "You thought I'd pitch a fit and refuse."

His eyes darkened. "What are you doin' here, Rose?"

"Mason is taking me to Magnolia tonight for dinner. He wants Jed to stay here until we get back into town." But I had to wonder how safe that was after J.R.'s threat.

A wicked grin lit up his face. "Does he now?"

"Skeeter. Don't."

"Don't what?" His smile faded into a glare. "Seems like he took you out to dinner last week—with a sheriff's deputy watching, no less—and you were snatched right out from under both their noses. If I didn't have my man watching you, you'd be dead right now."

"Like I said, that's the reason I came, but right before I came in, I got—"

"No."

My eyebrows shot up. "*No?*"

"*No.* I don't trust Deveraux for shit."

While I had been about to agree with him about keeping Jed around, he was ticking me off. "You don't have any right to tell me what to do."

"*I have every right after what happened in that restaurant!*" His voice boomed off the walls, and I fought the instinct to cringe.

I knew Skeeter held Mason responsible for my kidnapping. He also likely resented him for having suggested that Skeeter saw me as more than just an asset, that his feelings for me exceeded the bond of friendship. It was a subject we hadn't broached. "We need to talk about what happened. What Mason suggested . . ."

Skeeter shook his head. "There's nothing to discuss."

He wouldn't talk about his feelings for me, and I wasn't sure I was ready to go there with him, so I decided to focus on something else that had me worried. Especially before I told him about my call. "There's plenty to discuss, but right now I want to talk about J.R. I know you. There's no way you're content with letting J.R. sit behind bars. What are you planning?"

"What I'm planning is no damned business of yours."

"You and I both know it's very much my business."

"This is not your goddamned world!" he shouted, his voice ringing in my ears. "Just because you put on a damned hat does *not* make you a part of it!"

I stomped toward him and jabbed his chest. "You're my friend, and I care about you. I don't want you to do anything stupid."

Anger flashed in his eyes, but then a cold mask replaced it, his eyes looking deadly. "First of all, you and I are *not* friends. This was a business relationship, no more, no less. Do not for one second think you mean a *damn thing* to me."

My chest tightened, and I tried to hide my shock, even though I knew he didn't mean a single word of it. Just like Jed had warned me, he was lashing out. The problem was that he always knew exactly where to strike.

"And second, I should kill you where you stand for insinuating I'm stupid. I've done a helluva lot more to men for lesser insults."

I shook my head in disbelief. "If you don't care about me, then why are you having Jed and Merv watch out for me?"

"You are still my property," he said, walking back to his desk. "You agreed to pose as the Lady in Black for six months."

My mouth gaped. "You can't be serious."

He sat in his chair, lifting his face with a cold, hard stare. "Have you ever known me to joke?"

I put my hand on my hip. "You think you can parade me out as the Lady in Black after everything that happened? What about Mason?"

His eyes narrowed into slits. "Deveraux won't say a word."

"Why not?"

He turned to his computer and started typing.

"Skeeter, why won't he say anything?"

An ugly sneer spread across his face as he lifted his head. "We've reached an agreement, and I'm sure he'll keep his word."

A cold chill washed over me. "What did you do?" He turned back to his computer, and I stomped toward his desk, my hands fisted. "What did you do, Skeeter?"

He turned to me, his eyes so cold I would have been frightened of him if I hadn't known better. "I took care of my business and my *property*. Now get the hell out. I'll call you when I need your services."

I wanted to shake some sense into him, but I didn't trust myself to speak, so I turned around and stomped to the door. He was vastly mistaken if he thought I was going to play the Lady in Black ever again.

"Lady," he said, his voice just as chilly as before.

I spun around to look at him.

"Don't come back here again. If you do, I'll have you forcibly removed."

"Don't you worry, Skeeter Malcolm. I'm never comin' back here." Just before I spun back around, I saw a wave of emotions wash over his face—pain, then triumph, followed quickly by a mask of indifference.

As I walked out and slammed the door behind me, I realized I'd played right into his hands.

Skeeter may have won this round, but I wouldn't be so easily dissuaded.

Though part of me wondered why I even cared.

Chapter Six

J ed was sitting at the bar when I emerged from the back, and he jumped up from his stool. I shot him a scowl.

"I warned you," he said, following me as I made my way toward the door.

I shook my head. "I know. But I still had to see him."

"So who called you out in the parking lot?"

Well, crappy doodles. "I never got a chance to tell him."

"Then tell *me*. Who called you?"

"J.R."

"*What?*" he shouted loud enough to garner the attention of two guys shooting pool. One of the guys had been setting up his shot, but he stood upright at Jed's outburst, pulling the pool cue back and stabbing his buddy in his oversized belly.

Jed grabbed my arm and pulled me away from the door. "He called you right before you came in? What did he say?"

"Oh, the usual," I said, trying to play it off. "That he was coming for me . . . and Skeeter."

"Why the hell didn't you tell Skeeter?"

"I was goin' to," I said defensively. "Then he started calling me his property, and he ticked me off."

"I warned you that he was gonna lash out at you, so you're going to march right back in there and tell him about that call."

"I'll do no such thing. He made it very clear I'm not allowed to darken his doorstep again."

"You know he didn't mean that."

"He looked very serious to me."

"Trust me. He's gonna want to know about this."

"Fine," I said in a huff, rolling back my shoulders. "If you think it's so damn important, *you* go tell Skeeter. But as far as I'm concerned, it's not new information. We already knew J.R. would have it out for me, and he's been playing the long game with Skeeter for a while now. J.R. only called to confirm his mission hasn't changed."

"But now we know for certain. We'll step up surveillance."

"Why? So Skeeter doesn't lose his valuable property?" I asked, feeling like a witch. Jed hadn't done anything to deserve my attitude, and Skeeter had only acted out of self-preservation. But I wasn't ready to see Skeeter right now—his words still stung. "You go tell him. I need to call Joe."

Jed grabbed my arm before I could make it out the door.

I jerked against his hold. "Jed. Let me go."

He snorted. "You think tellin' Baby Simmons is a good idea?"

"And why wouldn't it be?"

"Who would you rather have watchin' over you? Me and Merv or Simmons's merry band of fools? Because you can't have both."

I pushed out a frustrated sigh. I hated to admit he had a point. "Then I need to talk to Mason. He was the one who called Skeeter in the first place. I'll let him decide."

Jed's eyes narrowed. "You're going to let the man who left you make your decision for you?"

Anger washed through me. "I'm trying to do the right thing here, Jed! I'm trying to keep from losing Mason."

"At the cost of your own life?"

"Dammit, Jed!"

But a grin spread across his face. "You know I'm right."

"Fine. You're right. But I'm still going to call Mason. J.R. threatened him, too."

He gave me a hard stare. "I could take your phone. I could drag you back there to tell Skeeter in person."

"But you won't," I said, pressing my lips together. "Because you don't think of me as Skeeter's property. You know I have a brain in my head that I'm capable of using."

He released a grunt and pointed to the empty bar. "Sit there and wait for me."

I lifted my eyebrows in defiance.

"*Please* sit there and wait for me. But before you consider walking out that front door alone, use that brain in your head to think about J.R.'s threat and how easy it would be for him to send someone to get you."

Shaking my head, I walked over to the bar and sat on a stool.

Jed pointed a finger at the bartender. "Keep an eye on her. If she leaves, you get your ass back to Skeeter's office to tell me."

The bartender swallowed hard, his face pale. "Yes, sir." His gaze followed Jed as he disappeared into the back. "Can I get you something?" he finally asked me.

"Water," I said, pulling out my phone.

He looked worried about what I might do with the phone, but he grabbed a glass and filled it with ice.

I considered sending Mason a text, but I was certain this fell under the *acceptable phone calls when you're taking a break* category.

Mason answered before the second ring. "Rose, are you okay?"

At least he didn't think this was a pathetic attempt to garner his attention. "I'm fine, but I received a phone call about ten minutes ago that I think you should know about."

"Was it from Joe?"

"No. But it *was* a Simmons."

"J.R.? How'd he get his hands on a phone?"

"I have no idea, but he called to tell me he's coming for me. And you."

"Where are you?" His voice was tight.

I hesitated, but I'd sworn there would be no more secrets or lies between us. "At Skeeter's pool hall. I came here to ask him to call Jed off for tonight."

"So Jed's still pulling surveillance?" I was surprised by how relieved he sounded.

"Yeah."

"We need to cancel dinner in Magnolia. It's not safe."

That was no surprise, but I was still disappointed. "Yeah, I suspect you're right." I hesitated. No secrets. "There's something else you need to know."

"Okay . . ."

"When J.R. threatened to kill me, he said he was going to make Skeeter watch before he killed him, too."

He didn't speak for several seconds. "I see."

"It's probably because Skeeter helped arrange the whole thing."

"Rose. Don't." His harsh tone made me wince. "We both know that's not why."

I couldn't deal with Mason's jealousy right now. "Jed doesn't think I should tell Joe. He says Skeeter's men can offer me better protection."

He was silent for several seconds. "There's no denying that the Fenton County Sheriff's Department isn't great at protecting people. I agree that Jed and his associates are better equipped to keep you safe from Simmons. Which means we can't tell Joe. And once again, I'm in a precarious situation." He sounded professional at first, as if he were talking about a case, but he was openly furious by the time he finished.

"Why are you getting so angry with me?" I demanded. "You're the one who called Skeeter in the first place!"

"But you're the one who put us both in this situation!"

I gasped. While he was right, he sounded so angry, so bitter that I knew in my heart he would never forgive me. I sucked in a breath and forced myself to sound strong. "Then let me make this easy for you, Mason. We're over."

"What are you talking about?"

"Exactly what it sounds like. You have someone watching you, right? The sheriff's department?"

He sounded confused. "Yes, but that—"

"So the only person whose safety you're concerned about right now is mine, right? And that's why you were forced to do something you didn't want to do—legally and morally—by calling Skeeter and asking him to protect me. Am I right?"

"Rose, you can't pigeonhole it like that. You have to—"

"True or false," I said, surprised at my cold tone. "The only reason you called Skeeter Malcolm was because of my safety."

"Rose," he said. "There was no way I could sit back—"

"*True or false?*"

"True." I heard the defeat in his voice, and it took everything in me not to cry.

"So the only reason you're still entangled in the underworld is because of me." I paused. "True or false?"

"Rose." The pain in his voice brought tears to my eyes.

"Answer the question."

"*Rose.*"

"I need you to answer, Mason. Just answer the damn question."

"True." In all my life, I'd never heard so much defeat in one word.

I took several breaths, trying to keep myself together. I had bigger issues to deal with than my silly love life. "Given everything goin' on right now, I think you should wait to get your things."

"Rose. Don't do this."

"Don't do what? Advance the time table on the inevitable?" I choked out the last words. "You and I both know how stubborn you are. I broke us. We might try to put us back together, but we'll never be the same."

He didn't answer.

"I love you, Mason"—my voice cracked from my tears,—"and I'm *so* sorry."

"Rose, please, sweetheart." He sounded so broken, I could hardly stand it. "Just think this through. Don't make such an important decision at a time like this."

I suddenly had a newfound respect for Neely Kate's decision. Somehow I'd landed myself in the same place. "You know I'm right." I could do this. I would survive this. But I had to set him free. I leaned forward, resting my forehead on my hand. "From this moment on, I am no longer your responsibility. I will no longer call you with information or requests, unless they are completely legal in nature."

"Rose!" he pleaded, panicked.

"I have only myself to blame for this. I know that, but I can't undo it. I wish you a happy life, Mason," I sobbed. "I want you to be happy."

"Rose! Sweetheart. Please, just listen to me! We can—"

But I hung up and held the phone to my chest, knowing I'd done the right thing.

Even if it had ripped my heart to shreds.

Chapter Seven

W hy the hell didn't you tell me about that phone call?" Skeeter shouted as he barreled around the corner toward me.

The bartender jumped at the sound of Skeeter's voice, his eyes widening in fright. He ducked behind the counter, grabbed a laminated menu from the counter, and held it over his head. One of the guys at the pool table in the corner froze while his buddy jerked his shirt sleeve, trying to get him to take cover under the pool table.

Taking a deep breath, I wiped my face and turned to look at him. My phone vibrated in my hand, but I stood and shoved it into my pocket.

"Because you were too busy treating me like your *property*," I said.

He paused in front of me, his upper lip curling in a sneer. "Have you been sitting out here crying?"

"Cry over you?" I asked. "Don't flatter yourself. I have far bigger issues than your PMS."

The exasperated look in his eyes told me that he wanted to counter my insult, but instead he motioned to my pocket and growled. "Did Simmons call you back?"

"No. I called Mason—not that it's any of your business. I wanted him to know about J.R.'s threat." I could see a tantrum brewing, so I cut him off at the pass. "Calm down. He's not going to tell Joe."

"How can you be sure of that?"

"Because he won't. He knows Jed is more qualified to protect me, so he doesn't feel he can risk it. You know I'm right. Mason came to you last week."

He studied me for a moment before nodding his head. "We shouldn't be discussing this out here. Come back to my office."

"What?" I demanded, putting my hands on my hips. "And risk getting thrown out?"

His eyes darkened. "Rose."

I pointed my finger at him. "Don't you *Rose* me. There's nothing more for us to discuss, so I'm going back to work."

I started to spin around, but he snagged my arm and lowered his face to mine. "We're not done," he said.

"Says you." I shook off his hold.

He tilted his head and gave me a look that told me he expected me to fall in line. "I'm taking you under my protection. I don't give a rat's ass what the D.A. says."

My mouth dropped open. "Wait. You discussed me going into hiding? With Mason?"

His forehead furrowed. "We need to have this discussion in my office. Anyone can hear us."

I wasn't sure who he thought was listening. The only patrons at the moment were the statue in the corner and his buddy, who was about to tip him over if he kept pulling on his shirtsleeve. "Answer the question, Skeeter!"

"Yes, we had that discussion last week. He wouldn't even consider it."

"Oh, my word!" I groaned. I spun away from him and shook my head in disbelief.

Thinking better of it, I turned back and poked my finger into his chest. "Let me make something perfectly clear, Skeeter Malcolm."

He took a step back, his eyes wide in surprise. But I kept jabbing as I spoke. "I am my own person. *You* do not own me. *Mason Deveraux* does not own me. *I* own me. Do you get that?"

A sly grin spread across his face. "If I say yes, will you stop poking me with your scrawny finger?" he asked.

I gave him one last poke for good measure. "I expected better of you."

He rubbed his chest, wearing a smirk that made him look like a cat who'd caught a barn full of mice. But when that grin faded, it was replaced by a seriousness I'd only seen a few times. This was the real Skeeter Malcolm, the man hiding behind the bravado, and I was fairly certain he didn't show it to many people.

"You're right. I should have discussed this with you, not him."

I nodded sharply, then pushed out a breath. "Thank you."

"But I really do think you should let me put you up in a safe house."

"For how long? J.R. could be a threat for years."

He shook his head. "No. Simmons will be dealt with sooner rather than later. The real question is whether or not your boyfriend will let you go."

I narrowed my eyes. It was easier to mask my pain with anger. "In case you haven't realized, this is the twenty-first century. This is *my* decision, not his. And I'm not going. I could be there for years. I don't have time for that nonsense."

He leaned closer again, his voice low. "I could protect you better there."

I looked up into his dark eyes. "Are you going, too?"

Skeeter snorted as if I'd asked him if he were joining a mime troupe. "Hell, no."

I shook my head and took a step back. "Then neither am I."

He let out an exasperated sigh. "You don't make things easy for me, do you?"

"No one asked you to watch over me." When he started to protest, I scowled. "*I* never asked you to watch me."

"If you think I'm leaving you alone, then you've got another think coming."

The fact that he cared made me feel better, a little less broken, like spackle over a gaping hole, and when I spoke again it was in a softer tone. "I really do need to get back to work."

He looked like he was wrestling with something, then said, sounding gruff, "Now that you know we're watching, it would be helpful if you gave Jed your schedule."

"Fine," I said in an angry huff, even though I agreed that it was a good idea. Right now it felt easier to be adversarial.

Skeeter shot Jed a laser-focused stare, then disappeared into the back. The bartender's head poked up from behind the counter like Punxsutawney Phil, the menu still lifted over his head. The man frozen in the corner looked like he'd actually turned to stone, but his friend, who was staring at us with a mouth like a guppy's, had finally stopped pulling his sleeve.

"What was that about?" I asked, walking to the exit.

"Nothing," he mumbled. "So are you really going back to work?"

"That's my plan. After that, I'm heading to the farm with Neely Kate."

"No dinner?" he asked smugly.

I narrowed my gaze, my jaw set with irritation. "You might want to rethink that gloating, or I'll make it ten times harder to follow me for the next few days."

I wouldn't, not really. I was scared to death of J.R., and knowing that Jed had my back made me feel a whole lot better.

Jed seemed to ponder my threat, then nodded as we walked out the door and toward our separate vehicles.

Now that I was alone, the knowledge that I'd broken up with Mason hit me square in the face. Somehow I'd just ended my relationship with the man I'd planned to marry. Where did I go from here?

All I wanted to do was go home, crawl into bed, and cry my eyes out. But I wouldn't give myself that luxury. I needed to focus on neutralizing J.R. Simmons.

The only strategy that came to mind was to check on the progress Maeve had made in decoding the shorthand on the lone remaining page of Dora's secret journal, recovered from the warehouse where she'd worked with Daddy and Paul all those years ago.

When I stopped at the next stoplight, I grabbed my phone out of my pocket. Swallowing the lump in my throat, I ignored the three missed calls from Mason and called his mother instead.

"Rose," she said, her voice warm and soothing.

Oh, mercy. A new thought hit me. Was I going to lose her, too? While I hadn't doubted she'd stick by me if Mason left me for good, the situation had changed. Would she change her mind when she found out that I was the one who'd broken up with him?

"Maeve," I said, my voice breaking. "Can I come over for a few minutes?"

"I'm at the nursery," she said, sounding distracted. "I'm filling in for Violet." Distantly, I heard her say, "The few pansies we have left are outside on the right." Then she said, "Sorry about that, Rose. I was helping a customer."

"It sounds like you're busy," I said, my voice tight. "I'll talk to you later."

"Rose, are you all right?"

"No." I said, choking on the word. I glanced in the rearview mirror at Jed in the sedan behind me. Now that I knew about my protective guard, he clearly didn't feel the need to hide any longer. But I looked away, not wanting him to see me upset. There was only one person I wanted to talk to about my breakup—it was the real reason I'd called her.

"I broke up with Mason."

"What?" She sounded dismayed. "Rose, what happened?"

I took a deep breath, fighting back my tears. "I'd rather talk about it in person, but I'm guessing Anna's there, right?"

"Yeah . . ."She sounded worried. "How's Mason?"

"I don't know," I said, fighting the urge to break down. "I did it over the phone."

"Rose." I heard the disappointment in her voice.

"I hadn't planned to do it, Maeve, but he was upset." I didn't want to drag her into the specifics. "Let's just say my ties to the criminal underworld are still very much in place, and Mason is upset at the position I've placed him in."

"Does he have any idea—"

"No, Maeve. Please don't be upset with him. He's a man of principles, and it's unfair to ask him to bend them, especially given his position."

"Once again you're saving him," she said, sounding sad.

I took a deep breath, hoping to soothe my frazzled nerves. "I did the right thing." *No matter how much it hurt.*

"I can see why you think so—"

"Maeve. It's done," I said, with a firmness I never used with her. "I wanted to talk to you for two reasons. The first is I wanted you to hear it from either me or Mason. I had no idea if he would tell you, so maybe you should reach out to him."

"Of course . . ."

"But second, I need to know what progress you've made on the journal page."

"I confess, I haven't gotten very far. It's not coming back to me as quickly as I'd hoped, and I've been covering for Violet." She paused. "How did your talk go earlier?"

"Do you know?" I asked, my voice breaking.

"Only that she's very sick and has to go to Houston."

"She's going to be okay," I said with determination.

"Of course she is," she said, as if there shouldn't be any doubt. "And we'll make sure we keep the store in great condition for her until she gets back."

"Will working at the nursery be too awkward for you?" I asked. "Because of me and Mason?" I hadn't even considered the ripple effect of our breakup, but I didn't want Violet to worry about anything other than getting better.

"Of course not, Rose. I still love you whether you're with Mason or not. I'll always be here for you."

My voice cracked. "Thank you."

"But don't rush into any snap decisions, okay? Give this some thought. You and Mason truly love each other."

She was right. We did love one another. But I had to wonder if love was enough.

"I'll talk to you tomorrow, Maeve."

"Okay."

I parked in front of the office, and Jed parked around the corner. I noticed him get out of his car and head toward the square.

The door chimed when I walked in the office, and Neely Kate looked up with a questioning glance.

"How did it go?" she asked.

"As well as could be expected," I said, heading toward my desk.

Bruce Wayne gave me a sympathetic look, but to his credit, he never even hinted at an *I told you so*.

At around five o'clock, I still had several estimates to prepare, so I handed Neely Kate the keys to my truck.

"Why don't you take my car home, and I'll stick around and get these plans done?" I asked.

I also needed to look at the finances to see about paying Maeve something for her work at the shop. Knowing her, she'd do more than she'd agreed to. We would also need to hire more help for our landscaping business soon. I'd expected the landscaping business to get off to a slow start, but it had exceeded our expectations.

Neely Kate's mouth dropped open. "What about your date with Mason?"

Oh, crap. I'd forgotten to tell her. I'd been too busy worrying about Violet and trying to figure out how to stop J.R.—anything to avoid thinking about the end of my relationship. And I sure didn't want to bring it up now.

"We're not goin', but I'll tell you about it later, okay? When I get home."

Neely Kate narrowed her eyes. "How about I stick around to keep you company?"

"You deserve a night off," I said, pulling her out of her seat and pushing her toward the exit. "Besides, Muffy's probably dying to go pee."

She broke free and turned around to look at me. "What's goin' on, Rose? What did Skeeter say? Did he threaten you?"

"Skeeter? Hardly. He's full of a lot of bark and little bite."

Bruce Wayne grabbed his coat off the coat rack, harrumphing. "Tell that to the guys who've gotten on his bad side."

He had a point. "Fair enough, but that's the way he is with *me*. I'm fine. I just need some time alone, okay? I'll explain it all when I get home."

Neely Kate sure didn't look happy, but she took the truck keys from my outstretched hand. "If you're not eating with Mason, then don't stay in town too long. I'll make a big pot of chili and some homemade cornbread."

"Is this one of your special recipes?" She'd been experimenting with the most God-awful combinations of foods lately, like peppermint meatloaf and French onion cheesecake. None of us had the heart to tell her how bad they were, but I wasn't sure I could choke down whatever she came up with tonight.

"No. I didn't have time to come up with something original, so I'm using my granny's recipe."

I tried to hide my relief. "I won't be too long."

"But if I leave you, how are you going to get home?"

"I'll have Jed bring me. He's tailing me anyway."

When her eyes bugged out, I added, "It's all out in the open. I don't see any reason for him to hide in the shadows."

"True." She wrapped her arms around me and squeezed. "Don't stay too long. You need to be with the people who love you."

I watched her as she headed for the front door. Did she know I'd broken up with Mason? Did she suspect?

Bruce Wayne stayed back, saying he'd forgotten something in the backroom that he needed to bring by the nursery the next morning.

I figured it was an excuse to grill me more about my encounter with Skeeter, so I wasn't prepared when he gave me a sad look and said, "I heard about your sister."

"How. . . ?" But as soon as the word was out of my mouth, I realized how.

"Anna." He'd been helping out at the nursery a lot lately, and Violet's assistant had taken a shine to him. "How much do you know?"

"Enough to know she's goin' to be gone for awhile. Do you need to take time off?"

I rubbed my hand over my forehead. "No. Not yet. Our Aunt Bessie is going to Houston with her, but I'll probably go down after things die down around here."

A wry smile twisted his lips. "Do things ever die down around here?"

"True enough."

"If you need to take off, Neely Kate and I can keep things goin'." He shifted his weight. "Neely Kate's picking it up so fast, I'll be out of a job soon."

I laughed. "Hardly. Once the weather starts warming up, you'll be working outside. We have so many jobs lined up, we're going to have to think about finding more help. Do you know anyone who might be interested?"

He studied my face for a moment. "Do you care if he has a criminal record?"

"You have a criminal record, and I hired you."

"Well, that was different. You knew I was innocent."

"Of committing murder. But I knew you'd done the other things—possession of pot, stealing. You said you wanted to change, though, and I believed in you. If the guy you're thinking about wants to change, too, and you think he's trustworthy, then hire him and tell him he can start mid-March."

Bruce Wayne looked shocked. "Don't you want to interview him?"

"Nope. You're a partner, Bruce Wayne. You interview him. You'll be the one who's ultimately in charge of him."

"I'll be his boss," he said in shock.

I laughed. "And he'll probably be the first employee of many. So get used to the idea."

A grin spread over his face, and I felt genuinely happy for him. He'd grown so much from the scared, beaten-down man I'd met last summer.

I locked the door behind him after he took off and then jumped when the sound of my cell phone broke the silence. I hurried over to my desk, wondering if it was Mason. I missed him something fierce and would be tempted to answer.

But it was Joe.

"Hey." I had to wonder if he was calling about Violet.

"I just wanted to give you a heads up. I suspect my dad won't be in county jail for long. I hear an indictment is coming from Little Rock in the next day or two."

"What will that mean?"

"It means they'll move him up to Little Rock and keep him there until his first trial." He paused. "Once we find other witnesses who are willing to attest to the things he's done, you'll be safer."

"You really believe that?"

"I have to."

I suspected I would never be safe from J.R. Simmons. I'd tricked him and trapped him using his own game, and he wasn't the sort of man to let bygones be bygones.

Joe cleared his throat. "Have you felt threatened in anyway? Have you felt like you're being watched?"

I hadn't noticed either Jed or Merv before today, so I wasn't too confident I could trust my skills of observation. And while I had noticed that strange man on Friday, I didn't want to tell Joe about that. Not when it might mess up my current protective duty. "No. But I'm being careful."

"Do you have your Taser?"

"Yeah, I keep it with me at all times. And there's a gun at the house." I didn't mention Neely Kate had hers in her purse, along with her concealed carry permit.

"Be careful with that gun. Don't go shooting the chief deputy sheriff when he shows up at your door makin' sure you're okay," he said with a grin in his voice.

"I'll try not to," I teased, but now that I had him on the phone and in a good mood, I decided to press my luck. "Now that your father has been arrested, when can I get Dora's journal back?"

His tone changed to all business. "It's no longer an issue."

"Has it been taken for evidence? Will it be used in the trial?"

His silence was all the confirmation I needed.

"That journal could contain information that would help keep your father in jail."

He groaned. "I've got it covered, Rose. I'm going to make sure he doesn't ever hurt anyone again, okay?"

What could I say? That I had trouble believing him? Those would be hard words for him to hear, but they were true. While I trusted him more than I had a week ago, I wasn't totally onboard the *Joe's going to protect me against his father* express.

"With all due respect, Joe, that's my property. If it's not being held for evidence, I want it back."

"Fine. It's evidence."

"Then why wasn't it logged in?"

He paused. "Who told you that?"

Mason had heard it from Deputy Miller, but there wasn't a snowball's chance in hades I was going to tell Joe that. "Maybe I had a vision."

"Of who?" he asked suspiciously.

"It doesn't matter. What matters is that I have no idea where *my property* is currently located, and I want it back."

"You'll get it back. I'm working on something that should play out soon, but I need the journal as bait."

"Bait? Bait for what? Is this official Fenton County business or personal?"

"That doesn't seem like it's any of your concern," Joe said, getting irritated.

"It is when you're using the book my birthmother left me as the lure."

"Rose, we're on the same side here. We both want the same thing."

I was pretty sure he believed that, but I wasn't so sure the sides were separated by a straight line. There were so many people out to make J.R. Simmons pay for his various misdeeds, I was fairly certain the lines were as twisted and contorted as an octagon.

But I was too tired to fight him, and I suddenly regretted my decision to stay at the office. I really just wanted to crawl into bed and sleep for a month or two—until the pain in my chest over my breakup with Mason had faded enough for me to breathe.

"I don't want to fight, Joe, but I'm going to ask you about it again soon."

"Fair enough . . . and Rose?" I heard the hesitation in his voice.

"Yeah?" I asked, worried about what was coming.

"I'm sorry to hear that you and Mason are separated. I hope you two work things out." Did he know we'd broken up? How?

Then I realized he was talking about Mason moving out. I fought back tears. "Thanks."

I waited for him to gloat or suggest we get back together, but he surprised me. "Have a good night, and let me know if you feel like you're in danger."

I didn't have it in me to remind him I was constantly in danger.

Chapter Eight

I tried to concentrate on a landscaping design for one of the houses in Violet's old neighborhood with the design program on my computer, but I gave up after it took me twenty minutes to place two trees. At this rate, it'd be next winter before I got to the beds around the house. When I got up and stretched, I realized it was already dark outside. The only light in the office was from the glow of my computer screen.

The streets were fairly deserted, but there was a man standing in front of the office window. I realized with a jolt that it was the guy I'd seen on Friday. Average height, dark brown jacket, jeans, and a dark gray knit hat on his head. He turned to meet my eyes, and we engaged in a staring contest that lasted a good two seconds. It also gave me a good look at the brown-pigmented birthmark on his cheek.

And a perfect set of scratch marks.

I was staring at Sam Teagen. The man who had posted my bail. The man who'd hired Eric Davidson, the manager of the Burger Shack, to run Mason off the road, steal his cell phone, and most likely kill him. Judging from the scratch marks on Teagen's cheek, he was also the man who had kidnapped me.

And in his hand, hanging at his side, was a gun.

I took a step back, wondering what to do. Should I call Joe? Jed? But before I could do anything, the man looked behind him and then took off running toward the antique store.

My cell phone started to ring. I snatched the Taser off my desk before answering the call with trembling fingers.

The screen showed a number I didn't recognize. "Hello?"

"Stay in your office, turn off all the lights, and make sure your door is locked," a man snarled, out of breath.

"Who is this?"

"Merv. Now do as I said!"

I turned off my computer monitor, casting the room in darkness, and checked the door even though I knew it was bolted.

I sat in my chair, feeling a little foolish. Should I be hiding?

A gunshot rang out, and I ducked, wishing I had the gun that Jed had given me last week. The one I'd used to shoot J.R. in the leg. But it had been taken for evidence. I regretted sending Neely Kate and her trusty revolver home.

Another shot rang out, followed by shouting. Sirens were next, although for the life of me, I had no idea why the Henryetta police would need to use sirens when their headquarters was on the other side of the square—although, common sense had never ranked high on their list of new-hire qualifications.

Someone pounded on my back door, and I ran back to open it. "Who's there?"

"Merv. Let me in."

I unlatched the deadbolt, and Merv stumbled in when I opened the door. The first clue something was wrong was the fact he wasn't standing upright.

"What happened?" I reached out to help him, but he flung his hand out to hold me off, his gun still in his grip. I backed away from it.

"The bastard shot me, that's what."

"Oh, mercy. Where?"

"In my damn leg. I need to call Skeeter."

My heart was in my throat as I shut and locked the door behind him. "I take it you want to hide from the police, but the only places to hide in here are the bathroom and the small storeroom."

"Bathroom."

I opened the bathroom door and turned on the light.

"Turn that off," he barked. "The damn police will come knockin', wantin' to question you."

I flipped the switch and closed the bathroom door, then used the flashlight on my phone to illuminate the small space. Merv hobbled to the toilet and sat on the lid, and as soon as he was situated, I shined the light on the hand that was pressed to his thigh. He lifted it to reveal a quickly spreading dark stain on his jeans.

"Ya got a towel?"

"Yeah." I told myself to calm down as I opened the cabinet under the sink and handed him two clean hand towels. "Do you want me to call Skeeter?"

"No. I'll do it." He pressed one of the towels to his leg as he pulled his phone out of his pocket and placed the call. "Skeeter. There's been trouble."

He flicked an expressionless gaze up to me and then looked back down at his leg. "No. She's fine. We're in the bathroom of her shop. Some guy was lurking out front. I chased him toward the alley, but he shot me in the leg, and now the police are swarming all over the square."

"It was Sam Teagen," I said.

His gaze lifted again. "What?"

"The man outside the shop—he was Sam Teagen."

"Who the hell's Sam Teagen?"

I snatched the phone and pressed the speaker button. "Skeeter, listen to me. It was the guy who posted my bail."

"You're certain?" he asked.

"I've seen two photos of him, and it's him. I'm sure of it."

"This ties Simmons to your kidnapping after all." Skeeter sounded pained to admit it.

"And there's something else," I added.

"What?"

"He had scratch marks on his cheek. I think he was also one of the men who kidnapped me."

"*What?* Did Merv get him?"

"He got away," Merv grumbled.

Skeeter cursed a blue streak, and I was shocked to see Merv cringe.

"Skeeter," I said, getting pissed. "Merv got shot in the leg. We need to address that right now—not the fact that Sam Teagen got away."

"Merv," Skeeter said, "did you leave a blood trail?"

"No," Merv answered. "I was careful."

I couldn't believe my ears. "Your employee was shot, and all you want to know is if he left *a blood trail?*"

"Yes," Skeeter said, sounding like he'd pinched off the word. "Because if they tie him to a shooting, he's probably goin' to jail, Lady!"

He paused for a moment, and when he spoke again, he sounded calmer. "Merv, how bad is it?"

"It hurts like hell, but I'll live." He shot me an angry glare. "It's nicked is all."

"So the place is already teeming with cops?" Skeeter asked.

"Yeah," Merv said.

"Then we can't get you out yet. Rose?"

"Yeah?"

"I need you to stay with him. There's a murderer on the loose, and I don't want you going home on your own. Besides, we can't let the cops know you're there."

"Why?"

"They'll want to question you, which means they'll probably want to come inside. It goes without saying that we don't want them knowin' Merv's holed up there, and we sure as hell don't want them knowing that you saw Teagen, let alone that you recognized him."

"I think we should—"

"Yeah, I know. Your boyfriend's gonna pitch a fit, but I'll make him see it my way."

And there it was—the pain I'd stuffed down all afternoon was rising up and demanding my attention. But I wasn't about to fall apart now. Not here in the bathroom of my office, with a man bleeding in front of me. I'd let myself cry later.

"Mason's not an issue at the moment. We're not telling him anything. Have I made myself clear?" I asked in a direct tone.

"Crystal." Skeeter said, clearly pissed.

"But won't the police figure out I'm here?"

"Your truck's not out front, since Neely Kate drove it to your farm. As far as they're concerned, you're nice and cozy in that farmhouse of yours."

"How do you—" I cut myself off. "Jed's watching Neely Kate, isn't he?"

"You let me worry about who's watching who. My point is that you need to hole up for a few hours, and then I'll come to get you."

"You think it's a good idea for *you* to come?" Merv asked. "Why don't you send one of the guys?"

"Are you telling me how to my damned job, Merv?" Skeeter demanded in a cold, ominous tone.

Merv was not immune to it. "No, sir."

"Good. Rose?"

"Yeah?"

"You sure you want to keep this from the D.A.? Because I'm playin' this differently if you do."

"I'm sure."

After a beat of silence, Skeeter said, "You both sit tight, and I'll let you know if I hear anything. You do the same."

"Okay," I said.

As soon as the line disconnected, Merv shot another angry look at me.

My back stiffened. "Go ahead and say what's on your mind."

"You're not worth all of this trouble."

"I never claimed to be."

"You're not even puttin' out, and he's still chasing you around."

I cringed. "It's not like that, and you know it. I provide a service that has helped Skeeter ferret out his enemies."

"I don't believe that hocus-pocus bullshit for a minute."

I gave him a haughty look. "Well, good thing for me it's not up to you to believe it or not."

"You're gonna ruin him."

I cracked the bathroom door open. "Not if I can help it."

"Where the hell do you think you're goin'?"

"I want to see what's goin' on out there."

"Like hell!" He reached for me as I slipped out the door and into the hall.

"Calm down, Merv," I said, closing the door but leaving it open a crack. "I'll be careful, and you know you'd be lookin' yourself if you could."

He grunted, which I took to be acceptance, and I plastered myself to the wall in the short hallway that opened to the office. Red lights swept across the darkened room, and through the edge of the front window, I could see several police cars spread out around the square. I squatted down and made my way to Neely Kate's desk. Hunkered down behind it, I had a much better view out of the front window.

Officer Ernie was standing on the sidewalk outside my front door, looking down the street while talking to an elderly man. Great. If Officer Ernie was working the case, the police were just as likely to offer Teagen a job as they were to arrest him. The elderly man pointed toward the courthouse, and then the two of them walked out of my view.

My phone vibrated in my pocket, and I pulled it out, not surprised to see Mason's name. I considered not answering, but

I couldn't do that to him—especially because I suspected I knew why he was calling.

"Hey, Mason," I said quietly, hiding in the hole under Neely Kate's desk.

"Where are you?" Worry sharpened his words.

"We broke up, Mason." I sounded as weary as I felt.

"Rose, there was a shooting by your office. I just want to make sure you're okay."

I squeezed my eyes shut. "I'm fine, but it's not your job to worry about me anymore."

"I'm not supposed to worry about you anymore because you broke up with me *four hours ago*?" he asked, incredulous. "My feelings for you are supposed to switch off just because you say so?"

"No." I pressed the palm of my hand into my forehead. "I don't know. Mason, no matter how much we love each other, we just don't work right now."

"Right *now*? Are you saying this is temporary?"

"I don't know. You can't deal with what's goin' on in my life, and I understand that. I really *do*. But I can't put that horse back in the barn. All I can do is step away. I'm trying not to involve you any more than I already have."

"Rose, I can handle it. I think I proved that at the cabin."

"No, you didn't. Not really. You were forced to be there . . . you left me the first chance you got."

"How can you say that? I left to get Joe. To get you out of your charges."

"I know." I squeezed my eyes shut, trying to keep my tears contained.

He was right. But so was I. It ripped Mason's conscience apart to straddle the law, and there was no denying that I was the reason for his straddling. While I was devastated over losing him, I knew I couldn't make him choose between the law and me. If he chose me, deep down he'd resent me for it, but if he didn't choose me, he'd regret it for the rest of his life. I had to be strong. For him.

"We don't work right now, Mason," I said again. "You know that. *That's* the real reason why you left me last Friday."

"I just needed time to think, Rose."

I leaned my head against the metal back of the desk. "I understand, I really do, but when were you planning on comin' back?"

He was silent for a moment. "I don't know."

"And that right there is your answer. Love is stickin' with someone in the good times and the bad. Love is being there."

"Are you claiming I don't *love you*?"

"No. I know you love me. Just not enough." I shook my head. "No. That's not right. You love the me you knew with all your heart. But not the Rose I turned out to be."

"Sweetheart, there's only one you."

I used to think so, too. But it was never actually true, I used to be two people—the Rose everyone knew and the Lady in Black—three, if you counted the fearful person I had been before Momma died.

Last week, those separate selves came together. I no longer knew where I stopped and where the Lady began. We'd merged, and I wasn't sure what Mason thought of this new part of me. From the reaction I'd seen last week, he didn't like it one bit. I couldn't blame him for that. My cooperation with Skeeter went against everything he believed in.

"I love you, Mason, but what I've done is unfair and selfish. I need to get myself out of this thing—without you—so I don't drag you in any deeper."

"What gives you the right to make that decision for both of us?" he asked, sounding angry.

"*You* made it, Mason," I said quietly. "You made it last Friday when you walked out of my office. I could understand if you'd left for one night, but you've been gone five days. You made the decision that we were done."

"That's not true."

I was on the verge of breaking down, and I couldn't risk that. Not with Merv bleeding in my bathroom and the police gathering outside my door.

"I can't do this right now. I have to go," I said.

"Will you at least agree to meet me in person to discuss this?"

I heard voices outside, which meant whoever was out there would be able to hear me, too. "Yeah. I'll let you know when," I whispered and then hung up.

I took several breaths to calm down. I needed to have my wits about me. I could fall apart later.

Crawling out of my hole, I moved to the edge of the desk, peered around the edge, and then gasped. Detective Taylor—the man who had a personal vendetta against me—was talking to Kate, of all people. I hadn't seen her since my kidnapping. She wore dark jeans with black boots and a canvas jacket. The light of the street lamp highlighted the blue streaks in her dark hair. I strained to hear what they were saying.

". . . and the suspect . . . corner?" Detective Taylor asked.

Kate had her back to me, but she turned and pointed in the opposite direction of the antique store. "He ran that way."

Detective Taylor wrote something in his notebook. "Can you give me a description?"

"Yeah," Kate said. "Really tall." She lifted her hand over her head to indicate a giant that would have dwarfed Sam Teagen. "Red jacket. Khaki pants. He looked like a kid, maybe seventeen."

"And you're sure you saw a gun?"

"I saw him shoot it toward the courthouse. Like he was aiming for a tree."

Kate was lying. A lot. Why would she lie?

Oh, my word.

Kate was working with him. The first time I'd seen Sam Teagen, he'd run toward the antique store—same as he'd done tonight. Kate lived above that antique store.

I'd bet ten bucks he was hiding there now.

I pulled out my phone and called Skeeter. "I have something," I whispered.

"What?"

"Kate Simmons told Detective Taylor she saw the shooter, but she's lying about what Sam Teagen looks like and which way he went. Both tonight and Friday, I saw him run toward the antique store and disappear. Kate's apartment is over the antique store—so I bet he's hiding there."

"Whoa. Back up a step. You said you saw him Friday?"

"Yeah, I saw him lurking around, but when I went to confront him, he took off toward the antique store and disappeared."

"Why didn't you tell me?" he shouted.

"Shh!" I hissed, moving further behind the desk. "Stop yelling!"

"Where the hell are you?" he demanded in a lower voice.

"I'm hiding behind Neely Kate's desk. Detective Taylor and Kate Simmons are on the sidewalk in front of my office."

"Where's Merv?"

"He's still bleedin' in my bathroom."

"Very bad?"

"Well, I'm no judge of gunshot wounds, but Jed bled a lot more from the one to his arm."

"Then Merv'll be fine," he said dismissively. "What else is goin' on?"

"You're not gonna tell me to run to the back and hide?"

"Why in the hell would I do that?" he demanded. "What's going on now?"

"Kate and Taylor are still talkin'."

"Can you see anyone else?"

"No . . . oh, wait. I see Joe and several deputies walkin' over to them. Detective Taylor doesn't look very happy."

Skeeter chuckled. "I'd love to see that."

"I suspect most of the Henryetta police officers are here, and it looks like there are four sheriff's deputies if you count Joe. Why would so many law enforcement officers show up to check out a couple of gunshots? The Henryetta P.D. is so territorial, I can't imagine why they're letting Joe and his deputies be part of this."

Skeeter was silent for a moment. "Shit. They're moving Simmons to the county jail. What's Simmons Jr. doin'?"

Joe was yelling at two of his deputies, and two more deputy cars pulled into the street. "Something's goin' on, Skeeter. Joe looks pretty ticked."

"Simmons is up to something."

I could see Joe pointing down the street, away from the courthouse. He was still yelling, but he'd switched the focus of his yelling to the detective. "Right now he's yelling at Taylor."

"Not *that* Simmons. His father."

Oh, crappy doodles. "He's not doin' what I think he's doin', is he?"

"Make a jailbreak? Yeah, I think he is. They must have a stack of evidence so high he knows he'll never crawl out from under it. Did Teagen see you?"

"Yes."

"Then that confirms it. We've got to get you out of there as soon as possible."

I gasped. "Surely he won't try something with all those police officers and deputies outside."

"I wouldn't put anything past that bastard," Skeeter growled. "Can you get to the roof?"

"Why?" I asked, my heart skipping a beat.

"That shit scraper can just walk in and snatch you is why."

"But the police—"

"*Shit*. Why didn't I see it before?"

"What?" I asked, starting to panic.

"It's all about distractions, Lady. Two pipe bombs went off about fifteen minutes ago. One by the ice cream shop and the other close to your friend's church."

"Jonah?"

"They're trying to get the police and the sheriff's deputies as frazzled as a mother with a houseful of toddlers. It'll give J.R. the perfect opportunity to not only slip out of custody, but also to pick up a package along the way."

"Me."

"Exactly. So you need to hide. *Now*. I'm positive it's all about to happen. So answer my question. Is there a way to the roof?"

Terror washed through my head, making me lightheaded. "There's a staircase in the back, but it's locked."

"Do you have a key?"

"Yeah, but what about Merv? I don't think he can climb the stairs."

"He's not. You're goin' on your own. Merv will lock the door behind you. Tell him to give you a gun."

My heart slammed into my ribcage. "I can't take his gun! I'll just use my Taser."

"Your Taser isn't gonna hold off Old Man Simmons. Take the gun."

"And leave him defenseless?"

"He's got two. Now do it. You're wastin' time."

"Joe's right out front. Why don't I run out there and tell him what's goin' on?"

"Do you totally trust him?"

"I don't think he'll hurt me . . ."

"But he's not tellin' you everything, is he? Listen, Rose, I'm gonna shoot it to you straight. J.R.'s escapin' police custody tonight, and he's sent Teagen to snatch you again. Simmons intends to kill you himself, and he won't be kind about it." He paused. "Remember that I spent six years under this man's tutelage. I know how he thinks, so I can outwit him before he makes his next move. His son might not condone the things he does, but he still sees him as his father."

My stomach spasmed. I believed every word Skeeter had said.

"Now, it's your choice," Skeeter said, his voiced tight with anxiety. "Stick with me—or go out to Joe."

I peered around the desk again, trying to see what was going on outside. Joe and Detective Taylor had moved across the street. If I went to Joe, he'd lock me up somewhere, and considering my luck, Officer Sprout would stand guard again. I'd nearly been killed the last time I was in protective custody. J.R. was a lot craftier than Daniel Crocker. It was an easy decision.

"You."

Chapter Nine

That's my girl. Now go to Merv. Tell him to give you his Glock."

"Okay." I wanted to argue with him some more about the gun, but I knew he was right.

"Can you get to the back without getting seen?"

"Yeah, they're all arguing across the street now."

"Then go."

"I have to get the key first." I crawled over to my desk, slid open the drawer, and then reached up and pulled out the key. Then I grabbed my coat off the back of my chair and stuffed my Taser in the pocket. My earbuds were in there, so I tugged them out and plugged them into my phone. I turned on my microphone, inserted one of the buds into my left ear, letting the other dangle, and then shoved the phone into my jeans pocket. Finally, I crawled to the back, staying low until I reached the cracked bathroom door.

My nerves were getting the better of me again. I suspected Merv wasn't going to be as gung-ho about this plan as his boss seemed to be.

I pushed the door open enough to see Merv sitting on toilet with a blood-soaked towel pressed to his leg. His phone was on the counter, its illuminated screen the only light in the small room.

"Merv," I said, stuffing my arm into my coat sleeve, "Skeeter wants you to give me your Glock."

"You'll have to pry it out of my cold, dead fingers if I don't hear it from the man himself."

A second later, the hold tone sounded in my ear and the phone on the counter began to bounce around.

Merv scowled as he answered. He didn't say anything, but I could hear Skeeter's voice yelling in Merv's ear.

"Got it," Merv said, then immediately hung up, smacking the phone on the counter. He pulled a gun out of his pocket and pointed it at me.

"Do you have it?" Skeeter asked in my ear as I slid my other arm into the coat.

I stared down the barrel of Merv's Glock, then lifted my gaze to meet his angry eyes. Surely he wouldn't be stupid enough to shoot me while his boss was on the line, listening to his every move. I took a breath to steady my nerves and held out my hand.

"Do you have the gun?" Skeeter repeated, sounding pissed. "Is Merv giving you trouble?"

I reached up and switched off the microphone, keeping my thumb and finger on the switch. "Skeeter's on my phone right now," I said quietly. "And he's asking if you've given me the gun. I'd like to keep this disagreement between us, but I'm going to turn the microphone back on now."

I slid the switch and extended my hand again. Merv's grip tightened on the weapon, and his scowl deepened before he let out a grunt. He turned the gun around and handed it to me, with the barrel pointed toward the ground.

"Rose!" Skeeter barked.

"I have it," I said, taking the gun and pulling out the clip to look at the shells inside. After setting the clip back into place, I stuffed the weapon into my right coat pocket. "I'm ready."

I spun around and used to the key to open the padlock securing the door to the spiral staircase that led up to the roof. At the last minute I remembered that Bruce Wayne kept a flashlight by the fuse box, also hidden here, since the power had

Denise Grover Swank

gone out so much during the first few weeks of our tenancy. I switched the flashlight on and shined it into the closet-sized room.

"What the hell is goin' on over there?" Skeeter demanded. "Give me an update."

"I found a flashlight," I said, exasperated, but then a new terror hit me. "Oh, mercy. After Merv locks the door, I'm gonna be trapped up there."

More gunshots filled the square outside, followed by several shouts and screams.

"I'll come get you," Skeeter barked. "Go. *Now.* Simmons is making his move. Tell Merv to be ready."

I started to say something, but Merv grunted, "Get goin'."

I stepped into the room, and Merv shut the door behind me. Fear almost crippled me as I heard the clink of the padlock locking into place. Memories of all the times my mother had locked me in a closet—a small, dark space like this one—as punishment for one of my visions came rushing back. I started breathing heavily as I stepped onto the first tread.

"Rose, talk to me," Skeeter said in a tight, low voice. "What's goin' on?"

I could give into my fear—and let Sam Teagen or whoever was coming for me hear me hyperventilating in the staircase—or I could keep going. I was pretty sure the wooden door wouldn't stop any bullets. Which meant I needed to get control of my nerves and get up on the roof. "I'm fine. I had to take a moment."

"You don't have a moment, Lady. *Go.*"

I knew he couldn't see me, but I nodded anyway. "I'm goin'."

I hurried up the two flights of stairs, trying to tread lightly so no one could hear me.

"I'm at the top," I whispered, shining the flashlight at the flat door over my head. Holding the flashlight in place with my shoulder, I climbed up the metal rungs that had been set into the concrete wall until I reached the door. I struggled to get the key to turn in the padlock, not surprising since I was sure it hadn't been opened in several years, but it finally turned with a rusty creak. I pulled off the lock and pushed up on the door, trying not to let it bang onto the roof as it dropped open.

The cold night air struck me in the face as I climbed out of the stairway, making me grateful I'd thought to grab my coat. Staying in a crouch, I flipped the door back over, then cringed when I heard more gunshots.

"Rose!" Skeeter shouted in my ear.

"I'm here," I said as I stuck the padlock into the pocket that held the Taser.

"Did I hear more gunshots?"

"Yeah."

"Can you see what's going on?"

"Let me get to the side of the roof."

"Keep your head down."

"I'm not stupid enough to let anyone see me," I grumped as I crawled on hands and knees to the edge.

"I'm more worried about stray bullets."

"Oh, yeah." I realized with a jolt that Joe was down there in the melee. I had to make sure he wasn't hurt. The ledge around the edge of the roof was less than three feet tall, so I stayed as flat to the ground as possible.

"The Henryetta police are hiding behind their open car doors." Officer Ernie's arm jutted out over the door's hinges, his gun pointed at the front of my office.

That was a bad sign.

"And where are the sheriff's deputies?" Skeeter asked.

"I don't see them."

"You mean they're hiding so well that you can't see them?"

"No, most of the sheriff cars are gone. There's no sign of Joe."

"He's makin' his move. Do you see anything else?"

I peered around the square, my stomach in knots. "No. Nothing."

"Make your way to the back of the building and check out the alley. Stay down. Simmons Sr. is gonna be a lot more sly then all them boys on the ground put together."

That's exactly what I was afraid of. I crawled across the roof, tiny scattered pebbles digging into my palms. When I got to the edge, I peered down into the alley. "I don't see anything."

"Whatever he's up to is goin' to happen in that alley. Keep an eye out."

"Okay."

"Do you have a coat?" he asked. "It's cold tonight."

I couldn't help grinning. "Yeah. I'm wearing it. Don't worry, I've survived worse. Sitting on top of a roof sure beats gettin' chased by a maniac through the snow-covered woods for two days."

"Crocker?"

"Yeah." That had marked the beginning of my relationship with Mason. Funny how it had started out with us both being chased by a maniac and ended the same way.

"You sure know how to find trouble," Skeeter teased.

I laughed, fighting tears. "So I've been told."

"You scared?" he asked softly.

"Yeah, but nothing I can't handle." I looked over the ledge again, searching for any sign of movement. I realized I could see Kate's fire escape from my vantage point. The one Neely Kate and I had used to make our escape after breaking into her apartment.

"That's what I like about you," he said. "You take the punches, but you don't back down."

"I was beaten down for too long," I said. "I got tired of not living my life, so now I'm gonna take on anyone who gets in my way."

He laughed. "I can't see you lettin' anyone beat you down."

"Then you must not remember meeting me nearly a year ago."

He laughed again, softer this time. "Oh, I remember. The woman I met was naïve and unworldly, but not beaten down."

"I guess I've changed a lot since then." Further proof I wasn't the woman Mason first met either.

I couldn't let myself think about him right now. I needed to focus on surviving.

I knelt on the roof, resting my hand on the ledge as I readjusted the earbud in my ear. Some movement to my left caught my eye, down below, close to the antiques store. It took a moment for me to register what I was seeing, but the shadows resolved into two men hurrying down the alley toward my shop. One looked like Teagen, and the other guy was dressed all in black. Both held high-powered rifles. Teagen wasn't playing around this time.

"Skeeter, they're comin'."

"Tell me what you see."

By the time I'd described them, they were already underneath me, standing at the back door. "They're at the door! What about Merv?"

"Don't you worry about Merv," Skeeter chuckled. "He's a tough old coot. Those boys'll be sorry they messed with him."

The guy dressed all in black bent over the door knob.

"I think they're picking the lock."

"Merv's waiting for 'em."

My heart was beating so hard against my ribcage I was sure it was gonna fly out and flop across the roof. "What if they get past him? Will they think to come up here?"

"It depends on whether they've been watching both entrances. If not, for all they know, you might have left."

"That padlock won't hold them, will it?"

He hesitated. "No."

I took a deep breath and looked around. My office building was connected to several adjoining ones, including the one housing the antique store on the opposite end. I noticed a small storage shed on top of the antique store building.

"I'm going to move," I said.

"Where do you think you can go?" Skeeter boomed out.

"I'm not going to sit around waiting to serve them tea when they come callin'," I said. "There's a storage shed on top of the building with the antique store. I can try to hole up there."

"Just sit tight for now and tell me what you see."

When I leaned over, I saw that the guy who was dressed all in black had stood up and that he and Teagen were opening the door.

Gunshots rang out, echoing off the brick buildings in the alley.

"They've gone inside," I whispered. I sat still, waiting for some sign, although I had no idea *what*. "The gunshots stopped. Do you think Merv's okay?"

Skeeter didn't answer me for several seconds. "Can you get to that shed?"

My pulse pounded in my head. "I think so. Is Merv okay?"

"He's not answering. Get going."

I tried not to think about the possibility of Merv getting killed. Because of me. "If I hadn't taken his other gun . . ."

"Merv was doin' the job I told him to do. Don't you even think about feeling guilty."

I started climbing over the ledge to the next building. Although the two buildings were attached, there was a two-foot drop between them. I landed with an *oomph* and stayed in a squat as I waddled to the next building. Sirens began to wail in the distance, from the area close to the county jail.

I couldn't stop thinking about Merv. "But if he hadn't been—"

"You stop right there. I need you to tell me what's going on in the square."

I moved closer to the front of the building to take a gander and discovered that the police had moved out from behind their car doors. They were now spread out in the street. Detective Taylor had jogged to the end of my street and was heading around the corner. No doubt his destination was my alley.

I relayed the information, then asked, "What will happen if they find Merv in my office?"

"You'll be in the clear, if you're worried about that," Skeeter said.

"I'm more worried about Merv."

"That's why I have Carter Hale on my retainer. To take care of these kinds of predicaments," he teased, but I heard the strain in his voice. He'd likely never admit it, but he was worried about Merv, too. "Are you still making your way to that shed?"

I started moving again, crawling on my hands and knees to move faster while remaining out of sight. "I have two more buildings to go," I said, climbing a short wall to get to the top of the next roof top. "Those men came from the direction of the antique store."

A new thought struck me, and I moved to the back edge of the building to verify my hunch. Sure enough, Kate's fire escape had been lowered.

I told Skeeter what I saw. "I think they came from Kate's apartment."

"You may very well be right. We'll deal with that later. Just get your ass to that shed."

"Why do you sound so anxious?" I asked.

"I still can't get through to Merv."

"Is Jed with Neely Kate?" I asked, starting to panic. "If they think I'm not at the office, they might go lookin' for me at the farm next."

"Already taken care of."

"Where is she?"

"Jed took Neely Kate and your dog to a safe house. She's fine. Now get your ass into that shed."

I climbed a one-foot incline to the final building, which was wider than the others and had a six-by-six structure in the middle. A small building in the back corner looked like it housed a staircase.

When I reached the door, I wasn't surprised to find the doorknob wouldn't turn. "It's locked."

Skeeter cursed. "What kind of lock? Deadbolt?"

I bent over and turned on my flashlight for a quick moment before flicking it off. "No, just a keyed doorknob."

"Are you wearing any hairpins?"

"What?" I asked, and then I realized what he wanted me to do. "I've never picked a lock before."

"No time like the present to learn. Do you have some?"

I didn't have any pins in my hair, but I felt three in my pocket. Thank goodness I tended to carry them in case I needed to go out and do an estimate on a windy day. "How many do I need?" I asked. "Two?"

He chuckled, but there was an anxious edge to it. "You've been watching cop shows. That's good. Yeah, bend one out flat. Keep the other like it is, but bend the hooked end at a forty-five degree angle. Tell me when you're ready."

I did as he instructed, but I had to stop a couple of times to rub my numb fingers together so I could finish the task. "Done."

"Okay, now listen close—you don't have much time. Turn the knob like you're trying to open it. Then slide the bent end of the hair pin in until you meet resistance."

I followed his instructions. "Okay."

"Good. Now take the other pin and gently slide it in over the other, keeping the knob turned. Again, stop when you meet resistance."

As I performed the maneuver, I tried not to think about the fact that two men with guns might appear at any time. I hoped to God this would work. "Okay."

"Now push up gently, and you'll feel it catch. Do you feel it?"

I closed my eyes and felt the pop. "I think so."

"Good, now push it deeper until you meet resistance."

Keeping my eyes closed, I tried to feel for the resistance. "That sounds like a bad *that's what she said* joke," I murmured as I felt the pin give. I slowly pushed deeper.

Skeeter chuckled. "Why, Rose Gardner, I expected you to be a blushing innocent."

"Haven't you figured out by now that I'm far from innocent? The fact that I'm picking a lock is proof enough of that." I felt another pin give, and then the knob turned and the door opened. "I did it!" I whisper-shouted in amazement. "It's open."

"Good. Get inside and lock the door. You're about to get company."

"How do you know?" I glanced over my shoulder as I opened the door wider.

"Merv sent me text. *Go.*"

I stumbled into the room, bumping into a table, and turned to shut and lock the door behind me. "What's to keep them from picking the lock?" I whispered, pulling the gun out of my pocket.

"Nothing. They could also shoot the lock, but I doubt they'll do either. They'll never expect you to be hiding in there, especially if they're hiding out in Kate's apartment. You just sit tight and wait them out."

"Is Merv okay?" I made my way along the edge of the table. It felt like it was made with 4x4s.

"He's been better, but you let me deal with Merv. You concentrate on what's going on around you. Do you hear anything?"

"No."

"Stay on your toes. I expect them to be quiet. They're hidin' from Henryetta's finest. They may think to hide in your shed, too."

"Oh, crap."

"What's in there with you?"

"Uh . . . I didn't see anything before I came in, but I bumped into a large table. About four feet long, I think. I figure I shouldn't turn on my flashlight in case they're close enough to see light at the bottom of the door."

"Good thinking. But use the light of your phone screen. It should be dim enough to keep you hidden. Look for someplace to hide in case they decide to join you in there."

I dug out my phone. The illuminated screen revealed a table constructed out of plywood and rough lumber, covered in stacks of papers. There was also a bottom ledge stacked with large cardboard boxes.

"I think I may have found a good spot," I said, moving around to the back of the table. I shifted two heavy boxes onto the floor. The table was wide enough that I could hide in the middle of the boxes and go undetected—unless they started searching. But it seemed like my best chance. "I found a place that should work unless they go snoopin'."

"Have your gun drawn just in case this all goes south," he said, his voice even and cool.

"Already done," I said as I moved the boxes back into place next to me. And I finished in the nick of time.

Seconds later, I heard low voices outside the shed, followed by the click of metal in the lock and the sound of the door swinging open. They were either experts at lock picking, or they had a key. Considering the familiar way they rushed into the room and shut the door behind them—neither of them hitting the table—I was going with the latter. Someone turned on a dim light, and I could hear their soft footsteps, pacing back and forth next to the table.

I struggled to keep my breath slow and steady. The last thing I needed was for them to hear me hyperventilating.

"Rose?" Skeeter whispered in my ear, reminding me that my phone was still in my hand. The screen was locked, but I turned it over just in case. I didn't dare tell Skeeter what was going on. He'd figure it out soon enough.

"Do you think he saw us?" one of them asked. He sounded like his vocal cords were made of sandpaper. I heard something metal clang on the table. He moved again, and I realized that he was the one wearing dark jeans.

"Nah," Sam Teagen said, his khaki-covered legs staying in place. "He was too distracted. Why do you think Malcolm has a guy at her office?"

"The bigger question is why did he help her take down Simmons? That's what she wants to find out."

"She ain't payin' us enough to deal with this shit," Teagen said. "I've already taken more chances than I would have liked."

"You've got that damn straight."

They were silent for a moment, then the sandpaper-voiced guy said, "I don't plan on spending all night in this shack."

"It's not like we have other options."

"Hell, yeah, we do. We could climb down to the fire escape and hang out in the apartment below us."

"She won't like that," Teagen growled.

"She's not the one dodging police and sheriff's deputies on the whims of a psychopath. We'll tell her we didn't have a choice."

"She'll want to know why we didn't hide out here in the shed."

I heard some more clinking of metal and plastic and realized they were reloading their guns.

"Tell her the police followed us up here. Hell, maybe we should burn the shed down."

My breath caught, and I could feel the tension radiating from the other side of the phone line.

"I suspect there's only one way out," Skeeter whispered.

The answer was obvious, not that I could respond.

"We ain't burnin' shit, idiot," Teagen said, and it sounded like he whacked the other guy in the back of the head. "Why would we want to call more attention to the fact that we're here in this block of buildings? Not to mention the ammo would explode." He paused. "Maybe we should head down to the apartment, though."

"No, listen. They're getting too close. We need to torch anything that even hints we're part of this."

"Huh . . ." Teagen murmured. "You might be right."

"Rose, you listen to me," Skeeter said. His voice rumbled in my head.

The other guy groaned. "She's not gonna be happy that we didn't get Rose Gardner. And Simmons is likely to kill us. We need to destroy everything linking us to her. Then it's her word against ours."

Skeeter continued with his instructions, adding, "You be prepared to shoot them."

My hand squeezed the handle of my gun.

"Yeah," Teagen said. "But where could Rose be? She couldn't have gone out the front . . ." He cursed. "I bet she was hiding in the apartment on the second floor of her building."

"But the door to the roof was unlocked."

"She probably did that to trick us. *Dammit.* We have to go back. If she hasn't gotten away already."

"What about burning the shack?"

"Let's wait until we check out that apartment. Then we'll torch it and hang out downstairs until we can escape in all the confusion.

The door opened and they both left, grumbling about what a pain in the ass I was.

"Are they gone?" Skeeter asked.

"Yeah." I pushed out a big breath and leaned forward, my heart beating so hard it hurt.

"Give them thirty seconds. Then crack the door. Watch them until they disappear back into your building."

"Then what?" I crawled out from under the table, thankful I could see what I was doing since they hadn't bothered to turn off the light. "I'm stuck on this roof."

"No, you can use the same fire escape they're planning to use, but you'll have to hurry."

When I cracked open the door, they were only halfway across the rooftops. I turned my attention to the interior of the room. The walls were lined with guns, but that didn't catch me off guard nearly as much as what was laying on top of the table.

I gasped.

"What?" Skeeter asked.

"All the evidence Neely Kate and I found in Kate Simmons's apartment was moved here." I flipped through a stack of documents and found Mason's case files.

"So?"

"So?" I asked in disbelief. "This proves Kate's involved."

"We've got Teagen and dipshit to prove that. You need to get the hell out of there before they come back."

I started rifling through the files and opened a folder at random. I was surprised to see a photo of an older African-American woman clipped to one side of the folder. A paper clipped to the other side read Roberta Miller. What did that have to do with Mason? As I looked over the paper, which listed her information in bullet points, I recognized the El Dorado, Arkansas, address of one of her previous employers. This woman didn't have anything to do with Mason.

This was a file on Joe's childhood housekeeper.

Chapter Ten

W hat are you doin', Rose?" Skeeter's voice pierced my ear.

"I'm looking in a file." The El Dorado address was the home of Joe's parents. Roberta had been Joe's housekeeper when he was a kid. He'd loved her like a grandmother, and it had devastated him when she'd up and left.

"You don't have time to look in a file. Get the hell out of there!"

I noticed a brown duffel bag on the floor, and without thinking, I grabbed the handles and dumped the heavy contents onto the floor. Guns and ammo spilled into the corner. I only hoped Teagen and his friend would be in too big of a hurry to burn the place to notice, but then I realized that what I was about to do would be *more* noticeable.

"There are a whole lot of guns in here, Skeeter," I said, stuffing Roberta's file into the bag, along with as many other files as I could grab.

"We heard that Gentry was moving guns into town, but we never could figure out where he was hiding them. No one would ever think to look there. How many do you see?"

"I just dumped ten or so out on the floor, but they're hanging on all the walls. I see at least fifty out in the open. And then all the boxes."

"Gentry," he confirmed. "Now get the hell out of there."

I crammed the last file into the bag, then struggled to zip it shut. When I picked it up, I groaned at the weight of it. How was I going to get it down the fire escape?

"Rose!"

I looped the strap over my shoulder. "I'm goin'." I ran over to the back edge of the building, but the hopelessness of my situation washed over me when I saw the distance between the roof and the fire escape platform. "I can't do it," I said. "It's too far."

"How far?"

"I don't know. Maybe eight feet."

"Shit." He paused. "You have to jump."

"Skeeter!"

"The way I see it, you have three choices. One, you stay there and get captured. Two, you hide in the shed and then shoot them when they open the door. Or three, you jump. Now which do you pick?"

"It's gonna make noise when I land on the metal grate, Skeeter. There are police officers milling around the alley. They're sure to notice."

"Give me thirty seconds, and there'll be a distraction. When you see it, jump."

"What is it?"

"You'll know when you see it. They should all clear out so you can lower the ladder and get to the street."

"It's already down." Further confirmation that they'd holed up in Kate's apartment. "Then what?"

"Head north on Lincoln and then go into the Greasy Spoon diner. Wait for me at a booth in the back."

I looked down at the fire escape again, shaking with fear. The landing was narrow. What if I missed?

He grunted, then his voice lowered. "I have to go, but wait for me there and try to keep a low profile."

"Skeeter!" I shouted, but he'd already hung up, leaving me terrified and alone. I hadn't realized how reassuring he'd been—even if it was just a voice in my ear—until he was gone.

About ten seconds later, an explosion lit up the night sky over by the square, sending pieces of burning debris raining down on the street. The police in the alley ran off to investigate, and I took that as my cue.

I dropped the bag first, aiming for the fire escape. Instead, it missed by a good three feet and landed in an open Dumpster with a loud thud. Thankfully, no one was around to notice.

Except . . . Shoot. That didn't bode well for my own leap.

I glanced back over my shoulder and saw a head popping out of the trap door on my building's roof.

Oh, *shit.*

I climbed onto the ledge, sucked in a deep breath, and then jumped, looking back just in time to see Sam Teagen staring right at me.

The fright of getting caught overrode my fear of jumping—not that I could have changed my mind midair. I landed in a crouch, hitting my shoulder against the metal siding hard enough to hurt—taking comfort that I wasn't in the trash bin—then scrambled up.

I didn't have much time to get down the ladder, around the alley, and out of sight. They were sure to see where I went.

Which gave me another idea.

I spun around and peered inside the dark apartment. *Kate's* dark apartment. When Neely Kate and I had broken into this very apartment last week, the fire escape had been our escape route. I was betting my life on a huge gamble, but if I pulled it off, I'd likely save my hide.

But first I had to get the window open. The window connected to the fire escape had been stuck last time, so I saw no reason to waste precious moments on it now. The next window over—the escape route I'd used with Neely Kate—was slightly open, hinting that Teagen and his friend had come that way, too. I leaned over the railing, slid my fingers under the one-inch crack at the bottom of the window, and jerked upward. The window slid up, but only by a foot.

Crap on a cracker.

I climbed onto the railing and, holding on to it with one hand for balance, used my free hand to grab the bottom of the window frame and shove it upward with all my strength. The window slid open with a jerk, making me lose my balance on the railing. I pitched forward—my chest and upper body landed in the opening, and the lower half of my body hung out of it.

I heard Teagen's friend yell, "She went over the edge!"

"Shut up, you idiot!" Teagen shouted, his voice much fainter.

I'd already suspected Teagen was craftier than half the criminals in the county, but his friend fell into the stupid category.

Pushing on the ledge, I pulled myself the rest of the way into the apartment and then spun around and pushed the window mostly shut, leaving the one-inch crack to throw Teagen off.

One of them shouted something incoherent. Panicked, I scrambled backward to the makeshift bathroom area that I remembered from my first "visit" to the apartment. I climbed into the tub and hid behind the shower curtains the owner had hung to stand in for makeshift bathroom walls. One of the men landed on the fire escape with a loud thud, which was quickly followed by an explosion that shook the floor beneath me. They'd set the fire.

There was another thud on the fire escape, followed by a groan. "Shit, I think I broke my ankle," the sandpaper voice whined.

"Get up, you wuss. She got away. Simmons is *really* gonna kill us if we don't track her down."

I strained to listen, thankful they weren't whispering.

"If you'd just killed her last week like you were supposed to, we wouldn't be in this mess."

"My job was to snatch her. The others were supposed to kill her. I did my part. I left her at the cabin, then went off to kill the assistant D.A."

"Which you didn't do."

"Shut up, Marshal. I couldn't find him!" Teagen whined. "It's like he vanished into thin air until they captured Simmons."

"That bitch wasn't happy before. She's already pissed she hasn't gotten her bail money back, so imagine how ugly she's gonna be now. We have to find that girl and quick."

"Then let's go find the girl," Teagen said. "And you better not bellyache about your foot."

"Ankle."

"Whatever. The fire's really burning now. We need to git."

He was right. Smoke was wafting down through cracks in the ceiling above me.

Their voices grew fainter as they descended the fire-escape staircase. Time to leave.

I ran to the front window and cursed when I saw how many people were gathered out front. How would I justify leaving Kate's apartment? The staircase to the street led only to this apartment.

But the answer quickly presented itself in the form of the elderly couple who owned the antique store downstairs. It couldn't be later than eight o'clock, but they were both ready for bed. Or had been when the alert went out. The husband was wearing a pair of overalls over a flannel pajama shirt along with a pair of dirty rain boots; the wife had on a nightgown over a pair of pants, and her thin gray hair was up in six or seven foam rollers. They pushed through the growing crowd, moving toward the front entrance of the store, yelling, "Get out of my way! We gotta save our stuff."

Officer Sprout tried to hold them back. "Nobody's goin' in there! It's for your own safety!"

"Let 'em go!" a man shouted. "This is America! They can go into their store if they wanna! The First Amendment says so!"

"Wrong amendment, dumbass," another man snarled. "That's our right to carry guns!" He aimed a rifle in the air and let off a round. The bullet ricocheted off the brick by the window closest to me, and the crowd screamed and ducked.

The roof over my head groaned, and smoke rolled through a growing crack.

The rowdy crowd was now back on their feet and surging forward. Someone threw a rock, and the sound of the shattering glass window filled the air as pieces of glass fell to the sidewalk.

Mass chaos broke out as the couple pushed past Officer Sprout. The crowd moved forward with them, rushing the store. That was my cue, which was a good thing since smoke was pouring into the apartment at an alarming rate from the ceiling, which appeared to be directly below the burning shack, burning my nose and throat. Covering my arm over the lower half of my face, I raced down the stairs.

Blending in with the crowd would have been easier if I'd had an armful of loot. Everywhere I looked, people were carting a variety of items out of the store. Two men hefted a battered, dirty beige sofa with yellow and brown stains onto their shoulders while a woman ran out behind them carrying a lamp that was shaped like a cow and painted to indicate the various cuts of meat. An older man tried to snatch it from her, but she lifted it over her head and began to beat him over the head with the lamp shade.

I pushed my way through the melee as a new fight broke out between two women over a bust of Justin Bieber—a fine antique if I ever saw one—and I narrowly missed getting hit in the head by a brass statuette of two dogs with clown wigs and noses, which a man had tossed out the window to his friend.

When I reached the safety of the corner, I hesitated. I needed to get to the Greasy Spoon, but it was three blocks away. Part of me wanted to stay in the anonymity of the crowd—rowdy as they were—but the rest of me was eager to get that bag out of the Dumpster and find Skeeter. I'd gotten a lot of potentially useful information from Teagen and his friend. I just needed to figure out what to do with it.

It quickly became apparent that the bag was not going to be easily retrieved. The fire department had parked a truck smack in the middle of the tight alley, and several fire fighters were trying to get to the roof. There was no way to get around them unnoticed. I only hoped the bag didn't get drenched.

Since the bag was a lost cause for now, I headed for the diner, passing several people hurrying toward the square.

"What's goin' on?" a woman asked, looking more excited than a person had any right to be considering the chaos unfolding in the center of town.

I considered not answering, not wanting to draw any attention to myself, but if I ignored her, I'd only make myself more conspicuous. "It's crazy. Gunshots and fires . . ." I said. "I'm headin' home."

"I hope we're not too late." A rapturous smile spread across the woman's face. It was clear this was the most exciting thing to ever happen to her.

Most of the people I passed were headed to the square, but I scanned their clothing, keeping an eye out for Sam Teagen and his friend.

The Greasy Spoon was known for being open late and for offering a menu that lived up to its name. According to town lore, it had originally opened up to serve the patrons of a bar that used to be next door. The greasy food was catered to customers who needed to sober up. But the bar had been closed for years, and the Greasy Spoon's patronage had dwindled to practically nothing. So it was no surprise there was only one other customer in the place when I walked in—an elderly man who was sitting at the counter with a cup of coffee, watching a TV mounted in the corner.

I slid into a booth at the back, choosing the side that faced the door. I was rubbing my hands for warmth when the waitress walked over. Middle-aged and slightly overweight, she looked like a stereotypical waitress from a TV sitcom, right down to her blue dress and white apron.

"Coffee to start, miss?"

I didn't have a single dollar on me, but Skeeter had said he was meeting me here. If he didn't show, I'd have bigger problems than an unpaid food bill. "Yeah, and do you serve breakfast this late?"

She put her hand on her hip and grinned. "We sure do."

"Then I'll take a stack of pancakes, bacon, and scrambled eggs."

The waitress chuckled and wandered toward the kitchen. "I'll get your coffee right out."

Way to not stand out.

I was nibbling a piece of bacon, having already made a good start on my pancakes, when the door jingled. My gaze flicked up to see Skeeter walk in, his dark gaze already fixed on me. He slid into the seat across from me and grinned as he took in my heaping plate.

"I love a woman who loves to eat." He turned up the empty coffee cup at his place setting and poured a cup of coffee from the carafe the waitress had left.

"Turns out running for your life makes you hungry." I sliced through the stack of three pancakes and took a big bite, then put down my fork and picked up my coffee, cradling the cup in my hands. "I learned a few things after our call."

He lifted his eyebrows. "Oh, really?" Shooting me a challenging stare, he picked up my fork, stabbed a section of my pancakes, and took a bite.

I laughed, then took a sip of my coffee. "Help yourself. You might as well get a bite since you're paying for it."

He chuckled as he set down the fork, then reached for a piece of bacon.

I slapped his hand away. "Get your own bacon. That's mine."

"So much for sharing." He lifted his hand, and the waitress came running, not that I was surprised. Skeeter looked less scary tonight, but he was still Skeeter. "I'll take what she's having." He motioned to my plate. "But with fried eggs and double the bacon."

"I'll have it right out."

Skeeter turned his attention back to me. "What happened after our call?"

"You tell me," I said. "Ten seconds after you hung up, there was an explosion."

He glanced around the room, quickly dismissing the old man. "Merv's car blew up."

"But how . . . ?"

"I took care of it."

I had a hard time picturing Skeeter doing his own dirty work. But I decided against asking for more details. I probably didn't want to know. "How's Merv?"

His good mood vanished. "He's been better."

"He's okay?"

He lifted his shoulder in a half-shrug, but I saw through his nonchalance. He was worried. "He got away and someone's lookin' after him."

Which meant he wasn't in a hospital. "Shouldn't you be with him?"

He stole a piece of my bacon and took a bite, his eyes lifting to mine in a challenge. "Do I look like a damn nurse to you?"

"No, but—"

"Merv doesn't want me there holdin' his hand. He wants me to catch the bastards who shot him." He dropped the bacon back on my plate, his mood even darker. "Tell me what you know."

"Teagen's friend's name is Marshal. They were both hired by a woman, but they ultimately answer to J.R. They kept saying she wouldn't be happy, but they sounded a heck of a lot more scared when they talked about Simmons."

"They damn well should be scared. J.R. Simmons does not suffer fools gladly."

"Marshal told Teagen that he should have killed me like he was supposed to, but Teagen said his job was just to snatch me and then go kill Mason."

Skeeter's scowl deepened and he nodded.

"The files in that shack were the same ones I saw in Kate's apartment. I think this proves she's been working for her father all along."

The waitress walked up and set a plate of food in front of Skeeter. "Here ya go, sugar."

Skeeter waited until she was out of sight before reaching for the syrup. "Kate never seemed interested in the family business before. She was a rebel, always challenging her father, but she was always a schemer. It could be that she realized working for Daddy was too lucrative to pass up."

I thought about it for a second. "What I don't understand is why she wanted me to get back with Joe if she was just gonna have me killed."

"It would make a lot of sense if she holds a grudge against him." He leaned forward. "Think about it. J.R. waited until I had everything I'd been working toward before he struck out at me. Maybe Kate Simmons was trying to do the same thing with Joe."

"But I wouldn't go back to him. So why go through with it?"

"She must have decided it would have to be enough. Why else have the video of your death sent to Deveraux while he was in Joe's office? And Kate was there to watch, don't forget."

I sat back in my seat, feeling lightheaded. "Oh, my word. How can someone be so cold?"

"They say the apple doesn't fall far from the tree," he said as he poured syrup over his pancakes.

The bitterness in his voice told me there was a story there. I decided to worm it out of him. "Scooter's your brother. He's friends with Bruce Wayne."

He looked up at me in surprise. "What's that got to do with anything?"

"Seems to me that you know a whole lot more about me than I know about you."

He turned his attention back to his plate. "And that's how it's supposed to be."

"Not if we're partners."

He sawed through his fried egg. "You turned that down."

"We may not be partners in your business, but we're partners in this mess."

He shook his head. "Not by a long shot."

He reached for his cup of coffee, but I snatched it before he could get to it.

"Skeeter, how can you say that?" I searched his eyes, trying not to let my temper get the best of me. "We're in this together. Do you consider me your underling?"

He remained silent, but his clenched jaw told me I was getting to him.

"Look, I know you're used to barkin' orders at people, but I'm sick to death of takin' orders, and you damn well know it. Now we're either partners in this, or I'm taking what I know and going home." I pointed my finger in his face. "And I'll send Jed and whoever else you assign to watch over me away."

The veins in his temples throbbed, but I held my ground, refusing to be the first to cave in our staring contest.

Five seconds later, he dropped his gaze and attacked his pancakes.

We stayed like that for a good minute or two, Skeeter eating like he was getting paid to do it while I crunched on the last of my bacon and cradled his coffee in my hand.

I studied him as he ignored me—except I realized that wasn't quite true. He was fully aware of what I was doing, just like he was aware of the waitress, the short order cook, and the man at the counter. He was even aware of the door, despite the fact that his back was to it. He'd suggested this place because there was a mirror on the wall behind me, giving him a view of the entire room.

Skeeter Malcolm was no fool.

But his personal life was also as well-guarded as Fort Knox. Jed seemed to be the only one who had access, and that was only granted because they shared a past. No, Skeeter wasn't ignoring me—he was fortifying his walls.

But then he surprised the bejiggers out of me. "Scooter's my younger brother. Not by much though." He kept his gaze on his plate. "Growing up, people always thought we were twins. They said I got all the brains and the brawn, and Scooter got the leftovers."

"Why would people say something so cruel?"

His gaze lifted to mine. "Why would your mother lock you in a closet?" He paused. "I learned very early on that it's human nature to be cruel. To attack the weak. I studied people. How they worked. Why they did what they did. And after I faced my father's bootstrap more times than I could count, I decided I'd never be under anyone's heel again."

"That's why you went to work for J.R. You saw it as your ticket out."

"I was tired of being dirt poor. I was known around here as one of the dirty Malcolm boys. I never stood a chance at being anything more. Unless I made it happen myself. So I left and never planned on coming back."

"Until J.R. made you."

He nodded. "Turns out I was still under someone's heel after all." He released a short laugh. "But I realized that everyone's under someone's heel. It's just a matter of how tolerable it is."

He didn't appear to be under anyone's heel at the moment, but I didn't want to ask anything that would get him to shut down again. "Did Scooter resent people being mean to him?"

He chuckled. "Have you ever met Scooter?"

"No."

A smile spread across his face. "Scooter's special. Not a mean bone in his body." He took a breath. "He wasn't born quite right. The cord was wrapped around his neck, and our mother said he came out looking like a ripe blueberry. That's why she named him Blue."

I blinked. "Wait. His name isn't Scooter?"

"It's his nickname."

My mouth dropped open. "So what's your given name?"

His smile dropped, and he studied me for a moment. "James."

"I had no idea . . ."

He laughed as he reached across the table and grabbed his coffee cup from my hands. "You think I was born with this name?"

The way he spat out the statement told me he hated it. "How'd you get saddled with Skeeter?"

He took a sip of his coffee. "My daddy was a mean ol' cuss. He beat my momma. He beat Scooter and me. I tried my best to spare my momma and Scooter from it, but one night . . ." His face darkened, and he looked down at the table. "He was drunk and he'd lost a shit ton of money on the horses, so he came home and took it out on us."

My chest tightened, and part of me wanted to show him sympathy, but I knew he didn't want it. He'd stop his story if I said anything or so much as touched him.

"He could hardly stand upright, but he was still beating the shit out of my mother with that damned bootstrap." His face tensed. "I grabbed his arm to stop him, but he was still strong enough to shake me off. He looked down at me, his eyes full of hate, and said, 'Boy, you ain't near strong enough to stop me. Yer nothing but a blood-suckin' skeeter the way you feed off me.' Then a fire lit his eyes, and he turned to Scooter and said, 'And you ain't got a lick of sense in your head. Yer as dumb as a damn scooter.'" He put down his cup. "Well, Scooter would have given his soul to get our father's attention. He took that stupid nickname to heart, telling everyone in creation that his name was now Scooter and I was Skeeter and they were all supposed to call us that from now on."

"How old were you?"

"Eight."

I couldn't imagine an eight-year-old having to defend his mother. But by the time I was eight, I'd been pretty beaten down by my mother. Violet, who wasn't much older, had stepped forward to defend me. "Why didn't you put a stop to it?"

He released a bitter laugh. "Oh, I could've if I'd wanted to. I didn't take shit from anybody, even back then. But I kept it."

"Why?"

His eyes glittered with dark emotion. "As a reminder."

"A reminder of what?"

"Of my failure." He refilled his cup, then set the empty carafe on the table and flagged down the waitress, who'd had the sense to keep her distance. "We need more coffee."

"Of course, Mr. Malcolm."

I flashed Skeeter a look, surprised the waitress knew him by name, but then all the pieces clicked together. We were having a private conversation in a public place—a public place that remained open despite the fact it was infamous for having hardly any customers. "You own this place, don't you?"

He shrugged and gave me a grin. "I own a lot of places." His grin spread. "You'd be surprised. I make far more money from my legitimate businesses than my illegal ones."

Obviously this place was one of his less profitable enterprises. "So why do it?"

He turned his grin on the waitress when she came over with a fresh carafe of coffee. "Sandra, this is Rose."

"Nice to meet you, Miss Rose."

"Oh, just Rose," I said with a smile.

"It's nice to see James with a lady friend," she said, beaming at him. "He's so focused on his business he says he doesn't have time for a girlfriend."

My eyes widened, but she walked away before I could explain we were just friends. "She knows your given name," I observed.

He shrugged. "She knew me growing up."

"So why did she call you Mr. Malcolm before?"

He grimaced. "She insists." He took a sip of coffee. "Before we started this stroll down memory lane, we were debating the possibility of Kate Simmons being behind your kidnapping. Did you hear anything else to corroborate it?"

"Yeah," I said, trying to switch gears. It was hard to associate the man I saw in this place with Skeeter Malcolm, crime boss. But it made sense that he wouldn't want any of this to get out for fear of tarnishing his reputation. Which meant he trusted me. I wanted to thank him for that, but Skeeter didn't respond to pretty words. He responded to action.

He lifted an eyebrow, waiting for me to continue.

"They said the woman who hired them also put up my bail money. And she's not happy she doesn't have it back yet."

"That was poor planning on her part . . . or maybe not. If you were dead, the charges would be dropped. She could get her money back nice and quiet."

"She must really hate Joe to bail me out with a million dollars just to have me killed."

"It's all sport for the Simmons family, although I confess that Joe seems to have been skipped over by the scheming gene. But his sister sure wasn't. Looks like she's all grown up and playing in the big leagues." He looked into my eyes. "The question is what do you want to do about it?"

"What are you suggesting?"

"Rose, the woman tried to have you killed in a horrific way. You think we're just going to let her get away with it?"

"We don't know that for certain," I protested. "Someone ran me off the road before she even got back into town."

He snorted. "You think she just started tuning in when she showed up in town?" He shook his head. "Hell, if it's revenge she wants, I guarantee you she's been watching her brother since she left, or at least had someone doing it for her."

"She had photos of me from last summer. Outside the courthouse with Joe and Mason. I figured she was photographing Mason because all the files on her table were about him."

His eyelid ticked. "Which burned up in the fire."

"Not necessarily. I stuffed most of them into a duffel bag."

"Where is it?"

I cocked my head and gave him a devious grin. "Are we partners in this or not?"

His eyes lit up. "You're really goin' to hold me to that? You know I'm never partners with anyone—they either outrank me or they're under me."

For the first time since I'd learned how he felt about me, I heard a hint of innuendo.

"I refuse to be under you, so it's either we're equals or I outrank you." My grin turned more innocent. "Your choice."

He burst out laughing, then shook his head. "I have never met anyone quite like you, Rose Gardner."

"I'm one of a kind. Now take it or leave it." I held out my hand to shake on it.

His eyebrows lifted, and he grabbed my hand and held on. "Oh, I'm definitely taking."

Chapter Eleven

I pulled my hand from his. "We need to lay some grounds rules."

"In case you haven't noticed, I've never been good with the rules," he said with a wink.

"Well, there's no time like the present to learn."

"You can't teach an old dog new tricks."

I sighed in exasperation. "Are we gonna speak in idioms all night, or are we gonna figure this out?"

"Fine, if you want to talk rules, then I have a few of my own."

"What are they?"

"Ladies first." He grinned, quite pleased with himself.

"You think you always have to get the last word, don't you?" I asked, grabbing a napkin from the dispenser on the table. "Do you have a pen?"

"What for?"

"We're putting this in writing."

He laughed as he handed me an ink pen. "Is this a contract?"

"Of sorts. When we first met, you claimed you weren't a man of your word. You've proved otherwise, but I feel a need for backup." I started writing. "We, Rose Gardner and James Malcolm—"

His hand descended on mine.

"It's your name, right? That's what I'm calling you from now on, so get used to it. No more yoke of shame"—I snatched my hand loose— "agree to the following. Number one, we are equals and partners." I glanced back at him, grinned at the scowl on his face, then returned my attention to the paper. "Number two, we share information even if we think it will hurt the other person."

He leaned back in his seat, his arms crossed over his broad chest, and nodded solemnly. I suspected he didn't think much could hurt him, so for him it was an easy concession.

"Three, we don't solve a situation with violence unless we have no other choice."

I glanced up, expecting an argument, but he simply nodded again.

"No argument?"

"When we're working together? No. I'll go your way."

"Why?"

He didn't uncross his arms, but his expression softened. "Because you couldn't live with yourself otherwise, and I won't ask you to compromise your principles."

"But you're . . ."

"A criminal?"

It was no secret, but we often glossed over his illegal activities.

"Let's just say I've doing a lot of thinking lately," he finally said. "I'm considering some restructuring."

"What does that mean?"

"What that means has no relation to this agreement." He sat up. "What else?"

I gave him a worried glance, then straightened my back. "Number four, we're just friends."

"Damn straight," he said. "You had your chance at a business partnership, and you passed." He winked. "Besides, what would your boyfriend think of you partnering up with a crime lord?"

A now familiar pain seized my heart, but there was no way I was going to tell Skeeter that Mason and I had broken up. I couldn't help tearing up, so I kept my gaze on the list.

"I have one," he said, his tone light. "*I* do the driving."

"What?" I asked, snapping out of my funk. "You think I'm incapable of driving? You let Jed drive!"

"But Jed's my underling. Are you saying you want to negate rule number one?" He tilted his head and grinned. "Fine, we'll share the driving." He pointed to the napkin. "Go on. Write it down."

We worked our way through a list of thirty-five rules, some ridiculous, some important—Rule #16, that I was only allowed to take part in illegal activities if absolutely necessary, was included at Skeeter's insistence.

"I've already got a criminal past, Rose. So if I get arrested, I'll take whatever punishment Carter can't get me out of."

Just when I thought we were done, Skeeter took the napkin from me and wrote "Rule #36: Rose's safety comes first. Always."

"That's hardly fair," I said after I read it.

"Rose, give me this one concession. I gave you Rule #27: no complaining if you have to stop to pee."

"That's different, James."

His eyes lit up. "I'm being a gentleman, and everyone knows that in the South, being a gentleman is more important than any contract."

"No one ever accused you of bein' a gentleman, James Malcolm," I teased.

He shrugged. "Maybe Skeeter Malcolm is incapable of it, but that doesn't mean James Malcolm is, too."

But I knew that to be false. He'd been a perfect gentleman to me multiple times.

Before I realized what he was doing, he signed his name at the bottom. James Daniel Malcolm. For some reason, it brought tears to my eyes. Maybe because he was sitting in front of me as *himself*, and I knew the list of people who ever saw him like this was probably nonexistent.

He handed me the pen, and I signed my name next to his. Rose Anne Gardner. Suddenly the napkin reminded me of the list I'd written on a hot May night long ago. The list that had set the wheels of change in motion. Only, I'd made that one alone.

I tried not to think of the significance of that as I folded the napkin and carefully tucked it into my coat pocket. "We'll find someplace safe to keep this."

He nodded, then leaned forward. "Now that we're partners, I'll do some digging into Kate Simmons. See if I can find her bank accounts. See if there was a major withdrawal."

"You can do that?"

He shrugged. "You just have to know the right people."

Why hadn't I thought of that before? Maybe his connections would help me solve another mystery.

"Do you think you can find me someone who can read shorthand?" I blurted out.

His eyebrows lifted in surprise.

"Remember me telling you about the book of evidence my birth mother had?"

"Joe Simmons took it."

"Yeah, but a photocopy of one of the pages was hidden in a safe at the factory. Mason's mother used to know shorthand, so we gave it to her to decipher. But she's forgotten most of it, and even though she bought a book to help, she's makin' slow progress. All we know is that it mentions something about a bank account, a shed, the police chief, and a key." I paused. "We found a key taped under one of Henry Buchanan's desk drawers."

"You think a journal from twenty-five years ago is gonna help us now?"

"I don't know, but several people have died over that journal—it has to be important. Not for a minute do I believe the police chief's death was a coincidence," I said, prepared to fight him over it.

He held up his hands, palms forward. "Whoa. Wait a minute. What police chief's death?"

"This happened about a week or so after J.R. came to Henryetta and threatened Dora in person. She went to see Henry Buchanan in his office with her baby—*me*—in her arms. According to her journal, she made a real ruckus and told him about J.R.'s threats. When he refused to do anything, she took off, but the factory burned down only days after that. Dora and Henry supposedly went to the police chief, Bill Niedermier, who said he was going to investigate the evidence they had on J.R., but he was murdered before anything came of it. Then my mother died in a car accident, and Henry hung himself."

Skeeter's eyes hardened. "Something stinks here."

"I know for a fact that Beverly killed Dora. She confessed in the factory, but she swore she didn't have anything to do with the police chief's death, and I believe that Henry killed himself."

"So Simmons had the police chief killed so his involvement would stay buried."

"Or in this case, taped underneath a baby bed for twenty-five years."

"We need the book."

I shook my head. "I have no earthly idea where it could be, but the page is at least a start."

He studied my plate as though it held the secrets of life before he lifted his gaze to mine. "Okay, I'll ask my bookkeeper. She knows anything from me is strictly hush-hush. She'll find the right person."

I should have come to Skeeter in the first place, but there was no denying that Mason was the reason I hadn't. It was further confirmation that I'd made the right decision to break up with him. I was going to do everything it took to bring J.R. Simmons to his knees and castrate him, and that was going to require some outside-the-law scheming.

My phone vibrated in my jeans pocket. I dug it out, cringing when I saw the name on the screen. I glanced into Skeeter's guarded eyes. "It's Joe."

"What's your gut instinct on that? Answer or let it go to voice mail?"

"After what went on at the square, he'll waste time and manpower if he thinks I'm in danger."

He gave a curt nod. "Answer it."

I hit accept and tried to sound breezy. "Hey, Joe."

"Rose, where are you?" He sounded anxious and exhausted.

I glanced at Skeeter. "Out."

"A lot's been going on downtown, some of it close to your office."

"Well, no need to be worried. I'm not there."

"I think someone is after you again. And I think it has to do with my father."

"Why would you think that?"

He paused. "Because my father escaped tonight."

Joe was only confirming what Skeeter had already surmised, but a shiver still ran down my back.

"How did your dad escape?" I asked, locking eyes with Skeeter.

His face hardened.

"During the transfer. They were ambushed while they were unloading him from the ambulance in front of the county jail. Two deputies and an EMT were shot."

"Oh, God," I choke out. "Who were the deputies?"

"I'm not allowed to say until we've notified the next of kin."

"Who were the deputies, Joe?" I asked, afraid of the answer.

"Rose."

"Is Randy Miller okay?"

He hesitated. "He's in the hospital. Last I heard, they were taking him to surgery, but they aren't sure if he's going to make it."

I squeezed my eyes closed. "Thank you for being honest with me."

"Why are you asking about Randy?"

Of course. He had no idea that we were friends. "He's always been so nice to me. I hate that this happened to him."

"I'd love to spare the manpower to watch you, but I'm—"

"I'm fine."

"Mason's still at his office. I know you two are fighting right now, but maybe you should go stay with him anyway."

"Yeah," I said, resting my forehead on my hand. "I'll give him a call."

"Rose, whatever you do, be careful. I know I don't have to tell you that my father is dangerous."

"Thanks." I hung up and put my phone on the table.

"A friend of yours get hurt?"

I sucked in a breath and wiped tears from the corners of my eyes. "Yeah. He's in surgery." I gave him a hard look. "How ironic that I'm friends with people on both sides of the law. You. Jed. Randy. Joe. Mason." My voice broke on Mason's name. "You're all sworn enemies, but I'd be devastated if anything happened to any of you."

"It's like I told you in the Gems parking lot when it was burning to the ground. You don't see black and white. You see gray. People aren't all good and bad. You have a way of bringing out the good."

I shook my head, thinking of J.R. Simmons, who didn't have a good bone in his body. "No. Not with everyone."

"Most people. That's what I like most about you . . . other than your determination to do what you think is right, even if everyone else around you thinks you're wrong. And the fact that you stand your ground, even with a scary asshole like me.

You're a woman of principles who wants to do the right thing." He slid out of the booth and stood, surprising me by tossing a hundred dollar bill on the table. "Let's go do the right thing."

As he ushered me out of the diner, I kept thinking about that hundred-dollar bill he'd left for the waitress in the restaurant he owned.

And I wondered if he was more like me than he thought.

Chapter Twelve

Skeeter wanted to go to his safe house, but after I told him about the duffel bag, we drove past the alley, slowing down to take in the fire fighters and police swarming the alley.

"There's no way we can get in there and get the bag," I said. "Unless you have someone on your payroll who works for the fire department."

"I do, but not someone close enough to trust with this."

I spun around to look at him. "I was kidding."

He remained silent.

"So what do we do?"

"The bag might be a lost cause, but maybe that's not such a big deal. You already saw everything that's in it, right?"

"Yeah, but not in great detail. But there was one file I hadn't seen before." I glanced at him again. "A file on Joe's old housekeeper."

"*Roberta?*"

My eyebrows rose in surprise. "You know her?"

"Yeah. Everyone loved Roberta. She was like the grandmother everyone wanted."

"I know Joe loved her," I said. "He told me she taught him how to cook."

"It was probably lonely to grow up a Simmons. From what I saw, she and Joe were close."

"Do you know why she left?"

He was quiet for a moment. "I was back in Fenton County by then, but once I heard, I checked into it. Apparently, it was very abrupt. I heard she'd left a note saying it was time for her to move on, but she'd given no notice whatsoever. She'd never even hinted that she was leaving. I heard the whole household was in an uproar after she left."

"Oh, my word. Did J.R. kill her?"

"No. Once I heard about her departure, I tracked her down in Memphis. She was scared to death to see me. She told me she'd been keeping her mouth shut, just like J.R. had told her to."

"Keeping her mouth shut about what?"

"She wouldn't say, but when I assured her that I would help her, she pretended like she'd never been scared at all and made me stay for dinner."

"She knew who you were and what you did," I murmured. "If she thought you were there to hurt her, then why would she invite you to dinner?"

"I assured her that no one would ever hurt her if I could help it." His voice hardened. "And I meant every word."

"You were willing to disobey J.R.?"

"J.R. was like the father I'd always wanted. He knew how to play that to his advantage. But I was startin' to see him for who he was."

"Is Roberta still alive?"

"No," he said softly. "She died from congestive heart failure about two years ago. She died in her sleep."

"And you're sure it wasn't foul play?" I asked. "Why else would Kate have a file on her housekeeper who died two years ago? When did it happen?"

"September, I think."

"September two years ago?" I said, turning in my seat to face him. "Joe said Kate disappeared in the early fall that year. She was living in Little Rock, and then she just up and vanished to California . . ." My eyes widened. "Without a word to anyone."

Skeeter cast me a sideways glance. "Are you suggesting Kate Simmons killed her old housekeeper eleven years after she left?"

"I'm not suggesting anything. But I am saying the timing is very coincidental."

He was quiet for a moment. "We could ask her granddaughter if she thinks something happened, but she never hinted that she suspected foul play when I saw her at the funeral."

"You went to Roberta's funeral?"

He squirmed in his seat. "I visited her at least once a month."

"Really?"

"Yeah."

There was so much I didn't know about this man. So much he kept hidden. "I think that's sweet."

"*Sweet?*" he asked in dismay. "There's not one *sweet* thing about me, not even a sweet tooth. It was for purely selfish reasons. She fed me a home-cooked dinner every first Tuesday of the month."

Yeah, right. "You know her granddaughter's name? You know how to contact her?"

"Her name is Anna Miller, but I lost contact with her about six months ago. I have no idea where she is."

"I do," I said, gasping in shock. "I know exactly where to find her."

"Where?" he asked in disbelief.

"Right under our noses." When he gave me a questioning glance, I added, "She works at my nursery."

He pulled to a stop at a street corner and turned to face me. "You're shittin' me."

"No. Violet hired her right after we reopened the nursery. She'd just moved to Henryetta, but she didn't say why. She said she was from Mississippi." I gasped. "I was covering for Violet in the shop a couple of weeks ago, and Hilary walked in. Anna kept her distance and acted nervous. Then Hilary saw her and got a funny look. She left in a bit of a hurry. Would Hilary know her?"

"I don't see how. I don't think Roberta ever even *mentioned* her family in that house, which is understandable. She was a smart woman. I'm fairly certain she only stayed with the family as long as she did because of the Simmons kids. She loved those kids, but she wasn't about to risk the safety of her own children and grandchild."

"So why is Anna here in Henryetta? It's not exactly the kind of place people move to on a lark. She's got a purpose, and it has to do with the Simmons family."

"Agreed."

"One more thing, Skeeter," I said, and he cast a glance in my direction. "Anna hates me. She's sweet to everyone else, but she doesn't bother to hide the fact that she doesn't like me."

"Why would you keep her as your employee if she's disrespectful?"

"I rarely work at the nursery, and Violet really likes her." I shrugged. "As long as she's doin' a good job, there's no reason to let her go. I'll talk to her tomorrow."

"No. Let me do it."

I narrowed my eyes. "You? Do you think scaring her is the best way to go about it?"

"Who says I'm gonna scare her?"

"Have you seen yourself?" I asked, rolling my eyes. "You're intimidating."

He grunted. "She knows me. And I know what to ask. I'm the one who should talk to her."

"Fine, but we need to come up with some kind of plan." I looked around at the landscape. "Where are we going?"

"I told you. The safe house."

"This isn't the way. It's south of town."

"Another one."

"How many safe houses do you have anyway?"

"As many as I need."

The safe house turned out to be a farmhouse set a good ways back from the road. As soon as Skeeter pulled into the driveway, the front door flew open and Neely Kate ran out, meeting me halfway to the door. Muffy came flying out behind her.

Neely Kate hugged me so tight I could barely breathe, and Muffy jumped around my legs.

"Oh, my stars and garters, Rose." My best friend squeezed me again. "You scared the snot out of me."

"I'm fine."

She released her hold and looked me up and down. "Jed said Merv was shot."

I nodded as I bent down and picked up my dog, rubbing her head. "More than once. I don't know how bad he got hit the second time. Skeeter wouldn't elaborate."

She looped her arm through mine and pulled me into the house. "From what little Jed said, I think he's gonna be okay."

Skeeter followed, but he stayed several steps behind, giving us space.

Jed stood in the doorway, looking very much like a guard with his holster slung over his shoulder. His expression was grim, but he gave me a nod when I walked past him.

This place was nicer than the ramshackle cabin we'd stayed in last week. The other safe house had looked like it either needed to be disinfected or torched. The farmhouse had a shabby-chic décor that was actually homey.

"Thank God you weren't hurt," Neely Kate said. "Joe was worried."

That reminded me of Joe's phone call. "Merv wasn't the only person who got shot tonight, Neely Kate."

She turned to face me, her eyes wide. "Who else?"

I took a breath, my nerves starting to catch up with me. "Deputy Miller."

She gasped. "What? How?"

"J.R. escaped and Deputy Miller was on duty. Joe said that he and another deputy and an EMT were shot by J.R.'s men. Deputy Miller's in surgery, and they're not sure he's gonna make it."

"Oh, no." Tears filled her eyes.

Suddenly, it was all too much. Mason. Running for my life. Deputy Miller. I couldn't take one more minute of this day. "I'm exhausted." I looked back at Skeeter. "Where are we sleepin'?"

As soon as the words left my mouth, I regretted it, expecting Skeeter to make a crude comment. But Jed spoke up before his boss could. "You and Neely Kate are sleeping in the bedroom on the right."

"I brought some of your things, Rose," Neely Kate said. "Do you want to take a shower?"

"No. I just want to go to bed."

"You don't have to worry," Skeeter said, catching my gaze. "No one knows about this place, and Jed and I will be taking turns standin' watch."

I followed Neely Kate down a short hall and into a small bedroom filled with a white wrought-iron bed, a dresser, and a nightstand with a lamp. The pale blue comforter looked as fluffy as a cloud, and I wanted nothing more than to fall asleep and wake up after everything was said and done.

I shut the door behind me and set Muffy down on the bed.

Neely Kate grabbed a bag off the dresser and handed it to me. "I put your comfy jammies in there. I'm going to go to the bathroom."

"Thanks." I found them at the top and changed while she was gone. By the time Neely Kate came back, I was already in bed.

We lay side by side for several long seconds before Neely Kate asked, "Are you really okay?"

Tears stung my eyes, a lump filled my throat, and I choked out the words. "No. I broke up with Mason."

She gasped and rolled onto her side to face me. "What happened?"

"I don't know," I said, trying to hold back my tears. "J.R. called to threaten me this afternoon. Then I called Mason to warn him, and he got peeved that we couldn't tell Joe."

"Why couldn't you?"

"Because then Joe would have insisted on watching me, and Mason had to admit that Jed would do a better job. But he was upset he'd have to compromise his principles . . . for me. I realized that as long as I'm in this mess, and as long as I'm working with Skeeter to fix it, I'm gonna have to keep dragging Mason into situations he can't handle. So I made it easy for him. I broke up with him." I rolled over onto my side to face her, tears streaming down my face. "I did it over the phone, Neely Kate. Who does that?"

"Oh, honey," she said, rubbing my arm. "Obviously this whole situation is far from ideal."

"I broke his heart, Neely Kate. He thought I was sweet Rose Gardner, but I turned out to be the Lady in Black. How come he hadn't already broken up with *me*?"

"Because he loves you?" she asked in a soft, teasing tone.

"He didn't want to break up, but I told him he'd already made his decision by leaving me and not coming back." I took a breath and hiccupped a sob. "He was the whole reason I agreed to continue this crazy scheme, but now I've lost him." I struggled to catch my breath. "I love him. I love him so much, but it's not enough. I'm not enough."

"You hush now," she said quietly. "You're plenty enough. But we both know Mason has his principles, and there's no disputin' you've crossed a heap of lines. He's just struggling to catch up is all."

"So you think I did the wrong thing?"

"That's not my decision to make. It's yours. But if you're asking what I would have done in your situation, then I'll tell you that I would have done the same."

I started crying harder. "I never should have gone to Skeeter for help last November. I should have just let my business fail."

She lifted my chin and looked into my eyes, her face covered with shadows in the darkened room. "Do you really believe that? Really? Are you're telling me that if you had to do it all over again, you would have let your business fail and let Mason get killed? Because going to Skeeter last November stopped both of those things from happening."

"No." I shook my head in confusion. "I don't know. I know what I've done is wrong and that I should feel guiltier than I do, but mostly I'm just so sad that I've lost him." My sobs were coming harder, as the true gravity of my loss hit me.

She pulled me close, stroking the back of my head. "Oh, honey. Sometimes you make some crazy leaps—and I'll admit, I thought you'd plum lost your mind when you went to Skeeter for help—but you followed your instincts, and look how it turned out."

"I lost Mason."

"You would have lost him anyway. Only, this way, he's alive."

I knew she was right, but it still felt like my heart had been ripped out of my chest and thrown across the room.

"Rose, you and me are so much alike. People beatin' us down when we were kids, telling us we were worthless and good for nothin'. We think we're supposed do what we're told, even when it doesn't feel right. We're supposed to be who they want us to be." She paused, searching my face. "Well, we can't go fittin' other people's molds. We can't allow ourselves to be untrue to the people we're supposed to be."

"But I want Mason. I lost him because I'm thoughtless and careless. I don't deserve him." I covered my face with my hands, still sobbing.

"You stop that talk right now," she admonished gently, pulling my hands from my face, and then brushing the hair from my eyes. "This has nothing to do with either of those things. Tell me about the Rose Gardner from a year ago today. Did she have many friends?"

"No."

"What were her dreams?"

I released a tiny laugh. "I wanted to go to Little Rock for a visit. I wanted to go back to school to become a teacher. I figured that would be the only way I could have kids in my life. Well, other than Ashley and Mikey."

"Why?" she asked in a teasing tone. "Because no man would want Crazy Rose Gardner?"

She was right, and we both knew it. No need to confirm it.

"Do you still want to become a teacher?"

"No. I love the landscaping company. I love owning my own business, even though I spend half my time worrying that it's gonna fail."

"What about going to Little Rock?"

I smiled through my tears. "You know I've already been. Multiple times."

"Look at how your dreams have grown, and in such a short time."

"People's dreams change, Neely Kate."

"True, but think about it. You have changed *so much* in less than a year. The you who broke up with Joe couldn't be more different than the you who broke up with Mason. Just like the me who met Ronnie is different than the me I am now. We were held back for so long, Rose, so as soon as the gate was opened, we just busted loose, no looking back. We're growing and changing so much it's not fair to ask a man to sit back and accept it. Maybe we need to figure out who we are, all on our own, before we know what we have to offer someone else."

"But I want Mason," I sobbed into her shoulder. "I'll fix it. I'll fix it all, and then I'll beg his forgiveness and ask him to take me back."

"Oh, honey," she cooed into my ear as she stroked my head.

I fell asleep crying, my heart broken from the knowledge that she was probably right.

Chapter Thirteen

W hen I awoke, my eyelids were heavy and my mouth dry. Daylight filtered in from the window, and when I rolled over, Neely Kate was gone.

I got out of bed and got dressed, then followed the smell of food to the kitchen. Neely Kate stood in front of the stove. Jed was leaned back in a kitchen chair, legs stretched out in front of him, eyes closed. Muffy was curled up under his chair, watching for Neely Kate to "accidentally" drop scraps.

"Good morning," I said, opening cabinets to look for a glass.

Muffy's head popped up, and she ran over to me, jumping up on my legs. I scooped her up and held her close, letting her lick my chin. She'd been missing Mason terribly, so she needed a little extra love from me. Not that it was a problem; it worked both ways.

Neely Kate turned to look at me, a spatula in her hand. "There's fresh coffee in the pot. And Muffy's already been outside." She pointed to the coffee pot on the counter. "I brought her leash from your house, and Skeeter walked her while she did her business." She turned back to the stove. "I know you worry she'll run off."

"*Skeeter* walked her?"

She shrugged.

"I need water before coffee," I croaked, opening another cabinet door and finding eight shiny glasses, all turned upside down and arranged in neat rows.

"There's cold water in the fridge."

I opened the refrigerator door and discovered a pitcher of water as well as plenty of food. I poured a glass, then looked around the cozy kitchen with its pale yellow walls and bright white cabinets and trim. Roosters were everywhere—rooster canisters, rooster wallpaper, even a set of rooster salt and pepper shakers on the wooden kitchen table. It looked like the lair of a rooster serial killer. This was the polar opposite of the cabin where Skeeter had taken me before. "What is this place?"

Jed's eyes were still closed, and I realized he was asleep.

Neely Kate started to answer, but I held a finger up to my lips and pointed to Jed.

She nodded, then lowered her voice as she flipped a pancake. "This house belongs to the grandma of a friend of Jed's."

"Where is she?"

"She's in Arizona for the winter. The friend stays here while she's gone to keep an eye on the place."

"Where's the friend?"

"Somewhere else," Skeeter said from behind me. "And he'll keep quiet, so we should be safe for now, but I'd rather wrap up this situation before anyone figures out where we're holed up."

"You mean J.R.?"

"Among other people." He scowled as his gaze landed on me. "I've had a few calls from your boyfriend, each one progressively more threatening."

I tried to steady my nerves.

"You need to call him and tell him I haven't abducted you before he sends the state police lookin' for you."

I nodded, setting Muffy down on the floor. "I'll take care of it."

I went back to the bedroom, but Muffy stayed close to my heels, so I picked her up and set her on the bed. I found my phone in the pocket of the jeans I'd left on the floor by the foot of the bed. I'd missed five calls from Mason and two from Joe, as well as multiple texts.

I sat down on the edge of the bed, rubbing Muffy behind the ears. Rather than listen to the messages, I called Mason straightaway.

"Rose?" he asked, sounding hopeful and worried. "Are you okay?"

Muffy's head popped up, and she looked up at the phone.

I stroked her head. "I'm fine."

"Are you with Skeeter?"

"Yeah." I wanted to apologize for that, but then I realized that's why I had broken up with him. So I wouldn't have to apologize. Then why did I still feel so guilty?

"Do you feel safe?"

"Yeah," I said, sounding as weary as I felt. "I'm safe."

Muffy rested her chin on my leg, looking so forlorn it brought tears to my eyes.

"Any word on Randy?" I asked.

"He's in ICU. It's touch and go."

We were both silent for a moment before Mason said, "Joe said he told you about J.R."

"Yeah. He did."

"Has J.R. called you again?"

I wanted to tell him about my horrific night, but then I'd be dragging him back into my mess. "I think the less you know the better."

"Goddammit, Rose! Don't do this!"

"Don't do what?" I asked, my anger rising to match his.

"I love you! You may have decided we're done, but I'm still scared to death for you. Don't make me sit here freaking out because I have no idea where you are or if you're safe." His voice broke. "Just think about how you'd feel if the situation were reversed. Would you just write me off if I told you I was breaking up with you to spare you some pain?"

"No, of course not."

"Then how do you expect me to do the same?"

"I don't know . . ." My voice shook as tears rolled down my cheek.

"Rose, sweetheart. I know it looked like I abandoned you." He cursed under his breath. "No. You're right. I *did* abandon you. You know I have a habit of taking off for a walk after an argument—and that's all this was, even if it was longer than I've ever been gone. It doesn't make it right, not one iota, but I've been absolutely miserable without you, Rose. And now that J.R. is on the loose, and I know he's coming for you . . . I'm going crazy. I can't eat. I can't sleep. I can't concentrate on my job. All I can do is worry and think about how much I let you down. How I failed you."

"Mason, stop."

"*No.* I'm not ready to give up on us."

"What about what I want?" I asked quietly.

He was silent for several seconds. "Yesterday you said you love me. Have you changed your mind since then?"

"No. Of course not. I love you so much I feel like my heart has been ripped into a tiny million pieces."

"Then what? You love Skeeter?"

I released a sardonic laugh. "No, Mason. I only love you."

"Sweetheart, listen. If we love each other, we can make this work."

"Are they appointing you as the D.A. permanently?"

He hesitated. "I don't know. Maybe. Probably."

"And what would happen if it ever got out that Skeeter helped me escape Sam Teagen and his cohort last night? Or that Merv got shot trying to protect me?"

"*What?*" he asked in a panic. "Are you okay?"

"I'm fine. Honest. Think about it." I paused. "Skeeter and I are piecing things together, and we're getting close to something. But I'm not doing this with Skeeter because I want to be with him. He can do things you and Joe can't. Besides, J.R. is after the two of us, and it makes sense for the two of us to work together to bring him down."

"Only a week ago, just the *two of us* was you and me." I heard the pain in his voice.

"I won't ask you to compromise your principles or ethics for me, Mason. Not anymore."

"So now you're involved in illegal activities?" His words were pinched.

"No. Not if I can help it, but you know that my connection to Skeeter would hurt you. If it ever got out, your career would be over. I can't do that to you."

"Splitting up is a huge decision, Rose. It affects both of our lives. You should let me have a say in it."

I knew he had a point, and now I was more confused than ever.

He was quiet for several seconds. "Rose, *please*. I understand why you're with Skeeter, and I know he'll do his best to keep you safe, so if you think this is the best way to bring J.R. down, I trust you."

"*What?*"

"I'm not going to deny that I'd rather you do it by the book. But we both know that doing it by the book won't work with J.R. Simmons. And if there are any two people out there who can bring him down, it's you and Skeeter Malcolm." He paused. "And you have no idea how hard it is to admit that."

"That I'm not doing it by the book?"

"No. That you're doing it with him," he barked, then continued in a softer voice. "I'm saying that as the Lady in Black, you proved that you are more than capable enough to take J.R. down. I have no doubt in your ability. It's still hard to accept that you are doing this with *him*. On multiple levels. But I've wrestled with this since you called me yesterday, and I've accepted it."

I couldn't believe what I was hearing.

"I know he loves you—that's why he's so protective of you. But—call me a fool—I also believe he'll never act on it unless you want him to."

"Like how things were with you and me last fall."

"Yeah. I want to trust you, Rose. Just be open and honest with me instead of trying to hide what you're doing. I *never* want you to feel trapped by me. So if working with Skeeter to bring J.R. down is our best option, then you have my full blessing and support." His voice broke. "But all I ask is that you come home to me when it's all said and done."

"Oh, Mason."

"You don't have to give me an answer. Just please give me updates, no matter how vague. Otherwise, I'll go crazy."

I could give him that. "No specifics."

"I can live with that." He paused. "I love you, Rose. I want this to work, but I know we need to fix some things. That's what I wanted to talk about last night—only, I did a piss-poor job of articulating myself yesterday afternoon. I want to fix us, so go get the bastard and come home to me so we can get started." Then he hung up before I could say another word.

Muffy started to whine, and I leaned over and rubbed her behind the ears. "Don't give up on us yet, Muff."

I felt like crying, but I smiled when she licked my nose.

Neely Kate appeared in the doorway to the bedroom. "Are you okay?"

"Yeah," I said, standing. I slid the phone into my front jeans pocket, then set Muffy on the floor. "I think I am."

Skeeter and Jed were already seated at the table with empty plates in front of them, and with heaping plates of pancakes and bacon in the middle. I got situated in one of the empty seats, and Neely Kate handed me a cup of coffee, giving me a worried look. I wanted to reassure her that I was fine, but I really didn't want to tip Skeeter or Jed off about my breakup with Mason. I needed to be on top of my game, and I sure didn't want them worrying that I would be distracted.

"We need to get the bag," I said, looking at Skeeter. I'd filled Neely Kate in on most of the details before we'd gone to sleep the night before. I could only presume Skeeter had done the same with Jed.

"I've already had one of my boys drive by the alley. It's still under surveillance. There's no way we can retrieve it yet."

I sighed as I took a sip of my coffee. "What are we gonna do?"

He grimaced as he heaped three pancakes onto his plate. "Seems to me that the most important file in the stack—or at least the most intriguing—is the one about the Simmons's housekeeper." He returned the platter to the middle of the table. "You're sure you didn't see it before in Kate Simmons's apartment?"

I looked at Neely Kate. "You saw more files than I did. Do you remember anything like that?"

She shook her head. "Nuh uh. I would have remembered because everything else had a direct connection to Mason."

"And you're sure you saw them all?" Skeeter asked. "Do you think you could have missed it?"

"Well, I suppose," Neely Kate said. "But I don't think so."

Skeeter nodded, then turned to me. "Do you remember what you saw?"

"Not much. I was running out of time, so I just stuffed it into the bag. I made the connection because I recognized the address of one of her previous employers as Joe's parents' house."

"So Kate's interest in Roberta is new?" Skeeter asked as he attacked his pancakes. "Maybe because Anna showed up? The real question is *why* she showed up."

"And also why Roberta left the Simmons's house in the first place," I added. "Do you think she told her granddaughter why she left?"

"No." Skeeter shook his head. "Not a chance. But I know someone we can ask."

"Who?" Neely Kate and I asked at the same time.

"Hilary Wilder. She might know something."

"I guess they grew up together, huh?" I asked.

"The way I heard it, Hilary spent more time at the Simmons house than her own," Skeeter confirmed. "I'm not surprised. Her momma was a conniver and a schemer. She was a difficult woman to be around for any length of time."

Neely Kate curled her upper lip. "Guess the apple doesn't fall far from the tree."

Skeeter shrugged. "Hilary was different back then—sweeter and naïve, as hard as that is to believe—and she took to Roberta, too. Everyone did."

I had a hard time envisioning a non-conniving Hilary, but it gave me hope that there was still a good person buried deep down. If her mother had been terrible, it was no wonder she'd grown attached to Roberta.

"Kind of like Maeve," I said to Neely Kate. "Everyone loves her like they loved Roberta."

"Hilary might know something," Skeeter said. "I think you should talk to her."

"*Me?* You knew her. *You* talk to her."

Skeeter shook his head. "Hilary's smart. She was always at the Simmons's house, and she saw me there with J.R. plenty of times. I wouldn't put it past her to recognize me. And if she does, she'd be too scared to tell me anything. It has to be you two."

"Well, there's no way she's talkin' to me," I protested. "She hates my guts."

"Get Violet to talk to her," Neely Kate said. "She and Hilary kind of became friends over the whole baby nursery thing."

The blood rushed from my face. How could I have forgotten about Violet's condition? "Violet can't talk to her," I said. "She's leaving for Texas tomorrow."

"Texas? What on God's green earth is she gonna do in Texas?" Neely Kate asked in disbelief.

"I . . . uh . . ."

"No," Skeeter barked. "I want it to be one of us."

"I'm telling you," I said, shaking my head, "she's never gonna talk to me."

"Then you're gonna have to find a way," he said, his eyes meeting mine.

"You're really gonna send me off to talk to Hilary while J.R. Simmons is on the loose?"

"Hell, no," he said with a snort. "Jed's gonna go with you."

"So we figure out how Roberta ties into all of this, then what?" Neely Kate asked. "Kate has to know her old housekeeper's granddaughter is in town." She turned her attention to me. "Remember last week when she said she was stickin' around for the show? She knows."

"That almost makes her sound like a bystander," I said. "Not an instigator."

"Not true," Skeeter said. "J.R. specializes in setting wheels in motion, then sitting back and watching his plan unfold. If Kate Simmons set this in motion, she is most definitely gonna stick around to see how it plays out."

"But why would she warn me that I was about to get arrested?" I asked. "When she knew I'd have no idea what she was talkin' about until after the fact."

"It's all part of the game," Skeeter said.

"Let's move onto something else," Jed said, speaking for the first time since we'd sat down for breakfast. "Tell us what you know about Sam Teagen's friend—Marshal, was it?" he asked me.

"Yeah, he seemed like an older guy, scratchy voice. But it was clear Teagen was in charge." I took a sip of my coffee and then set it down as another thought struck me. "Oh! And unless they're really fast at pickin' a lock, they had a key to the shed."

I gasped, overcome with horror as I remembered the few words Maeve had been able to translate from shorthand. "Oh, my word."

"What?" Neely Kate asked.

I turned to her. "Key. Shed. Sound familiar?"

Her eyes flew wide. "The journal page."

"Whatever was hidden in there would have been destroyed in the fire."

Skeeter set down his fork. "Even if it's the same shed, you're presuming that whatever Dora was referring to was still in there."

"Let's assume it was," I said. "Whoever owned that building twenty-five years ago would have owned the shed, too, right? They either put something in that shed or rented it to someone who did."

"If they're still alive," Jed countered.

"True."

"I can find out who owned it," Neely Kate said. "I still have my sources at the courthouse. We could know by lunchtime."

"Back to Teagen and Marshal," Jed said. "We need to figure out more about their connections."

"I know I'm stating the obvious," I said, pushing my plate away. "But Sam Teagen's dangerous. He not only kidnapped me to have me murdered, but he was going to kill Mason. And I think he killed Eric Davidson."

"Why would he have offed Davidson?" Jed asked.

"Neely Kate and I talked to a kid at Burger Shack, where Eric worked. He remembered Teagen comin' in to meet with Eric. After that, Eric started tellin' everyone who'd listen that he was workin' for someone big. A few days later, Mason was run off the road and his phone was stolen. Mason remembers seeing a gun pointed at him, but someone else approached the car to check on him, and the gunman hightailed it out of there. Eric was found dead in his garage soon after. They said it was suicide, but I never believed it."

"You're right," Jed agreed. "If Davidson chickened out and didn't finish his job, it makes sense that Teagen would try and cover his tracks."

"Eric couldn't be the one who ran me off the road last month. He was already dead."

Skeeter's lips pinched. "It could have been Teagen or his friend. What do we know about Teagen?"

Jed studied his fork. "Not much. Teagen's done some petty theft of his own, but he's never really tied himself to anyone before. As for Marshal? Never heard of him." He lifted his gaze to me. "Did you get a look at him?"

"I saw them from a distance when they were running down the alley to my back door. He was wearing all black and had a hat on. I only saw their legs in the shed. And then when I was about to jump off the building—"

Jed and Neely Kate stared at me like I'd sprouted snakes on top of my head.

"—I only saw Teagen," I continued. "Oh! Marshal thought he broke his ankle when he jumped. And I noticed he was the one who picked the lock on the back door to my office. They had high-powered rifles, so they weren't playin' around." I gasped, remembering what they'd done with those high-powered rifles. "How's Merv?"

Skeeter's eyes hardened. "It's touch and go."

"Who's runnin' things while you two are holed up here?" I asked.

"That's none of your damn concern!" Skeeter shouted.

Jed turned to face me and lowered his voice. "We don't have to be out in the open to run things. We can work remotely for a few days, and we're hoping it won't take longer than that to flush Simmons out."

"I would suggest usin' me for bait again, but I suspect it won't go as smoothly as it did last time."

"No one is gettin' used as bait," Skeeter said in a tone that suggested he expected our full cooperation.

Lucky for him, I agreed. "I'll talk to Anna, see what I can find. And I'll also see about retrieving the bag. I suspect the page you found from Dora's journal might be a dead end, but I'll talk to my bookkeeper about finding someone to translate it. Leave no stone unturned, my great-grandma used to say."

A grin tugged at the corner of his lips. "Jed, you have our sources look into Kate Simmons's finances, specifically if she made a million-dollar withdrawal recently, and see if the investigator can find out what she was doing in California for two years . . . if she was even there."

Jed nodded.

"Rose, you and Neely Kate find out who used to own that building, and then talk to Hilary and see what you can find out about Roberta. Jed's gonna drive you, and I want you both in the backseat. *Do not stand out.* We don't want to make it easy for Simmons to up and snatch you."

"Okay," I said. "Then we'll meet back here and share what we've learned."

Skeeter stood and placed his plate in the sink. "Let's get goin'. We have things to do, and they ain't gonna get done on their own."

Then he went out the back door, slamming the door behind him.

Chapter Fourteen

Y ou realize this will never work," Neely Kate said.
"Hey, you're the one who always tries to convince me that we're capable of uncovering anything."

"I still say we should get Violet to do it before she leaves on her trip."

Jed glanced back at me in the rearview mirror, narrowing his eyes, but I beat him to it.

"No. We leave Violet out of it. She has enough on her plate right now." Not to mention I refused to put her in any type of danger. If Kate realized we were talking to Hilary, who knew what she'd do. "We're two smart women. Surely we can come up with something."

Neely Kate tapped her finger to her lips as she stared out the window, then turned to face Jed. "Stop by Dena's Bakery."

"We just had breakfast," Jed said. "You really think you need cupcakes right now?"

"No. It's for Hilary." Her eyes glittered with excitement. "We take her cupcakes as a truce gift. Tell her we're sorry that we got off on the wrong foot and want to be her friends since she's here all alone and Joe won't give her the time of day."

I narrowed my gaze. "Did you hit your head sometime after breakfast? Maybe while I was outside with Muffy? Because there's no way in tarnation she's gonna buy *that*."

"Well, do you have a better idea?" She cocked her eyebrow, giving me attitude.

I scowled. "No."

"Then we'll try my plan."

"We might only have one shot at this." I thought for a moment. "Maybe I should call Joe. I could ask him."

"You always said he was tight-lipped about anything from his past. What did he tell you about Roberta?"

"That she was like a surrogate mother to him. They were very close. He never said why she quit, just that she left abruptly and that he felt like he'd lost the one person who kept him grounded."

"Wait a minute." She held up her hands. "If Joe's part owner of the nursery, how does he not know Roberta's granddaughter is working for him?"

I shrugged. "Violet did the hiring, and he's hardly ever there." I pushed out a breath. It terrified me that I had no idea when I'd see my sister again . . . if ever again. "I have to stop to see Violet."

"Why?"

"She's leaving tomorrow."

"So? It's not like you two are on the best of terms right now."

Violet didn't want people to know about her illness, but I couldn't keep this from my best friend. "Because I don't know when I'll see her again."

Neely Kate's eyes sparked with anger. "You stop talkin' like that, Rose Gardner. You're gonna survive this."

"Not me, Neely Kate. Violet." I licked my bottom lip. "She's sick. That's why she's goin' to Texas. For treatment."

She gasped. "Why didn't you tell me?"

"I just found out yesterday after lunch, and I was still processing it all. She doesn't want people to know."

A hurt look filled her eyes.

"Neely Kate, of course I was gonna tell you. I just did. It's not something you just blurt out like the weather. 'It's gonna be cloudy today with a chance of rain. Oh, by the way, my sister is dying of cancer.'"

"Dyin'?"

"It's bad, Neely Kate. She needs a bone marrow transplant. Before I came back to the office yesterday, I went to have a blood test to see if I can be a donor."

"But you . . ."

"I know." I sighed, leaning back in my seat. "We might not share the same father."

"Did you tell her?"

"I had to. And no, the answer to your next question is that she did not take it very well. She's already worried that she's going to leave Ashley and Mikey without a mother. Now she thinks she's all alone in this world. I told her we're sisters no matter what, but we're not as close as we used to be. I can see why she would think that."

"It was her own doin', Rose. Don't you dare feel guilty about that."

"She's still my sister, and she's hurting." We drove in silence for several seconds before I remembered my purse was at the office. "Oh crap."

"What?" Neely Kate asked.

Somehow I'd forgotten that the office that had been broken into last night. "Oh! Double crap! Was Bruce Wayne coming into the office this morning?"

"No. He was going to help out at the nursery for a little while. Oh."

"Yeah. I have no idea what the inside of our office looks like. Jed, do you know if the police checked out my office?"

Jed looked at me in the mirror. "Did you hear from Joe Simmons?"

I cringed. "I had some missed calls from him, but I didn't check my messages." I grabbed my phone out of my purse. He'd left me two voicemails. I played the oldest one first.

"Rose, I'm just checking to make sure you're okay. Mason said you're not with him. Call me."

The next message came after my call to Mason. "Rose, I need you to tell me where you are. Mason says you're safe, but I want to know where, because you're sure as hell not at the farmhouse. And by some coincidence, Skeeter Malcolm is laying low, too." He paused. "I don't know what you're up to, but my father is not to be messed with. He will chew you up and spit you out for dinner. Back off, Rose, before you get yourself killed."

I replayed the last message on speakerphone, looking into the rearview mirror.

"Your call, Lady," Jed said. "We can hide you somewhere in Louisiana until this mess is over. Just say the word, and Skeeter will make it happen. Neither Simmons would ever think to look for you there."

I shook my head. "No. I'm tired of backin' down to bullies, and that's exactly what J.R. Simmons is—a bully. We're gonna finish what we started."

An idea sparked in my head. I knew it wasn't the best or brightest, but I decided I didn't much care. "I need to stop by the office to get my purse, Jed."

His eyes darkened. "They're bound to be watchin'."

"Let 'em watch. Do you think they'll try to abduct me in broad daylight? No. And we know they won't flat-out kill me. So we're going to waltz into the place like nothin' ever happened. It'll piss them off even more."

"And you plan to let them follow us all over town?"

"Not if I can help it." I turned to Neely Kate. "I hate to ask you this, but I need you to be prepared to shoot your gun if necessary."

"That's not a problem," she said, tossing her hair over her shoulder.

146

Once again, I had to wonder about her past, but now was not the time to ask.

"This is not a good idea," Jed said. "They're bound to be watchin' your office. They'll be less likely to be watching the bakery. Why not send Bruce Wayne to get your purse?"

I knew he was right, but there was something about flipping off J.R. that appealed to me. "Maybe it's not very smart, but I think we can make it work. If it pisses off J.R., I call it a win. Besides, you know they'll never expect it."

"Skeeter's not gonna be happy."

"Once it's done, he'll appreciate the gesture."

Jed's eyes held mine in the mirror. "I suppose there's no chance of changin' your mind?"

"Not even a little one."

He cursed under his breath. "I'm going in with you."

"You can go into the bakery, but you can't follow us into the office. That's where we're going to lose them."

"And just how do you propose to do that?"

"We'll slip out the back door and walk down the alley toward the county jail."

"That's blocks away. And you'll be crossing two streets."

"If you're out front watching the office, they'll be watching *you*."

Jed pushed out a long breath. "This is crazy."

I grinned. "And that's why it's gonna work."

He was quiet for a moment. "Fine. But if anything goes sideways, you're both staying with me."

"I can live with that."

Jed parked across the street from the landscaping office, then followed Neely Kate and me into the bakery. Dena's eyes widened when she saw him trailing behind us. I cast a glance back at him, realizing what a formidable presence he was—tall, broad-chested, a no-nonsense look on his face. But she wasn't looking at him with fear, I realized. No, it was pure, unadulterated lust.

"Rose, Neely Kate," she said, her gaze still on Jed. "You brought a friend."

"Yeah . . ."

"Aren't you going to introduce us?"

I looked back at Jed, unsure if he wanted me to share his name.

He shrugged, leaving it to me to decide.

I wasn't ashamed of him, and I wasn't going to pretend otherwise. "Dena, this is my friend, Jed."

"Your friend?" I heard the unspoken question in her voice. "What kind of friend? I thought you were with Mason."

Instant pain shot through my heart, but I managed not to cringe. "No, Jed's just hanging out with me and Neely Kate today."

"Like a bodyguard?" When I gave her a questioning look, she added, "I heard about J.R. Simmons bustin' loose, and I know you helped put him behind bars. If I were you, I wouldn't mind having someone like Jed around to protect me." She winked at him. "Of course, I wouldn't mind havin' you around anyway."

Jed's only visible reaction was to narrow his eyes.

"Um . . . we're here for some cupcakes," I said.

"Are they for Jed? Because I have a special recipe I'd like to share with him."

My eyes widened as I cast a glance at Neely Kate. I never would have expected Dena to lose her head like this over a man, let alone my friend. The shrug Neely Kate gave me told me she was surprised, too.

"Actually," Neely Kate said, as she moved in front of the glass case, "we're taking cupcakes to a friend of ours. You might know her, actually."

Dena crossed her arms over her chest. "This isn't like the time you wanted to accuse poor Marta Gray of murder but decided to butter her up with her favorite cupcakes instead, is it?"

"For the record," Neely Kate said with a hint of sass, "we never accused her of murder."

"That's right," I added. "It was easy to see she couldn't hurt a fly. In fact, we offered to be her friends."

Dena uncrossed her arms, but she still looked suspicious. "So who are you trying to butter up this time, and why?"

"Maybe we're just trying to be nice," Neely Kate said.

"Not likely," Dena retorted.

"No, *really*," I said, crossing my fingers behind my back. "We're trying to cheer someone up. We heard poor Hilary Wilder was feeling under the weather, and what pregnant woman doesn't like cupcakes?"

Neely Kate flinched enough for me to know it still stung that Hilary, who was the source of so much contention, still carried her baby while Neely Kate had miscarried her twins and most likely would never be able to get pregnant again.

Dena looked like she was almost convinced.

Neely Kate pushed out an exaggerated breath. "Of course, we could always go to Ima Jean's shop."

Dena snorted. "Sure you will. If you want to give her cupcakes that taste like dirt. Besides, she shut down her shop after her daughter died. Even if she opened it back up, I suspect she wouldn't want to see *you* there."

I sighed. She was right. Not only had I been there to witness her daughter's death, but there was a chance she might be my grandmother. I wasn't up to dealing with that right now. "We want a dozen cupcakes," I said. "But I need two of them in a separate box. For Hilary. One vanilla bean and one chocolate."

Dena pursed her lips and shook her head.

"Wrong choice?"

"Are you really trying to cheer her up?"

I couldn't make myself lie, not even with my fingers crossed. "We—"

Neely Kate butted in front of me. "What pregnant woman wouldn't want cupcakes? And yours to boot! What kind should we bring her?"

Dena studied the two of us for a moment, then sighed in defeat. "She's been craving raspberry lemon."

I smiled. "Then we'll take two of those."

Dena boxed those up before grabbing a bigger box for the rest of our treats. "And the others?"

Neely Kate and I selected an assortment, and then Neely Kate paid since I didn't have my purse.

"I'll pay you back," I promised.

Neely Kate shot me an ornery grin. "You sure will."

I was in a heap of trouble. And it wasn't just from J.R. and his nonsense. Neely Kate would find a way to make me pay, all right.

Dena gave Jed a final lingering look as we walked out of the bakery.

Neely Kate laughed as soon as the door shut behind us. "If you're lookin' for a girlfriend, Jed, looks like you have someone jumpin' at the bit to apply for the role."

"Not interested," he grunted.

She laughed as we walked over to his car. "It's good to have options."

"Not interested."

"You got a girlfriend?" she asked. "Significant other?"

He gave her a look that suggested he wanted to swat her away like a fly. Instead, he grunted again. "No. Now drop it."

Obviously he didn't know my best friend very well. His comment only encouraged her to run through a list of the available women in a twenty-mile radius.

"Maddie Hershey is cute, but she's more gossipy than a hen house. I don't suppose that would work with your career choice. Then again, it *might* as long as the information had a one-way valve, if you know what I mean."

His glare only made her laugh.

"You need a woman, Jed. And I'm going to find you one." She held up her hands as though viewing a sign. "Neely Kate Colson, woman of many trades: landscape designer, detective, and matchmaker."

She turned to me. "Do you think any of those will make me rich?"

"Not unless you can make matches for millionaires," I said, looking around for suspicious characters. The square seemed pretty innocuous, but I knew better than to accept that at face value. "But you won't find many of those here in Fenton County. You might have to branch out."

She pursed her lips. "No, if Kate really bailed Rose out, she's lost her million, and Skeeter seems to have his hands full with strippers and bimbos."

Jed gave her questioning glance.

"What? It's not hard to figure out he has money. He was gonna bail Rose out, right?" she whispered. "And everybody knows he goes through strippers at his club like a crying woman goes through tissues."

While I had no doubt that was true, I hated that she thought she had him pegged. The man I knew was more than the sleazy kingpin she was describing. Then again, that was probably the perception he wanted the world to have of him. It was so much easier to underestimate him that way.

When we reached the car, Neely Kate set both cupcake boxes on the front passenger seat. My gaze shot to a darkened spot on the asphalt outside the hardware store, several parking spaces down. It was surrounded by yellow crime scene tape, but Merv's car had already been towed away.

"You sure you want to do this, Rose?" Jed asked quietly, leaning into my ear.

I lifted my chin and turned to look him in the eye. "Yes." I knew I should be nervous, but I was mostly pissed. "I have my reasons."

He nodded with a grim expression. "I'll walk you to the door, and then I'll sit across the street in the car. Text me when you go out the back, and I'll meet you around the corner on the side street. That way, if anyone's watching the office from a lower vantage point, they won't be able to see us."

Jed stood close, trying to shield my back as we crossed the street, but I knew it wasn't necessary. J.R. wanted me to be terrified when I was taken. A sunny February morning in southern Arkansas was anything but terrifying.

No, he'd wait until I let my guard down.

Neely Kate unlocked the door, and Jed practically shoved me inside.

"Keep the lights off," he said, filling the open space with his body. "We can use the sunlight to our advantage. If it's darker inside than out, no one will be able to see you two leave out the back unless they're pressing their noses to the window."

"You're not comin' in?"

Jed studied my face for a minute. "No," he finally said, a slow smile stretching across his face. "You were right. You gallivantin' all over town like nothing happened is gonna piss Simmons off more than you can possibly know. I say we do it."

Neely Kate broke into a huge grin. "I'm in."

"We're all crazy," I said, dabbing the corner of my eyes. "This is dangerous."

"But exciting," Neely Kate said. "Let's do it."

"Okay."

Jed nodded, then waited until Neely Kate locked the door before he walked across the street and sat in his car.

Neely Kate gave me a long look. "Okay, it's just you and me now. Why were you really so insistent about coming into the office? Shoot, I could have run in to get your purse."

"I don't know," I said, walking past her desk and looking down at the space I'd crawled into to hide. "I needed to see it in the daylight. So I'm not afraid of it." I paused. "Neely Kate, Sam Teagen stood in that window with a gun, the both of us staring at each other. He would have busted in and taken me if Merv hadn't run him off." I walked to the back room, and opened the door to the toilet. A blood-stained towel lay in the sink, and there was a spatter of blood on the wall. "Merv was shot in our office, protecting me." I looked back at her. "He doesn't even like me very much. That just doesn't seem right."

When she started to protest, I held up my hand. "That's not why I'm here. He works for Skeeter, and I know he was doing his job. I may still feel guilty, but he knew the risk he was taking."

"Then why are you here?"

"Because those derelicts came into *my* business—*our* business. I'm not going to let them put their slimy stamp on it so that I'm scared to come into my own office. I'm not going to let them or J.R. Simmons—or anyone—make me cower in the dark. So I had to come here and face it, because I *am* scared. And I *am* intimidated. But I don't want to let them have that power over me anymore. So I'm here, confronting it. This is me saying you can't steal my life, J.R. Simmons, no matter how much you try."

She watched me for a second. "You really have grown so much from the woman I met last July."

"I have, haven't I?" I asked, my eyes tearing up again. "But I've lost so much."

"Nothin' worth havin' is easy. You know that," she said quietly. "We both know that. And I understand needin' to make a stand, no matter how foolish it might look. What do you think I'm doing with Ronnie?"

"I'm sorry I gave you a hard time about filing for divorce. I just want you to be happy, Neely Kate. You deserve it."

"I don't know that I want what I truly deserve, but I'm gonna take a stand anyway. So if you need to ride through town like Lady Godiva, I'll be waitin' with a robe for when you climb down."

I pulled her into a hug. "You're the best friend I could ever hope to have."

"You too." She gave me a squeeze, then leaned back to look into my face. "Now why else are we here?"

I laughed as I dropped my arms. "What makes you say that?"

"Because I know you. There's something else." Her grin spread. "You wanted to come here for another reason. What is it?"

"I want to go back up."

"On the roof? Why?"

"I want to see if the duffel bag is still in the Dumpster."

"But Skeeter says the alley is under surveillance. And I thought the shed blew a hole in the roof."

"But he didn't say the roof was under surveillance, and I can check out the Dumpster from the building next door."

"But Skeeter is supposed to be checking out the Dumpster," she protested.

"We're already here, so why shouldn't we look? Besides, I'm done taking orders from men."

"So why not tell Jed?"

"He'd insist on coming, which would blow our cover," I said."They'd know we were up to something."

"They?"

"You know someone's watching us for J.R."

"But won't they see us up on the roof?" Neely Kate asked.

"Do you really think they'll be looking?"

"What if the police are up there? If there are as many guns in that shed as you said, they're sure to keep a close watch."

"If they're up there, we'll leave. But J.R.'s escape is probably their top priority, so they must be stretched thin."

Neely Kate nodded resolutely. "Well, there's only one way to find out."

As soon as I opened the unlocked door to the staircase, I was hit by a blast of cold air.

"I bet they didn't close the trap door," I said as I led the way up the two flights of spiral stairs.

I climbed the rungs in the wall and poked my head out of the hatch, which was indeed open. The shed had collapsed, and the roof was covered with black soot that surrounded the hole where the shed had stood. But while the entire area was cordoned off with police tape, no one was standing around. "It's clear."

We both climbed out and squatted next to the opening. "Unfortunately, I don't think we can just walk right over," I said with a grimace. "I think we'll have to squat and crawl."

She rolled her eyes. "I already figured that out." But, rather than make her way to the next roof, she crawled over to the side of the building that faced the square. "You sure can see a lot up here."

I nodded, taking in the view. If J.R. had someone watching the office, they weren't out in the open. So where were they? "We need to find Teagen and Marshal. It's not enough to just take J.R. down, especially if Kate's involved. We need to figure the whole thing out and wrap it up in a nice tidy bow."

We crawled over the multiple buildings separating us from the building that housed the antique store. The middle of the roof had completely collapsed, and the rest of the ceiling looked about ready to fall in, making it impossible to get closer. I squatted in the corner and scanned the alley. Both ends were blocked with crime scene tape, but I didn't see any law enforcement officials. I also couldn't get a good look inside the Dumpster.

"Can you see anything?" Neely Kate asked.

"No." I had to get closer.

Taking a deep breath, I crawled onto the foot-wide ledge of the antique store building.

"Rose! What do you think you're doin'?"

"We need that bag." I didn't crawl very far. I definitely didn't have a death wish, but I was far enough that I could peer inside.

"Well?" she asked.

"I don't see it." Disappointment was heavy in my voice.

"Okay, don't get upset yet," Neely Kate said. "Maybe it sunk into the trash. I bet a bunch of water went inside the Dumpster and all those cardboard boxes and papers would have fallen apart."

"But if it all flattened, wouldn't the bag be on top?" I crawled backward, then lowered myself to the roof of the building next door. "I'm pretty sure the insurance office next door didn't start throwing bags of shredded paper on top of it in the middle of a fire—oh crap! They know." I dug out my phone and dialed Skeeter.

"Who knows what?" Neely Kate asked, looking worried.

"Everything okay?" Skeeter asked when he answered.

"I don't know," I said. "Have you talked to Anna?"

He was silent for a moment. "I can't find her."

I sucked in a breath, trying not to panic. "Did you go by the nursery?"

"Yeah. Deveraux's mother is working. She said Anna was outside helpin' your partner with some mulch. One minute Anna and your partner, Decker, were there, the next they were gone. She has no idea where they went."

"Oh shit," I said in panic. "They know we know."

"Whoa. Slow down," Skeeter said in a tight voice. "What are you talkin' about?"

"James, think about it," I said, ignoring Neely Kate's startled look. "Teagen saw me jump off the side of the roof. He and Marshal left the shed unlocked before heading back to my building. Even if they didn't know I was in the shed while they were, they might think I went in after them. The files were missing after they were in the shed the first time—after they saw me jump. And now I don't see the bag in the Dumpster—"

"What do you mean you don't see the bag in the Dumpster? Where the hell are you?"

"I stopped by my office, so I decided to check the trash bin from the roof. Now, before you say anything, I'm perfectly safe."

He was quiet for a beat before he asked, "You're sure the bag's gone?"

"Yeah, I'm sure." I pushed out a breath of frustration. "What if Teagen saw me drop it? Roberta's file was in there, James. If they found it, they know that *we* know there's something goin' on."

Skeeter grunted. "What if J.R. and Kate started the file after they realized Anna was back in town—working for you, no less. Now they know you're onto them, so they snatched her, and Decker tried to play hero, so they took him, too."

I hated to admit it, but that was the likely scenario.

"I'm gonna swing back by the nursery to see if Deveraux's mother has any leads on where to look for them."

"Okay," I said. "Sounds good."

"Now get the hell off that roof," he barked, and then the decibel level of his voice decreased significantly. "And get the journal page. My bookkeeper thinks she has someone to read it for us. Jed'll know where to drop it off."

I could ask Maeve, but she was at the shop. Besides, Bruce Wayne and Anna had been abducted out from under her nose, and I didn't want to put her in any more danger. But I knew someone else who had a copy. If he left it for me somewhere, no one would be the wiser.

"I'll get it." I hung up, then stuffed my phone into my back pocket. "Come on," I said, determination in my voice. I was getting Bruce Wayne back, and I was going to take that slimy bastard down for the count.

"Where are we goin'?" Neely Kate asked, following me as I strode upright across the rooftop—no reason to hide being up here now.

"To see Mason."

Chapter Fifteen

W hat do you mean we're going to see Mason? Why?"
I climbed over a ledge to the next roof top, moving
in the direction of the landscaping office.

"*Rose!* Why?"

I stopped and ran a hand over my head. I needed to think this through. If I wanted to keep Mason safe, it would be better to call him and tell him what I needed than to show up at his office. I dug my phone back out.

"Anna and Bruce Wayne are missing," I explained to Neely Kate, finding the speed dial for Mason's number. "I think Teagen found the duffel bag. Which means he knows we saw the file on Roberta. They probably snatched Anna from behind the nursery to find out the reason she's working for me."

"But *we* don't even know the reason."

"Exactly, but they probably think we're colluding, which is bad." I sounded so matter-of-fact, as though I were discussing the weather, but I was trying my best not to panic. If Bruce Wayne had been kidnapped, I was partially responsible. I wasn't sure I could live with that.

"Bruce Wayne was snatched, too?" Her voice rose in panic.

"We don't know that for certain, but there's a good chance."

"So why do you need to see Mason?"

"Maeve's working and Mason has a copy of the journal page in his office. I'm going to ask him for it."

"And what makes you think he'll just give it to you?"

"Because it's *mine*." I took a deep breath to quell my fear. "While I'm calling Mason, why don't you try calling Bruce Wayne's phone to see if he answers?"

Nodding, she dug her phone out of her purse. "Good idea."

I began to pace while the phone rang. When Mason answered, he sounded worried. "Everything okay?"

"No, it's not, but I'll spare you the details and tell you that *I* am fine. But I need your copy of the journal page."

"Why not get it from my mother?"

"Because she's working for Violet, and honestly, trouble is following me like a black cloud, and I don't want to lead it to her door." Disappointment sank through my body like a rock. This meant I needed to stay away from Violet, too. But I didn't have time to think about that right now. "I know you took a copy to the office. Can you put it somewhere for me to pick up so I'm not seen with you or in your office?"

"You're not out in the open, are you?" he asked in a panic. "You really need to be hiding."

"No questions, Mason. The less you know, the better. But we're onto something big. I need that page."

"So you found someone to translate?"

"No questions."

"This concerns me, too, Rose." He groaned. "I know all this secrecy was the agreement, but please let me help you. I'll meet you somewhere, and we'll work on this together."

"Not this time, Mason. I have to do things the dirty way. It's our only hope for getting through this, and you know it. You told me the same thing two months ago—only, I was too naïve to listen." Would things be different now if I had? No use looking back. "Will you put a copy somewhere for me to find?"

"I'll meet you somewhere."

"No, I need you to leave it somewhere. I don't want you tied to me in any way from here on out."

"I don't feel comfortable just leaving it somewhere, especially if we're being watched. But I'm pretty sure there's somewhere we won't be seen. Meet me at my car in the parking garage."

"Why?"

"I have something I need to give you, and I can't do it in the courthouse. Can you get there without risking yourself too much? How close are you?"

I hesitated. "Close."

"Give me ten minutes. And come alone. Be careful, sweetheart." He hung up before I could answer, but then, what could I have said? Reminded him that we were broken up? I couldn't deny that it felt good to know he cared.

But I had bigger things to deal with than my love life.

Neely Kate was shoving her phone into her pocket with a grim expression.

"No answer?" I asked.

"No."

"Then we really need to talk to Hilary. I just hope she knows something."

"And that she'll share it with us."

"That too."

We made our way back to the office building and then headed downstairs. Jed was standing outside the picture window—exactly where I'd seen Sam Teagen the night before—his back to us as he scanned the street. He had either talked to Skeeter or seen us on the roof. Maybe both. He turned around and stared at me, and a look was all it took to know he wasn't very happy with me. Not that I blamed him.

Neely Kate unlocked the door, and Jed came inside.

"What the hell did you two think you were doing?"

"Looking for the bag."

"That wasn't part of the plan."

"I had a chance to look, so I took it. The bag was gone from the Dumpster. Which means Teagen and his buddy probably found it. So they know we know about the file on Roberta."

He scowled. "Skeeter told me about the granddaughter and Bruce Wayne."

Tears burned behind my eyes, but I wasn't giving in to them. "We're gonna find them. They'll be just fine. We need to talk to Hilary pronto, but first I have to pick up a copy of the journal page from Mason."

He stared at me without saying a word.

"No protest?" I asked.

Jed's eyebrows rose. "Would it do any good?"

I snorted. "No."

"Then why waste my breath? What's the plan?"

"I'm meeting Mason in the parking garage. At his car. He has an assigned space, so I know where it is."

"Okay, we can cover you while you meet him."

"No, I'm going alone."

"What? No way."

I put my hands on my hips. "No? You don't get to boss me around, Jed Carlisle. *Nobody* gets to boss me around." I had to admit that I liked the freedom of not having to answer to anyone. There was no need to seek permission or approval. But the utter selfishness of the thought wasn't lost on me. "I'm meeting Mason by his car—alone. I'm getting the photocopy—then we're going to track down Hilary, and we're going to bring the page from the journal to Skeeter's bookkeeper. Now, you can come to the garage entrance, Jed, but that's it."

"It could be a trap," Neely Kate said.

"With Mason?" I asked in disbelief.

She didn't say anything.

"It's Mason, Neely Kate."

"I just think you shouldn't trust anyone right now," she said.

"Except for us."

"Don't be ridiculous," I said, grabbing my purse from my desk. "I'm goin'." There was no way on God's green Earth that Mason would hurt or betray me. I refused to entertain the idea. "Neely Kate, why don't you track down Hilary so we can go see her when I'm done? If anyone can figure out where to find her, it's you."

The parking garage had been added to the square about five years ago. It was on the other side of the street from the courthouse, connected to it by an underground tunnel—the same one that led to the county jail. The small garage was reserved for courthouse employees, and Mason had finally gotten his own parking space a few months earlier. While it protected the vehicles from the elements, it was dark and creepy.

I walked down the street, not caring who saw me. Since the tunnel under the road opened up and then split to the jail and the parking garage, I decided to go in through the county jail entrance and backtrack to the garage.

Jed grudgingly admitted it was a good idea. "If Teagen's watching, he might think you're going to see Deputy Simmons. He'll never suspect where you're really going."

Nevertheless, he decided to wait for me at the part of the tunnel that opened to the basement level of the garage. I had to admit that the lack of sunlight or sky made me slightly claustrophobic—but I pushed on anyway. My fears weren't going to hold me back anymore.

Mason was standing next to his car, looking toward the entrance to the street. I stopped to take in the sight of him, noticing how anxious he looked. The heels of my boots made my approach surprisingly quiet. Mason didn't hear me until I was a car's length away. The look of relief that covered his face when he saw me stole my breath away. He wrapped his arms around me and held me close, resting his cheek on top of my head.

I clung to him, afraid to give into my feelings, but this was Mason. No matter what had transpired between us over the past week, I still wanted him to hold me close and tell me everything would be okay.

He tilted my head back so I was looking up at him and then searched my eyes. "What happened last night?" he asked.

I slowly shook my head. "Off limits."

Despite his obvious frustration, he nodded. Then he lowered his mouth to mine, giving me a soft kiss. His hand sank into my hair, pulling me closer as his mouth became more demanding, but before the kiss could become too heated, he lifted his head.

"What you're doing scares me to death," he said in a ragged whisper. "But you're right. You saved us both as the Lady in Black. *You* took down J.R. Simmons."

He paused. "Like I said earlier, I've done a lot of soul-searching since yesterday afternoon, and I realized that I have to trust you to finish this. It's important that you know that."

I couldn't believe my ears. "Thank you," I said.

"I've got a lot of things to figure out when this is all said and done, but you are not one of them," he said. "You are the only thing I want. I'll give up all the rest as long as I'm with you."

I sighed. "Mason."

"I know. You broke up with me, and I understand your reasoning, but I'm here, Rose. I'm here waiting for you. I need you to know that."

"Thank you." I pressed my cheek against his chest. He had always been the reward at the end of this craziness. What would it mean if that changed? Would it all have been for nothing?

I gave myself a good thirty seconds to enjoy the comfort of his arms around me before I pulled free. "Did you bring the page?"

"Yes, and like I said, I brought you something else, too." He gestured toward the car. "But I need to give it to you inside the car."

I hesitated for a second, wondering what it could be, but I decided to give him the benefit of the doubt. I walked around to the passenger side and climbed in; Mason sat in the driver's seat. I shut the door and gave him a strained smile. "You're not going to drive off with me, are you?"

A smile tugged at his lips as he reached into his coat and pulled out a folded sheet of paper. "If I thought I could get away with it, I might try. But I know that running isn't the answer."

I opened the page, confirming it was a copy of the page from Dora's journal.

"You really think it might come into play?" he asked as I folded it back up and stowed it in my purse.

"It might. That's all we really know just yet."

He nodded. "J.R. is out for blood, Rose. I'm not sure it's a good idea for you to be walking around as free as you please."

"I know. But I'm also tired of someone dictating what I can and cannot do."

"Is that how you see me?" he asked quietly. "As someone who dictates what you can and cannot do?"

"No, Mason. No." I grabbed his hand and held it close. "I've always felt like an equal with you. You make me feel like I can do anything. But you love your job, and I'm not gonna compromise that anymore."

"Rose, Mom called me. I'm guessing you might have heard this since she already talked to Skeeter, but Bruce Wayne's missing. He was out back with Anna, and they both vanished into thin air. She called Joe, and he's over there talking to her now. But we both know that could be you next."

I shook my head. "No, Jed's with me. He's just inside the doorway behind us."

"But what if he wasn't? You need to be able to protect yourself." He leaned over my legs and opened the glove compartment. I gasped when he pulled out a small handgun. "I bought this last week, but I've been waiting on the paperwork.

It's small enough for you to carry in your purse, but it'll do the job if you need to use it."

I looked up into his face in shock. "It looks just like the gun Jed gave me. I thought it was taken for evidence."

"It was. Same make, different gun. I know Neely Kate showed you how to use that gun, and I figured it would be best for you to have a similar one."

"Mason, I . . ."

"You still have your Taser?"

"Yeah . . ."

"Good, but it's not enough. Not with J.R. I pulled some strings and got you a concealed carry permit."

"Mason!"

He shook his head. "A Taser won't stop him, Rose. If it comes to a confrontation, you're going to have to shoot him." He paused, searching my eyes. "Promise me that you'll protect yourself if it comes down to it."

He was asking me to promise to kill a man. While I'd killed a man in self-defense before, it was still a hard promise to make.

But I nodded. "I will."

"Thank you." He gave me a hard kiss, then pulled a box of ammunition out from his seat. He opened it, pulled out a clip, and handed it to me with the gun. "Go ahead and load it."

I felt self-conscious doing it in front of him, but I pointed the gun toward the windshield and forced myself to slide the clip into place.

"You need to keep it loaded at all times. Keep the safety on, but if you think you're in a dangerous situation, turn it off and be ready to use it." Fear edged his words.

I made sure the safety was on and put the gun in my purse, along with the box of bullets and the permit.

"I'm gonna be fine, Mason." I turned to him. "Thank you for this, but I hate that you broke the rules to do it."

He grabbed my hand. "I should be helping you. I'm part of this, too. After what he did to my sister . . ."

I shook my head, tears in my eyes. "No. This county needs someone who's honest and dedicated to making things right again. If you get caught up in this, you won't be able to do what needs to be done later. So let me handle it."

"It hardly seems right for you to take on all the responsibility."

"And you think the Fenton County District Attorney can go gallivanting around chasing a jail escapee?" I gave him a sad smile. "You have your job, and I have mine. Remember when you gave me that money last month when I was broke? You said you were investing in me. Well, this is me investing in us. We'll never be free of that man unless we put a stop to him."

I reached for the door handle. "I have to go."

"Wait." He grabbed the back of my head and kissed me.

When he pulled back, he searched my face. "You said you were doing this for us. Does that mean there's hope?"

"You know I still love you. But let's figure all of this out before we try to figure us out."

"I can live with that," Mason said.

We both got out of the car, and he met me at the rear. He pulled me close and tucked a stray strand of hair behind my ear. "I love you, Rose Gardner. Promise me you'll be safe."

"You're asking for a lot of promises today." I placed my hand on his chest, rubbing the cloth of his dress shirt with my fingertips. "This will have to be enough for now."

He gave me one last kiss and then dropped his hold on me.

He nodded toward the entrance to the tunnel. "You go ahead. I'll make sure you're not followed."

"I love you."

He nodded again and then shifted his gaze to the garage entrance, keeping watch as I hurried toward the tunnel.

Chapter Sixteen

Jed remained expressionless when I emerged from the garage, but Neely Kate had joined him—and she didn't waste any time before pouncing on me.

"Why did he insist you come alone?"

"Because he wanted to give me something."

"What?" Neely Kate sounded suspicious.

I opened the wide mouth to my purse, showing her the contents.

"He gave you a gun?" She looked up at me. "The gun Jed gave you?"

"Shh." I closed my purse and looked around the short tunnel before heading for the door to the jail. "It's a different gun, but he said he thought it would be best for me to have a familiar model."

Jed's eyes hardened. "While I'm all for you carrying protection, we don't want you caught with an illegal weapon."

"He got me a concealed carry permit."

"How?" Neely Kate asked. "He'd have to break the rules to do that."

I gave her a half-shrug and then started walking, not surprised when they followed. I needed to keep moving, anything to help me stop thinking about Mason breaking more rules for me. "What did you find out about Hilary?"

"She's not at home," Neely Kate said. "She's volunteering at the food pantry at Jonah's church."

"Hilary? Volunteering at a food pantry?"

"Giving back to the less fortunate and undeserving is part of the socialite life," Neely Kate said in a fake genteel drawl. "She's keepin' up appearances."

"Well, if she's keepin' up appearances, maybe she'll be forced to be nice to us."

"Does that mean we get to keep all of the cupcakes?" Neely Kate asked.

"You know Dena didn't trust us with those cupcakes in the first place. If we don't give them to Hilary, she's likely never to sell us cupcakes for bribery purposes again."

Neely Kate grinned. "Are you sayin' we'll need to bribe people in the future?"

I rolled my eyes. "Let's just say I'm not ruling anything out."

"I'm gonna take that as a positive sign."

"You girls are gonna drive me to drink," Jed grumbled. "I'm goin' to get the car. You two stay inside the jail entrance. Surely you'll be safe waiting for me here."

"I don't know," I said. "Mason thought it was safe to leave me in the reception area of the sheriff's office, but I was kidnapped from there at gunpoint. And not a single person noticed."

"Well, try not to get snatched this time."

Neely Kate gave him an ornery grin. "We'll do our best."

"Tell me again why she's here," Jed said dryly, but with the hint of a grin.

"Because she's actually pretty useful when she's not being a pain in the backside. You go on. We'll come out when you pull up."

Jed took off, grumbling under his breath that being confined to a work camp in Siberia was starting to sound pretty good, and left us in the empty reception area of the county jail.

"You shouldn't give him such a hard time, Neely Kate," I admonished. "You're gonna give the man an ulcer."

"Pfft, he loves it. Besides, you give him plenty of grief."

She had a point.

"Well, let's try to be nicer for the rest of the day. It's the least I can do after he's saved my life so many times."

Neely Kate's smile faded as her eyes focused on something outside the front door. "What do you think would happen if Joe happened to find you standing here?"

"Nothing good." I tried to look around her and out the door. "Is he coming in?"

She gave me a shove. "You go hide in the tunnel, and I'll try to keep him busy. When I say something about galoshes, it's the signal that you can slip past and get in Jed's car when I say something about galoshes."

"Galoshes?"

She gave me another hard shove. *"Go!"*

I dashed around the corner as I heard her say in a cheery voice, "Why Joe Simmons, fancy meeting you at the county jail."

"Uh . . . I'm the chief deputy sheriff. It's part of my job."

"Oh, that's right. Silly me."

"Cut the crap, Neely Kate. What are you doin' here?"

"Well . . . I wanted to come check on the status of your daddy breakin' out of jail. My best friend is a fugitive from the slime ball, after all. I wanted to see if he was back in custody yet."

"No, not yet."

"Well, why are you standing here then?" she asked, sounding belligerent. "Why aren't you out there tryin' to catch him? Unless you *want* him to go free."

"I can't believe you're standing there accusing me of that, when I was the one to lock him up."

"Well, you didn't really lock him up, now did you? You just sent him to the Henryetta hospital. Then he ran off, free as a bird."

"Does this have a point?" he asked, starting to sound pissed. Not that I could blame him.

"Oh, my stars and garters," she exclaimed. "Are all those photos on the wall men you're lookin' for?"

"Well, not just me. They're men who have warrants out for their arrest."

"Where's your father's photo? He's running around like a sailor on shore leave after six months at sea. Why isn't he up there?"

"Because he just broke out last night. We're hoping to have him back in custody before we need to put his photo up."

"Hmm . . ." she said, her voice growing fainter. "Speaking of a sailor on shore leave, do you think those men are running from lockup because they're worried about the lack of female company?"

"What?" He sounded genuinely puzzled.

"I've heard that they . . . you know . . . get together themselves when they're behind bars. Do you think that's safe? Do y'all provide them with *galoshes*?"

And that was my cue. I peeked around the corner and saw Joe and Neely Kate standing in front of a bulletin board plastered with wanted posters.

"*What?*" Joe asked, shaking his head.

I started for the front door, glancing back over my shoulder to see if I was going to get caught.

Neely Kate tapped a photo of a bald guy with tattoos running from his neck to his jaw. "That guy right there. He looks like he should have a case of 'em."

"A case of what?

"Condoms."

"What the hell are you talkin' about?" poor Joe asked, but I was already slipping out the door and running toward Jed's car, parked parallel to the street.

"Rose!" Joe shouted after me.

Oh, crap.

Ignoring him, I opened the back door of the car and practically dove in, slamming the door shut. "Go!"

But Jed had already figured that part out. He was pulling away from the curb and driving down the street before I got even that one-syllable word out.

"What about Neely Kate?" Jed asked, watching me in the rearview mirror.

"We'll let her assess the damage, and then we'll figure out where to pick her up." I pulled out my phone and sent her a text. *Is he coming after me?*

She immediately typed back. *No.* A good thirty seconds later she sent: *But he's good and ticked.* A good minute after that she sent: *I'm walking to our office. I'll let you know when the coast is clear.*

"Would he arrest you?" Jed asked. We didn't have a destination, so he started driving in a big square several blocks around the courthouse.

"No. He wouldn't have any grounds to, would he?"

"If he knew you were anywhere around that shed, he could arrest you for impeding an investigation."

Hell's bells. Jed was right. For all I knew, Joe might try to pull such a gambit to keep me from his father. "Well, he tried it once, and I didn't take it well. It almost cost us our friendship. I hope he'd have better sense this time."

Jed didn't answer.

We drove past the nursery, and the sight of a sheriff's car parked out back made my heart stop. Even though Mason had told me Joe was investigating the matter, it felt different to see the evidence of it in front of my face. Had Bruce Wayne and Anna really been kidnapped? I'd thought Bruce Wayne had been kidnapped before, but both times he'd left of his own free will. Maybe this was a similar situation. I could only hope.

I called Maeve.

"Oh, Rose. It's just horrible. I'm sure you've heard, but Joe thinks Anna and Bruce Wayne may have been kidnapped."

"I heard Joe came by?" I asked.

"Yes. He didn't say anything about what he found, but he said he was sending a deputy over to do a formal look-over. They're out back now."

"What happened, Maeve?"

"I don't really know. Bruce Wayne was working out back, shoveling a fresh batch of mulch. We were all caught up inside, so Anna went to check on him, although you and I both know it's probably because she likes him."

"Yeah, and he likes her," I said. "So they were both out back. Did you see anything?"

"I saw a dark van turn onto the side street next to the nursery. I remember it because it was moving so slowly. I was sure it was going to turn into the parking lot, but then it sped up and went around back."

"Do you remember what time that was?"

"Um . . . about nine thirty."

"Did you see the van again?"

"Yes. It came back on the same side street and turned right, heading south."

"Did you see who was driving? Was there someone in the passenger seat?"

"Yeah, a younger man, maybe in his twenties, wearing a gray stocking cap."

Sounded a lot like Sam Teagen. "And the passenger?"

"An older guy, black coat. No hat."

Marshal. This didn't sound good. "Did you hear any shouts or anything?"

"Not a peep. I went back there to check on them at around ten. They were gone, but both of their cars are still here."

"Do you remember anything about the van?"

"It was black with darkened windows in the back. Like those old conversion vans. I saw an image on the passenger side that looked like it had been covered with black spray paint."

"Could you tell what it was?"

"Just the top was still showing. It kind of looked like wings. Large ones."

"No license plate or anything?"

"No, but I wasn't looking. I only paid attention because it was moving so slowly and the two guys looked into the shop. Oh, wait! There *was* something else. It had one of those things on the hood that all the street cars have, you know with all the pipes. Only they looked defective. The ones in the middle were shorter than the ones on the ends."

"Thanks, Maeve. That's really helpful."

"I hope they're okay."

"Me too. We're looking into it. Can you give me a call if you think of anything else?" I asked.

"Of course . . . Rose?"

"Yeah."

"I talked to Mason this morning."

"He told me."

"You talked to him, too?"

"Yeah." I saw no reason to elaborate.

"I know you have bigger things to worry about, but he regrets so many things."

I didn't say anything. I didn't want to get into it right now.

"I know I told you this once, but it bears saying again. No matter what path you choose, I'll still be here for you."

My voice broke. "Thanks, Maeve."

"There's one more thing," she said, with hesitation. "Skeeter Malcolm came by the shop looking for Anna and asking questions. Twice."

My back stiffened. Was she going to demand answers? "That's what I heard from Mason."

"I didn't tell him much. Mason told me to keep everything to myself and share it only with Joe and you."

Mason was looking out for me. While he might trust Skeeter to keep me safe, that didn't mean he trusted him with information.

"Thanks, Maeve."

"Now you be safe, okay?"

"Yes, ma'am." I hung up and stared out the window. The day was much too bright and sunny to be so full of sadness and despair.

"Nothin' usable?" Jed asked.

"Actually, there was." I described the van to him, strange pipes, covered-up wings, and all.

"An air cooler on a conversion van?"

I shrugged. "That's what Maeve said."

"That should be easy to spot."

"I've never seen it before."

"Maybe we can ask around at a couple shops, see if they know anything about Teagen and Marshal."

I sucked in a sharp breath, and Jed's gaze lifted in the mirror. "Ted's Garage, where Neely Kate's husband works. Her cousin works with him, and he said some of the guys there pledged themselves to Mick Gentry. Teagen's working for Kate and J.R., so he might have gone there."

Jed looked furious. "Looks like we need to drop in and pay them a visit."

"You can't do that, Jed," I said in disbelief. "Nobody's goin' to tell you anything."

"Believe it or not, I've actually done this a time or two."

"How do you know they won't just tell you what they think you want to know?"

"I have ways."

I shuddered when I thought about what his ways might encompass. "How about you let Neely Kate and me try first, and if we don't get anywhere, you can come in and work your magic?"

To my surprise, he didn't fight me on it. "As soon as we pick up Neely Kate we'll head to the food pantry, then Skeeter's accountant's office to drop off your paper, then to Ted's Garage."

"What's Skeeter doing?"

He remained silent.

It was probably just as well that Skeeter was off doing his own thing. This kind of scurrying around seemed beneath the Fenton County crime lord, and he had such an intimidating presence that he'd probably scare off everyone we tried to talk to. Jed was bad enough.

Neely Kate texted a few seconds later, asking us to pick her up at the hardware store.

Jed gave me a weird look when I told him where she was, but he remained silent. He was definitely learning.

She was waiting outside on a bench, sitting under a scrawny maple tree with a plastic bag in her lap. When she saw us, she hopped up and made a beeline for the car.

"That was close," she said as soon as she slid into the car, bag in hand. "Joe was madder than a cat thrown into the bath water."

"Did he say why?" I asked as Jed took off.

She laughed. "He was mad at me for tricking him, and he yelled something about how he thought we'd moved past this stage of our relationship, as though we have one," she scoffed. "Mostly he was mad at you for running around like a first-grader set loose on her first school field trip."

I grimaced.

"He threatened to arrest me for tricking him, but someone told him he couldn't keep me, so he let me go. The last thing he said was for me to tell you to go to Mason's office and stay put."

"We learned some things while you were gone." I shared everything Maeve had told me. "Jed thinks we might be able to get a lead on Teagen or Marshal if we can figure out where they had that air intake system put in."

"Ted's Garage," she said matter-of-factly. "They had a special on them a couple of months ago. They were screwed up and nonreturnable. Vern had a good deal on them. We need to go there and ask around."

I gaped at her. "Are you sure you want to go?" I'd already mentioned the idea to Jed, but I hadn't been prepared for Neely Kate to so readily accept the idea.

"Why? Because of Ronnie? Maybe we can get a lead on him so I can serve him the divorce papers."

"Are you sure?" I asked.

"Why wouldn't I be? I already told you I wanted a divorce." She shook her head in dismissal. "So Hilary first, then Ted's?"

I explained the stop we were planning to make at Skeeter's accountant's office.

Neely Kate nodded. "If we pick up food at Big Bill's before we head to the garage, we might be able to butter the guys up," she said.

"Good idea."

"I hope you don't expect me to pay for it," Jed grumbled. "I ain't feedin' a bunch of turncoats."

"I'll pay for it," Neely Kate said in a snit, but I seriously wondered if she had enough money to cover it.

"So what's with the bag?" I finally asked.

She reached into the opening. "Bungee cords." She set a package of six bright pink cords of various sizes on the seat between us. "Duct tape."

"Nice print," I said as she set the pink and white polka-dot tape on top of the cords.

"Some rope and some zip ties." She lifted them out next— all of them pink.

I pointed to the pile and joked, "You have the tools for a kidnapping there."

She lifted her chin and grinned. "Exactly."

My eyes bugged open. "Just who are you plannin' on kidnapping?"

"J.R. Simmons, of course."

Chapter Seventeen

I was too shocked by Neely Kate's pronouncement to give much thought to the fact that Jed had just pulled into Jonah's church parking lot, but then he slammed the brakes so hard, Neely Kate's kidnapping kit fell onto the floorboard.

"Jed!" she shouted.

He shoved the gearshift into park and then spun around so fast that surely he was going to need to see a chiropractor to have his spine realigned. "What the hell are you talkin' about?"

She rolled her eyes as she grabbed the items off the floor and stuffed them back into her bag. "Come on, Jed. What's our endgame here? What are we gonna do once we find him?"

"I'm sure as hell not wrapping him up in pink and white polka-dot duct tape!"

"Nobody asked you to. Rose and I will do it."

I wasn't sure I wanted to be included in that part of her crazy scheme, but it didn't seem like a good time to contradict her. Besides, I couldn't help thinking she had a point. We needed an endgame plan, but we needed information first. "Before we can do any such thing, we have to get close to J.R. Simmons, and right now, he might as well be holed up in the North Pole, workin' in Santa's workshop. So let's talk to Hilary to see if she knows anything about Roberta."

"She might even know how to find the big guy himself," Neely Kate said, grabbing both boxes of cupcakes—which had somehow survived the abrupt stop.

"Santa?" I asked hopefully.

"Yeah, right."

I started to open the car door, but then stopped. "Jed, I think you should stay out here."

"I already figured that part out. I doubt Teagen or Marshal are gonna be helpin' at the food pantry. I plan to make a few calls while you're inside."

I climbed out and followed Neely Kate, who was already halfway up the steps to the front door.

"Neely Kate! Wait!"

She kept going until she reached the top step, then turned to stare down at me with a determined look in her eyes.

"Look," I said as I climbed the last few steps. "You know her. We can't just waltz in there and ask her anything we want. We have to warm her up."

"Hello." She lifted the small cupcake box. "That's what this is for."

"But shouldn't we at least have some kind of plan?" I asked, starting to panic.

She pushed out an exasperated breath. "I let you take the lead when we questioned that kid at the Burger Shack last week. Trust me to do it this time."

I studied her for a second. While she seemed to be pushing boundaries lately, she'd always had good instincts, and she'd done most of the interrogating up to this point.

"Of course I trust you. You haven't led us astray yet."

A warm smile lit up her face. "Thanks." She handed me the smaller cupcake box and said, "Let's do this."

I sure hoped she didn't expect me to be the one to butter up Hilary.

I opened the door for her and let her take the lead. She headed straight for Jonah's office, moving with all the confidence of someone who'd been invited. His secretary and now girlfriend,

Jessica, gave us a bright smile from behind her desk in the outer office. Jonah's office was through a door to the left.

"Neely Kate! Rose! How wonderful for you to stop by. We haven't seen you here in a few weeks."

"We've been busy," I said. I didn't add that entrapping a criminal mastermind took more time than most people thought.

"Is Jonah here?" Neely Kate asked, leaning to the side, trying to get a view of the interior of his office.

Jessica flinched and her smile became forced. "Actually, he's down at the food pantry."

"I'd completely forgotten about the new food pantry," Neely Kate said. "What a great idea. Have you had many volunteers?"

"A few . . ." The look on her face made it clear she wasn't happy with the volunteers. "I'm worried the ones we have takin' charge will scare everyone else away, but as Jonah says, everyone is welcome in the Lord's house."

That sounded like Hilary all right.

Neely Kate's smile beamed sunshine. "Ain't that the truth. And if anyone can lead them onto the straight and narrow, it's Jonah."

I knew that wasn't just a platitude. Neely Kate and I both knew Jonah worked with ex-cons to help them turn their lives around. The fact that Jonah was a semi-popular televangelist led many people to discount him as a grandstander—his good looks and charm didn't help. To my shame, I'd fallen into the judging camp before I took the time to really look and see his compassionate heart.

Neely Kate stepped closer, holding out the bigger cupcake box and opening the lid. "Would you like a cupcake? We wanted to bring a little treat to you and Jonah to show y'all how much we appreciate you and everything you do for the community."

"Isn't that so sweet of you?" Jessica asked as she grabbed a strawberry shortcake cupcake. "Thank you, Rose and Neely Kate."

"You're welcome," Neely Kate said.

I was feeling guilty. I really did appreciate everything they did, so I hated lying about why we'd come here.

But Neely Kate had already moved to the door and waved to Jessica, "We'll go find Jonah. Good to see you, Jessica."

"You too," she called after us. "Let's do lunch soon."

"We'd love to," I said before we reached the hall.

When we were several feet from the doorway, I lowered my voice so Jessica couldn't hear. "This doesn't feel right, Neely Kate."

"We might not have bought those cupcakes for them," she whispered back, "but we *do* appreciate what they do, so there's nothing wrong with offering them."

She had a point, but it still felt wrong to be so devious in the Lord's house.

Neely Kate continued down the hall, moving past the church hall and toward the kitchen.

We heard Hilary before we saw her. Her tone was sharp and bossy, and she was arguing with someone else whose voice I also recognized.

I groaned.

Neely Kate grinned ear to ear. She had obviously chosen to keep this piece of the puzzle a secret.

"A little advance notice would have been nice," I grumbled as we came to a stop in the hallway outside the storeroom.

"Now what would be the fun in that?"

"Ladies," Jonah said in exasperation. "Can't we just compromise on this one? It seems logical to keep the canned goods sorted by food category—beans, soups, vegetables, and the like, instead of arranging them alphabetically."

"I told you so," Hilary said smugly.

"Maybe that's how you do it in the big city of El Dorado," Miss Mildred sneered, "But that's not how we've been doing it around here. This ain't my first food pantry, missy, so I know what I'm doin'. And shame on you, Reverend Jonah," she added. "Siding with an outsider. She's not even plannin' on stayin'. She's only dropped in to get her baby daddy to marry her. Then she's gonna grab him by the collar and flit on out of here."

It was like watching a duel between two supervillains, and I had no idea who to root for. While I would have loved to keep listening from afar, I felt the need to save Jonah from accidently instigating World War III.

I turned to Neely Kate and lifted my eyebrows, tilting my head toward the storage room. She rolled her eyes and let her shoulders sink, signaling that she'd wanted to stay there and listen, too.

Then she lifted her chin and stepped into the room. "Jonah! There you are. We heard you were hard at work, and look at this room. You sure are getting it organized."

I followed behind and almost asked if she'd learned her version of "organized" from *Hoarders*, but wisely kept my mouth shut. The large storage room—previously the choir robe room—was filled with floor-to-ceiling metal restaurant shelving, but food was scattered everywhere, making it look like a bomb had just exploded boxes and canned goods all over the place.

Jonah's eyes filled with desperation. "Neely Kate! Rose! How wonderful of you two to stop by for a visit." His head swiveled from Hilary to Miss Mildred and back. "How about we take a short break?"

"But we just got started," Hilary said, planting her hands on her narrow hips. I had no idea how she'd ever push a baby through that tiny pelvis.

"I need to talk to Neely Kate about something important," Jonah said, scrambling to climb over a huge pile of instant macaroni and cheese boxes and packages of ramen noodles. "This will only take a minute or two."

"Leave it to Rose Gardner to go stirrin' up trouble," Miss Mildred grumbled.

"Something we actually agree on," Hilary murmured.

"Hey, he needed to talk to Neely Kate," I said as Jonah hurried past me. "I'm just following my friend around."

The glare on Miss Mildred's face assured me she wasn't buying it.

I was only going to make things worse if I stayed, so I followed Neely Kate and Jonah twenty feet down the hall into the kitchen.

"I really could use a little something extra in this today," he said as he poured himself a cup of coffee. He took a sip, and his gaze wandered between the two of us. "Do you either of you have anything on you?"

"Like a flask?" I asked in disbelief.

Neely Kate reached into her purse, pulled out a mini bottle of Jack Daniels, and then handed it to him. "Here you go."

My mouth dropped open as if it were on a hinge.

"Before you judge"—Jonah said, dumping the entire contents of the bottle into his coffee before burying the bottle under a stack of paper towels in the trash— "you spend an hour with the two of them. You'd either need a shot of whiskey or a Xanax."

He had a point.

Neely Kate set the cupcake box on the counter and opened the lid. "Maybe this will help."

"You're just full of wonders today," Jonah said, reaching for a chocolate cupcake. "I love Dena's cupcakes."

"Who doesn't?" she asked.

Let's hope they'll work as well on Hilary.

"So what are you two doin' here?" he asked, then turned to me. "I thought you'd be hiding, with J.R. Simmons on the loose."

"Well, we could use a favor . . ." Neely Kate said.

His gaze shifted between the two of us. "I would think you'd need more than a favor with J.R. Simmons running loose. You need divine intervention." He swung his attention to me. "I can't believe Joe's just lettin' you *walk around*."

I pushed out a sigh. "He's not too happy, but I'm tired of sitting around, waiting for the officials to take care of business. So I'm"—I glanced at Neely Kate— "*we're* trying to find out more information to bring him down for good."

"Do you think that's a good idea?" he asked, worry wrinkling his brow. "He's capable of anything, and you two . . ."

"Are protected," I said quietly.

His eyes rounded with understanding. "Skeeter."

When I didn't respond, he asked, "And Mason. . . ?"

Since that was a complicated answer, I gave the simplest one I had. "Mason isn't an issue at the moment."

His gaze softened. "Rose, I'm sorry."

I shook my head vigorously, trying to settle my grief back into place. While Mason said he wanted to work things out, I knew it wouldn't be that easy. But now was not the time to think about our relationship.

"It's for the best this way." I rolled my shoulders. I needed to focus. I could fall apart later. "We're here because we need to talk to Hilary."

"Ask and you shall receive," a voice said from behind me.

I spun around to stare into the annoyed face of Hilary herself.

Chapter Eighteen

How long had Hilary been standing there? I went back over our conversation, looking for what she could have overheard.

But Neely Kate didn't look fazed in the least. "Hilary, you're gonna spoil our surprise. We brought you a peace offering, and we were just beggin' Jonah to let us steal you for a few minutes so we could give it to you."

She remained expressionless. "Well, isn't *that* quite the surprise."

Neely Kate picked up the small box and held it out to her. "We got you Dena's cupcakes. We asked her for your favorite flavor."

"Why would you do that?" she asked in a guarded tone, her hand resting on her small belly as if she were protecting her baby from us.

"Because you and I are more alike than you seem to think," Neely Kate said. "And you're alone in this town. We haven't treated you very well, and I'd like to make it up to you."

She cast a wary glance at us.

"She's right," I said, meaning every word. "We've all said some ugly things to one another, but I'd really like to put that behind us. If you're stayin' in Henryetta, we should all try to get along, if only for the poor baby's sake. You don't want all this animosity around him or her."

"Havin' a baby should be a joyous occasion," Neely Kate said quietly. "It's bad enough the way Joe is treatin' you. You don't need any more ugliness in your life."

To my surprise, Hilary's eyes filled with tears.

"How can I trust you?" she asked.

I took a step forward. "I mean every word." I glanced back at Jonah and nodded to assure him I did. "I hate bein' enemies with you. Maybe we can't be friends, but all of this turmoil with Violet and my birthmother has made me realize the importance of family. Your baby needs Joe—and you do, too. Maybe we can help you make things right with him."

"I still don't understand why you would help me after everything you've said and done." She sounded wary and I didn't blame her. I'd certainly be suspicious if I were in her shoes.

Truth be told, she'd always been the instigator, but pointing that out now wouldn't help with our quest.

"Why can't we let bygones be bygones?" Neely Kate asked, holding her hands out at her sides.

"Even after you went around town telling everyone that I'm eighty-five years old, and only keep my youth by drinking the blood of baby raccoons?"

Neely Kate grimaced. "Well . . ."

"Or that I dance in the woods—"

Neely Kate shrugged. "There's not a doggone thing wrong with dancing."

"In Dark Hollow Grove. Naked and under a full moon?"

Neely Kate pointed her finger at Hilary. "I never said Dark Hollow Grove. People tend to make things up as the story goes along." Then a guilty look spread across her face. "So I might have said a few things I regret . . . but maybe you have, too."

Hilary didn't answer, yet her anger seemed to have faded.

"Let's just start simple. With cupcakes," Neely Kate said, gesturing to the box. "Why don't you sit down and take a rest, and maybe we can have a chat?"

Tears filled Hilary's eyes, and when she blinked, two streams rolled down her cheeks.

Damn her. She was even a pretty crier.

Hilary glanced back at Jonah for confirmation, and I decided this bridge we were building was too important for us to blow it up. Especially when there was little chance of her knowing anything about Joe's housekeeper. I just needed to tell Neely Kate.

I motioned to the table. "Why don't you two have a seat, and I'll take this other box to Miss Mildred to see if she wants one."

Neely Kate gave me an odd look, but I picked up the box and slipped out into the hall.

I pulled out my phone and quickly sent Neely Kate a text: *We need to think long term here and not blow it with H. If the opportunity comes up to bring up Roberta, do it. Otherwise, let it be. I meant what I said about getting along.*

She texted back moments later. *Got it.*

Was that just an acknowledgment, or did she agree?

"What in the Sam Hill is takin' so long?" Miss Mildred grumped behind me.

I stuffed my phone into my pocket and turned to face my perpetually grumpy ex-neighbor. "Hilary is takin' a break. We figured she might need one with the baby and all. But I was just heading back here to find you."

"Back in my day, you kept on workin' until it was time to have the kid. Then you got yourself to the hospital where they knocked you out, and when you woke up, you had a kid."

I wasn't sure what any of that had to do with Hilary and her break, but I just nodded and opened the lid of the box.

"Would you like a cupcake?" I asked.

She leaned forward and peered into the box. "Those don't look like Ima Jean's cupcakes."

"That's because they're Dena's."

She wrinkled her nose. "I don't eat her cupcakes."

"Why not?" I asked. "They taste a whole lot better than Ima Jean's."

She pointed her bony finger at me. "And that's precisely why. Too much of a good thing is bad."

"Okay . . ." I had to wonder if Miss Mildred was turning senile. In what world were good cupcakes a *bad* thing?

I closed the lid. "Miss Mildred, have you talked to Violet lately?"

"Of course. I saw her the day before last."

"Did she tell you that she's gonna be gone for a while?"

"Of course. Something about a gardening class in Texas. A month or so. Who would have thought up such a thing? I offered to teach her everything I know, but she refused to take any more of my help."

I gave her a weak smile. Miss Mildred had always loved my sister.

"Well, you know Violet."

She nodded, and then her eyes turned glassy. "You tell your sister not to worry about the house. I'll be watching. She needs to devote all her energy to her . . . class."

My eyes widened.

"She's been looking under the weather lately. I hope that Texas sunshine helps her while she's down there."

I tried to swallow the lump in my throat. She knew.

"I hope it does, too," I choked out.

Then to my surprise, Miss Mildred put her hand on mine and patted it. "Violet comes from good stock. Both of you girls do. You're fighters. You can overcome anything. Even a cantankerous old woman."

Then, before I could say anything, she pushed past me and continued down the hall. "Jonah! If that new woman is takin' a break, then you and I can discuss the offering plates," she shouted into the empty hallway, although we both knew he likely heard her.

I was fairly certain that the figure I'd seen darting out of sight at the end of the hallway was him.

"I do not approve of passing around wicker baskets like we're some poor church. I know darn good and well you have some perfectly usable silver-plated ones in the closet," Miss Mildred continued.

Her voice faded as I started to slip back into the kitchen, surprised to find Neely Kate and Hilary deep in conversation. They were sitting at the table, and of both of them had cupcakes and bottles of water in front of them. I decided to stay put in the hall, peering around the corner. Hilary was more likely to spill things to Neely Kate if I wasn't around.

"Dena's Bakery is better than Ima Jean's ever was," Neely Kate said. "Dena is the first person brave enough to take Ima Jean on."

"I made the mistake of eating a brownie from Ima Jean's once," Hilary said, looking embarrassed. "My pregnancy hormones didn't give me constipation problems for *days*. I think I lost a pound or two." Hilary cringed. "Oh, Neely Kate. I'm sorry. That was so insensitive of me. How are you doing?" She lowered her voice. "*Really.*"

Neely Kate looked confused by the sincerity in Hilary's voice. "I have my good days and my bad."

"Honestly, it's a wonder you're even here talking to me," Hilary said softly. "I'm ashamed to say I'm not sure I'd be talking to you if our roles were reversed. This baby means everything to me. I don't think I could go on without him."

Her voice broke, and Neely Kate hesitated before patting her hand.

"You'd find a way," she said to Hilary. "It's still hard. I think about them all the time. They were so small. Most people wouldn't think of them as real babies, but they sure as shoot were real to me."

Hilary looked into her eyes. "I understand. And I am so sorry you lost them. You would have made a wonderful mother." She paused and looked down at her cupcake, then pinched off a tiny piece and lifted it to her lips. "Maybe it would hurt more than help, but once little Joe is born, you're welcome to come hold him anytime you want." Hilary paused. "But no pressure, okay? You just do what feels best for you."

Neely Kate stared at her in apparent shock.

"I know you're best friends with Rose, and Rose and I haven't been on good terms, but I really like you, Neely Kate. So I'm going to work extra hard to get along with Rose."

"Why?"

"Because she seems to want to mend bridges, too. And, well . . . it's silly, really." Hilary pinched off another piece of cupcake. "Me being jealous of Rose when she's clearly so in love with Mason."

"Rose and Mason broke up," Neely Kate said with a little more bite than was fitting for the *be nice* approach.

Hilary nodded. "I heard."

"But you just said—"

"Even so, it's obvious she only has eyes for Mason. I was insecure before, but Violet helped me realize I had nothing to worry about. And I want to live here in Henryetta. We might not be together right now, but I want my baby to be close to Joe. Violet helped me realize I need to make more of an effort to fit in."

"That Violet's been a busy girl."

"In any case, since you and Rose seem so genuine, I want to extend the olive branch. One day maybe we can even be friends."

"Well," Neely Kate drawled. "I guess we'll just have to work on it. But it's hard to imagine that someone like you would want to have anything to do with me. I spent the first twelve years of my life livin' in a trailer while you were probably livin' in a mansion with servants. You'd be slummin' to associate with me." Surprisingly, her tone was non-confrontational.

Hilary looked down at her barely eaten cupcake, then up at Neely Kate. "I can see how you might think that, but before Rose took those cupcakes to Miss Mildred, you said you thought we were more alike than I might realize. I think you were right. I really want to try to be your friend."

"Forgive me, Hilary, but after the way you've treated Rose and me, that's hard to believe."

"I know I've been more than intolerable. As I said, jealousy and insecurity got the better of me. I'm not proud of it, but there it is." She shifted in her seat, looking uncomfortable. "I'm willing to make an effort if you are."

Neely Kate pursed her lips. "Joe's mother called Rose Fenton County white trash. You don't think the same?"

Hilary's cheeks turned a soft pink that made her glow. "I admit that I came to Henryetta with a few preconceived ideas. But those ideas were wrong."

"How can someone with so much money relate to someone like me? You had everything you ever wanted. You were raised in paradise."

"Paradise . . ." Hilary gave her a sad smile. "My life hasn't been as wonderful as you think. Just because a person has lots of money doesn't mean they have lots of love."

I had to hand it to Neely Kate. She had just steered the conversation exactly where we needed it to go. But, hearing the pain in Hilary's voice, it felt wrong. Then I reminded myself that Bruce Wayne and Anna's lives might depend on what she knew.

"And I had neither," Neely Kate said in a guarded voice. "I've spent my whole life scraping by for everything—food, clothes, my mother's attention. What I got instead was a little more attention from her boyfriends than I ever wanted, if you know what I mean."

Hilary's eyes flooded with tears. "I do."

Neely Kate's back stiffened. "You . . ."

Hilary grabbed a tissue from her purse. "See? We really are more alike than either of us thought. We had money, but my house was cold and sterile. Love was just another commodity to be bought and sold. My parents had my life's purpose planned out before I was even born. I've been groomed to become Joe's wife for as long as I can remember."

"You're kidding me," Neely Kate gasped.

"I wish I were." She gave her a weak smile. "I know it's hard to imagine an arranged marriage in the twenty-first century—in the United States anyway—and I actually agreed to it." She released a tinkling laugh. "But it was what my parents wanted. It was all I knew. Joe was clueless to the whole thing until we were in high school. By then, he was busy sowing his wild oats. He said he wanted to get it out of his system before we got married."

"And you still agreed to it?"

She shrugged. "It was all I knew. My father cheated on my mother." A dark cloud crossed her features. "Joe's father cheated on *his* mother." She glanced down at the table, brushing a few crumbs toward the cupcake wrapper. "And maybe you find it hard to believe, but I loved him."

She glanced at Neely Kate with a new earnestness in her eyes. "I truly loved him. He's the only man I've ever loved . . . even if he's not the only man I've ever slept with." She gave a sly smile. "What's good for the gander is good for the goose."

Neely Kate grinned. "Good for you. But what about now? Do you still love him?"

Hilary didn't answer for a few seconds, gazing at a spot on the wall several feet away. "Would you think I was crazy if I said yes? But not like before, not the starry-eyed love of youth."

"What if Joe never decides to come back to you?" Neely Kate asked.

"I have to believe that he will. Maybe he'll change his mind once the baby comes."

"Maybe . . ." Neely Kate said, but she didn't sound convinced. "We both grew up in dysfunctional families, but I have to think it was easier with money. I hated goin' to school in hand-me-downs. I bet you had all kinds of pretty dresses."

Hilary lifted an eyebrow and nodded. "I did, but I was only allowed to wear them once before they went to the thrift store. I could re-wear my private school uniform, but anything for a party or a public appearance was disposable. God forbid we create the impression we couldn't afford to buy something new."

"Did you have housekeepers?" Neely Kate asked. "This summer, Joe used to talk nonstop about his housekeeper. What was her name? Rowena?"

"Roberta," Hilary said softly, looking away.

My stomach clenched, not only at the prospect of finding information, but also at the pain in Hilary's voice.

"Yeah, that's it. The way he talked about her made me think she took more care of him than his own momma."

She placed her hands in her lap and laced her fingers tightly. "Betsy was a hands-off mother, just like mine. Only I didn't have a Roberta at home. I spent most of my time at the Simmons house, and Roberta took me under her wing just like she did Joe and Kate. She treated me the same as she treated them. She protected me more times than I can remember."

"Protected you?" Neely Kate asked in surprise. "How?"

Hilary just shook her head.

Neely Kate stayed silent for a moment. "Joe said Roberta just up and left one day. He has no idea why. I told Rose that it was a wonder she lasted so long with J.R. Simmons as her boss."

Hilary's face paled. "What are you talking about?"

Neely Kate shook her head. "I'm surprised she didn't quit sooner. Doing the cookin' and the cleanin' *and* raisin' the Simmons kids. That's too much for one person, especially if the house is as big as Rose described it."

"She didn't do it all alone," Hilary said in a quiet voice. "She had help, but they came and went. Only Roberta stayed. She always stayed."

"Until she left, right? How long did Roberta work for the Simmons?

"Um . . . I think she came on when was Joe as a toddler, so about fifteen years." Her tone turned suspicious. "Why are you asking about Roberta?"

Neely Kate shrugged. "Like I said, I'm curious. Joe talked about her so much, and it's obvious you loved her. It sounds like she loved y'all, too, so it's weird that she would stay for so long, only to up and leave without any warning."

Hilary's face paled and her eyes filled with tears.

Her reaction caught me by surprise. It wasn't the behavior of a grieving woman. She looked like she was scared.

Neely Kate pressed on. "What do *you* think happened?"

Hilary stood, starting to cry.

"She loved us. She would have done anything to protect us." She pushed back in her chair, her fingers shaking. "I have to go. Tell Jonah I don't feel well and that I'll come back tomorrow."

With that, she ran out the door.

I had nowhere to hide, but she ignored me as she hurried down the hall toward the front doors.

I walked into the kitchen, unsure whether to be happy that we had new information or upset that Hilary seemed so distraught. I went with both.

195

"I didn't mean to make her cry, Rose," Neely Kate said, rising from her chair. "I had no idea she'd get so emotional."

"I need to call Joe," I said, digging out my phone.

"Why?"

"She's really upset, Neely Kate." I shook my head. "Not just upset. Scared. If you felt like that, you'd turn to me, but Hilary has no one. Plus, there's the baby to think about. I need to tell him."

Surprisingly, she didn't stop me.

Joe was raging when he answered.

"If you're in some kind of trouble and expect me to come bail you out, you've got another think coming."

"No," I said. "This is about Hilary."

"Oh, God. What has she done now?"

"Nothing, Joe. I'm worried about her. Neely Kate and I told her we wanted to try to get along, let bygones be bygones. She seemed fine with the idea. In fact, she and Neely Kate were getting along really well, but then Neely Kate asked her about Roberta."

"Roberta?" he asked in surprise. "What brought that up?"

"Well . . ." I hedged. "There might have been an ulterior motive," I confessed.

"What on earth could be her motive behind asking about my old housekeeper?"

"Because the nursery's new employee—Anna Miller—is Roberta's granddaughter."

"*What?*"

"I just found out last night."

"What? Wait. Start at the beginning."

There was no way I could tell him the entire story, so I kept to the bare minimum. "She moved to Henryetta around the first of the year, and she applied for a job at the nursery. She said she moved from Mississippi, but we had no idea who she was or why she was even in Henryetta. Violet and I joked that it was a big mystery."

"Violet told me she hired a new employee and cleared it with you. I honestly didn't pay much attention, since I was knee-deep in shit with my father. How'd you make the connection to Roberta?"

"Remember those files Neely Kate and I found in Kate's apartment?"

He groaned. "Not that again."

"Well, I found a file on Roberta. I just thought of it last night, but before I could go ask her about it today, Maeve told me that she and Bruce Wayne had disappeared."

"Why didn't you say anything earlier?"

"You knew about them disappearing before I did."

"Not that. About the file."

I knew I should confess where I'd found it, but I wasn't ready to tip my hat yet.

"I guess I forgot," I said.

His "hmph" told me he didn't quite believe me.

Then he asked, "Are we sure they didn't just run off together? Two kids in love just wanting to spend the day together?"

"First of all, Bruce Wayne is older than you, and second, I can't see Bruce Wayne doin' that. At least not without some kind of notice. Not since I made him part owner."

"It sure would have made my job easier if he had." Then he quickly added, "Sorry. That was a piss-poor joke."

"Any news about your father?"

"Nothing."

"Do you think he's still around?"

"Yep. He's got unfinished business, which is why you need to let me put you under protection."

"Tell you what—when Randy gets out of the hospital, I'll let *him* watch over me. Until then, not a chance."

"Well, at least quit gallivanting around the county. You're making it easy for him to find you."

"I doubt it. *You* haven't managed to find me."

That pissed him off. "Goodbye, Rose."

"Wait!" I'd almost forgotten why I'd called him.

He paused. "I'm waiting."

"I really meant it when I said I was worried about Hilary. She got really upset when Neely Kate asked her about Roberta leaving. She looked close to passing out."

"Well," he said, "she did take the news pretty hard when she found out Roberta left, come to think about it. She locked herself in her bedroom and wouldn't let anyone in until I stopped by."

I hadn't expected to get answers from Joe—this had been a call to alert him to Hilary's distress. But, now that he'd opened the door, I figured I might as well walk on through. "And you were both seventeen? Doesn't that seem excessive considerin' Roberta wasn't even her housekeeper?"

"You didn't know Roberta. She was like a mother to all of us. Even Hilary."

"Even so, isn't it weird she got so upset about it all these years later?" I asked.

"Maybe it's pregnancy hormones," Joe said. "She's been pretty weepy the last week or two."

"You've been talkin' to her?"

He hesitated. "I'm trying to make an effort. Planned or not, she's pregnant with my baby. So we've been spending some time together and . . . she's different. It's like the baby's calmed her down." He sounded guilty.

"That's great, Joe," I said, surprised I meant it. "That baby needs you, and things will go so much better if you two are friends."

"Yeah . . ."

"Nevertheless, I think there's more to it than hormones. She didn't just act upset. She seemed scared."

"Scared? Why would she act scared?"

"I don't know," I said, feeling wary. I couldn't help thinking it all tied back to J.R., but I just couldn't figure out how. "But she's never gonna tell us. Can you talk to her?"

"Rose."

"You know that Anna didn't just accidentally show up in the same town you and your sister are now living in. Kate showin' up at the same time is more than fishy. Something's goin' on."

"*Fine.* I'll ask."

"And text me so I know she's okay."

"Are you really worried about her? Or are you just snoopin' into something that doesn't concern you?"

Part of me was offended, but after everything I'd been through with his ex-girlfriend, I could understand his skepticism.

"Yeah, I'm worried enough that I'd follow her home to check on her if I didn't think it would upset her more. I'd send someone else, but as far as I know, there *is* no one else." But as soon as I said the words, I knew that wasn't quite true.

"Fine, if you're really worried, I'll check on her," he said, not sounding as sympathetic as I would have liked—but then, he'd lived through a lifetime of her manipulation. I could see how he'd think this was just one more chapter.

For all I knew, it was.

I stuffed my phone back into my pocket. We hadn't found out much, but we'd found out something. Hilary knew more than she was letting on. We just had to figure out what that something was.

Which was why I was going to turn to Jonah.

Chapter Nineteen

I found Jonah trapped by the water fountain close to his office, Miss Mildred peppering him with questions.

"I think the church lawn needs to be mowed more often. What do you plan to do about that?"

He stared at her as if an alien had popped out of her chest. "Uh . . ."

"And the ushers are much too slow when they are passing out the communion plates," she continued. "I'm sure it's due to those flimsy wicker baskets. There's no reason not to use the silver ones."

He gave Neely Kate and I a puppy-dog look as we approached.

"Hilary had to leave," Neely Kate said. "She says she'll be back tomorrow."

"What?" Miss Mildred screeched. "She's done for the day already?"

Neely Kate shrugged. "She wasn't feeling well."

Miss Mildred looked suspicious. "She was feeling just fine when we were goin' toe to toe. What did you do to her?"

Neely Kate lifted her hand to her chest. "I have no idea what you're talkin' about. We were just chatting, and she was eatin' her cupcake, and the next thing I knew, she said she felt poorly and was goin' home."

"I knew it!" Miss Mildred half-shouted. "It's those blasted cupcakes! Now I'm glad I didn't eat one of those health hazards."

Neely Kate's eyes widened. "Oh, no! It wasn't the cupcake! I'm sure it was her hormones. Maybe some lingering morning sickness."

A fire lit up the older woman's eyes. She had a new cause to fight for. "Jonah," she said, turning to the minister. "If that hussy can leave, then I'm gonna do the same. I have work to do. I'm gonna put that woman out of business."

Miss Mildred hurried to the front entrance as quickly as her cane would allow, which turned out to be surprisingly fast.

We all stood in stunned silence until Neely Kate muttered under her breath, "Oh, my stars and garters. What have I done?"

"You know Miss Mildred," I said. "She's not happy unless she's fighting some kind of evil. But usually the evil is me."

"I'll call Dena and warn her," Neely Kate said, digging in her purse for her phone.

"Good idea," I said, grabbing Jonah's arm and dragging him aside. "Jonah, I'm really worried about Hilary."

He looked surprised—not that I blamed him. Practically everyone in Henryetta knew about our rocky history.

"She and Neely Kate were having a good conversation. Then the topic turned to Joe's old housekeeper, Roberta." I told him what little Joe had told me about her, then added in Hilary's reaction. "We both know that's not normal. Even if we take her pregnancy into account."

"Why the interest in Joe's old housekeeper?"

I considered fibbing my way through it, or more like fibbing by omission, but I wanted Jonah's help. "Anna, Violet's new employee at the nursery, is Roberta's granddaughter."

"Oh." He looked as stunned as I had felt when I came to the realization.

"We didn't know. She didn't tell us, but it's pretty odd that she came to town around the same time Kate did. Plus, we found out some suspicious information about Kate. Then Anna and Bruce Wayne disappeared from behind the nursery this morning."

"What?"

"We think they were kidnapped by J.R. Simmons's guys."

"Why?"

"We're not sure. Maybe the kidnappers think she knows something. Or maybe they were trying to keep me from figuring out why she's here."

Jonah studied me for a moment, then said, "You're forgetting a possibility."

"What?"

"That *she's* the one who kidnapped *him.*"

I gasped and took a step back. "Oh, my word."

He looked grim. "Maybe she was sent to spy on you. You have to consider it."

That actually relieved some of my anxiety. "She likes Bruce Wayne. If that's true, surely she won't hurt him."

"Maybe. Maybe not. What does Joe think?"

"Oh, you know Joe," I hedged. "He's not very forthcoming with information." Time to change the subject. "But that brings us back to Hilary. Can you help?"

His eyes were guarded. "Let me guess. You want me to go find out more information from her."

"Believe it or not, I mostly just want you to go make sure she's okay. She really has no one to turn to here. I think she needs someone. The fact that she picked this church means she's open to lettin' you help her."

A grin tugged at his lips. "Or that she wanted to join your church to spy on you." He laughed. "Don't look so surprised. I work with criminals. I know how devious minds work. But

202

don't worry, I'll still go check on her. I believe that everyone has the ability to change and seek forgiveness."

He paused. "And speakin' of forgiveness. What's really goin' on with you and Mason?"

My stomach cramped. I might as well tell him the truth. "I broke up with him."

His eyes widened. "Rose."

"I knew I was only goin' to hurt him," I said. "Workin' with Skeeter is the only way I can bring J.R. down, I'm sure of it, but it was making Mason uncomfortable to work outside of the law. I hated putting him in that position, so I told him it was over. That way I don't feel obligated to tell him what I'm doin', and I don't feel guilty about hiding it from him. It's better this way."

"How did he take it?"

"Not well." I shrugged, trying to look nonchalant, even though my heart ached. "Who knows? Maybe when this is all settled, we can get back together and lead normal, boring lives. So boring that there won't be a single thing I would even consider hiding from him."

"You really believe that?" he asked, sounding dubious.

"I'd like to."

He gave me a kind smile. "Rose, I suspect chaos will find you wherever you go—and unfortunately for you, that chaos tends to be criminal in nature." He paused. "Would you like my two cents?"

"Always."

"You and Neely Kate always seem to find yourselves in these crazy situations, and I have no reason to believe that will change. Not everything you've been through the last year has been related to J.R. Simmons. If anything, most of it hasn't been. So while you may hope your life will calm down after Simmons is caught, it might not be what fate has in store for you. What good is a relationship you're tip-toeing through?

Hidin' parts of your life? I worry that you'll feel caught in the middle."

Tears stung my eyes. "But you like Mason."

"I do. Very much. And I think he's a much better match for you than Joe. But given the nature of Mason's job, I fear you'll always be forced to keep secrets from him. You see what happened when the Lady in Black blew up."

I pushed out a breath, trying not to panic. He was right.

"I'm not telling you not to get back together with Mason, only that the possibility needs more examination. Otherwise, I worry you'll be back in this same situation in the near future—Mason feeling hurt and betrayed by your secrets, and you resenting him for feeling that way."

"I don't resent Mason for being hurt and angry."

He gave me a sad look. "Are you sure about that?"

Neely Kate came bustling over, shaking her head. "Can you believe that Miss Mildred is in the process of getting a group of picketers to stand outside Dena's Bakery and protest that it's a health hazard?"

I was still reeling from Jonah's question. "Uh . . .no one will believe it. Even if they did, Dena's cupcakes are like crack. They could be dropped in dog poo and people would still eat them."

"Fair enough."

I turned to Jonah and gave him a hug. "Thank you for your help, my friend."

"There's no need for you to make any big decisions about your future right now, but I care about you, Rose. You've made great progress over the last year. I'd hate to see anything interfere with that."

I nodded, not sure if I could speak past the lump in my throat.

"And I'll let you know how it goes with Hilary," he said. "I'll share what I can without jeopardizing Hilary's confidence."

"That's all I would ever ask of you."

He nodded and headed back to his office as I made a beeline for the front door, Neely Kate trailing behind.

"What was Jonah talking about?" Neely Kate asked.

"A lot of things. But he said one thing that I want to run by Jed and Skeeter. What if Anna wasn't kidnapped? What if she's the one who snatched Bruce Wayne? She did move up here around the same time as Kate . . ."

Neely Kate stopped on the stairs. "Oh, my stars and garters!"

"Come on. Let's go talk to Jed and Skeeter."

Jed looked relieved when we climbed into the car.

"I need to call Skeeter," I said, leaning over the front seat. "Jonah gave me something else to think on."

He nodded and pulled out his phone and placed the call.

"I'm putting you on speaker," he said as he pressed the button and held out the phone.

Skeeter answered within seconds. "What's the latest?"

"James, it's me," I said. Jed's eyes widened in shock, but I ignored him and continued. "I found several things I think you need to know about.

"Okay."

"First, Neely Kate talked to Hilary. She looked really upset when Neely Kate brought up Roberta."

Neely Kate leaned forward, resting her hand on the seat. "If she was acting, then she should be in Hollywood. She was shaking like an unbalanced washing machine."

"Did she say anything we can use?"

"She said Roberta protected her," I said. "What does that mean?"

"Did she say who she protected her from?"

"No, but it was related to what I . . ." Neely Kate paused, looking uncomfortable. I covered her hand with my own.

"Neely Kate shared that her mother's boyfriends showed more interest in her than she would have liked. Hilary alluded to having experienced the same thing."

Skeeter was quiet for a moment, and when he spoke, I could hear the fury in his voice. "The fucking bastard."

"What?" I asked.

Neely Kate looked down, her face expressionless.

"J.R. often had closed-door meetings," Skeeter said. "I have no idea what went on behind those closed doors, but I could guess on some of them."

"Do you think he . . ." My voice trailed off.

"After Roberta left? Yeah."

"So Hilary got upset because her protector left, making her fair game?" I asked.

"Seems likely," Skeeter said. "But that still doesn't tell us why Roberta left. I suspect Hilary knows. And if Anna is in town, then she probably knows, too."

"Which brings me to my next point," I said. "What if Anna wasn't snatched? What if she kidnapped Bruce Wayne?"

"Why would she do that?"

"I don't know," I said in exasperation. "Maybe he was askin' questions and got too close to the truth."

"Maybe . . ." He didn't sound convinced.

"If Anna's workin' with Kate, it would explain why she doesn't seem to like me."

Skeeter remained silent.

Jed shook his head. "We don't even know what part the housekeeper plays in all this." His voice was heavy with irritation. "I think we should focus on finding Teagen and Marshal. They'll lead us to Simmons, which is our ultimate goal. The housekeeper is a moot point as long as we get him."

"Not necessarily," Neely Kate countered. "We can't forget Kate in all of this."

"Well, Kate's nowhere to be found," Skeeter said. "I decided to pay her a visit, but her apartment is toast due to the fire, and no one knows where she is."

"Well, in all fairness," Neely Kate said. "It's not like she has a lot of friends in this town."

"So we focus on Simmons and hope his daughter is there when we catch him," Skeeter said.

It wasn't ideal, but he and Jed had a point.

"We spent more time than planned at the church," I said. "We're gonna miss lunchtime at the garage."

"What are you talkin' about?" Skeeter asked.

I cringed. I wasn't sure what he'd think about this part. "I got a better description of the van that drove past the nursery. It had air intake pipes, so we're going to stop by Ted's Garage and see if anyone knows anything. We thought we'd butter 'em up with some chicken wings from Big Bill's."

"The shop where Neely Kate's husband works?"

Jed gave me a pointed look. "Don't look so shocked that he knows," he said. "You think Neely Kate would be here if we didn't know all about her?"

She lifted her chin in defiance. "Not *all* about me."

Jed held her gaze. "More than you probably think."

I glanced between the two of them. "What does that mean?"

"It doesn't mean shit," Skeeter barked. "We need to stay on task. My bookkeeper is waiting for you. Just drop the photocopy off with Mellie before you head over to the shop."

"What are you doin'?" I asked.

"I'm doin' my own real damn job," he snapped. "The whole damn county is fallin' to shit." Then he hung up.

"Someone's crabby," Neely Kate grumbled.

"He's under a lot of stress." Jed pocketed the phone and started the car. "He's not only dealing with Simmons's breakout, but with all the men who had sided with Mick Gentry.

They're crawling back like the cockroaches they are, begging for mercy."

My breath caught. This was the side of Skeeter I liked to pretend didn't exist. "Will he give it to them?"

"Skeeter's in a tough spot. He hates to dole out harsh discipline, but if he lets them off scot-free, he'll be seen as weak and some upstart will try to take over."

"So he needs a punishment harsh enough to discourage disloyalty," I said. "But not harsh enough to make them hate him even more."

He looked at me in the mirror. "He was right to choose you."

I didn't know what to say. I could take the intended meaning of his statement a half-dozen different ways, but I was pretty sure he was referring to Skeeter's offer to make me a partner in his business.

Neely Kate gave me a strange look but didn't say a word.

The bookkeeper's office was on the west side of town, which happened to be in the area of Big Bill's Barbeque. As with most businesses around town, Mellie's Accounting was in a repurposed house off County Rd 24.

Jed pulled into the gravel parking lot, which had replaced the front yard, and got out of the car. "You ladies go on in," he said, pulling out his phone. "I'll stay out here and place some calls."

Mellie was waiting for us when we walked through the door.

"I'm Rose," I said, clutching my purse to my side, adjusting to the weight of the weapon inside. I'd left it in the car for our visit to the church, so the sensation of carrying a gun was still totally new and foreign. "Skeeter said you might be able to help us."

"You're the girl with the shorthand message that needs translating, right?"

"Yeah."

"It's like a treasure hunt," she said, walking around her desk and moving toward us.

"I guess," I said, digging the paper out of my purse. "Do you think you can just read it to me?"

Neely Kate stood behind me, uncharacteristically quiet.

Mellie laughed. "Oh, honey, I don't know diddly about shorthand. My friend Ruthie is coming over to take a gander at it."

She reached out her hand, but I didn't let loose my grip.

"I'm not sure what Skeeter told you, but if this got into the wrong hands—"

She gave me a patronizing glare. "I know all about discretion, missy. My job depends on it. And Ruthie won't be talkin' about it either. You're just insultin' me."

"I'm sorry," I said, surprised to hear the venom in her voice. "This is just really important, is all."

Her gaze softened. "I'm just gonna assume you're used to working with amateurs and imbeciles. I can assure you that I wouldn't be working with Mr. Malcolm if I were either of those things."

I supposed not, but I was still having a hard time letting it go. "Could I make a copy of it before I drop it off?" I asked. "It's my only copy at the moment. And just in case . . ."

"I lose it?" she asked in a dry tone, then burst out laughing. "I'm not gonna lose it, but it don't hurt to have a Plan B."

She took the paper from me, unfolded it, and placed it on the scanner of her printer. "I appreciate having a Plan B." Once the copy rolled out, she handed the original page back to me with a grin. "I should have a translation for you by the end of the day."

"Thank you, Mellie."

"Anything for Mr. Malcolm."

Jed was still on the side of the house, deep in conversation on his phone, when we left the office.

"What do you think he's talking about?" Neely Kate asked.

"Good question. But it looks serious."

Jed nodded at us but stayed where he was while he finished his call.

"How come I never noticed how built Jed is until Dena started drooling over him?" Neely Kate asked.

His dark brown hair was cropped close, and he had a bit of stubble on his face, making it apparent he hadn't shaved today. He was dressed in fitted jeans, a solid black T-shirt stretched tight over his muscles, and a black leather jacket.

I shrugged. "Probably because he sticks to the background and lets Skeeter take the spotlight."

"Maybe."

Jed hung up and made a move toward us. His expression was grim. "We need to get goin'."

"What happened?" I asked. When Jed tried to move past me, I grabbed his arm and pulled him to a halt. "*What happened?*"

He gave me a long look—a war waging in his eyes—before he said, "Skeeter just heard from Simmons."

A band squeezed around my chest, but I forced out, "Simmons Senior, I take it."

He nodded. "He gave Skeeter an ultimatum."

He reached out to open the car door, but I blocked him. "What's the ultimatum, Jed?"

His eyes hardened. "We need to focus on finding Teagen and Marshal."

"Don't you dare do that. Don't try to hide things from me. I expect more than that from you."

"Rose, let it go."

"I can find out on my own, you know," I said. "I can force a vision." But I didn't want to. I was scared of what Jed knew and even warier of going into a vision blind.

When he didn't say anything, I asked, "Was Skeeter gonna tell me?"

He paused, his shoulders tensing. "He's thinking it over."

If neither Jed nor Skeeter wanted to tell me, it couldn't be good. "Why? What did he say?"

Jed pushed out a heavy sigh. "He wants you. He wants you delivered to the barn where the auction was held by ten tonight."

I shook my head, trying to hide my fear. "What was the threat?"

"He didn't specify."

"That's malarkey if I've ever heard it. If someone gives you an ultimatum, it usually comes with a threat to force the person to comply. What's the threat?"

He studied my face, his eyes emotionless. "Someone you care about will pay the price."

I sucked in a breath. "Who?"

"He didn't say."

"Bruce Wayne," Neely Kate said quietly. "Anna snatched him for J.R. Or J.R. snatched them both."

I put my hand to my forehead, suddenly feeling lightheaded. "Why didn't J.R. call me? He obviously has my number. Why call Skeeter?"

Jed hesitated. "I'm guessing it was a test," he said. "To see if he'd tell you."

That surprised me. Why would J.R. care whether he did or not? "Did he threaten Skeeter?"

"He didn't have to." When I gave him a questioning look, he added, "You're Skeeter's threat. Simmons knows he'll go to great lengths to protect you."

"Thus Skeeter's test." I pressed my back against the car. "Would he have told me?"

Jed opened his mouth to answer, but my phone started to vibrate in my pocket. I lifted my hand to hold him off, then pulled out the phone, not surprised to see Skeeter's name on the caller ID.

"Hey, James," I answered, my heart heavy.

"Jed told you." His voice was stone cold.

"Not everything, but enough. I forced it out of him."

His grunt implied he wasn't entirely convinced.

"What did J.R. say? Who is he going to hurt?"

"He didn't specify. But he says you'll regret not goin'."

"Bruce Wayne," I said.

"Maybe. Probably."

"So what do you propose we do?" I asked. "Callin' his bluff isn't a good idea, but I'm not fond of the idea of just handin' myself over to him."

"That is not an option," he said tersely. "We'll track the bastard down and get to him first. You head out to that garage, and I'll work on some things on my end."

I knew he was about to hang up, so I called out, "James. Wait."

He paused, waiting.

"How's Merv?"

"He'll survive."

I felt a load of guilt roll off my back. "Tell him thank you."

"You tell him yourself the next time you see him," Skeeter said. Then he hung up.

We had a timetable now, but we weren't much closer to finding J.R. It was time to bring in reinforcements. We'd focus on our end of the investigating and hand another piece off to someone else.

I called Joe on the way to Big Bill's, not giving Jed the chance to stop me.

"Rose," Joe said when he answered, "You can't keep calling me. I'm ass-deep in shit."

"A half hour ago, you were only knee-deep, Joe."

Jed's eyes were dark as he jerked around to glare at me. This was why I hadn't warned him about who I was calling.

Joe sighed. "Well, the shit just keeps pilin' up."

I cringed. "I'm about to make it deeper."

"What now?"

I needed to tell him what I knew, but the less he knew about my collaboration with Skeeter, the better.

"Your father has my number, Joe. He called me yesterday before he escaped."

"Why the hell didn't you tell me that before?" he demanded.

"It didn't seem important."

"Don't bullshit me, Rose."

"Okay, fine. Because I knew your answer would be to put me under some type of police custody. Your deputies need to focus on catching him, not babysitting me."

"Then for God's sake, go sit with Mason."

"No. I'm not hiding anymore."

"Rose!"

"Listen to me, Joe. I'm being careful. Believe it or not, I feel safer right now than I would tucked away in some safe house like a sitting duck. I'm on the move, and he has no idea where I am. You need to focus on finding him. I may have a lead for you."

Jed looked furious.

I paused, then pushed out a breath. I was about to piss Jed off even more, but we really did need to pool our resources to stop J.R.

"You need to be looking for Sam Teagen."

Jed jerked his head around to glare at me.

"Who the hell is Sam Teagen?" Joe barked.

"The man who kidnapped me."

"What? *Why are you just now telling me?*"

"I just figured it out."

"How?"

"Never mind about that part. You need to look for Teagen and work on figurin' out where your father is going to make his move." I hung up before he could ask more questions.

"Why'd you tell him about Teagen?" Neely Kate asked.

"Because we need all the help we can get. It didn't feel right keepin' it from him."

"But not Marshal?"

"Jed and Skeeter don't know who Marshal is. I highly doubt his name would be helpful to Joe."

"So why not tell him about Kate and the shed?"

"I told him about the files in her apartment, and he pooh-poohed the whole thing after he didn't find anything when he dropped in. Do you really think he'd believe me?"

"No."

"Exactly, so no use tipping our hand. We'll play it close to the vest until we have more information."

Jed still looked furious, but he didn't say a word on the drive to the restaurant.

Just like I'd suspected, Neely Kate didn't have enough money to cover the wings from Big Bill's. Jed grumbled and pushed her to the side, then paid for the entire order. She grinned at me, but wisely kept her mouth shut.

Ted's Garage was on the south side of town, so I had plenty of time to stew about how much we had riding on this random drop-in visit. If we didn't get any useable information about Teagen or Marshal, we were at a dead end.

Jed parked in the lot but left the car running. Turning around to face us, he said, "I'd like to go in there with you, but as Rose pointed out, if those guys have turned on Skeeter, they'll clam up at the sight of me. Doesn't matter that their ring leader showed up at the pool hall this morning to pledge his allegiance to Skeeter, claiming none of them never wavered in their loyalty."

Neely Kate rolled her eyes. "Yeah, right."

He paused and searched my friend's face. "I agree. They're saving their skin, which means they can't be trusted. I'm gonna ask you straight, Neely Kate. Do you feel safe goin' in there? I know you're separated from your husband right now. Does that mean they'll turn on you?"

"No. Ronnie would kill anyone who dared lay a finger on me."

He nodded, looking grave. "What about Rose?"

Her mouth twisted as she cast a glance at me. "Rose is a bit trickier."

My back stiffened. "I'm goin' in there with you."

Jed turned his attention to me. "You might need to use the gun Deveraux gave you to get yourself out of there."

"We both have guns," Neely Kate said. "I doubt they'll be brandishing weapons in a mechanic shop with customers coming and going. If they try to take Rose, they'll use brute force. If it comes to that, we'll use our weapons."

"I'd rather try my Taser first," I said. "It's less lethal."

"Don't try it if you're outnumbered," Jed said. "Keep your gun in your coat pocket, safety off. I want you to call me and stay on the line like you did with Skeeter last night. If I can hear what's goin' on, I'll know if you need me to come in or not."

"Okay," I said, trying to steady my nerves. I transferred the gun to my coat pocket, then set up the call like Jed had suggested, tucking my phone into my jeans pocket with the microphone end sticking out. "Let's go do this."

"At least we'll have the element of surprise," Neely Kate said as she slipped out of the backseat.

"Rose," Jed called after me.

I turned back to face him, my hand on the door handle.

"Be careful."

I was sure going to try.

Chapter Twenty

W'e're going to play this like we have no idea anyone here might have it out for you," Neely Kate said, leading the way with the bags of chicken wings.

I trailed a step behind. "Yeah. That's good."

"And let me do the talkin'."

"I'm not gonna fight you for this one."

She gave me a tight grin and then, bold as brass, walked under an open garage door, ignoring the customer entrance. The garage had six bays, each one occupied by a car, several of them up on lifts. I could see four men spread out around the garage, all of them wearing gray coveralls stained with various amounts of grease. One of the cars was being fitted with a set of air intake pipes just like the ones described by Maeve.

We were at the right place, all right.

"Good afternoon, boys," Neely Kate called out in a semi-confrontational tone.

A middle-aged man stepped out from behind an old station wagon, its hood gaping open, and wiped his hands on his coveralls.

"Neely Kate, what in tarnation are you doin' here?" His eyes grew even wider when he saw me.

"I'm lookin' for my husband, Vern."

A look of disgust covered his face. "Your lazy-ass husband hasn't bothered to show his face here in darn near a week."

"Well, you can't blame a girl for tryin'." She hefted the two paper bags. "But I still have a mess of wings that I can't eat. Mind if I take them back to the break room?"

"You know we ain't gonna turn down Big Bill's wings, but you must be desperate if you're pullin' out the big guns."

"Well . . ." Her voice trailed off as she walked around a newer model pickup truck. "I guess maybe I am."

I followed her down a short hall to a square-shaped room with a rectangular table and chairs on one side, and a sink, microwave, and fridge on the other. Two windows were centered on the wall to the right, overlooking a gravel parking lot full of cars.

"I didn't see Witt," I whispered. I knew Neely Kate's cousin worked at Ted's Garage, and I was hoping I'd have at least one other ally there.

"He's off today since he's workin' Saturday."

Well, crap.

Three men sat at the table, and they all looked up when we entered. While Vern had seemed harmless, two of these three men didn't.

Neely Kate set the bags on the table with a loud thud. "Tiny. Big Mo. Fancy seeing you here. Seems to me you'd be hiding under the same rock as my husband."

The two scary-looking men scowled, and I had to wonder which one was Tiny and which was Big Mo. Both were muscular and tall. The bald one had a goatee and a hoop earring in his left ear while the other guy had tattoo sleeves and hair cropped so close I could see his scalp. The one with the tattoos looked vaguely familiar, but I couldn't figure out how I knew him.

"What the hell are you doin' here, Neely Kate?" the bald guy asked.

"What's it look like?" she asked in a condescending tone. "I brought lunch."

"Why would you do that?"

"Because I was hopin' to find my husband and eat with him. The leftovers were for the rest of you."

"And what about her?" the other guy asked.

"She came along to keep me company."

"We ain't stupid, Neely Kate. That's Rose Gardner," the bald guy said. "Hangin' out with her is likely to be bad for your health."

Neely Kate's eyes narrowed, making her look all kinds of scary. "Are you threatening me, Tiny?"

He lifted a shoulder in a half-shrug. "Just statin' the facts."

"I suppose you're entitled to your opinion." She moved over to the cabinets and curled up her nose as she grabbed paper plates from a shelf thick with dust and crumbs. "You boys ever think about cleanin' up after yourselves?"

"That's a good one, Neely Kate," Tiny laughed.

"We ain't doin' women's work," Big Mo chortled.

The third guy, who was tall and skinny and looked like he'd fall over in a big gust of wind, wisely kept his mouth shut.

Neely Kate handed me a plate, kept one for herself, and then tossed a small stack on the table. "Seeing as how there are no women around, I guess you all like to live in filth."

"We ain't livin' here," Big Mo said with a gap-toothed grin as he leaned over and grabbed a couple of plates. He handed one to his friend, but the skinny guy was left to fend for himself.

"Vern hires someone to clean up," the skinny guy said, hesitantly reaching for the stack of plates.

Neely Kate grabbed one and handed it to him. "Why's he have to shrug that off on someone else, John Paul? What? You're not responsible enough to clean up after yourself?"

His face reddened. "No, ma'am. I mean, yes, ma'am. I am."

I expected Neely Kate to go off on him for calling her ma'am, but the boy looked like he was about to pee his pants, so maybe she decided to take mercy on him. Either that or she was too busy going after her real targets.

She grabbed several wings and plopped them on my plate, then added a couple to hers before sliding the bags over to John Paul.

Tiny reached for the bag, but Neely Kate slapped his hand away. "You wait your turn. John Paul's the only one with manners around here, so he gets first dibs."

John Paul grabbed a few, then hurriedly pushed the bags toward the other guys.

Neely Kate sat in a chair opposite Tiny and Big Mo, motioning for me to sit next to her.

I hesitated. These two men intimidated the bejiggers out of me. But then I reminded myself that I'd faced far scarier men in my role as the Lady in Black. The only difference was that this time I'd left the hat in my bedroom closet. I suspected I was going to have to force a vision. The fact was I should have probably forced half a dozen by now, but for some reason I couldn't fathom, I was scared to do it. Maybe I was worried my luck with J.R. had run out.

"I hear things are a mess around here," Neely Kate said, taking a bite from one of her wings. "And I'm not talkin' about the kitchen."

"Things are always a mess," Tiny said.

"They have to be pretty bad if Ronnie and Al are both missin'."

Rather than answer, they devoted their full attention to their wings.

"You givin' your allegiance back to Skeeter Malcolm?" Neely Kate asked.

"I don't see how it's any business of yers," Big Mo grunted while gnawing on a wing like a starving dog with a bone.

"It's my business if my husband's caught up in the middle of it."

Tiny released a short laugh. "You really think we're gonna tell you anything in front of her?" He pointed a greasy, sauce-covered finger at me while still holding his wing. "She's just gonna go tell her boyfriend, the D.A."

"In case you hadn't heard," Neely Kate said with an air of nonchalance, "she's not with the D.A. anymore. They split up."

The two men studied me with narrowed eyes.

"It's true," I said, feeling my Lady persona slipping into place like a well-worn glove. "Difference of opinion. I tend to think the rules aren't so black and white."

"Did you work with Crocker?" John Paul asked in a quiet voice, eyeing me as if I were a sideshow oddity. "Did you hire him to kill your mother like they said you did?"

"No," I said, turning to him. "But I killed *him*."

"And you shot J.R. Simmons," Tiny said, pushing his plate away with a wary look. "You're working with Skeeter Malcolm, ain't you?"

I was standing at a crossroads. I didn't have my veil to hide behind, but I needed all the bravado it gave me. And watching these two, I suspected I was going to have to out myself. I wished I had more time to think about how this was going to affect everyone else in my circle, especially Mason.

"I am," I said in a direct voice, holding eye contact with him. I felt naked and exposed, but I reminded myself that it was the same me. Lady and Rose were the same. Besides, it was no secret that I'd helped Skeeter and Jed entrap J.R. "Do either of you know Sam Teagen or his buddy Marshal?"

Neely Kate shot me an exasperated look, but it was clear her idea of buttering them up wasn't going to work—these guys had only two settings, mean and meaner.

"And who wants to know?" Big Mo asked with a humorless laugh.

"Skeeter Malcolm. I'm here on his behalf."

Both men laughed. "Skeeter sent you?" Tiny asked. "Yeah, right."

I glanced at Neely Kate, and she nodded her head, giving me her blessing. I was risking a lot, and I knew it, but we needed answers. Besides, I was pretty sure they weren't going to share out of the kindness of their hearts.

"She's right," Neely Kate said. "And as you can imagine, Skeeter's madder than a wet hornet at your betrayal, so you ought to do yourself a favor and cooperate."

Tiny burst out laughing. "Her? She's with Malcolm?"

Neely Kate put down her food, wiped her fingers on a napkin, and then rested her forearm on the table. "You can believe me or not, but I can guarantee you that she has his ear."

He snorted. "Yeah, right."

I slid my chair away from my untouched plate and crossed my legs, staring Tiny down. "I'm not sure why you're so surprised. Skeeter and I teamed up to get J.R. arrested."

Tiny pointed a greasy finger toward me and started laughing. "Maybe she's the Lady in Black."

"She's not the Lady in Black," Big Mo protested, glancing at me for confirmation. "She ain't rich enough."

I shrugged, forcing myself to look bored. "I don't really care who you think I am, but I do know one thing. You *will* tell us what we want to know."

Tiny started laughing, but Big Mo and John Paul eyed me with new interest.

"The Lady in Black wears a black dress and a black hat. She's got a big scar on her face," Tiny grunted.

"As I said, it doesn't matter if I am or not. All you need to know is that I'm here as Skeeter's representative right now. You will give me your cooperation, or Skeeter Malcolm will not be inclined to show you mercy when you go crawling back to him, beggin' for his forgiveness."

Tiny gave me a look of disgust. "Like he cares what you think."

I turned my attention to Big Mo, suddenly realizing where I'd seen him before. "You know I'm right. And I know that your loyalty twists in the wind like a broken kite. You were with Crocker's men. Y'all came to my farm to hunt me and Mason down. Then you turned your loyalty to Mick Gentry." I didn't add that I'd also seen him in the warehouse where I'd met Mick Gentry the week before. I cocked my head. "I suspect you're a terrible gambler, Big Mo. You have a tendency for picking the losing side."

Big Mo's face turned red, and he looked like he was about to climb over the table to wring my neck, but I held his gaze, calm on the outside even though my heart was racing faster than a jack rabbit's.

"I would take a seat if I were you, Mr. Mo," I said in a deceptively calm voice. "Skeeter's quite protective of his assets, and I can assure you that if I go back to him with one hair out of place, you will face a wrath the likes of which you have never seen before."

"If you're the Lady in Black, where's Carlisle?" Tiny asked, still looking skeptical. "I hear the Lady don't take a shit without him at her side."

"I never said I was the Lady in Black, but I can call Jed if you like. I'm sure he'll be more than happy to come in and say hello." I gave him a tiny smile. "Although he probably won't be nearly as friendly as Neely Kate and me."

"What do you want?" Big Mo asked.

I turned to face him. "Like I said, we want to know about Sam Teagen and his friend Marshal."

"How can we tell you shit when we've never heard of 'em?" Tiny asked, wearing a smart-ass grin and holding his hands out to his sides.

"See," I said, resting my hand on the table, "I don't believe that. I know for a fact that Teagen brought his van here, not to mention that *he* picked the wrong side like you did. Only, you two fellows seem like you might have wised up and seen the error of your ways, and Teagen and Marshal still believe the Easter Bunny's bringin' them a giant basket full of chocolate eggs. So why don't you help your case with Skeeter by tellin' us what we want to know?"

The four of us had a staring match for several seconds. Big Mo was the first to break. He cursed under his breath and said, "You swear you'll put in a good word for us?"

"Mo!" Tiny growled.

Big Mo turned to him, his jaw set. "I'm tellin' you, Tiny. I saw the Lady once, and she's her."

"How can you tell?"

He waved his hand toward me in exasperation. "I just can. She might not be wearin' the hat and the clothes, but it's her— the haughty attitude, the stare down. Veil or no veil, it's her."

Tiny stared at me in open awe. "How the hell did the girlfriend of the assistant district attorney become the Lady in Black?"

I gave him a cold stare. "I'm the one asking the questions here. Now are you going to tell us what we want to know, or do I need to call Skeeter?" I pulled my phone out of my jeans pocket and set it on the table, facedown. How much had Jed heard? It was a wonder he hadn't burst in yet. I could only imagine how Skeeter would react to my stunt.

Tiny cursed again, shaking his head.

"We ain't seen much of Teagen here at the garage," John Paul said, his face a pale shade of gray. "Only when he brought his van in. But he went to the poker games."

Probably the same poker games Ronnie went to, but Neely Kate remained cool as a cucumber.

"How many times did he go to the games?" I asked John Paul.

"I don't know, ma'am," he said in a shaky voice. "I'm not invited to 'em, and that's the God's honest truth."

I turned back to Big Mo. "I'm sure you two went. Someone who is so poor at taking gambles would surely keep turning up, hoping to win his money back. Am I right?"

The look on Big Mo's face made it clear we weren't going to be friends when this was all said and done.

"Let me ask this again—how many times did Sam Teagen show up at your poker games?"

Big Mo shot Neely Kate a hateful glare. "Ask your man, Neely Kate. He was there."

"Yeah, I'd do that," she said in a dry tone. "If I knew where he was. So we're askin' *you*. How many times?"

"You think I'm the man's damn keeper?"

I drummed my fingers on the table, pushing out a sigh. "You see, Mr. Mo. I don't believe you." I shrugged. "But then, maybe you don't know. It's pretty obvious you don't have the wits to be a card counter. Maybe you simply can't count that high."

"The only thing keepin' me from rippin' your head off right now is Skeeter Malcolm," Big Mo spat out, spittle landing on the table.

I gave him a bored stare. "Frankly, I don't care about your impulse control issues, Mr. Mo. What I want is information about Teagen and Marshal. Now, John Paul was helpful enough to let me know Teagen attended your poker games, and I'll be sure to tell Skeeter how cooperative he was." I pursed my lips and gave a slight shake of my head. "So far *you two* aren't getting a favorable report. Now you boys have three seconds to start talking, or I'm going to call Skeeter and inform him that you aren't ready to be brought into the fold. The count starts now. One."

Both men shot daggers of hate at me. I was sure the fact that a woman had so much power over them was getting their goat.

"Two."

John Paul looked like he was about to throw up, and Big Mo looked like he was close to having a stroke.

"Three." Disappointment rose through me as I picked up my phone and stood. Neely Kate got to her feet as well. "Gentleman, I wish you the best of luck," I said. "You're gonna need it."

Movement caught my eye as I turned to leave. Neely Kate whipped out her gun and trained it on Big Mo, who had pulled out a large pocketknife.

"Mr. Mo," I said, sounding like a disapproving schoolteacher. "That is disappointing. I suggest you sit yourself in that chair and place your knife on the table before somebody gets hurt."

"I don't have to do a damn thing you say, you bitch," Tiny said. "If you were *her*—hell, if you were anywhere close to being in Skeeter Malcolm's back pocket—Carlisle would be on us like white on rice."

The back door slammed open, and Jed appeared in the opening with a gun in his hand and an expression on his face that made it clear that two of the men in the room were in deep shit. "Do as she says."

The men's eyes widened as they turned to face their newest threat.

Tiny lifted his hands. "I didn't threaten her."

"*Sit your asses in those chairs,*" Jed snarled.

Tiny sat down so fast he almost fell off the edge of his chair, but Big Mo stood his ground, the knife still in his hand, blade extended.

Jed shook his head in disgust and shoved the table against the wall.

"While Rose likes to take a genteel approach, you'll find me much more direct." He lowered the tip of his gun. "This is your last warning, Tompkins, or you're losin' a knee cap."

Cursing, Big Mo tossed the knife onto the floor and sat down.

Jed shut the door he'd burst through and bent down to pick up Big Mo's knife. He tucked the blade away with one hand, keeping his gun trained on the men as he moved closer to them. He motioned for John Paul to move his chair next to Big Mo's so they were all facing him in a rough line.

Neely Kate walked around them before coming to a stop next to Jed, her gun still in her hand. I joined them, and Jed handed me the knife, giving them a disappointing stare all the while.

"Skeeter's not going to be happy to hear about this," Jed said.

"We didn't know she was the Lady in Black," Tiny said. "Otherwise, we would have been more respectful."

"Yeah, see . . ." Jed drawled, "I'm not buying that. And neither will Skeeter."

Fear filled Tiny's eyes, but Big Mo still looked furious.

"Now we're gonna try this again," Jed said, cocking his head to the side. "Rose is gonna ask you questions, and the level of your cooperation will help when you plead your case with Skeeter."

"I'll help," Tiny burst out. "Teagen came to four poker games. He was the one who recruited us to work with Gentry."

That surprised me, but Jed and Neely Kate remained expressionless.

"What did he say to convince you?" I asked.

"He said Gentry may have lost the auction, but he had backing from some big wigs. He refused to tell us who—he only said to think bigger than big. But Teagen didn't work for Gentry. He said he worked for the woman who had the big wig's ear."

"What did he want you to do?"

He cast a glance at Jed before returning his attention to me. "Support Gentry."

"What exactly did that entail?"

"Gentry planned to have some kind of turf war, but Teagen admitted that was just smoke and mirrors. The big guy and the woman were after four people," he said, casting a glance in my direction. "Well, I guess it turns out maybe it was really three."

"So I'm guessing me and the Lady in Black count as two of them?" I asked.

"Shut up, you idiot," Big Mo spat out in disgust. "You're as good as dead if you tell her."

I held Tiny's gaze. "I give you my word that Skeeter won't kill you. No matter what you have to tell me."

"He might not kill us, but he can still make us suffer."

"Then I promise that your punishment will be humane. Your fate depends on the level of your cooperation, as well as how repentant you truly are."

I cast a side-glance at Jed, and he gave a slight nod.

"You can trust her word," Jed said, although he didn't look too happy about it. "She has Malcolm's ear. He trusts her judgment."

Tiny hesitated before he said, "The other two on the list were Mason Deveraux and Malcolm himself, although Teagen set it up to make it look like Malcolm tortured Scott Humphrey and Marcus Tilton."

While we'd already figured that out, it was good to have confirmation, especially of Teagen's direct involvement. "What do you know about the attempts on my life and Mason Deveraux's?" I asked. "And don't tell me you don't know anything."

He squirmed in his seat.

"I'll work on getting you nearly full amnesty if you tell me everything you know."

"Rose," Jed snarled. Leaning into my ear, he growled, "What are you *doin'*? I suspect these two pieces of trash helped try to kill you."

Putting my mouth to Jed's ear, I whispered back, "I don't want to turn myself in to J.R. tonight, so we're running out of time to get a lead on Teagen. We need to find out as much as we can as soon as possible. Now you just told them Skeeter trusts my judgment. You need to do the same."

He grunted, clenching his jaw. "Fine."

I turned back around to face the two men. Big Mo looked no less angry than he had a few minutes ago, and a new wariness filled Tiny's eyes.

"Go on, Tiny," I said. "You were just about to tell me what you knew about the attempts on my life and Mason Deveraux's."

He shrugged and looked away. "I don't recall."

"You've tried to kill so many people they've all just blended together?" I asked, raising an eyebrow.

But he gave me a smart-ass grin.

He'd just made his own bed with Skeeter, but that didn't help me now. John Paul squirmed in his seat, making him look like a kindergartner trying to keep a secret.

I turned my attention to him. "Tell me what you know, John Paul."

"*Me?*"

"Who's working with Teagen?"

His eyes widened, and his gaze flickered to Neely Kate before returning to me.

"Ronnie's workin' with him, right?" I asked. "And Tiny and Big Mo. Who else?"

He swallowed, then said, "Al Moberly. He and Ronnie are with Teagen now."

"And Eric Davidson worked with him, too, correct?" I asked.

He nodded, his eyes wide. "Yes, ma'am."

"Teagen hired Eric to run Mason off the road. But Eric doesn't work at Ted's. How'd he get hooked up with Teagen?"

He paused for a moment, shooting a sidelong glance at his two coworkers.

Jed's body tensed. "Your buddies aren't gonna help you, kid. Your best bet is to answer the lady."

John Paul nodded, then looked down at his lap. "Eric was recruited after meeting Teagen at a poker game in early December. Eric told me all about it. He was still smartin' after losin' all that money at the auction, and 'cause Gentry had promised him all kinds of things. But even though Gentry was lookin' to strike back at Malcolm, Eric didn't have the stomach to go through another potential loss."

"Until he met Teagen," I prodded. "What did he tell Eric to make him change his mind?"

John Paul looked up at me. "He promised him money and power. He told Eric that his big wig lady boss was stringin' Mick Gentry along, but if Eric just did a simple job, he'd be part of the inner circle when it was all said and done."

I stared him in the eye, and he dropped his gaze.

"And that simple job was runnin' Mason off the road?" I asked.

He was shaking when he lifted his eyes to meet mine. "Eric knew I wanted an in with the poker games. He told me that if I got in tight with Teagen, I could earn the guy's respect. That's what he was doin'. Only he was pretty upset about his assignment. He didn't want no part of killin' the assistant district attorney."

"But Eric decided to go through with it anyway?" It seemed so hard to believe. The man I'd met hadn't seemed like a cold-blooded killer.

"Yeah, but he couldn't do it in the end. He was supposed to run Deveraux off the road, steal his phone, and make sure he was dead, but Eric told me he couldn't go through with it when it came time to pull the trigger. So he ran instead."

"Then Teagen killed him," I said. "So he wouldn't tell anyone."

John Paul nodded. "As a lesson to anyone else who was thinkin' about not following orders."

"If I can guarantee that you won't be charged with anything, will you give your testimony to Mr. Deveraux in exchange for protection?"

Jed's angry eyes whipped toward me, but I ignored him.

"I don't know," John Paul stammered.

"We're gonna take care of this one way or the other, but I suspect this isn't the life you want. You don't look very happy workin' with these two. Shoot, they won't even let you come to their poker games. You can either turn to Skeeter for protection, or I can arrange for you to talk to the D.A. One way or the other, we'll get you out of this mess."

"Rose," Jed said in a low voice, "think about what you're doin'."

Sure, I was working outside the law right now, but that didn't mean I planned to totally disregard it. I respected Mason too much for that. Plus, I still wanted to believe in it.

"How about we see how this plays out?" I suggested. "In the meantime, Jed, what can we do to make sure John Paul stays safe?"

"We can put him under our protection." He turned to the frightened man. "We can take you someplace safe, or you can stay here. Your choice."

John Paul swallowed. "Mr. Malcolm's not gonna squash me?"

"Now why would he do that?" I asked.

He looked me straight in the eye. "Because I was the one who ran *you* off the road."

Chapter-Twenty-One

Jed started to lunge for John Paul, but I put a hand on his arm, holding him back.

Big Mo and Tiny looked disappointed. I suspected they'd hoped to use the distraction to get away.

"You're the one who ran me off the road back in January, when I was in Mason's car? Driving out to the farm?"

He nodded, casting a fearful glance at Jed.

"And the notes on the windshield?"

He looked over at me, guilt in his eyes. "Teagen gave 'em to me to put there."

"Who's Teagen work for?"

"We didn't know, but now we're guessing it's J.R. Simmons."

"And the woman?"

"No idea. Never seen her, and Teagen doesn't say anything about her other than to call her the boss lady."

I racked my brain trying to come up with more questions, but Neely Kate beat me to it. "So if you were following Rose around, leavin' notes on her car and runnin' her off the road, why'd you stop?"

His bony shoulders lifted to his ears. "I was just doin' what I was told when I was told."

"Did you ever snoop around at her farm?" Neely Kate asked.

"No, ma'am."

Neely Kate gave me an exasperated look.

Jed slightly lifted the gun in his hand. "So who's Marshal?"

"Dunno. Never met him."

"But you've heard of him?"

He nodded.

"So what have you heard?" Jed asked.

John Paul swallowed, his Adam's apple bobbing up and down. "I think he's from someplace else because he just showed up last week."

I cast a glance toward Jed. Was Marshal one of J.R.'s men? Maybe one of his Twelve? I quickly cast the second thought aside. I'd seen him in action. He wasn't smart enough to be one of J.R.'s twelve most important men in the state.

Jed turned his attention to the other two men. "Do you two know anything about Marshal?"

"Screw you, Carlisle," Tiny sneered.

"I think I'll take a pass," Jed said with a grin, then turned to face Big Mo. "Tompkins. Last chance to cooperate."

He leaned back in his chair and stuck out his legs, crossing them at the ankles.

While we had confirmation of things we'd long suspected, we didn't have any new leads to help us find Teagen or J.R.

I turned back to John Paul. "When Teagen gave you orders, how did you communicate?"

"He called me."

"So you have his number?"

"No." He shook his head. "His number is always blocked."

"Do you have any idea where he's hiding out? Gentry was in Columbia County. Is he up there?"

"I'm guessing he's here in Fenton County, maybe down south. Teagen and Gentry didn't get along, so I doubt they'd be anywhere close to each other. I think Gentry got his orders from Simmons, but Teagen got his from the boss lady."

"When was the last time Teagen called you?" Jed asked.

"Yesterday."

Big Mo kicked John Paul's chair leg. "Shut up, runt."

Jed's face hardened and he moved closer, pressing the tip of his gun to Big Mo's forehead. "Got anything else to say, Tompkins? Because the gentleman and I are having a conversation."

Big Mo had just enough sense to stay silent, but he looked downright pissed.

Jed took a step back, but he kept the gun trained at Big Mo's chest as he once again addressed John Paul. "What did Teagen say when he called you?"

"That things were about to start happening," John Paul said.

"What things?" Jed asked.

"The end of Malcolm's reign."

"Did he ask you to do anything?"

John Paul looked sheepish but didn't answer.

"John Paul," I said. "Which bomb did you set off last night to create a diversion for J.R. Simmons's escape?"

His eyes widened. "How—"

I rolled my eyes. "Please. Don't insult me. Which one?"

He lowered his gaze. "The one at the ice cream shop."

"Did you make it yourself?" Jed asked.

"No, Teagen had 'em already made. We just had to pick them up."

"We? Who is we?" I asked.

"Me and them two." He motioned to Tiny and Big Mo.

The two men's faces turned red with anger.

"How'd you get the bombs?" Jed asked.

"He told us where to pick 'em up. He didn't meet us. They were behind a Dumpster on the Moore For Less used car lot."

If Teagen had used these men last night, there was a chance he'd call them again. I held out my hand. "I'm gonna need your phones, boys."

Big Mo snorted. "There ain't no way I'm gonna—"

Jed shoved the gun in Big Mo's face, but Big Mo was prepared. He lifted his hand to swat it away—a risky move, in my opinion—but Jed was prepared. He grabbed the back of Big Mo's head and slammed it down against his own upright knee.

Jed let go and stepped back while Big Mo wavered in his seat, blood gushing from his now busted nose.

"Let's make this perfectly clear," Jed growled, his eyes hard with anger. "You are only still alive due to Rose's interference on your behalf. One more attempt to disobey will be met with the gift of a few bullets. Got it?"

John Paul and Tiny nodded, murmuring, "Got it," but Big Mo looked too dazed to respond.

"Now, Rose asked for your phones, so I suggest you get them out—slowly—or I won't have any qualms with pulling them off your dead bodies."

John Paul handed over his phone with shaky fingers, but Tiny took his time, looking like he was hoping for an opportunity to get his revenge. At Jed's demand, John Paul retrieved Big Mo's phone from his pocket. As he handed it over, I had to wonder what Jed had planned. We couldn't just leave them here. They could—and would—warn Teagen.

Jed pulled his own phone out and pressed a button, then held it up to his ear. "Yeah, we're ready."

Seconds later, the back door opened and two beefy men brandishing guns came through the opening. I didn't recognize either of them.

Jed gave a slight nod of acknowledgment. "I'll let you boys take it from here."

He motioned for us to go out the back door, but Neely Kate ignored him and bustled up to Tiny.

"Where's my husband?"

"Damned if I know," he grunted.

A fire lit up my best friend's eyes, and she grabbed his earlobe and twisted. "Try again."

"I really don't know, Neely Kate. Stop!"

"Take a guess."

"He's with Teagen."

"I already figured that part out. Why's Ronnie with him and not with you imbeciles?"

"Teagen took a special shine to him."

"Why?"

Tiny cast a glance in my direction.

Neely Kate twisted harder.

"Oww!"

"Because of her?" Neely Kate asked. "He wanted to use my friendship with Rose to get closer to her?"

"I don't know! I guess!"

Neely Kate gave another tug before dropping her hold. "You come near my friend and I'll kill you myself, got it?"

"Yeah," he muttered rubbing his ear. "I got it."

Neely Kate stomped toward the back door, and I followed, my head reeling. I *knew* Ronnie. Mason and I had gone out with him and Neely Kate multiple times. I'd seen the terror in his eyes in the hospital waiting room while we waited to hear the news about his babies and his wife. I had a hard time seeing our *friend* choosing to plot against us.

"There has to be some explanation," I said, hurrying to catch up to her as she walked around the side of the building, heading for the parking lot in the front. "Neely Kate!"

But she didn't stop until she opened the back door of Jed's car and slid onto the seat. I slid in beside her, and Jed got into the driver's seat and started the car.

Silence hung between us for several moments, and I was the one to break it. "Neely Kate," I said. "You know Ronnie—"

She glared at me. "I don't want to talk about it."

"Okay." I'd give her a little bit to cool down. I could only imagine how I'd feel if Mason had taken off with some guy who was out to kill *her*. I turned to Jed. "Thanks for coming inside when you did."

He grimaced. "Skeeter would probably be pissed that I didn't get in there sooner."

"What he doesn't know won't hurt him." I held out all the cell phones I'd gathered. "Where do we want to keep these?"

Jed took them and set them on the passenger seat. "This seems good for now. We'll babysit them until one of them rings. Good call on grabbing them."

"If Teagen's got those guys doin' his dirty work, it makes sense he'll call them again."

"It seems more likely that Simmons and the boss lady will want Teagen to be at the barn, where they asked you to meet them. It would make sense they'd want a whole lot of fire power—Teagen and a whole lot of other men." I gave him a questioning look, and he added, "He knows that if you're comin', you won't be alone. Simmons is counting on it."

"So other than wait for one or all of those phones to ring, what do we do now?" I asked. "Seems like we've hit a dead end."

"Not necessarily," Neely Kate said, holding up her hand. "My friend texted while we were inside. I know who owned the antique store building twenty-five years ago."

"Who?"

"The same couple who owns it now. Timothy and Sharon Pelgers."

"That makes sense," I said. "They seem as old as time, and that store's been there as long as I remember."

"So we go ask them questions," Neely Kate said. "I think we need to split up."

"What are you talkin' about?" I asked. "You're not thinking about going after Ronnie on your own, are you?"

"What if they're tailing me, trying to get to you? That rat bastard Teagen targeted my husband because I'm friends with you. That's why Ronnie kept telling me to stay away from you. He was trying to protect both of us."

More like protecting his wife . . . not that I could blame him. I suspected Ronnie had gotten caught up in something he wanted no part of—only, he'd gotten himself good and stuck. He'd done the only thing he knew to protect Neely Kate—try to keep her away from me. But he had to have known all along that his headstrong wife wasn't the type to follow orders.

What a mess.

I turned to study my best friend. Neely Kate loved her husband, no matter what she claimed. Why had she been so quick to file for divorce? I couldn't help wondering if she was hiding something. But why? Surely she would tell us everything she knew to help get us out of this predicament. But what if she was trying to save Ronnie, too?

"Neely Kate," I said softly, "I need to ask you some questions about Ronnie."

Her angry gaze lifted to mine. "I told you I don't want to talk about it."

I couldn't outright accuse her of hiding anything from me. That would tick her off. But there had to be a way around it. "Neely Kate, you know we need any information we can get. If Ronnie's with Teagen, then maybe we should all go lookin' for *him*."

I gasped. I suddenly realized why she'd filed for divorce so hastily.

"You knew," I said, making sure to keep any accusation out of my voice. "You knew Ronnie was with Teagen."

Jed stiffened in the seat in front of us.

"That's why you filed for divorce," I continued. "You knew Carter would have to find him to have him served, and the person servin' him would know his location. Then we'd be able to find Teagen."

Tears filled her eyes. "I didn't know it was Teagen. I swear. But I figured Ronnie was with the guys servin' J.R. Simmons, and if I found him, then I'd find them, too."

"Neely Kate," I sighed. "Why didn't you tell me?"

"And admit to suspectin' my husband is out to kill my best friend? Besides, that alone seems divorce-worthy to me."

"I personally have my doubts that your husband is out to kill me."

"The proof is in the pudding, Rose."

"I think he's being coerced." But Carter needed to know the real reason why Neely Kate had filed in such a hurry. It no longer seemed like such a great plan for his slowest man to be on the job.

She shook her head and looked away. "I don't know what to believe anymore."

We were silent for a moment, and then I said, "I think we should stick together for now, and since we have no other leads to follow, we need to find the Pelgers and have a chat."

"My friend sent me their address," Neely Kate said. "It's only a couple of blocks from their store. So we have a starting place to look for them."

"Jed," I sighed. "Those sleaze balls think I'm Lady. How long do you think that secret will be kept under wraps?"

His gaze held mine. "We can make sure it stays a secret."

"And kill those men to do it? No," I said, although I had to wonder how much longer Tiny and Big Mo had left on this earth considering their crappy attitudes and their association with Sam Teagen. "So I said I was working on Skeeter's behalf, so what?"

"It could mean trouble for your boyfriend. It could ruin his integrity."

"I think Mason would prefer for the truth to come out than to always be lookin' over his shoulder, waiting for it to catch up to him. Even if it means losing me in the process." But I couldn't help thinking I should warn Mason.

I gave Jed a weak smile. "If it gets out more widely, I'll do whatever I can to make sure people know he had nothing to do with it."

"I'll pay a visit to the Pelgers." Jed announced, his tone suggesting it wasn't up for debate. "I'm dropping you two off at the pool hall. All three of us ganging up on them might make them less chatty. Beside, Skeeter thinks you two should lie low for a bit and come up with a plan for where to go from here." Jed glanced over his shoulder. "Neely Kate? You good with that?"

"Yeah," she said, sounding distracted as she watched the passing landscape. I could tell she was tangled up with her own demons.

That was the thing about demons. They never wanted to let you go.

Chapter Twenty-Two

I told Neely Kate to call Carter and fill him in on her reasons for filing for divorce so he'd know the entire story—without telling her about my chat with Carter. Then I sent Mason a text while she was tied up on the phone.

Some of Gentry's men are figuring out my connection to Lady. I wanted to give you a warning . . . in case you get caught in the backlash.

He responded within a minute. *Rose, it's bound to come out. Do what you need to do and don't worry about me. Be safe.*

Was it bound to come out? What would be the repercussions for Mason? I reminded myself that was part of the reason I'd broken up with him—so I didn't have to worry about things like that. But I was fooling myself. There was no way I could stop worrying about him. Love wasn't the kind of thing you could just turn off.

Not surprisingly, the pool hall was fairly empty on a Thursday afternoon. Jed followed us inside, and I was shocked to find Skeeter at the bar, nursing a glass of clear liquid.

Skeeter set down his glass and turned to Jed. "Feck and Hodges got the three turncoats under control, so I can spare one of them to meet you after your social call to the couple who owns the antique store. You sure you want to go out there afterward?"

Jed nodded.

What on earth was he talking about?

Skeeter shook his head. "There's little chance of finding anything. It's probably been trampled or taken as evidence."

Jed's jaw set and a fire filled his eyes. "I still want to look."

Skeeter gave him a quick nod.

"Where's he going?" I asked Skeeter, not bothering to keep the suspicion out of my voice.

"The barn where Humphrey and Tilton were killed."

"Why?"

Skeeter shrugged. "Beats the hell out of me. I think it's a dead end, but Jed insists. It's not like we have many other leads."

Jed took off without a backward glance.

Skeeter chuckled. "You've had a busy morning and an even busier afternoon. I really should put you girls on the payroll."

I sat on the empty stool next to him. "Do you serve food here? Because I'm starving. We left all those good wings at the garage."

Neely Kate scowled. "It seemed like a good idea at the time."

Skeeter waved a hand. "Live and learn, NK. Let it go."

I had to wonder how much he knew about what had just happened at Ted's Garage. Probably all of it.

"And yes," he said with a grin. "We serve food."

"Good. I want a hamburger and fries."

He looked over at my friend. "NK?"

She scowled. "The same."

He flagged down the bartender and gave him our orders, and then he said to me, "I heard you outed yourself."

I picked up the glass of water the bartender had just set in front of me. "I never admitted to anything, but they made suppositions."

"And how do you feel about that?"

I shrugged. "What's done is done." I took a sip and set down my glass. "Am I sorry we questioned those guys? Not one iota."

Looking down at his drink, he grinned.

"But we're not too much closer to finding Teagen," I said. "Tonight—"

"You will *not* be going to that barn tonight," Skeeter said in a tight voice.

"I don't want to. But I might not have a choice. What if they hurt Bruce Wayne?"

He turned and looked into my face with darkened eyes. "I can assure you that you won't have a choice in goin'. I'll lock you up if I have to."

"James," I groaned. "Don't pull that chauvinistic crap on me."

"I assure you it has nothing to do with you being a woman and everything to do with you being hunted by a psychopath. If the bastard wanted Jed, I'd lock him up to keep him from goin', too."

"You expect me to let them hurt or kill Bruce Wayne?"

"You don't even know if he has Bruce Wayne. He only said he'd hurt someone you care about," Skeeter countered. "He never said who."

"And you didn't think to ask him?"

Skeeter's eyes narrowed. "It wasn't exactly a chatty conversation."

Irritation burned in my chest. "What kind of conversation *was* it?"

"It was a performance, Lady. And a weapon."

"What does that mean?"

"Did you stop to think about why he called me?"

"Yeah," I said offhandedly. "As a test to see if you'd tell me."

"And also as a wedge. He hates that we're working together. He wants to sow the seeds of distrust between us. Which is why he was purposely vague. So you'd think I was hiding the truth from you."

His explanation made sense. "So what did he say?"

"He called and said he hoped I was enjoying the chase."

I nodded. J.R. got off on the game.

"He told me that I'd brought this on myself. Then he made his ultimatum."

"And what did *you* say?"

He held my gaze. "I said there was no way in hell I was letting you walk into that barn with an army, let alone by yourself. Then he said he was counting on it and hung up."

I watched him for several seconds. "What does that mean? That he didn't expect you to tell me?"

"It's J.R. Simmons. Who can tell?"

"Were you going to tell me?"

He scowled. "I called you, didn't I?"

"Because you knew Jed would end up telling me," I said. The defiance in his eyes confirmed my statement. "So why *did* you call me?"

He hesitated. "Because you deserve to be able to make your own decisions. I'd kill anyone who made mine for me." His expression softened, and a teasing glint filled his eyes. "Besides, on more than one occasion you've hinted at what you'd do to the family jewels if I crossed you." He winked. "If you're ever in the vicinity, I'd prefer for you to be there for other reasons." Then he laughed and took a drink.

Neely Kate choked on her drink, and I spun around to pat her back. She rounded her shoulders and said, "Maybe she *should* go. Maybe we can figure out a way to work it in our favor."

"No." Skeeter set down his glass with a thud, his good mood gone. "Playin' into J.R. Simmons's hands has never once worked for anyone. Hell is littered with the fools who have tried to best him."

I pushed out an exasperated sigh. "So what am I supposed to do?"

"Nothing," he said. "You wait."

"I can't just sit back and let something happen to Bruce Wayne."

"Maybe Jed will get a lead from the owners of that building."

"Maybe." But it seemed like we were all looking for needles in a haystack. What if they didn't remember who'd rented the shack twenty-five years ago? What if Jed didn't even find them?

We spent the next hour at the pool hall. Jed had called and said the Pelgers weren't home, but he was going to try again after he visited the barn. After we ate, Neely Kate became more like her usual bubbly self, although I was starting to wonder if that was just a persona she used to hide all the pain beneath the surface. She challenged Skeeter to a game of pool, and they went several rounds before Neely Kate squeaked by with the most wins.

Skeeter had just ordered her a congratulatory beer when my cell phone rang. It was a number I didn't recognize.

"Rose," the woman said in a cheery voice after I answered. "This is Mellie. We've got your paper translated already."

"Really?" I asked, trying to contain my excitement. I wasn't sure how a twenty-five-year-old clue could help us now, but at least it was more than what we had at the moment. "Anything interesting?"

"Oh, sugar, I didn't look at it," she said. "I know better than that. How do you think I manage to keep my job with Mr. Malcolm?"

"I'm not sure when I can get out there, Miss Mellie."

Skeeter's face perked up. "Is she done?"

I nodded.

"Tell her we'll be out there in less than half an hour."

I gave him a surprised look, then did as he'd said.

"I'll be here waitin' for ya," Mellie said before she hung up.

I looked Skeeter square in the face. "And how are we gettin' out there?"

"I'll take you."

"You? Shouldn't you and I stay out of the public eye together?"

"You're hangin' out in my pool hall. That's pretty public."

"True . . ."

"Trust me," he said. "If it's Simmons you're worried about, he isn't going to snatch you right now. He's excited about seeing you slink into that barn tonight. He loves the smell of fear and anxiety. He gets off on it. We're safe for now, but tomorrow will be another story, so we might as well take advantage of it."

He had a point.

We were at the bookkeeper's office within twenty minutes. Skeeter parked in the lot, and he and Neely Kate waited in the car while I ran inside. When Mellie handed me a sealed envelope, I opened my purse and grabbed my wallet. "How much do I owe you?"

She waved her hand and laughed. "Put your money away. It's been taken care of. Mr. Malcolm told me to put it on his bill."

That didn't surprise me, but I hated relying on Skeeter's money. "How much will you charge Mr. Malcolm?"

A teasing grin lit up her eyes. "He warned me you might ask, and I'm supposed to say not to worry. It's taken care of."

Of course he had.

"Thank you, Mellie," I said as I walked out the front door.

Playing pool with Skeeter had seemed to pull Neely Kate out of her doldrums, and now she was practically bouncing in the backseat of his sedan. "What's it say?"

"I don't know. It's still sealed."

"Well, open it!"

I got the envelope open and pulled out three papers. One was the original copy Mellie had made. The second was a copy that had words filled in around the shorthand. The third was the translated version. I started with that one and read out loud: *He is not to be taken lightly. He has killed for lesser things. He will kill again.*

"Sounds like J.R.," Neely Kate murmured.

I nodded and then continued.

I have been gathering information. I have two copies. One is under the baby bed. The other is in my barn. Use this key in the trap door. If anything happens to me, give it to the police chief.

I looked up. "Maeve thought it said shed. She must have misread barn."

"Rose," Neely Kate said. "You keep finding people in your barn. Mason searched out there forever—"

"He said he didn't find anything."

"Then Joe."

"He said he was checking on us to make sure we were safe."

"You've heard noises out there before."

"True . . ."

Skeeter spoke up. "We need to head out there. We need to search your barn."

"I agree."

Skeeter pulled out of the lot and turned in the direction of my farm. "Keep reading. What else does it say?"

I continued.

The journal lists important meetings, including who attended and what was discussed. It goes into detail I don't dare mention here. I trust you to do the right thing. In the name of your son, the father of your grandchild. And if anything should happen to me, I ask that you make sure she is loved and cared for.

I stumbled over that last sentence, and Neely Kate put her hand on my shoulder.

"She could have wanted him to believe that, Rose. Her options were the rich factory owner or the barely-getting-by factory worker with a shrew for a wife."

"He wasn't rich," I said quietly. "And his wife was just as shrewish. She had no reason to lie. I can't help Violet. I won't be a bone marrow match."

Skeeter glanced over his shoulder at me. "What are you talking about?"

"Yesterday, my sister, Violet, told me she has cancer. She's going to Texas for treatment, but she needs a bone marrow transplant."

"And you were tested?"

I nodded, swallowing the lump in my throat. "It would be a long shot for half-siblings to be a match, but if Paul Buchanan is my father . . ." I gave him a weak smile. "Violet didn't take it well."

"Because you can't save her?" he asked.

"Mostly because she thinks it changes things between us, no matter how much I tell her our DNA means nothing."

"You are both gettin' all upset over nothing," Neely Kate said, shaking her head. "I don't believe it. Your visions have to be from your grandmother. Your father's mother."

"Maybe. Maybe not. We can't forget that Violet and I look nothing alike. I only slightly resemble my father."

"Have you seen photos of Paul Buchanan?" she asked. "I don't think we can trust her word, Rose. She wanted the best for you, even if she had to lie to get it."

"That makes her sound like a horrible person." I knew she'd done illegal things, but from all appearances, she'd been trying to make things right.

"Not at all," Neely Kate said, her hand gently squeezing my shoulder. "She sounds like a mother who was doing everything she could to make sure her baby had the best life possible."

"It didn't matter in the end," I said. "Henry Buchanan must not have told the police chief. He was killed, and then Henry killed himself. He left me as a Gardner."

"You said your mother's best friend and your father thought it was safer for the world to think you were a Gardner. To protect you from the Buchanans."

I shook my head. "I don't know what to believe. And honestly, none of it matters. It doesn't change a blessed thing. Other than it might affect my ability to help save Violet's life."

"Rose is right," Skeeter said. "The only real consequence of which man's DNA she carries is her sister's life." He paused. "We can't choose our blood, but we can choose the people we trust. That's always meant a whole lot more than blood to me."

"Like Jed?" Neely Kate asked.

He hesitated for so long, I didn't think he'd answer. "I've known Jed since we were kids. We both came from shit families, and we agreed to stick together. And we did, except for those years I worked for J.R. When I came back, it was a little rough. I couldn't tell him where I'd been. He resented me for keeping it secret, but we stuck together anyway. And now he knows everything. I trust him with my life . . . and with everything that means something to me. That means more than the blood flowing through my brother Scooter's veins." He slid his hand over the top of the steering wheel. "What else does the paper say?"

"There are a couple of bank account numbers and balances, but the translator made a note on the side that she has no idea what banks they're with or who they belong to."

"If they have a routing number, wouldn't she have been able to figure it out?" Neely Kate asked.

"My people know I value my privacy," Skeeter said. "Unless I specifically asked her to look for the banks, she would never have thought to do it."

I gave the paper a tiny shake. "There are two sets of numbers for each of them. Some of which are the same. I'm guessing those are routing numbers, so we can ask, right?"

"Yes."

"The real trick is finding out who owns the accounts," Neely Kate said. "If they're even still open."

"That will have to wait." Skeeter caught my eye in the rearview mirror. "First we need to search a barn."

Chapter Twenty-Three

Since we would drive past our current safe house, I convinced Skeeter to stop and pick up Muffy so she wouldn't be all alone.

"It's a damn dog, Rose," he grumbled. "They're used to being alone."

"Not Muffy. She's all by herself in a house she doesn't know. She's bound to be scared."

"We're wasting time."

"As far as I can tell, there's no timetable here," I said in a snit. "We're on a wild goose chase. If I'm dying tonight, at least let me spend a few hours with my dog."

"*Nobody's dyin' tonight!*" he boomed loud enough to make Neely Kate jump.

He stopped at the safe house, of course, but that didn't stop him from grumbling about me and my damned priorities all the way to my farm.

When he pulled down the drive, I told him to park in front of the house. "If something's hidden in the barn, I bet we'll need the key we found in the warehouse to open it."

I dug out my house key and opened the front door while Muffy ran around like a crazy dog in the front yard.

Skeeter watched in horror as she started rolling around on her back in the grass. "Does she always do that?"

"She's happy to be home," I said, stepping inside. An immediate feeling of relief and belonging washed over me, as welcoming as the smell of fresh-baked cookies.

Neely Kate brushed past him and laughed. "You don't have any pets, do you?" she asked, but she didn't wait for an answer before heading upstairs to use the bathroom.

Muffy ran in through the open door, but Skeeter lingered on the porch with a wary look on his face.

"You can come in, James," I said, holding the side of the open door. "All this domestication isn't catching."

His eyes found mine. "I don't think I belong in there."

"That's bull crap if I ever heard it. Get your butt inside. You're letting the cold in."

Something about his demeanor changed as he crossed over the threshold. It was like some of the wildness bled out of him.

I shut the door behind him, then led the way to the office's French doors. "The key is in Mason's desk drawer." I pushed one of the doors open and hesitated. "He still has paperwork here. Maybe you should stay out of this room."

He gave a sharp nod as he came to a stop outside the office. "You inherited this house," he said, surveying the living room décor.

"That's right. But I only found out about it last June. I moved in after the whole Crocker mess."

He smirked. "*Which* Crocker mess?"

I grinned as I opened the drawer and pulled out the key. "Good point. The one in November."

His smile fell, but his eyes were sharp. "You and Deveraux escaped and eluded Crocker and his men in the woods. In a snowstorm."

"Until we were caught," I murmured, clutching the key in my hand as I closed the drawer.

"But you held your own. You killed the bastard."

I walked to the door and stopped next to him. "I didn't hold my own at first. He almost . . ." I shook my head. "I only killed him to save Mason."

"And yourself."

I didn't like thinking about the day I killed Daniel Crocker. A shiver ran through my body.

"What happened in that house, Rose?" he asked quietly.

My breathing sped up. "Why are you asking me this?"

He ignored my question. "You said you didn't hold your own at first. What happened?"

"He dragged me out of the closet, and he . . ." I closed my eyes. "And then Joe showed up."

"And Deveraux was locked in the closet."

I wasn't surprised he knew the details. The real question was why he was asking me to retell them. I opened my eyes, glaring at him. "What's your point, James?"

"How did you feel when Crocker dragged you out of the closet? Before Joe showed up?"

Fear made me lightheaded. "Do you really need to ask me this?"

"*Yes.* How did you feel?"

A list of emotions rushed through my head. "Scared. Helpless."

He nodded his acknowledgment. "And how did you feel last week at Gentry's house? When you were facing down Simmons. Did you feel helpless then?"

"No."

He leaned closer and lowered his voice. "J.R. Simmons is a hell of a lot scarier than Daniel Crocker and ten times as deadly. Simmons doesn't just want to kill us. He wants to make us suffer on a scale that not even a sadistic son of a bitch like Crocker could have envisioned. There's only a fifty-fifty chance of us coming out ahead. And that's generous." His eyes turned serious. "If we find ourselves in a defensive position, you need to remember that you aren't the scared woman who walked into my pool hall last summer. You're a fighter. You're a survivor. You are *not* helpless. The best way to get J.R. Simmons's goat is to not only survive, but to show bravery and courage. Show him no fear. Just like you did last week."

My stomach churned with nausea. "This won't end well, will it?"

His face hardened. "Someone's goin' down before this is all said and done. We need to make sure it's not us."

I nodded, swallowing bile.

"You two ready to search the barn?" Neely Kate asked from the bottom of the stairs, her hands on her hips.

Taking a step back, I spun to face her. After Skeeter's little *pep talk*, looking through a barn that had been searched many times over suddenly seemed like a waste of time. The fact that Skeeter was on board with the scavenger hunt was the only thing that convinced me to go through with it.

"Mason and I have looked through that barn multiple times, and neither of us found a blessed thing. I'm worried whatever used to be there is gone."

"The only way to find out is to start searchin'," Skeeter said. "Let's get to it."

I headed into the kitchen and grabbed two flashlights out of junk drawer. Although it was mid-afternoon, the sparse lighting in the barn made it difficult to see into the nooks and crannies. We needed all the assistance we could get.

I told a disappointed Muffy that she had to stay in the house, but I was worried she'd get in the way, especially since she was being more attention-seeking than usual. I led the way to the barn, trying to ignore her forlorn barks. At least I couldn't see her face pressed up against the glass. Instead, I cast a glance at the fence posts Neely Kate and I had used for target practice the week before. The gun Mason had given me was in my pocket, and I suspected I was going to need it sometime soon. Too bad I wasn't very good at shooting.

When we reached the barn, I started to open the heavy door, but Skeeter swung it open instead, then motioned for Neely Kate and me to enter.

He started to close it behind him, so I said, "We'll be able to see better if we open both doors."

He shook his head. "We don't want to clue anyone that we're back here."

"But your car's out front," Neely Kate said.

"The chances of anyone finding us are slim," Skeeter said. "They would have already looked for you at the farm. If someone drives up, we'll hear the car. Keepin' the doors closed will buy us more time because they're sure to start at the house."

"Like when Crocker came," I said. "Mason and I hid in the barn, then went out the back door and escaped into the woods. But we didn't go straight into the woods. We skirted the back property line before going in further south. To throw them off our trail."

It was surreal that I was back in a similar situation. Just a different megalomaniac.

Neely Kate studied me with curiosity. I hadn't shared much about our escape, and uncharacteristically, she hadn't pried.

Skeeter flipped on his flashlight. "Smart move."

As I turned on my own flashlight and moved toward the beat-up pickup I'd inherited with the barn, I considered confessing that it had been Mason's idea, but Skeeter had already moved on.

"Tell me what you know about this barn. How old is it? What was it used for?"

I rubbed my temple. "I think it was built in the early 1900s. I know my grandparents kept horses. There are a few beat-up stalls over there." I pointed to the left. "I think they sold the last of the horses about thirty years ago. I'm not sure what else they've used it for. I know this truck has been here for decades." I patted the rusty side.

"And where have you searched?" he asked as he swung the flashlight into a corner by the front doors.

"I've only snooped around trying to find out more about my birthmother and my grandparents. Mason was the one who did a thorough search."

Skeeter walked the length of the wall, shining his flashlight on the crack where it met the dirt floor. "And what did he find?"

"Absolutely nothing. He was out here for hours last week. The night I was released from jail. He'd hit another dead end and was frustrated. I think he was doin' what we're doing—searching to keep us busy because there's nothing else we can do."

"I can't speak for the counselor's intentions," Skeeter said derisively. "But that's not why I'm here." He stopped and turned to look at me, his back stiffening. "If you thought the shorthand on the page said the information was in a shed, why would Deveraux spend so much time looking in the barn?" His voice was steady, but I heard an undercurrent of accusation.

"He was desperate. We had three weeks until the trial. I'd just told him about finding the journal under the baby bed. Maybe he thought he'd find something out here."

"In the barn. Where'd you get the translation that told you it was a *shed*?" The accusation in his voice was clearer this time.

My blood turned to ice. "His mother."

Without a word, he continued following the wall with his flashlight beam, but his shoulders had tensed.

I planted my hands on my hips. "Spit it out, James. You don't think Mason has my best interests in mind."

Skeeter stopped and slowly turned around. "I don't know the man like you do, so you tell me—do you think he's really so shiny and clean?"

"Joe thought he was using you," Neely Kate said quietly. "Remember? To get even."

Skeeter's voice was deceptively calm. "To get even for what?"

Neely Kate turned to him. "Joe was certain Mason stole Rose from him in retaliation for Joe's role in Savannah's death."

Anger burned in my gut. "First of all, no one *stole* me. I have something called free will, and Joe had already broken up with me. But more importantly, Mason would never do such a thing. He loves me. He's proven that time and time again."

"He left you when you needed him more than ever," Skeeter said in a harsh tone. "He left you defenseless."

"He didn't leave me defenseless," I said in exasperation. "He called *you* to make sure I was watched."

He took a step toward me, his eyes glittering with menace. "Why would he call *me*—a man he's sworn to put away—to watch after his own girlfriend?"

I pointed my finger at him. "You stop that right now, James Daniel Malcolm. You know darn good and well why he called you." I snuck a glance at Neely Kate, hoping to find support there, but she was frowning. Trying to regroup, I returned my gaze to Skeeter and started over in a calmer voice. "You and I were the ones to instigate the plan to bring down J.R. Mason knew you had a vested interest in me as Lady. He knew you would protect me."

He shook his head and took two steps closer. "No. He knows that Simmons wants us both, and how convenient—we're here together. To prove my point, Deveraux knows how I feel about you, and he still asked me to keep an eye on you. What man would do that?"

I crossed my arms. "A man who loves unconditionally."

"But he *didn't* love you unconditionally," Skeeter continued, taking another step. "He left you."

I shook my head, getting angrier by the second. "What are you saying, James? I want to hear you say the words."

"I think Deveraux's been using you and is betraying you even as we speak."

I dropped my hands to my sides and clenched my fists, livid. "Have you plum lost your mind?"

"What if he's right?" Neely Kate asked. "What if he's setting you up for J.R.?"

I spun to face her. "That's crazy, Neely Kate! That man loves me. You saw how devastated he was when I was in jail."

"What if it was an act?" Skeeter countered. "You insisted on reaching out to Deveraux before sending him that video of your supposed death. You said he'd be good at playing along. And he was."

My eyebrows nearly shot to my hairline. "Are you saying he was in on that, too?"

The muscles on his jaw line tightened. "I think we should be suspicious of everyone and everything right now."

I looked at Neely Kate.

She gave me a sympathetic grimace. "He has a point."

"*Neely Kate!*"

She reached for me, but I took a step back. I could barely see her face through the pool of unshed tears in my eyes.

"Rose. I know you love him, but you have to put aside your feelings for him and look at the facts. I've had to do the same with Ronnie."

I found myself in too much shock to do anything other than nod my head.

Skeeter moved up behind her.

"We knew that J.R. was the one who sent him here to Henryetta," Neely Kate said.

"We can only speculate that," I said.

Skeeter's hard eyes sought mine. "You knew damn good and well it's true."

Neely Kate grabbed my hand. "Mason hates Joe. And he hates J.R. for sending him to Fenton County in exile."

"And both those things contradict your speculation," I said in a firm voice. "What you're suggesting would mean he's working with J.R. He would never do that after discovering J.R. was behind his sister's murder. On top of that, why would J.R. want to hurt Joe?"

"You *know* why. Punishment," Skeeter said matter-of-factly. "To teach him a lesson for not following orders. For picking the wrong woman again. J.R.'s just going to keep upping the stakes for his disobedience. And Deveraux just discovered J.R.'s involvement in his sister's death." He paused. "Maybe Simmons convinced him I'm lying. Maybe he convinced him that *I* was the mastermind behind it."

I shook my head, trying not to cry.

"Then there's Hilary," Neely Kate said.

My eyes narrowed as my anger blazed again. "What about her?"

"Kate told you they have a history."

"Mason explained it to me."

"*His* side. But what about hers?"

I jerked my hand from hers, so furious I was seeing red. "I am not falling for any of this. I know that man. He would *never* hurt me."

"Rose," Neely Kate said, her voice full of sympathy. "I never in a million years thought Ronnie capable of siding with people out to hurt you. Maybe you should try to be objective."

"It would be a betrayal to even consider it, and I've betrayed him enough!"

Skeeter pushed Neely Kate aside and gave me a cold, hard stare. "No. You put you first. Above everything else."

I returned his stare. "You've been puttin' yourself first for thirty-nine years, Skeeter Malcolm. How's that workin' out for you?"

His nostrils flared, but he held my gaze. "I'm still alive, so I'd say it's workin' pretty well."

Until me. But I couldn't deal with that guilt. I already had enough on my plate.

I lifted my chin and said in defiance, "I know Mason. I trust him."

He held my gaze, his jaw tight. "You are the most stubborn woman I've ever met."

I pushed his shoulder and walked past him. "And you like me that way. End of discussion." I took a breath and shined my light on the opposite wall. "So presuming what we're looking for is still here, where should we look? Because the obvious places have all been searched."

Both remained silent for a good three seconds before Skeeter took a step into the middle of the room. "Let's act as though it's the first time it's been searched."

We'd been searching for fifteen minutes when I heard a loud groan of splitting wood. My mouth dropped open when I saw that Skeeter had ripped an empty tack cabinet off the wall with a crowbar.

"What on earth. . . ?" I gasped.

"Time to start lookin' in the *non*-obvious places." He'd tossed his jacket into the corner and was wearing a dark gray Henley that clung to his thick arms and wide chest.

His eyebrows rose in a challenge. "You got a problem with it?"

"No," I said, with a hand on my hip. "I was thinking about remodeling anyway."

If he caught my joke, he didn't let on. Instead, he continued ripping off the cabinet to reveal the wood planks behind it.

I watched him for several seconds before Neely Kate flashed me a grin. *What on earth was she so happy about?*

She pointed her thumb behind her. "I'm going to check the loft."

My head was still spinning after their earlier confrontation. I'd told them my trust in Mason was unwavering, but a small part of me kept wondering if there was a kernel of truth to their accusations. And that made me feel so guilty I could hardly bear it.

I had to nip these stray thoughts in the bud.

Feeling like a traitor, I brushed my dirty hands on my jeans. "I'm going to the house to check on Muffy and get some bottles of water. I'll be back."

Skeeter gave me a sideways look of disgust. "You always dote on that dog this much?"

"Yes, not that it's any of your business," I said. My snotty response caught me off guard, but he'd helped plant these annoying seeds of doubt. I realized I was more than a little ticked at the both of them.

"Next thing you know, you'll be carryin' it around in your damn purse. Or in one of those baby carriers," he grumbled, then ripped a cabinet clean off the wall. It occurred to me that he was pissed, too.

"What a great idea," I sneered. "I think I'll go order one online right now." Then I flung the barn door open with more force than necessary. The door bounced off the wall, and I looked back to see Neely Kate's stunned face peering over the edge of the loft.

If I'd had any notion of surprising Muffy, it was quickly dismissed. Her face was still peering out the window, and she started barking and jumping up on the window the moment she saw me. I slipped through the back door and scooped her up, nuzzling her head with my cheek.

"Mason would never betray us, would he, Muffy?"

She assured me he wouldn't by licking my chin. Unfortunately, that didn't quiet the whispers of doubt floating through my head.

Setting her down, I walked into Mason's office and sat in his chair. My shaken faith was a betrayal, and what I was about to do was even worse. Never once since he'd moved into the farmhouse had I gone through his desk. I'd given him the room for his private, professional use, and I'd always respected that boundary. Honestly, I was surprised he hadn't come back to clean it out. He'd come by the house to pick up some clothes, but those files were on his desk. And I suspected there were more in the drawers.

I had no idea what the contents held. Mason Deveraux could never be accused of being careless, so if they were criminal files, I knew they couldn't be too serious. The best way to find out was to start looking.

Taking a deep breath, I grabbed the folder on top of the stack and opened. It contained a file on a sixteen-year-old boy who had shoplifted at Walmart. The teen was a repeat offender, but a cursory glance told me Mason had worked with the boy's case worker to get him into an anger management class and community service rather than a youth detention center. The rest of the files on the desk were similar—minor crimes, often repeat offenders.

In each, there was evidence of Mason's fair-mindedness. He'd offered smaller punishments in plea bargains to the offenders who complied with counseling and community service. He'd referred several defendants to Jonah's support group.

I closed the last file and took a deep breath. This was not the behavior of a man hell-bent on revenge, let alone a man who'd use a woman he claimed to love. I had a choice—I either trusted Mason or I didn't—and I had to choose right now.

I was following my heart.

With my decision made, I hurried into the kitchen and grabbed three bottles of water from the fridge. I was about to go out the back door when my phone rang. When I pulled it out of my pocket, I was surprised to see Neely Kate's name on the caller ID.

The moment I answered, her breathless voice filled my ear.

"You need to get out here. We found something."

Chapter Twenty-Four

I dropped the bottles on the table and ran out the back door, Muffy hot on my heels. I didn't stop until I opened the door and found Neely Kate standing outside a horse stall. The cabinets on the other side of the room had been completely removed, but Skeeter was nowhere to be found.

She looked over at me with a horrified expression on her face.

"What did you find?"

"Do you have the key?" Skeeter called out, his voice muffled. I was pretty sure he was behind the horse stall.

For the life of me, I couldn't figure out why Neely Kate was so freaked out. We'd already turned the barn inside out. What could they have found? And, more importantly, *where*?

"Yeah." I pulled it out of my front jeans pocket as I walked toward the stall. Muffy stayed at my feet, acting subdued. "What did you find?"

I rounded the corner and found Skeeter had ripped out the feed trough, which now lay on its side. "Are you seriously going to tear my barn apart?"

"Rose," Neely Kate said, "he found something."

"You already said that. Why don't you look happier?"

"I found a trap door," Skeeter said, reaching out his hand. "Let me try the key in the lock."

I moved closer and realized he'd discovered a two-foot square door that was flush with the dirt, and which looked to be encased by concrete. The door had a deadbolt with a keyhole and a handle. There was a shallow hole next to the concrete box, but Skeeter's body and the darkness obscured my view. Both the hole and the box looked to have been previously covered by the feed trough.

"This is a good thing, right?" I asked. "Why are you so freaked out?"

"Skeeter found something along with it."

"What?"

"A body."

I gasped and took a step back, turning my attention to Skeeter. "*What?*"

Skeeter grunted his impatience. "It looks like it's been there for years. He's not goin' anywhere. We need to see what's in the box. Give me the key."

I handed it to him and tried to look around him into the hole. How could I have lived here—been in this barn multiple times—without knowing there was a dead body buried under the rusted tin trough?

"How'd you know to turn over the feed trough?" I asked, trying to catch my breath as my mind whirled. "It was bolted down."

He looked up and winked, apparently unbothered by the fact that he was squatting next to a corpse. "A trick from the depression. People didn't trust banks, so they hid their money in lots of hidey holes. My great-grandmother used to hide things under her feed trough along with a whole lot of other places. I suspect the trap door was already here, but this lock looks like it's only twenty to thirty years old. The grave was probably dug at around the same time."

I heard a pop of metal, and Skeeter grabbed the handle on the door and lifted. He peered inside and pulled out a soft covered journal, folded over on itself and wrapped up with leather strings.

"How many journals can a damn person have?" he grumbled.

"Maybe she was an aspiring writer," Neely Kate mused. "Maybe she thought she could write a memoir."

"Or maybe she wanted to keep me from knowing this seedy part," I countered. "The journal I found in her drawer was all personal stuff, nothing about any of the mess she was in except for vague insinuations. The journal in shorthand looked to be dates and figures with text."

"So what about this one?" Neely Kate asked.

Skeeter handed it to me. "Only one way to find out."

I took it, glancing over his shoulder. I could see clothing, but it was partially covered by dirt. "What about the body?"

"You take a look in the book, and I'll see what I can find out. The safe seemed more pressing."

I nodded and unwrapped the cords with slightly shaky fingers. I had no idea what to expect.

Neely Kate moved next to me while I unfolded the book and opened the cover.

"It's in regular English," she said in surprise.

I was equally stunned but also relieved to see that the writing was in Dora's script in legible English, not the shorthand of the other journal and the page in the safe.

I've become more and more suspicious of the things going on at Atchison Manufacturing. Before it was just me, but now I have my baby to protect. With that in mind, I plan to create a record of how J.R. Simmons was introduced to Henry Buchanan and what occurred afterward.

I have done so many things wrong. I am not blameless in any of this. But I hope to find redemption. For my baby.

"What does it say?" Skeeter asked as he shined his flashlight into the hole.

"I don't know yet," I said, flipping the page. "It's a whole separate journal."

"But this one reads like a book," Neely Kate said. "See? I told you she might be an aspiring writer."

She was right, about the reading like a book part anyway. The next page started like a story. I read out loud, "The first time I first met J.R. Simmons, I was mesmerized by his good looks and charm."

Skeeter snorted. "He's like the angel of light, Lucifer himself. Is there anything we can use?"

"I don't know yet. I'm not even sure what to look for. Sure, we can give this journal to the state police, but that won't help us tonight."

"The Fenton County chief deputy sheriff took the other journal, and no one knows where it went," he said. "You really think handing this one over is a good idea?"

He had a good point.

He leaned down into the hole, rooting around. "If this won't help us, then we find something that does. Leverage."

"Oh, my stars and garters," Neely Kate moaned. "Are you touching that dead body?"

"Gotta find out who he was." He rose to a squat with a wallet in his dirty hand. "Whoever buried him did a piss-poor job. They must have been in a hurry. Looks like they dug just deep enough to stuff him under the trough, then filled the cracks with dirt. But the body's decomposed, so some of the dirt on the sides has fallen in on him."

I cringed and swallowed my nausea.

"How do you know it's a man?" Neely Kate asked, inching closer.

"His clothes. His hair."

"Hair?" she screeched, moving next to the grave.

Skeeter shined the light into the hole. "See his hair? It's short but dark, so he was probably young. He's wearing men's jeans and work boots. Look, see the blood on his shirt? I think he was shot."

Neely Kate looked over his shoulder. "How do you know he wasn't stabbed?"

"Because of the small holes in the cloth."

"So he died from gunshot wounds to the gut?"

"No. I suspect he died from a bullet to the head. See the hole in his forehead?"

I shuddered. "How can you be discussing a man's death so coldly?"

He glanced over at me. "He's been dead for quite some time, Lady. I'm sure it's not a coincidence he's here next to the safe." He opened the wallet. "Thaddeus Brooke. His license expired a year after the factory fire and Dora's death, so if he died in that period of time, he was thirty-five. He lived in Henryetta, and based on his photo, he was plenty rough around the edges."

"You think he was here in the barn looking for the book?" I asked.

"There's a good chance. I think we need to do some diggin' into poor Thaddeus while you skim the journal."

He leaned over again and dug into the grave, pulling out a set of keys and a money clip. "You girls head into the house. I'll be inside in a minute."

"What are you gonna do?" Neely Kate asked.

"See if there's anything underneath him. It's bound to get messy."

Neely Kate made a beeline for the door, and Muffy, who'd been so quiet at my feet that I'd nearly forgotten her, took off in a sprint after her.

I paused at the edge of the stall, suddenly feeling the weight of Skeeter's discovery. "We're gonna have to kill J.R., aren't we?"

Skeeter had jumped into the shallow grave, but he looked up at me with a serious expression. "*You* won't be killin' anyone. I'll take care of it."

That should have made me feel better, but it only terrified me.

"What's our endgame, James? We know J.R.'s plan is to torture and kill us. We've been on the defensive, trying to outwit him, but what's our goal? It can't just be survival. We have to best him, and the only way I know how to do that is to kill him, because as long as J.R. Simmons is drawing a breath, he's a threat to everyone. So what's our plan?" My voice broke, frustrating the hell out of me. This wasn't the time to fall apart, but I couldn't believe what I was suggesting. When had I crossed the line to condoning murder?

"You're right. I have an endgame in mind, but I haven't shared it because I'm sure you would never approve. I plan to show the bastard no mercy."

"That's murder."

"Not if it's in self-defense."

"I suppose that's how it's goin' to end anyway. The two of us starin' down the barrel of his gun."

He held my gaze for several seconds, then turned his attention to the grave. "Not if I can help it."

I headed into the house to find that Neely Kate had started a pot of coffee and set the remains of one of Maeve's lemon pound cakes on the table. I grabbed one of Mason's empty legal pads, a pen, and my laptop, and sat down at the table with the journal.

"I think we should write down anything that looks important, then figure out how it might fit in."

Neely Kate nodded. "How about you read and I'll take notes?"

"Actually," I said, opening the book, "why don't you search the Internet for anything you can find about Thaddeus Brooke?"

We'd been at it for ten minutes before Skeeter walked in the back door, covered in dirt.

"You find anything?" Neely Kate asked.

"No." He glanced at the book. "What about you?"

I rubbed the back of my neck. "I've found a host of things that will interest the state police, like the dates and times J.R. and Henry Buchanan met, but nothing that will help us tonight."

Neely Kate looked up from the computer screen. "And I've been searching for anything I can find about Thaddeus Brooke, which isn't much, so I've sent texts to a few friends at the courthouse to see what they can find."

"Keep diggin'," he said as he walked across the room. "I'm gonna take a shower. Jed should be here in a bit with a change of clothes."

"He struck out at the barn, too?" Neely Kate asked.

"It doesn't look too promising. He'll tell us when he gets here. Is your shower upstairs?"

"Second door on the right," Neely Kate said, giving me a worried look. Once we heard his footsteps on the stairs, she said, "So far we have a fat lot of nothing to help us for tonight. I think we need to try tracking down Anna and Bruce Wayne. If we can find Anna, we'll find Bruce Wayne."

I sighed. "You might be right, but it seems a little late for us to try findin' her now. I wouldn't even know where to look. That's the reason we went this direction."

"I think Hilary knows more. I texted Jonah, but apparently she wasn't home when he stopped by her house. The question is what's the connection between Anna and Hilary? You said Anna acted strange when Hilary walked into the shop."

"Yeah, but Hilary didn't seem to recognize her."

Neely Kate was quiet for a moment. "Hilary was pretty upset over Roberta leaving. It was obvious from the way she acted earlier, and Joe even said as much. What if Hilary had something to do with it? What if Anna is here because of that?"

I shook my head. "That seems like a reach, but we don't have *any* idea why she's here." I tapped my pen on the table and flipped the legal pad page over. "We're gonna write down everything we know and try to tie it all together."

"Good idea." She grabbed the notebook and pen from me. "Let's start with Kate. She disappeared from Little Rock two years ago, right around the time Roberta died in Memphis."

"Yeah."

"Then she says she went to California, but she dropped off the face of the earth when she left. She didn't even tell Joe how to find her."

"Right."

"But we know she'd been keepin' tabs on Mason since July—she has photos of him outside the courthouse with you and Joe."

"Right."

"She showed up in town right after Christmas. But why?"

I nodded my head. "Good question."

She sighed. "Okay, let's move on to Hilary. She showed up pregnant with Joe's baby in November . . ."

I jumped in. "And Kate showed up a month later, eager for me to get back together with Joe."

"Hilary and Kate seem to hate each other."

I paused for a moment. "We know how Joe and Hilary felt about Roberta leaving, but what about Kate? How did she react?"

Neely Kate released a loud groan. "This seems pointless." Tears filled her eyes. "That monster is going to hurt Bruce Wayne or worse. And we're sitting here talkin' about a housekeeper who worked for the Simmons family thirteen years ago!"

I stood and began to pace. "We know why J.R. is here—revenge against Skeeter. I'm collateral damage. And Mason . . . Why Mason?" I stopped and looked at her. "The fact that Mason's name was on J.R.'s hit list proves he's not involved."

"Unless he's on the list to throw you off."

I shook my head and pulled out my phone. "This is ridiculous. Why would J.R. go to so much effort?"

"Because it would be quite the reveal at the showdown, wouldn't it? I don't want to believe that Mason's part of this, but after Ronnie, I don't trust anyone but you, Skeeter, and Jed. But think about it—Mason standing by J.R's side. How much drama would that be? And you've said it before—J.R. Simmons loves a big show."

I gaped at her. I couldn't believe she would turn on Mason so easily. "You really believe Mason would do that?"

"Did I think Ronnie would be part of a plot to kill you? Hell, no." She took a breath, then lowered her voice. "Look, I'm not saying Mason's part of it. I don't want to think he is. But you can't ignore some of the red flags. Just like I'd ignored them with Ronnie." When I started to protest, she held up her hand. "All I know is that we can't trust *anyone*, Rose. Only each other."

I could see why she'd say that. She'd been used and lied to for years, so in her eyes, this was just more of the same. But I had plenty of trouble believing either man was capable of such a thing.

"We've talked to Hilary, and we've talked to Joe," I said. "We need to talk to Kate."

Her eyes flew open. "What? Are you crazy? That witch tried to kill you!"

"Kate doesn't know we're onto her."

"That's not true. If Teagen knows you were in the shed, he surely told her."

"I still want to talk to her. We really have nothing to lose."

Neely Kate studied me for several seconds before nodding. "This is crazy . . . but I'm game."

I slipped my phone out of my pocket. "I have her number from when she called me after the warehouse incident." I looked up her number and pressed send.

Kate sounded surprised when she answered. "Well, well, well . . . little Rosie's calling *me*. To what do I owe the pleasure?"

"I have a few questions to ask."

"Do you now?" She sounded amused.

"I want to know if you—"

"Stop right there."

I tried to quell my disappointment. "So you refuse to talk to me?"

"No. Not at all. I just want to be able to look at you while we chat. Meet me at Merilee's at four, one minute late and I'm leaving. Bring Neely Kate with you, but be sure to leave your bodyguards behind. Otherwise, no conversation," she said. Then she hung up.

My mouth dropped open.

"So she wouldn't talk to you?"

"She wants to do it in person." I glanced at the clock on the wall. "At Merilee's in thirty minutes. But just the two of us."

"If we're gonna make that, we need to leave soon." She gave me a dry look. "Which one of us is going to tell Skeeter?"

I twisted my mouth as I considered. "He's in the shower, and I'm not gonna interrupt him." I paused, thinking it through. "We'll leave and then call him on the way into town. He can catch up."

"You're forgetting that we don't have a car," Neely Kate said.

I grinned. "But we *do* have a car."

"You want to steal Skeeter's car?"

"Not steal it. Borrow it. Besides, Jed's already on his way."

Grimacing, she shook her head. "For the record, I think this is a bad idea. How do we know she won't kill or kidnap us?"

"Because J.R. wants me to show up of my own free will. He wants to see me slink in and beg him to spare Bruce Wayne. It would be far less rewarding if he has to capture me first."

"Unless he does it to make Skeeter show up."

"No, he knows Skeeter will walk in with me. I don't know why she wants to meet us, but I'm not gonna pass up the chance. Maybe we'll get something we can use to help us tonight."

"Or she's looking for something to use against us."

"Then we'll just have to be smarter than she is." I grinned. "We're pretty smart."

Chapter Twenty-Five

Getting away was easier than I'd expected. Skeeter had left the keys in his ignition in case we needed to make a quick getaway.

Muffy and I climbed into the backseat. I had no idea when I'd be back, and I couldn't bear to leave her behind.

As soon as I closed the door, Neely Kate put the car in reverse and the car sped backwards before she hit the brakes. "Whoa. Skeeter's car has some serious horsepower."

Then she put it in drive and shot down the driveway.

"I suppose he needs it for his getaways," I said, looking out the back window. I hadn't sent Skeeter a message yet to let him know where we went. I wouldn't put it past Skeeter to strut around my house in a towel, which meant if he heard someone taking his car, he could be chasing us out the front door at any moment. Maybe even naked. "He's gonna be livid when he realizes we left without tellin' him first."

"Good thing he can't run as fast as his car," Neely Kate said as she turned onto the highway. She looked in the rearview mirror. "Maybe you should call him and try to butter him up."

I grabbed my phone. "I have to figure out what to do with Muffy."

"You want to take her to the safe house?"

I looked out the window at the passing landscape. I had no idea how tonight was going to turn out and no idea when I'd be back to the safe house. What if I never came back at all? What would happen to Muffy then? "No," I said quietly. "I'm gonna ask Maeve if she'll look after her."

"Do we have time for that?"

I glanced at the speedometer, stunned to see she was driving over eighty miles per hour. "If you keep driving that fast, we'll end up in town five minutes before we left. I think we can make the time."

She shrugged, but was grinning ear to ear. "I can't help it. I love me a fast car."

I still needed to send Skeeter a text.

Neely Kate and I went to Merilee's to talk to Kate. We'll meet you and Jed later. She says no bodyguards or she won't talk.

I called Maeve before he could respond, and she answered right away. "Rose! Have you heard the news?"

I blinked, nearly choking on fear. "What news?"

"Deputy Miller has woken up and is doing well. They're moving him out of ICU. He's going to be just fine."

I pushed out a sigh of relief. "Oh, thank God. We could really use some good news right now." I looked up front. "Neely Kate. They're moving Randy out of ICU. He's going to be fine."

She smiled. "Well, of course he is."

"Maeve," I said, feeling guilty, "I have a favor to ask."

"Of course, Rose. You know I'll help you in any way I can."

"Can you watch Muffy for me? Overnight?"

"Of course. You know I love that little dog," she said. "She helps keep me company. Are you up to more investigating?"

"Uh . . ." It was a simple question, but my friends' seeds of doubt had me feeling paranoid. Still, this was Maeve, and if I couldn't trust her, I couldn't trust anyone. "Let's just say I'm busy. I'm not sure when I'll be back to get her."

"I can keep her as long as necessary. In fact, I can bring her back to the nursery with me in the morning if need be. She loves greeting the customers." She paused. "I was thinking about going over and telling Violet goodbye in the morning. I know she's leaving at eight. Will you be able to see her off?"

A lump filled my throat. Would I? What if it was the last time I ever saw my sister? Or worse, what if I didn't survive the evening to see her off? But I swallowed my grief and worry. I was going into this with a positive attitude. Fretting was wasted energy. "Yes." I nodded even though she couldn't see me. "I'll be there." I wiped away a tear that escaped the corner of my eye. "Are you still at the nursery?"

"Yes. It's been a long day with Anna missing."

More worry churned in my gut. "No word, I guess."

"No."

I expected as much, but the disappointment still stung. "We'll be by in a bit."

I hung up and told Neely Kate to stop by the nursery, then said, "I have to go see Violet tomorrow before she leaves. She's taking off at eight."

Neely Kate kept her eyes on the road, but her face tensed and her hands tightened on the steering wheel. "That shouldn't be a problem." Her gaze flicked to mine in the mirror. "I know you're not typically an early riser, but surely you can be up and about to make that."

I put my hand on her shoulder and squeezed. "Thank you. For everything." I heaved a breath. "I couldn't do this without you."

She covered my hand with hers. "I told you," she teased. "We were meant to do this together."

"Try to escape a psychopath?"

"Live a life of adventure and mystery."

"Well, I want peace and quiet, thank you very much."

"You'd be bored to tears."

That's what I was afraid of.

My phone rang, and I cringed when I saw Skeeter's name.

"Hey," I answered, putting the phone on speaker as I prepared to be chewed out.

"What the hell do you girls think you're doin'? How did this meeting with Kate get set up?"

"I had a call with her."

"Kate called *you*?"

"No . . . I called her and told her I wanted to ask a few questions, but she suggested an in-person meeting—just me and Neely Kate. No one else."

"And you're on your way *now*? Have you lost your mind? Why didn't you wait for me or Jed?"

"She said we had to be there by four or she was leaving. I sure wasn't walking in on you in the shower, and we had no idea when Jed would show up."

"Here's an idea," he said, his voice tight. "You could have called him."

"It was all so spur of the moment," I said. "I didn't want to lose the chance to talk to her."

He was quiet for several seconds before he said, "What do you hope to get from her?"

"Anything that will help us tonight. Maybe get her take on Roberta." Getting her to confess her and her father's scheme would be great, but I'd take what I could get.

"She's gonna figure out you know about Anna if you do that."

"Does it really matter?"

"No," he said slowly, as though he was thinking out loud. "I'm not sure it does at this point."

"No lectures?" I asked in disbelief. "No threats and ultimatums?"

"You're a grown-ass woman, not a five-year-old."

I was momentarily stunned by his pronouncement, and then I grinned. "You're only okay with this because I pointed out all the reasons I'd be safe."

He chuckled. "Plus the fact that you're not really alone. Jed's been tailing you for a few minutes."

"What?" I spun around in my seat to look out the back window. Sure enough, I could see Jed's car two cars behind us. "We can't have anyone with us, Skeeter."

"You're insulting me with your insinuation that my associate's an amateur."

"I just don't want to screw this up."

"She'll never know anyone is there. Call me when you're done."

Neely Kate glanced over her shoulder. "That went better than expected."

"Yeah, I agree."

"Let's hope our chat with Kate goes equally well."

Muffy sat in my lap the rest of the way into town, a pretty short trip given Neely Kate's lead foot. I continued to read the journal, getting increasingly frustrated—it was interesting, but interesting wasn't going to keep us alive.

Neely Kate pulled into the nursery parking lot, and Muffy jumped off my lap and planted her front paws on the window, excited to see Maeve inside the building. I was just about to close the book when a name caught my eye.

Thaddeus Brooke.

"Whoa. Neely Kate. Wait."

She had opened her car door and closed it again. "Did you change your mind about dropping off Muffy?"

"No. Dora wrote about the guy in the barn."

"What?" She leaned over the seat back to see.

I held up the book. "Look, right here. *Steyer sent a man named Thaddeus Brooke to see me today.*"

"Who is Steyer?" Neely Kate asked.

"I don't know. But this says Thaddeus Brooke threatened her if she continued to make waves."

"Did she say how he threatened her?"

"No."

Maeve was waiting at the door of the nursery now, and Muffy began to bark her head off.

"Let's drop off Muffy. I'll look at it more on the way to the restaurant," I said, opening the door and picking up my little dog. I stuffed the book into my purse, which I slung over my shoulder. I sure wasn't letting it out of my sight.

Muffy didn't want any part of being carried, but I didn't feel like putting on her leash. She practically leapt out of my arms the moment we walked through the door.

Maeve laughed when Muffy jumped up on her legs, begging for attention.

"I guess I don't have to worry about her being upset that I'm leaving her," I said, trying to keep the hurt out of my voice.

"She's just used to staying with me now," Maeve said as she squatted to rub Muffy's head. "That and the homemade dog biscuits I make her." Maeve stood and smiled. "She knows who her mommy is. Besides, you'll see her tomorrow."

But what if I didn't? What if tonight didn't go well?

"Maeve," I said. "If anything happens to me—"

"You stop that right now," she admonished. "Nothing's going to happen to you."

"But if it were to . . ." I looked down at my dog, who had begun to sniff around.

"I would be honored to take care of Muffy. But that's something we don't have to worry about for a very long time."

I gave her a smile. "Thanks." I looked out into the parking lot, wondering how Bruce Wayne and possibly Anna had been snatched in broad daylight.

"I'm sure they're just fine," Maeve said softly behind me. She wrapped her arms around my front and gave me a hug. "I'm sure everything's gonna be just fine."

"Is this a feeling?" I asked hopefully. Maeve occasionally had feelings that were more like premonitions, and they often came true.

"No, I just have to believe everything will work out."

I sure hoped so, but my usual optimism had been jaded by the impossible situation we were in.

Neely Kate could see me tearing up, so she tugged on Maeve's arm and hugged her. As soon as she set Maeve free, Neely Kate grabbed my arm. "We're going to be late for our appointment."

Maeve kissed my cheek, and a warm smile lit up her face. "We'll see you tomorrow morning."

When we got to the car, I sat in front with Neely Kate, starting to get nervous about meeting Kate.

"See if you can find out more from the journal," Neely Kate said. "You have about five minutes to search."

I grabbed the book out of my purse and quickly got to work, skimming the text until I came across something several pages later.

"Oh. This is different than everything else. It's much more personal. Like her diary." I started to read out loud:

One day in September, I had just gotten off work and was heading to my car when I saw a teenage girl I knew from church. She was sitting on the hood of a beat-up car, staring at the factory like it held the secret to life. She was so intent on her staring that she jumped when I asked her if she was okay. She said no, and when I asked her if she needed any help, she said it was too late. So I said, Jenny Lynn Rivers, it's never too late. I'm proof enough of that.

Neely Kate jerked upright. "*What?*"

"Jenny Lynn Rivers." Realization washed through me. "Oh, my word. That's your mother." I turned to face her. "What do you know about her life before she moved away?"

"Not much. She ran from Henryetta when she was seventeen and never came back until she dumped me on my grandmother's doorstep."

I hesitated before asking, "And your father?"

Her face paled. "Absolutely nothing."

"What do you want me to do? Would you rather read this yourself? What if it's personal?"

"No. *Your* mother wrote it. Keep going." She paused. "Besides, you know I'd probably turn around and tell you anyway."

I nodded and continued reading out loud, but I felt like I'd landed in my best friend's business.

She seemed thinner than usual, so I told her I'd buy her dinner if she met me at the diner. She met me there—which surprised me considering she'd looked liable to bolt with fright. I bought her a cheeseburger and fries and watched her inhale her food, wondering when I should broach the way she'd been sitting in the factory parking lot.

But she beat me to it. She looked up at me and asked, "Have you ever struggled with doin' the right thing?"

I started laughing until tears ran out of my eyes, but she was getting downright angry. If she hadn't been waiting on her dessert, she probably would have walked out then and there.

"Jenny Lynn," I said, putting my hand over hers. "I'm smack dab in the middle of doing the right thing myself."

She looked down at my huge belly and asked, "Is it hard? Having a baby all by yourself?"

I smiled. "I don't know. I haven't had one yet."

She grinned at that, then looked down at her plate. "But is it hard not being married? The women in this town don't take to sinnin' much. And they sure don't approve of unwed mothers who don't claim the father."

I hesitated. I wasn't surprised she knew all that about me. I was the best scandal to hit Henryetta in years. "That's a complicated question."

The dessert came, but before she started eating her cake, she said, "I think he'll kill me if he finds out."

"The father of your baby?" I asked. She looked surprised since she obviously wasn't showing and clearly didn't suffer from morning sickness based on the way she inhaled her dinner. "Surely you're exaggerating."

"He's killed people before," she said matter-of-factly. "I'm pretty sure he don't want this hangin' over his head."

"But that's so drastic." Surely I'd misunderstood her.

She shrugged, concentrating on her cake.

"Have you gone to the police? They could protect you."

She laughed. "The police won't care about a Rivers. We stir up too much trouble. They'd probably be happy to have one less of us messin' up their pretty town."

That seemed drastic, too, but the Rivers family did have a reputation. And while the police chief seemed fair, a good portion of the officers were judgmental pricks. "Have you thought about . . . ending it?"

She looked up at me with big blue eyes. "You mean stop seeing him?"

"That too, but I was talking about, you know, the baby."

"Oh." Her eyes flicked down before rising again to meet mine. "No. Have you ever wanted someone to love you for you? A baby don't know any better. They just love you. You're their everything and they don't leave." She shook her head and took another bite of her cake. "No. I want this baby."

"How old are you, Jenny Lynn?"

"Seventeen."

"Are you still in school?"

She nodded. "I'm a senior."

"*What about your hopes and dreams?*" *I asked.* "*Don't you want to go to college?*"

She released a bitter laugh. "*I can't afford no college. He says he could pay for it, but I'm too stupid to go.*"

I gasped. "*He? Your boyfriend? Jenny Lynn, don't let* any *boy get away with telling you something like that.*"

"*He's a man, not a boy,*" *she said defensively, lifting her chin.* "*And he's a successful business man. So he knows what he's talking about.*"

I took a moment to glance over at Neely Kate. She was twenty-four with a birthday coming up, which made the timing right. She'd already pulled into a parking spot in front of our landscaping office. Her hands gripped the steering wheel, and her face was pale.

"Go on," she said, her chin trembling. "Finish it."

I took a breath and tried to quell my nausea as I continued reading, knowing this wouldn't end well.

A successful business man. A shiver ran down my back, but I forced myself to ask, "*Does he live around here?*"

"*No,*" *she said.* "*He lives in El Dorado, but he comes here every few weeks for business and I stay with him then. He has an apartment.*" *Tears filled her eyes.* "*He gave me money for birth control pills, but I used it for something else. He doesn't want to use condoms. And now . . .*"

"*How far along are you?*" *I asked.*

"*Not far.*" *She shrugged, trying to look nonchalant, but I could see the fear in her eyes.* "*Maybe two months.*"

"*It's not too late to—*"

"*No.*" *Her tone made it clear she wouldn't tolerate discussing it.* "*I'm keeping my baby.*"

"*Okay,*" *I said quietly.* "*He's gonna find out eventually. What's your plan?*"

"*I know a guy. He's in a band and he's about to go on tour.*" *She looked up at me with a sad smile.* "*He has a thing for me. He asked me to go.*"

"*Do you like this guy?*"

She sighed, looking indifferent. "*They're all the same. That's why I like being with* him.*" A wicked grin lit up her eyes.* "*He ain't no boy. He's all man. And he's powerful.*"

"*But he'll kill you if he finds out about the baby?*"

"*Yeah.*"

"*So why not just leave this man? What's his name?*"

She shook her head. "*It's a secret. I'm not allowed to tell anyone. He likes his women young, and he says people just don't understand.*"

"*But you stay with him when he comes to town? You skip school?*" *When she nodded, I asked,* "*What if you just stopped going to his apartment when he comes to town?*"

Fear filled her eyes. "*No one tells him no. He'd have one of Steyer's men hunt me down. I'll have to run far away if I want to stop seeing, J—*" *The horror in her voice as she cut herself off broke my heart.* "*I didn't tell you his name.*" *Her eyes were wide with fear.*

I tried to keep calm now that I was 99% certain I knew the father of her baby. "*Jenny Lynn, you didn't tell me anything, but I think I know who it is. I'm trying to get him arrested. Let me help you.*"

"*No!*" *She shook her head violently.* "*You'll only make it worse.*"

"*You can't just do nothing.*"

She took a breath and her eyes hardened. "*Dustin's leaving at the end of the week. And I'm going with him. He's heading out to Virginia. He'll never think to look for me there.*"

I considered trying to talk her out of it, but I knew it was wasted breath. Besides, if I was right about her baby's father, running was probably for the best. "So what were you doin' in the parking lot at the factory?"

Tears filled her eyes. "I wanted to see the place that changed my life. I never would have met him if it weren't for that place."

Then she got up and left. I heard at church the next Sunday that she'd run away with Dustin Hargrove. And her momma never even tried to hunt her down.

I swear I'll do better by my baby girl.

But I can't stop the wave of guilt swallowing me whole. Jenny Lynn Rivers is just one more casualty from the mess I created. And I'm clueless about how to fix it.

I stopped reading and looked over at Neely Kate. Tears were streaming down her face.

"Neely Kate, you don't know that he's your father."

"I'm not sure we need much more proof," she said. Then she wiped her face and opened the car door. "We don't have time for this. Let's go see my half-sister."

Chapter Twenty-Six

I hurried to catch up with Neely Kate, who seemed remarkably calm after hearing such earth-shattering news. Like she'd just stepped into her next role.

"Neely Kate, I think you goin' in to meet Kate right now is a bad idea."

She stopped in her tracks. "Why?"

I sighed in exasperation. "Because you just found out something life-altering. When I found out about Dora, I fell to pieces."

"With all due respect, Rose," she said in a tight voice, "I'm much stronger than you were then."

I gasped.

Her eyes softened. "You have no idea what my life has been like. I've hardly told a soul any of it, especially the two years I left after high school, but I promise you that finding out that boll weevil is my father changes nothin'."

I didn't believe her for a second. "Do you think Kate knows?"

It was her turn to gasp. "Why would she know?"

"Think about it. Whenever we see her, she's really taken with you."

Neely Kate looked stunned.

"Plus, she insisted that you come to this meeting." I studied her face. "Are you planning on saying something to her?"

She sucked in her bottom lip, suddenly looking more vulnerable. "I don't know yet."

I pulled her into a hug. "Just think about it for a spell, okay? Don't rush into anything. Let this sit for a bit."

She backed up and looked me in the eye, her mask of indifference back in place. "We have far bigger things to worry about than who provided half of my DNA."

"Maybe or maybe not, but you're entitled to your feelings."

She ignored me, hustling across the street and leaving me to trail behind her.

"Neely Kate!"

"We're late." She didn't slow down until she stepped into the restaurant.

Kate was already sitting at a table for four by the window, wearing her trademark sarcastic grin. Her dark hair had grown since she'd come to town, but she'd touched up the blue streaks. She was dressed in a long-sleeved black T-shirt, jeans, and boots. Her canvas jacket hung on the back of her chair. A plate with half a sandwich and some chips sat in front of her, along with a glass of water. "You two were having a heartfelt moment out there."

"It's called friendship," Neely Kate spat out as she sat across from her. "You might want to try it sometime."

Kate's grin spread, and she made a scratching motion with her curled fingers. "Someone's feeling bitchy today. I like it. It's a good look on you."

"Cut the shit, Kate," my friend said with more venom than I'd ever heard in her voice. "Why are we here?"

She leaned back in her chair and slightly tilted her head, her smile gone. "We're *here* because your friend said she has questions. So I'm letting her ask them."

Neely Kate started to say something, but I grabbed her hand under the table and squeezed. I could only imagine what was going through her head right now. I should have made her stay in the office.

A waitress walked over with her order pad. "What can I get for you two girls?"

"Water for me," I said, then glanced at Neely Kate before adding, "And a sweet tea for Neely Kate."

When the waitress walked away, I turned my attention to Joe's sister. "Why did you come to Henryetta?"

Kate laughed and sat up. "No beatin' around the bush for you, Rosie. Just get right to it. Good for you."

"Answer the question."

She gave me a pouty look. "I missed my brother."

"You expect me to believe that?"

"Am I supposed to care that you don't?"

Crap. This was going to be a waste of time. I had to figure out why she was interested in me. I thought it was because of my past relationship with Joe, but what if she was trying to get to Neely Kate through me? What if her sudden appearance in town was really all about Neely Kate? I had to be smart with my questions. It was best to start with the obvious. "Do you really want me and Joe back together?"

She burst out laughing. When she settled down, she asked, "Of all the questions you could come up with, that's the one you ask?" She shook her head. "Maybe I pegged you wrong. Maybe you're just like that cow after all."

"Hilary?"

She rolled her eyes. "How many cows do you know?"

Neely Kate narrowed her eyes. "I'm looking at one right now."

Oh, crap on a cracker. This was going downhill fast.

But Kate just laughed. "What's eatin' you today, NK? You upset about your man leavin' you?" She laughed at Neely Kate's look of surprise. "Yeah. I know about that. Chin up. No man's worth the grief."

"You ever been in love, Kate?" I asked.

She groaned and placed her palms on the table with a bang. "What is your obsession with love, Rose Gardner? This isn't some damn romance novel."

"You said I could ask anything I wanted. So I'm asking." I leaned forward. "Have you ever been in love?"

Her eyes softened for a split second, and she sat up taller in her seat but didn't answer.

I pressed on anyway. "What happened?"

"Who said anything happened?"

"It's obvious you're a free agent," I said, sweeping my hand over the table. "No man in sight, but you're obsessed with your brother's love life. Trying to live vicariously through him?"

"You have no idea what you're talking about," she spat out.

"What's your obsession with Mason?" I asked.

She released a short laugh. "Who said I'm obsessed with your *ex*-boyfriend?" She gave me a mocking grin. "Yeah, I know about that, too."

"Wow," Neely Kate said, "You're awfully tuned in to Fenton County gossip for a newcomer. Who's your source?"

Kate wagged her finger tsking. "A lady never talks."

"True," Neely Kate drawled. "So why aren't you talkin'?"

Kate burst out laughing. "You two have a lot of piss water and vinegar for two girls on the defensive."

"Well," I said, giving her a cold stare, "let's get a few things straight. First, we're women, not girls. And second, we are not on the *defensive*." The moment the last sentence left my mouth, a shiver ran down my back. Shoot. I'd just played a hand I hadn't meant to reveal. We needed to let J.R. think we were walking into his trap. But we'd probably played our hand anyway—the very fact that we were here questioning Kate was an admission that we weren't taking this lying down. "Let's cut the bull, Kate. I know you have a more-than-healthy interest in Mason Deveraux."

"You're barking up the wrong tree, sweetie pie."

"What's that mean?" Neely Kate asked.

She shrugged. "Figure it out for yourself."

The waitress brought our drinks and asked if we wanted to order any food, but we told her we were good.

As soon as she walked away, Neely Kate asked, "So you're denying you're interested in Mason?"

Kate laughed. "I wasn't, but maybe I'll take a stab at him now that he's unshackled." Her eyes lit up as a wicked grin spread across her face. "The straight-laced ones tend to be a bit dark and wild in the bedroom. Did you find that to be true, Rose Petal?"

My face burned.

She leaned forward. "I had the perfect view of him in his office. I thought about dropping in on him and paying him a visit . . ." Her eyes danced. "Kind of like you used to do, but it looked pretty vanilla. I'd show him what it's like with a *real* woman."

I gasped, but Neely Kate jumped in. "What's your father's end goal?"

"*Seriously?*" Kate shook her head. "Have you suffered a traumatic brain injury recently? Any fool can figure out what he wants. Freedom. Revenge. The usual."

"Who did you fall in love with?" I asked.

Both women looked at me like I'd lost my mind.

"We're back to that?" Kate asked in disbelief, but the look in her eyes confirmed I was on the right track.

"Come on, it's girl talk. I share, you share. Isn't that how it works?" I asked.

Kate chuckled. "You're really going to share your sexy times with me? *You?*"

I hoped to God I didn't regret this. "How about we take turns asking questions? But we have to answer truthfully."

Kate rested her forearms on the table, grinning from ear to ear. "It's like our own truth or dare, only just the truth. Too bad we don't have any tequila."

I didn't share that sentiment. I suspected I'd never drink tequila again after my experience with Daniel Crocker eight months ago. But the memory only confirmed that I wasn't the same blushing virgin who'd feared her own shadow. I could do this. I *would* do this if it helped us survive. After all, talking about intimate matters with Kate paled in comparison to the other challenges I'd faced.

I leaned forward and asked again, "How many times have you been in love?"

She gave me a haughty grin. "Once. Now my turn." Her grin turned wicked. "What's Mason's favorite position?"

"You don't want to ask me how many times I've been in love?" I countered, trying to stall.

She snorted. "Hell, no. Why would I ask you a question that I could answer myself?"

"Do you think I was in love with Joe?"

She lifted her finger and wagged it at me. "It's not your turn. You answer *my* question now." She grinned. "Mason's favorite position."

I took a breath. "I don't know that he has one." I felt my face getting hot. "We often switch."

"Do tell." She grinned. "What are they?"

I fought to hold her gaze. "Me on top and missionary."

She lifted an eyebrow. "What about a reverse cowgirl?"

I was going to die of embarrassment. "No."

She shook her head, tsking. "Note to self: Show Mason Deveraux a reverse cowgirl and ride him *hard*."

Jealously struck fast and furious, but Neely Kate put her hand on my knee and squeezed hard.

I had to phrase my next question carefully, because it didn't take a genius to see that the closer I got to her secret, the more she would try to shake me up with humiliating questions. "Why did you break up with the man you loved?"

Her eyes were guarded. "Difference of opinion."

"Sorry," Neely Kate said, "you'll need to expand on who had the difference of opinion."

Anger washed over Kate's face before she finally spat out, "My father."

I wasn't sure why that caught me by surprise. Her father hadn't approved of Joe's previous girlfriends. It made sense he'd be just as critical of Kate's choices. Especially if she'd found someone more fringe like her. He would have been an embarrassment.

"My turn," she said, not trying to disguise her desire to hurt me. "How big is he?"

"Excuse me?" I choked out.

"How big is Mason. I suspect he's got a python under those sexy pants."

I shot a quick glance at Neely Kate. Her face said it all. *Don't do it. It's not worth it.* But it was. I suspected Kate's involvement in this whole mess was tied up with her lost love. All I had to do was get through this answer, and then I could ask my final question, and we could start researching the rest without her.

I channeled some inner strength and gave her a sexy smile. "Oh, he's big. Plenty big enough to get the job done *over* and *over* and *over* again." When she started to protest, I added. "Let's just say your reverse cowgirl would leave you sore—but satisfied—for days."

A wicked grin spread across her face. "Something to look forward to."

Not if I had anything to do with it.

I gave her a coy smile. "The man you were in love with—what was his name?"

She blinked, the only sign I'd gotten to her. "Why would you want to know his name?"

"I don't know . . . Maybe so I'll know what to call him when I start asking about his sexual preferences."

She grinned, but her eyes were cold. "He liked it rough and kinky. If you'd like, I can demonstrate later. I have a pair of handcuffs and a dildo that survived the fire."

I couldn't hide my shock, but her belligerence only proved I was digging into something she didn't want to share.

"While that sounds fun," Neely Kate said in a dry voice, "you'll have to pencil us in for later this week. We can't be double-booked for tonight."

She tapped her fingernail on the table. "What could be more pressing than learning kinky ways to be sexually satisfied?"

Was she serious? I forced myself to hold my gaze on her. Did she really not know about her father's little get-together tonight? Had J.R. double-crossed her? Or was she just bluffing?

"You didn't answer my question," I said. "His name."

She broke eye contact and glanced down at the table.

"His name," Neely Kate barked.

Kate glanced up with a defiant look in her eyes. "I could lie."

"But you won't," Neely Kate said in a low voice. "Rose was honest with her answers, and you will be, too. Otherwise, you'll be walking away without those blue streaks in your hair, and I won't use scissors to take 'em off."

I expected Kate to get even angrier, but it was like all the fight oozed out of her, leaving her in a puddle of sadness. "Nick."

"Nick what?" Neely Kate asked in a softer voice.

"Nick Thorn."

"What happened?" Neely Kate asked. "What did your father do to him?"

Her gaze shot up. "Who said my father did something to him?"

"It's pretty obvious."

Tears shimmered in Kate's eyes. "He thought he could buy Nick off, that Nick would take money over me. Because my father only value things based on their monetary worth. Everything has a price tag for him. He couldn't fathom that a man would pick *me* over a few hundred thousand dollars. So when Nick didn't take the deal, it only confirmed to Daddy Dearest that he was unworthy of a *Simmons*." She spat the name in disgust. "And things that are defective must be eliminated." She turned her gaze to me. "Surely, you've figured that out by now."

J.R. had killed Kate's boyfriend. No wonder she'd taken off. No wonder she was bitter. But how could she be working for her father?

"So what did trying to get me and Joe back together have to do with it?"

Anger filled her eyes. "Because you were my one shot at getting even with the bastard. You were the only one with the guts to stand up to him and tell him to fuck off. But you wouldn't leave that stuck-up prick in the courthouse. You just kept falling deeper and deeper into my father's trap."

"Rose was your revenge," Neely Kate said.

Kate shook her head. "You couldn't just go along with it, could you?"

The hate in her voice was shocking.

"How close were you to Roberta?" Neely Kate asked out of the blue.

Kate's head swung to face her. "Who?"

"Roberta. Your housekeeper."

Her face scrunched in disgust. "Why in the hell are you asking about *her*?"

"Her granddaughter is working in Rose's nursery. Why is she there?"

Her eyes widened in mock surprise. "Do I look like I'm in charge of the personnel at my brother's pet business project? Ask *him*."

"You didn't answer the question," Neely Kate said. "How close were you to Roberta?"

"She was a great nanny, but she had a soft spot for Hilary, which made me distrust her."

"Why?" Neely Kate asked.

Kate's eyes filled with rage. "Because I hated Hilary. She spent nearly as much time at our house as we did. She and Joe were allies, leaving me out of everything. Do you have any idea what it was like growing up in that house?"

"No," Neely Kate said softly. "None at all."

"I didn't wish Roberta gone, but I wasn't sorry to see her go either. Hilary was devastated, which made it all the sweeter."

I stared at the woman in front of me in disbelief. How could someone carry so much hatred?

"But Hilmonster's about to get what's comin' to her," Kate said with a grin. "And she's going to be plenty surprised." Kate stood. "I think we're done here." Then she walked out the door without a backward glance.

Chapter Twenty-Seven

We sat in silence for nearly half a minute. I was trying to process everything Kate had said, and I was sure Neely Kate was doing the same, only through a slightly different lens. She had to be thinking she'd dodged a bullet by not growing up in that house. I know I sure would have felt that way.

"I think she just threatened Hilary," I finally said.

Neely Kate laughed. "That's your takeaway from that conversation?"

"It seems the most pressing."

"Your upcoming date with *my daddy* seems more pressing to me."

Pain shot through my chest. How much more could Neely Kate take? "Oh, honey."

Neely Kate waved me off. "I'm fine. Just a bad joke. But I still say tonight takes priority. We don't have time to worry about *Hilmonster*."

I turned in my seat. "Kate just admitted that she hates Hilary and that she's about to get what's coming to her."

"She's hated her for years and hasn't done a thing. What's one more day?"

Neely Kate had a point, but something still nagged at me. I just wasn't sure what.

The waitress brought over the bill. "Your friend said to put it on your tab."

"Of course she did," Neely Kate grumbled. "I can't believe I'm related to that psycho."

"Maybe you're not—" But the look on her face told me not to argue. And I could see her point. The evidence was pretty damning.

I grabbed some cash out of my wallet and tossed it on the table. "We need to get some paying jobs soon. Mason was the one paying the bills, and now I'm down to fifteen dollars."

While we had jobs lined up, the deposits covered the expense of the plants. But the real profit didn't come until we finished the job and collected the balance.

Neely Kate stood. "Maybe I can collect on back allowance. How much do you think the Simmons kids made?"

"Not enough," I grumbled as I followed her out the door, surprised she could joke about it. Then again, what else was she going to do? I'd never seen anything really get her down with the exception of her miscarriage.

"I think we should stop by the courthouse first," Neely Kate said as we started across the street. "None of my friends have gotten back to me yet, but if they're busy, we can just look for information on Thaddeus Brooke ourselves."

"And Nick Thorn?" I asked.

She frowned. "I suspect what we're looking for isn't in Fenton County. Good call goin' down that rabbit hole, by the way."

"It just made sense to follow my instinct."

We hid our guns in the car, then went through the courthouse security. I couldn't help wondering how smart it was to just waltz into the courthouse, but Neely Kate was right. J.R. wasn't going to do a thing to us. Not until later tonight.

While Neely Kate headed to the records room to look for her cohorts, I made my way to the deserted staircase and sat on a step. I needed to call Skeeter and fill him in on what we'd learned.

I told him everything with the exception of Neely Kate's discovery, which seemed too personal to share with him. This needed to be strictly business, and Neely Kate's parentage had nothing to do with this mess.

But after I mentioned Kate's ominous threat, I said, "I'm worried about Hilary."

I was dead wrong if I'd hoped to find a sympathetic ear.

"That bitch is like a cat," Skeeter said. "She always lands on her feet and has nine lives. She's fine."

"But she's pregnant. There's a baby to think about."

"Not my problem and not yours either. What are you two doin' now?"

"We're at the courthouse looking up information about Thaddeus Brooke and Nick Thorn."

"By the time Kate left for California, I hadn't worked for Simmons for years. I've never heard of Thorn. But I suspect you'll be able to find something with an Internet search. We'll do some ☐etting' on our end, too. Keep in touch. Let me know if you find anything else."

"Okay." I hung up and closed my eyes, needing a moment to decompress after all the news I'd been bombarded with throughout the day. I needed to get my anxiety under control. I was so focused on the breathing exercises Jonah had taught me that I didn't hear him approach.

"Rose," Mason asked quietly. "Are you okay?"

My eyes flew open, and I saw him standing in from of me, worry on his face.

I hopped off the steps and threw myself at him, wrapping my arms around his neck before I could remind myself I wasn't supposed to do that anymore.

But Mason didn't seem to remember either. "Sweetheart, what's going on?" he asked, holding me against his chest. "What are you doing here?"

I blinked back tears. I couldn't deny that Mason made me feel stronger, but was that a good thing? Shouldn't I be able to stand on my own? But I didn't have time to dwell on my weakness. I only knew that I needed him right now. Any lingering suspicions over his character flittered away. This man loved me, of that I was sure.

"Rose?"

I leaned back and looked up into his face, cupping his cheeks. "I'm fine now."

He kissed me. His lips were gentle but firm, giving me the courage I needed to stay focused on this crazy task. Giving me the hope that I'd find the happiness I so desperately craved at the end of the tunnel.

When he lifted his head, I looked into his eyes. "Promise me—no matter what," I said, "that you'll never let that witch Kate Simmons reverse cowgirl you."

"What?" he asked in horror, jerking back.

But I held him in place. "Promise."

A soft grin lit up his face. "That's an easy promise to make."

I pressed my flushed cheek to his chest, letting the sound of his heartbeat in my ear fill me with reassurance.

"Rose, what's goin' on?"

"I'm not sure what I can tell you."

"Because of my job?"

I nodded.

He pulled loose and grabbed my hand, then led me to the stairs, where we sat side by side.

"It kills me that you're doing this alone," he said. "Tell me what's going on, my job be damned."

I sat up and shook my head. How on earth was I going to tell him there was a dead body in my barn? But I knew there was something I could tell him. The thing I couldn't stop thinking about. I had no idea how Neely Kate was scouring files for information while I was sitting in a stairwell, still reeling in shock. I knew it wasn't my secret to tell, but this was the man I'd planned to marry, my best friend other than Neely Kate. I needed to confide in someone, and I knew he'd give me the support I needed.

"We figured out who Neely Kate's father is."

Mason shook his head. "I had no idea she was even looking."

"She wasn't. It just fell into our laps."

"Where? How?"

"I had the shorthand page transcribed. Your momma got part of it wrong. It wasn't a shed. It was a barn." I watched him closely to gauge his reaction.

"*Your* barn? You found something?" he asked in surprise.

I nodded.

"I searched that barn high and low last week and never found a thing."

"We found another journal from Dora. Under the feed trough in a horse stall."

"How'd you think to look there? Those things were bolted down."

I grimaced. "I had some help."

He turned somber. "I see."

"Dora wrote about Neely Kate's momma. I guess Dora knew her from church. Jenny Lynn was pregnant."

"She told Dora who her father is?"

"Kind of." I looked into his face. "He was a powerful businessman from El Dorado who came to town every few weeks to handle his business at Atchison Manufacturing."

His eyes widened. "Oh, God. *J.R.?*"

I nodded.

He took a moment to recover from the shock. "How's she dealing with the news?"

"She's kind dazed and stunned, but she's ignoring it to focus on other things."

"Yeah. I can see her doing that."

"We also talked to Kate."

He looked worried, but he forced a grin. "Hence the cowgirl comment." When I nodded, he said, "Did she admit to having the files?"

"I didn't even try that tactic," I said. "I took a different route."

"And what did you find?"

"Kate's out for revenge, but maybe not entirely as we suspected. I thought she was working with J.R., but now I'm pretty sure she's trying to get even with her father. She had a boyfriend, and J.R. offered him several hundred thousand dollars to leave her, but her boyfriend refused. Kate says her father had him *eliminated*. I was only allowed a few questions, so I don't know many details. His name is Nick Thorn, and my gut says he's the reason Kate left Little Rock two years ago."

"Why's she here now?"

"Me."

"She admitted she wants to hurt you?" he asked in alarm.

"No. She wanted me to get back together with Joe because she thought I was the one who'd stand up to her father. But she realizes that won't happen, so now I think she's goin' after Hilary."

"What do you think she has planned?"

"I don't know, but I don't trust her. Maybe I should tell Joe." That idea sparked another. "He might know more about Kate's boyfriend, too."

Mason gave me a hesitant grin. "Maybe you should have Neely Kate talk to him. You're not his favorite person right now."

"I'm not sure that's a good idea either. I was worried she was going to lose it talkin' to Kate. For all I know, she'd break the news that she's Joe's half-sister over the phone."

Mason cringed. "She's that much of a loose cannon?"

"I don't know. I love her, but I'm not sure I trust her to let this sit."

"Okay, so maybe *you* call him. In the meantime, I'll focus my attention on finding out everything I can about Nick Thorn."

"Really?" I asked in surprise.

"How much time do you have left on your ticking clock?" he asked.

I blinked in surprise. "What ticking clock?"

He tucked a stray hair behind my ear, a soft smile lifting his mouth. "I can read you, Rose. You're tense, which tells me you're working with a deadline."

"Maybe I'm just worried about Bruce Wayne."

His smile turned sad. "I suspect the deadline has something to do with him."

He'd always been pretty perceptive. With everything other than the Lady in Black. "You've told me before that the courthouse is like Fort Knox. Do you still believe that's true?"

"Yes. I'd say this is a good place to hole up." He looked down at me. "You want to stay here? You and Neely Kate are both welcome to hang out with me in my office tonight."

"No, but I need *you* to stay here tonight."

"Why?" he asked suspiciously.

"Because. It's safe."

"What time is your deadline?"

"Ten."

"I take it you expect me to hide in here until after everything goes down. Has J.R. threatened me?"

I gave him a hopeful look. "He hasn't threatened you *today*. But it doesn't hurt to be too careful."

He lifted his hand to my cheek and lightly stroked my jaw with his thumb. A soft smile lit up his eyes, but I also saw his sadness. "I love you, Rose. When this is over, please remember that."

I turned serious. "I love you, too." When it was all said and done, I still wasn't sure we would work, but there was no denying that I loved him.

He stood and tugged me up, pulling me flush against his body. He pressed a hand to the small of my back while his other hand cupped my cheek. He leaned forward and kissed me gently, but then it turned hungry and demanding. "Let me come with you."

"You can't," I murmured against his lips, then gave him one last kiss before stepping back and pushing him away. "You have your job to do, and I have mine. I need you to find out what you can about Nick Thorn. You're more important to me here."

I could see he wanted to protest, but then he nodded, solemn and serious. He studied me with a deep sorrow. "I'll let you know when I find something." Before I could respond, he bounded up the stairs, leaving me on the stairwell landing.

I found Neely Kate in the records room, digging through a filing cabinet. She looked up at me and rolled her eyes. "I really wish Fenton County would digitalize their records."

"No luck?" I asked.

"Actually, Lori had already found a few things, but I've added more. Thaddeus Brooke had several prior arrests—breaking and entering, larceny, assault."

"Sounds like a nice guy," I said. Skeeter had said the photo on his license made him look rough, and apparently he wasn't far off.

"Exactly. He was reported missing right after Thanksgiving twenty-five years ago. Around the time of the factory fire."

"Anything else?"

"I looked up anyone with the name Steyer from that time period."

"And?" I asked.

"Allen Steyer owned the fertilizer plant and several other businesses."

"Why would he be involved with Thaddeus Brooke?"

"I don't know, but he died around the same time. I found his obituary."

My eyebrows rose in surprise. "What? Why didn't someone from the state come investigate if all these people died or went missing?"

"You know the answer to that."

"J.R."

She nodded, then leaned her head closer to mine and whispered, "Rose, think about it. Steyer was rich and powerful and obviously dirty."

The answer hit me like a ton of bricks. "Oh, my word. Allen Steyer was one of J.R. Simmons's Twelve. Skeeter didn't know who he was, but he said he thinks the man who covered this area disappeared around the time of the factory fire. Instead, he died. It fits."

"Yeah, I think so, too."

"Find out anything about Nick Thorn?"

She shook her head. "No record of him here, but I suspect he's from Little Rock anyway."

"Agreed." I had to confess that I'd just seen Mason, but I didn't want to upset her. "I have someone looking into him. Someone with the resources to get information fast."

"Skeeter?"

I shook my head. "Although I suspect he's lookin'."

"Joe?"

"No. But he's next on my list for a chat." I paused. "I saw Mason."

"*What?*"

The two women working in the room looked over at us, so Neely Kate grabbed my arm and dragged me down a short, empty hall. "You told him about Nick Thorn? Are you crazy?"

I straightened my back and gave her a defiant look. "I trust him." When she started to protest, I held up my hand. "I know you and Skeeter don't, but if I've learned one thing, it's to go with my gut. And my gut tells me that Mason Deveraux would sooner die than put me in harm's way." I paused. "And if you can't accept me sharing information with him, maybe we need to tackle this separately."

Her mouth dropped open. "You would do that? You would let a man come between us?"

"No. This is no different than if you'd asked me to stop trusting Jonah. Or Bruce Wayne. Mason can help us."

"Well, we don't have a heap of evidence implicating either of them."

"Everything you have is circumstantial and hearsay."

She put her hand on her hip. "I thought he didn't want to be caught in the middle."

I shrugged. "There's nothing shady about looking up some information. We need all the help we can get."

"But can you trust him?"

I looked her in the eye. "I would bet my life on it."

"You just did. Let's hope you picked the winning side."

Chapter Twenty-Eight

When we left the courthouse, Neely Kate called Skeeter to fill him in on what she'd discovered. She hung up grinning.

"What did he say?"

"He said he'd look into Allen Steyer and get back to us." Her grin spread.

"What else did he say?"

"He said if we didn't get off the damn street, Jed was gonna hang out with us again."

I laughed and spotted Jed sitting in his parked car. "Let's go to the office. It's after five o'clock, which means we have less than five hours. We need to figure out what to do next."

"We keep □etting'," Neely Kate said, stopping by Skeeter's car. She stuffed our guns into her purse. "We keep looking until it's time."

I dug out my keys and unlocked the door to the landscaping office.

"I say our next task should be to find out who rented that shed twenty-five years ago," Neely Kate said.

"But do we need to do that?" I asked as I locked the door behind us. "We were only looking into it because we thought the storage unit might be the shed mentioned in the shorthand page."

"Maybe so, but my gut tells me to keep digging. If you're listening to your gut, then we should listen to mine, too." She shrugged. "Besides, we've got nothing else to do, but I think we should wait another hour until it's dark."

"Why?" I asked. "Jed couldn't find the Pelgers. What are you ☐etting☐g'?"

She grinned and plopped down on the sofa by the front door. "We're going to snoop in the Pelgers' office."

"In the *antique store*?"

"Yeah. And the beauty of it is that we aren't *breaking* and entering, because the place was already broken into when the crowd looted the store. We're only entering, which sounds so much less illegal."

My eyebrows rose as I sat down next to her. "And yet it *is* illegal."

"So you want to sit this one out?" she asked.

"Shoot, no. I'm comin'."

"So now we need to figure out what to do for the next hour."

I studied her for a moment. I suspected she wasn't going to like what I was about to propose. "I need to talk to Joe."

Her eyes narrowed. "Why?"

I sighed. "I want to ask him what he knows about Kate and her boyfriend. And to make sure he knows about her threat against Hilary." And while that was all true, I had other reasons. Would Neely Kate understand? "There's more . . . I have no idea what's gonna happen tonight. If anything happens to me, I realized there are too many things left unsettled between us."

Her mouth pinched tight. "You're not dyin', Rose Gardner, so stop talking like that."

"They still need to be said, Neely Kate," I said softly.

She was silent for several seconds before she said, "So what are you ☐etting☐g'? It doesn't sound like you're talking about a phone call."

"No. I need to talk to him in person."

She nodded, then a grin spread across her face, and she jabbed my arm with her elbow. "Hey! If you get back together with Joe, we'll be related. Maybe I should support that endeavor."

I grinned back. "We don't need blood or legal binds to hold us together." I grabbed her hand, turning serious. "What we have runs deeper than either of those things. No matter who your father is."

Tears filled her eyes. "He's a monster, Rose. And look at all of his children."

"I know Kate is loony tunes, but Joe's coming around. He's breaking free of his father's hold. He's really trying to be his own man." I grinned. "And you're stronger than the two of them put together."

"Well, of course I am," she said with attitude, and then her voice softened. "He would have killed my mother. He would have killed us both. That's why she moved around so much. All these years, she was trying to keep me safe."

From what little I knew about Jenny Lynn Rivers, she had probably put herself as number one on the list of importance. I only hoped Neely Kate had been number two. But I wasn't about to point out all the shortcomings of Neely Kate's mother. Hopefully we'd have years to revisit the topic.

"It's a lot to take in, Neely Kate. Trust me, I know. Give it some time."

"I want to talk to my granny. I want to ask her some questions."

"Now?"

She turned to look at me. "Sure, why not? You need privacy to talk to Joe. Besides, maybe my granny knows something that will help us. I'll call and see if she's home."

"Okay." I didn't like the thought of her going off without me, but she was right about me needing privacy when I talked to Joe. She started to call her grandmother, so I sent Joe a text.

Truce?

He sent back a text within seconds. *What are you up to?*

Can we talk? In person?

The little text bubble kept popping up and disappearing on my phone before he finally sent: *Why?*

Because we need to clear the air. Hence the "truce."

Fine. How about in a few days?

No. Tonight. I'm in my office. Can you come now? When he didn't answer after ten seconds, I added, *You need to eat dinner. We can meet at Merilee's if you'd like, but I'd hoped to talk in private. I can pick something up.*

He answered right away. *Call something in for both of us— you know what I like. I'll pick it up and be there in twenty minutes.*

Thanks.

"Granny's got two fortune-telling clients back to back," Neely Kate said. "She can't see us until later. What did Joe say?"

I grimaced. "He'll be here in twenty minutes. I'm calling a dinner order in to Merilee's, and he's gonna pick it up."

A wicked grin lit up her eyes. "So what to do with me, right?"

"Neely Kate—"

Waving her hand, she laughed. "I'm teasing. I'll have Jed take me to get something. He can't say no to leaving you alone with the chief deputy sheriff."

"Are you sure?"

"Totally. You better call in that order if you want it to be ready when Joe gets there."

I picked up my phone and called the restaurant, ordering a bowl of potato soup for me and meatloaf and mashed potatoes for Joe.

"That's not what you usually get for Mr. Deveraux," the waitress taking the order said. "He trying something different tonight?"

"No," I said, feeling like I was cheating on Mason even though I wasn't. "It's for Chief Deputy Simmons. In fact, he'll be picking it up."

"Oh," she said, sounding scandalized. "I see."

Obviously she didn't, but pointing that out would only draw more attention to the situation. "Thank you."

Neely Kate had called Jed, who'd at first balked at the idea of leaving me under Joe's watch, but she'd successfully convinced him. When she hung up, she sat at the round table we used to make presentations to customers. I was rearranging stacks of gardening magazines and papers to make room for my dinner with Joe.

"Are you nervous?" she asked.

"About tonight with J.R.?" I was terrified, but I wasn't sure I could let myself admit it.

"No. With Joe."

I shook my head. "No, I think this talk has been a long time coming."

"Aren't you worried Joe will try and put you into protective custody?"

"No. I think he finally respects me enough to take my opinion into consideration." Or at least I hoped so.

She just nodded, a thoughtful look on her face.

I went into the bathroom to clean up the mess from Merv's incident the night before. I sure didn't want Joe to discover my role in last night's events.

I'd just finished when I heard a knock on the front door and then Neely Kate's voice. "Hey, Joe."

"Neely Kate," Joe said, sounding miffed.

"You're not gonna have bad feelings, are you?"

"That depends on whether or not you continue to impede official investigations."

I walked out of the bathroom to find Neely Kate with her hands on her hips.

"It's a free country, Joe Simmons. I didn't break any laws," she said.

"Neely Kate," I said as I approached them. "Let's give Joe a break."

It suddenly hit me that they were constantly bickering. Just like siblings. The thought brought a lump to my throat. How would Joe react when he discovered Neely Kate was his sister?

"Thanks for agreeing to see me," I said, noticing the bag in his hand. He was wearing his sheriff's uniform and a leather coat. The dark circles under his eyes were a testament to his exhaustion. "And for picking up dinner."

"And that's my cue to leave." Neely Kate grabbed her coat and her purse and dashed out the front door.

I walked over and locked the door behind her.

"Do you think it's a good idea for her to be out there alone with my father on the loose?"

I turned around to face him. "You're worried about her?"

"Well . . . yeah. I am."

Part of me ached to tell him what I knew. With his wackadoodle sister Kate, his evil father, and his controlling mother, Joe needed family who would actually care about him and support him. But it wasn't my place to tell.

I motioned to the table. "I thought we could eat at the table."

He nodded as he walked over and sat in a chair. "I have to say I was surprised to get your text."

"We've had so many ups and downs lately—more downs than I'd like—I thought it might be nice to clear the air . . . but over dinner. And without our usual yelling."

He unpacked the two containers and set the bowl in front of me. "Why do I think there's an ulterior motive here?"

I opened the lid to my soup and sighed. "Given the last few months, I can see why you would think that." I reached for a plastic spoon.

He opened the lid to his container and grinned. "Meatloaf and Merilee's garlic mashed potatoes. Exactly what I needed right now." He scooped a forkful of potatoes and shoved it into his mouth.

"How's the search for your father going?"

He stopped his fork midair and then scowled as he cut off a piece of his meatloaf. "Is that why you asked me here? You could have asked about my father on the phone."

"No, that's definitely not why I asked to see you. I assumed you'd tell me what you can when you can."

His eyes widened. "I'm surprised to hear you say that."

I nodded. "Which is why I thought we should talk."

A wary look filled his eyes. "I'm listening."

After taking a couple of slurps of soup, I put my spoon down, suddenly unsure where to start or what to say. "I hate that we've come to this—the fighting and distrust. We've both said we want to be friends, but it seems like we're adversaries more than anything else."

"Rose." He set his fork down.

I put my hand on his. "Joe, just listen to me first. I want to be your friend. We're business partners, and now that Violet's goin' to Texas for who knows how long . . . well, I'm going to need you more than ever. But I need you to respect me. I need you to see me as a grown woman and not the scared girl you met on your front porch last May. I know you think I'm foolhardy, but I know what I'm doin'. You wouldn't even begin to imagine the things I've done the last several months."

He looked me in the eye. "Like the Lady in Black?"

"Do you think the woman you met last year could actually be the Lady?"

He shook his head. "No." I tried to curb my disappointment, but he continued. "Because you're not the woman you were last year. You've changed. While you made quite an impression on Crocker in that warehouse last summer, that woman was nowhere close to the woman who faced my father last week. I barely recognized you."

I cocked an eyebrow. "Is that good or bad?"

He gave me a sad smile. "It's neither. It just is."

We ate in silence for another half-minute before Joe said, "I loved you, Rose. It's important you believe that."

I put my spoon down and searched his eyes. "I've never doubted that for a minute."

He grinned, but there was something sad about it. "I believe you've said a few things to contradict that."

"I think we've both said a few things we regret."

We were silent for a moment before Joe said, "I've thinking about last week, that night in your barn. Everything you said . . ."

"I was angry, Joe."

"But you meant every word."

I couldn't deny it.

"When I thought you died, I kept replaying that conversation over and over in my head. And I realized you were right. I was so desperate to hold onto you that I lost sight of everything."

"I know you loved me, Joe, but I can't help thinkin' you loved the idea of you *with* me. Joe McAllister living in a small town and living a simple life."

"No, Rose," he said quietly. "I loved *you.*"

I looked into his eyes. "Loved? Past tense?"

"You're not the woman I met and fell in love with. That woman is gone. I think my desperation to hold onto you has been part of my grief over that."

While part of me was relieved to hear him say that, it was also like a knife to the heart.

"Rose, when I lost you, I thought I had nothing left."

"That's not true, Joe."

He shook his head. "No, it actually was. I'd made you my entire world. But right after Thanksgiving, Maeve said something to me that left an impression. She told me I had to find peace and strength in *myself* before I could find happiness with someone else. It took awhile for that to really sink in, but after our conversation in the barn . . . well, I think I get it now."

"So what about Hilary?"

"I don't want to get back together with her, but like I said on the phone, I'm making an effort to get along. We're having a baby, and I want to be a part of his or her life. The problem is that Hilary can't see the possibility of us being friends. For her, it's an all or nothing deal, and she got it into her head that you were the reason we weren't together. But now that I've started making more of an effort, she's acting less paranoid and seems to have leveled out."

"How do you feel about the baby now?"

"To say I was unhappy about the baby is an understatement, but now that I've gotten used to the idea . . ." He frowned. "Neely Kate's miscarriage really shook me up, and after I found out about Savannah, I realized I *do* want the baby. I want a family, Rose. I've never made a secret of that. And while it's true that I'll never have a traditional family with Hilary, I think I'll be a damn good dad."

I smiled. "I know you will, Joe. You're nothing like your father."

He grimaced.

"I talked to Kate about an hour ago."

Joe momentarily froze, then stabbed his meatloaf. "How did that go?"

"It was rocky, but she confided a few things."

"Are you sure we're talking about *my sister*?"

"Yeah," I said, chuckling. But then I sobered, reminded that he had another sister. I hoped he wouldn't reject her when he discovered the truth. I wasn't sure Neely Kate could handle any more rejection.

Joe leaned forward, resting his elbow on the table. "And what did Kate confide?"

"That she was in love with a man named Nick Thorn."

He shook his head. "Kate told you that? I find that hard to believe."

"She didn't share it willingly," I confessed. "There may have been some bargaining involved. Did you know about him?"

"No."

"Really?"

"Rose," he sighed. "When you and I were together, I told you that Kate and I were never close. Our relationship was turbulent at best. But she'd been making an effort before she took off a couple of years ago. She hinted that she was seeing someone, and she seemed . . . happy."

"And then she disappeared?"

"Yeah, which is why I was especially worried. She'd been happier than I'd seen her since she was a kid."

"Joe, I asked her what happened to Nick, and she said your father didn't approve of him. She says he tried to pay him off with hundreds of thousands of dollars, but her boyfriend turned him down. So your father had him eliminated."

His face paled as he sat up. "Oh, God. Why didn't she tell me?"

"I don't know, but she said that when she found out about me, she thought I might have a shot at standing up to your father—hence her obsession with getting you and me back together."

He looked lost in thought. "If she wanted us back together, then Mason would have been a roadblock."

Oh, my word. Why hadn't I thought *that* part through? "Road block enough to hire Sam Teagen to hire Eric Davidson to run Mason off the road?"

His eyes narrowed. "*What?*"

"I'm 99% positive Kate hired Sam Teagen to do her dirty work."

"What the hell are you talking about, Rose?"

I put my hand on his. "Joe. Listen to me. You know Neely Kate and I saw those files in Kate's apartment—"

"But there was nothing there when I went to check."

"That's because she moved them."

"Moved them where?"

"To the shed on top of the antique store. The one that burned."

He cocked his head and gave me a suspicious look. "And how would you know that?"

"I saw them in there."

He gave me a dubious look.

"Not to mention I heard Sam Teagen talking. He said he was hired by a woman to kidnap me, then kill Mason." Which brought up another issue. She'd obviously hired Teagen, but he also answered to J.R. How did *that* work? Was she planning to double-cross him?

"When and where did you hear him talking?"

"I . . . uh . . ."

"*Rose.* Quit playing games and answer the question."

What were the ramifications of telling him everything? "When I was kidnapped, I reached up and scratched the cheek of my capturer. Then I saw a suspicious character watching me last Friday. But I thought I was paranoid. Until I saw Sam Teagen yesterday with healing scratch marks on his face."

"How do you know his name?"

I couldn't bring myself to tell him everything. "I heard his friend call him by name."

"And he just happened to confess to kidnapping you?"

I cringed. "It was last night. I was in my office when I saw Sam Teagen outside the front window with a gun in his hand. I think he was there to kidnap me and take me to your father. His friend told him they wouldn't have to have been there if Teagen had gotten it right the week before."

Joe sat back in his seat with a pained expression. "Shit. How'd you get away?"

"The explosions scared them off." Not exactly true, but I didn't want to drag Merv into this. "But not before he told his friend he was hired by a woman—a woman who wasn't happy with the way things were going. They knew about the files in the shed, Joe. The same files that were in Kate's apartment."

Joe got a far-off look in his eyes, then rubbed his mouth with the side of his hand. "You realize you're accusing my sister of some very serious crimes?"

"I know, Joe, and I'm sorry, but there's more."

He shook his head. "Go on."

"Before Kate left this afternoon, she mentioned how much she hated Hilary. We asked her about Roberta, and she said she hadn't been sorry to see your housekeeper go. Hilary was devastated when Roberta left, so that made Kate happy."

"She said that?"

I nodded. "Then she said that Hilary was going to get what was coming to her."

"That could mean anything."

"I know, but I really feel like we need to warn Hilary. I'd do it myself, but she'll think I'm trying to trick her. Will you talk to her?"

"Yeah." He ran his hands over his head, still looking dazed. "I guess I should talk to my sister again, too."

"I'm sorry."

He shook his head.

"This isn't your fault," I insisted.

But he looked devastated. "My father's a piece of shit. My mother is a manipulative bitch. My sister . . ." He looked into my face. "I have no one, Rose."

I ached to tell him about Neely Kate, but it wasn't my secret to share. At least not with him. Instead, I covered his hand with mine. "No. That's not true, Joe. You and I may not be together, but I'm still your friend. I care about you. And you have other friends. People who would do anything for you."

He stood and grabbed his coat and shoved his arms into his sleeves. "I need to go."

"Thanks for taking the time to talk to me."

A sad smile lifted the corners of his lips. "No. Thanks for this. It's given me the closure I needed to move on."

I stepped toward him and pulled him into a hug. "Thank you seems so inadequate. When we met, you saw the potential in me that no one else could see." I pulled back and smiled even though my eyes burned. "You were with me when I started this crazy journey."

He grinned. "You and your wish list."

I wiped a tear from my cheek. "There were so many firsts with you, Joe."

"You have no idea how much I loved watching you break free." He wiped another of my tears. A soft smile lit up my face "You gave me the courage to believe I could be happy and free from my father. I will always love you for that, Rose, but I'm ready to let you go."

I nodded through my tears, shocked at how much this hurt.

He pressed a lingering kiss to my forehead, then stepped away. "Lock the door behind me. And please, for the love of God, go sit with Mason in the courthouse. I have a feeling something big's going down tonight, and I don't want you to be in the middle of it."

I nodded again, then pushed past the lump in my throat, "Be careful, Joe."

Joe walked out the front door, and I followed behind and turned the deadbolt. As hard as that had been, I knew it was only the prelude to the big finale.

Chapter Twenty-Nine

I sent Neely Kate a text to let her know that Joe had left. When she still hadn't responded a full minute later, I was starting to get worried, but then I heard banging at the back door.

"Rose!" Neely Kate called out, her voice muffled by the door. "Let us in!"

I ran to the back door and unlocked it. Neely Kate and Jed tumbled in, and I shut the door behind them. "What in tarnation are you two doin'?"

"We've been digging in the Pelgers's office," Neely Kate said.

"Without me?"

Jed grinned. "Don't sound so disappointed."

"Did you find anything?"

"Yep. Twenty-five years ago, the Pelgers rented the apartment and the storage building to Allen Steyer."

I tilted my head. "Why would the owner of the fertilizer plant rent an apartment on the square? Wouldn't he own his own house?"

A smug grin spread across Jed's face. "Skeeter thinks he rented it for J.R."

"What?"

"Your momma's journal said he stayed somewhere," Neely Kate said. "Skeeter says it makes sense that J.R. wouldn't rent a place under his own name. But one of his Twelve could rent it for him."

"That's great and all," I grumbled, "but again, it's not very useful for tonight."

"I disagree," Skeeter said, strutting in through the back door like he owned the place. "You can never have too much information. You never know when you're gonna discover something that will save your ass later."

I knew he had a point, but it still felt hopeless. "So we're just walking into a trap?"

"No." The amusement bled from his face. "I've got men surrounding that barn even as we speak. I'll have my own show of force waiting for the bastard."

"And what?" I asked. "They'll ambush them?"

"No, they'll let Simmons do his thing, but I'll be prepared to face him."

"Just you?" I asked.

His eyes hardened. "This is between him and me. I've always been one to cut through the shit, but we know J.R. likes pomp and circumstance."

"You know it won't be that easy."

"Nothing worth fightin' for ever is."

Neely Kate's cell phone started to ring. She dug her phone out of her coat pocket and pressed it to her ear. "Hey, Granny." She was silent for several moments, then said, "Okay. See you soon." As she hung up, she glanced over at me. "Her second fortune-telling appointment cancelled."

"And she didn't see that coming?" Jed asked, his face splitting into a grin. "What kind of fortune teller is she?"

Neely Kate put her hands on her hips. "She can only read other people's futures, not her own. And besides, she has to look for it. With tea leaves. We'll have her read your future before we leave her house."

"Me?" He sounded horrified.

"You might as well come inside with us," she teased. "And Granny *loves* doing tea readings."

"Do her predictions ever come true?" Jed asked, sounding fearful. Smart man.

"Sometimes." Neely Kate's eyes clouded over. I knew she had to be thinking about her granny seeing the miscarriage of twins—even though Neely Kate's doctor hadn't seen her ectopic pregnancy in her early ultrasound.

Skeeter grinned. "Jed, you take the ladies to see Neely Kate's granny, and I'll head out to the barn to check on things."

The thought of him going out there alone scared the bejiggers out of me, but then, he wouldn't really be alone. He'd have the company of his gun-toting loyal employees.

Jed nodded and motioned for us to head toward the front door, but I looked back at the man still standing larger than life in my short hallway.

"James, be careful."

His grin widened. "You don't have to tell me to be careful, Lady, or wish me luck. I make my own luck." Then he took off out the back door.

"Cocky bastard," Neely Kate murmured.

I grinned. She was right, but he had the brute strength, both his own and his men's, to back it up. His cockiness gave me confidence.

Neely Kate's granny lived southwest of town. I had never been to her farm, although I'd heard plenty about it. Neely Kate's cousins ran the cattle she kept there, but from everything Neely Kate had told me, they could have been more profitable if they'd put some gumption into it. If the Rivers family had been known for trouble when Jenny Lynn Rivers had haunted the county, they were better known for their laziness now. While they did stir up plenty of trouble, they were just as likely to let someone else do the dirty work for them.

With that in mind, I wasn't all that shocked to see that Granny Rivers's farm looked like an abandoned homestead rather than a working farm. It was hard to see it all in the dark, but the shoddily mended fences lining the gravel drive were proof that Neely Kate's cousins only did what they absolutely had to.

"Your grandmother lives here?" Jed asked in disbelief, parking the car in front of the worn one-story house. While my farmhouse had a wrap-around porch, this one had a stoop without even an overhang to protect against the rain. So little remained of the white peeling paint that the house looked brown from the underside of the clapboard siding.

"Yeah," Neely Kate grumbled as she climbed out of the car. "Let's get this over with."

We followed her to the door, and I heard a dog howl in the distance. I flinched and Jed glanced down at me, not looking very relaxed either. I held my purse tight to my side, and then as an afterthought, I pulled out my gun and put it in my pocket. Something didn't feel right, even if I couldn't put my finger on what it was. Jed caught the movement, lifting his brow, but Neely Kate was too focused on knocking on the door to pay me any mind.

"Granny?"

"In the kitchen."

We walked through a room that looked be a makeshift mud room, filled with muddy rain boots and coats. It was also full of an array of gardening tools—a few rakes and shovels, a hoe, and a pitchfork.

Neely Kate glanced over her shoulder. "Home protection."

"From zombies?" Jed whispered to me with a smirk.

"I heard that," Neely Kate said dryly.

We entered a small kitchen, the counters stacked high with dirty dishes and pots. A small round table covered with a lace tablecloth was pushed close to the wall, and three empty mismatched wooden chairs were gathered around it. A fourth chair was occupied by Neely Kate's grandmother, who wore a brightly colored turban on her head.

She held her hands out when she saw us. "Welcome to your future."

"We're not here for a reading, Granny," Neely Kate said, looking back at us and gesturing to the chairs.

Jed's eyes widened, and I couldn't say I blamed him. I had my doubts one of those rickety chairs would hold his bulky frame.

Neely Kate plopped onto the chair next to her grandmother. "Jed, you sit in the corner. I need Rose over here." She pointed to the chair between them. When he hesitated, she grumped, "Oh, have a seat, you big baby."

I couldn't say I blamed her poor attitude, and I also understood why she was so eager to stay with me out at my farm. Five minutes in this place would make me grumpy, too.

Jed scooted between the table and the wall, his legs bumping the edge, pushing it toward Neely Kate's granny. He shot my friend a look that said she was a dead woman when we left.

Neely Kate just chuckled.

"You did that on purpose," I whispered.

"Paybacks bite you in the keister. We'll see if he ever suggests I'm incapable of a little light burglary again."

This obviously had something to do with their visit to the Pelgers's office, but I knew better than to ask now.

Neely Kate's grandmother stood, and her gazed flitted around the table before coming to rest on Jed. "And who might you be?"

"Granny," Neely Kate said, "this is Jed."

"Jed what?"

Jed gave her a wary smile. "Jed Carlisle, ma'am."

"Well, Jed Carlisle, this is your lucky day. I'm gonna tell you your future."

Jed's eyes flew wide open. "That's not necessary ma'am."

"Nonsense," she said, moving over to her stove and grabbing a worn red tea kettle. She hobbled over to the sink and pushed a pan out of the way to fill the pot. "Have you ever had your tea leaves read before?"

"No, ma'am."

She glanced over her shoulder and smiled. "Then today really *is* your lucky day. I'll even do it at a discount price."

"You'll do it for *free*, Granny," Neely Kate said, shooting her a warning look.

"You don't need to do it at all," Jed insisted.

Granny shot Neely Kate a frown before putting the kettle on the stove. "Of course I'll do it for free. My introductory special."

It was obvious Jed did *not* want to know his future. I found it amusing considering all the dangerous situations I'd seen him navigate without so much as breaking a sweat, not to mention the fact that I'd told him his changeable future many times.

But whatever his reason, I decided to help him out. Lord knew he'd helped me plenty. "Ms. Rivers, can you read my tea leaves instead?"

The older woman moved closer, putting her gnarled hand on my cheek. "No, your future is too uncertain."

Neely Kate looked alarmed. "What does that mean, Granny?"

Her grandmother's back stiffened. "It means just what I said." She picked up a tea cup and rinsed it in the sink.

"Why would her future be uncertain?" Neely Kate asked.

The older woman put the cup and saucer on the table. "Because she's a seer. All seers' futures are unclear because they carry the futures of so many others."

I shot a questioning look at Neely Kate, but she shook her head.

"I didn't tell her," she said.

Neely Kate's granny laughed. "She didn't have to tell me. I can see it in your aura."

"Granny, we're not here for you to read either of their futures. I'm here because I need to ask you a few questions about Momma."

The older woman's smile fell, and she suddenly looked nervous. "Oh."

"Momma was seeing someone before she left. Do you know anything about him?"

She waved her hand in dismissal, but she wouldn't look her granddaughter in the eyes. "That kid in the band."

"No, Granny. She was seeing someone else."

Her grandmother froze. "What makes you say that?"

I cast a glance at Jed to see if he'd picked up on her strange behavior. His previous anxiety was gone, replaced with the face he used to face Skeeter's adversaries in meetings.

"I found out some information about Momma . . . before she left," Neely Kate said. "She was pregnant. You always told me she got pregnant later."

Her grandmother sat in her chair and covered Neely Kate's hands with her own. "You don't know what you're messin' with, baby girl. You need to leave this alone."

"What are you talkin' about?" Neely Kate asked.

"You just accept that fool boy as your father and go on with your life."

"Momma never told me who my father was. She always said it didn't matter."

Her grandmother nodded, but I saw the fear in her eyes. "This is the one time your Momma and I agree on ⬜etting⬜g', and given what a rarity that is, you should listen."

"No, Granny. I need to know."

Anger flashed in the older woman's eyes. "No, you don't! You just let sleepin' dogs lie, Neely Kate Rivers. Your very life depends on it!"

We were all silent for a moment before Neely Kate said in a calm, clear voice. "I know that J.R. Simmons is my father."

Her grandmother shook her head violently. "No, Neely Kate. No."

"Yes, Granny," she continued. "It's true. Now I need you to tell me what you know." Neely Kate grew impatient when her grandmother didn't answer. "Granny!"

"There was a woman here . . . recent. She was asking about you." She started to shake. "You're not supposed to know about it."

Neely Kate gasped. "What? Who?"

My heart slammed into my chest. Had Kate been to see Neely Kate's grandmother?

Neely Kate looked over her shoulder at me, then back at her grandmother. "Just tell me what she looked like, okay?" Neely Kate asked in an amazingly calm voice. "What color was her hair? That couldn't hurt anything, could it?"

The older woman was clearly flustered. "She told me not to tell anyone. She told me not to say."

"Granny, this is important. I *need* to know."

"No!" Granny Rivers's face turned red. "She said she'd kill you if I told! I failed Jenny Lynn. I'm not failing you, too."

The older woman clearly knew more about what had happened to her daughter than she was letting on, but I was worried she wouldn't tell us anything.

Neely Kate stood and began to pace, and Jed's eyes had darkened. "Ma'am, I know you think you're protecting Neely Kate," he said, "but she'll be in more danger if we don't know who came to see you and why."

She pressed her lips together and shook her head.

"Granny Rivers," I said softly as I slid over to sit in Neely Kate's vacated chair. "She said not tell us what she said, right?"

She nodded.

"How about I ask you a few things, and you only answer if you feel comfortable?"

She hesitated, eyeing me closely as though trying to figure out if it was a trick.

"I won't force you to tell me anything you don't want to. Can we just try it?"

She nodded.

"Okay." I smiled. "Let's talk about the time before Jenny Lynn left." When she didn't protest, I continued, "Did you know she was seeing an older man?"

"I knew she was hiding something, but I didn't know what. She wouldn't come home for days, and she'd show up with things—once a necklace and another time a pair of earrings."

"From him? The man she was seeing?"

Granny Rivers shrugged. "She never said. I almost accused her of stealing, but I knew better. Jenny Lynn was a lot of things before she left, but a thief wasn't one of them."

"Did she ever act scared of him?"

"She was jumpy at the end. Easily spooked and lookin' out the windows at night. The last week was the worst, and that's when she finally told me the whole story."

"And can you tell me the whole story?" I asked.

"No. She told me not to."

"The woman who came to see you?"

Granny Rivers nodded.

"That's okay," I said softly. "Did the woman want the whole story?" She started getting agitated, so I added, "You're not telling me what you two talked about. It's okay."

She nodded, grabbing a tissue from a box on the table. "She wanted the whole story."

"Did you know who Neely Kate's father was before Jenny Lynn left?"

She hesitated.

"You don't have to say it out loud," I suggested. "You can just nod or shake your head."

She nodded.

"Did anyone come lookin' for her after she left?"

She nodded again.

There was no way J.R. would have shown up to do his own dirty work. He would have sent someone else.

"Do you know the name of the person who came to see you?"

She looked away. "No."

"If I show you a picture, do you think you can tell me if it was him?"

Despite her dubious expression, she nodded and said, "I'll never forget that man."

I pulled out my phone and sent Skeeter a text:

I need you to send pic of Thaddeus Brooke's photo on his driver's license.

He didn't respond for a good half-minute, but then he sent the photo, no questions asked.

I held the screen in front of Neely Kate's grandmother. "Is this him?"

Tears filled her eyes, and I stared at her in shock. This was not the woman I'd met in the bingo hall. I had never expected anything to terrify that feisty woman.

"So this is him?"

She nodded.

"He showed up lookin' for Jenny Lynn?"

"Her too."

"So he was looking for something else?" I asked in surprise.

When she didn't answer, Neely Kate blew her stack. "For God's sake, Granny, I know you think you're helpin' me, but you're hurtin' me more by not telling me! What was he lookin' for?"

Her grandmother stood up and shouted, "A gun! He was looking for the gun Jenny Lynn took from that man!"

Neely Kate gasped. "A *gun*?"

The older woman started to sob. "Jenny Lynn took if for insurance."

"You mean protection?" I asked.

"No, *insurance*. She said he'd shot and killed a man with it. She took it to use for blackmail. I told the man who showed up that if he or the man who'd used Jenny Lynn tried to find her, we'd turn the gun in to the police."

I sucked in a breath.

Granny Rivers wiped her nose with her tissue. "I told him that she took it with her. He banged me up a bit, then said he'd be back in a week to get it or else. But he never came back. Then the police chief got shot in his house. A burglary gone wrong, they said. Who's gonna fall for that? The police chief! After the same thing had happened to the owner of the fertilizer plant the week before . . . Everyone thought there was a dangerous criminal on the loose, but I knew that rich guy from El Dorado had ☐etting☐g' to do with it."

"Where's the gun now, Granny?" Neely Kate asked.

She started crying harder. "She took it with her."

"Momma took it?"

"No, that woman. She knew I had it, and she demanded I give it to her."

Neely Kate glanced at me. "How'd Kate know about the gun, and why would she want it?"

I shrugged. "I don't know. Maybe she wanted it for more evidence against her father."

"So why'd she threaten Granny if she told anybody about her showing up and askin' questions?"

"I don't know." I looked over at Jed. "Any ideas?"

"Not a one, but I agree it sounds like Kate. Still, it would be good if we could get your grandmother to help confirm it."

Neely Kate squatted next to her grandmother's chair. "Granny, listen to me. Can you tell me something about the woman? We can make it yes or no, just like the questions you answered for Rose."

The old woman looked suspicious, but Neely Kate forged on anyway. "Did she have dark hair?"

Her grandmother hesitated before giving a slight nod.

"See?" Neely Kate said. "That wasn't hard. Now tell me this: did she have blue streaks in her hair?" Neely Kate grew frustrated when the woman didn't answer. "Granny, did she have blue streaks in her hair?"

"I don't know," she said, her body shaking as she started to cry. "Her hair was covered with a hat. I could only see the ends of her dark hair sticking out."

I heard the door behind us open.

"Hey, Granny," Neely Kate's cousin Witt called out. "Sorry I got held up. I know you think I was trying to get out of fixin' your hot water heater."

"What did the hat look like, Granny?" Neely Kate said, her voice rising. "*What was she wearing?* Tell me!"

"What in the hell is goin' on here?" Witt stomped into the room with fury in his eyes. "What are you *doin'*, Neely Kate?"

Neely Kate stood and turned to face him, looking like she was ready for a showdown. "A woman was here askin' about me and my momma, but she threatened to kill me if Granny told anyone. I need to know what she asked and what Granny told her."

"So you're just lightin' into her?" he asked in disbelief. "She's liable to have another spell."

"I need to know, Witt!"

"Well, this isn't the way to do it!"

I put an arm around Neely Kate's shoulders and gave her a comforting squeeze. "It's okay, Neely Kate. We have enough."

"No, we don't!" She turned to face me. "We don't know who he killed with that gun!"

"We don't need to," I said quietly, trying to calm her down. "It's enough to know that Kate's ☐etting' desperate. She has to be if she's threatening an old woman just to make a move on her father."

"Rose is right," Jed added, rising from his chair. "We've got enough for now."

"No—"

"*Neely Kate,*" Jed said, firmly. "That's enough."

She nodded, and then her entire body slumped against me.

"Jed . . ." I called out in a panic.

"I got her." He was around the table in an instant, scooping Neely Kate up in his arms. "I'm takin' her out to the car."

"I don't need you to do that, Jed Carlisle," Neely Kate protested. "I can walk on my own two feet." She swatted his chest, but she didn't struggle very hard to get loose as he carried her outside.

"Rose," Witt said. "What's goin' on?"

I moved next to him and lowered my voice. "Neely Kate has stumbled onto the truth about her birth father, and it's a dangerous mess."

Pride filled Witt's eyes. "Of course it is. It's Neely Kate."

"And now that she knows someone came to see your granny . . . Well, Neely Kate has just had one shock right after another today, and I suspect she hasn't eaten in hours, which explains why Jed is carryin' her."

Witt winked. "Or the fact that he's a strappin' young man."

I shook my head, wondering how much of his suggestion was true. "In any case, we're gonna take her with us to keep her safe, but you might take your granny somewhere else tonight. To be on the safe side."

"Just how big of a mess has Neely Kate stumbled into?"

"A huge, nasty pile of poo."

He shook his head in amazement. "You've got your work cut out for you. You take care of Neely Kate, and I've got Granny covered."

"Thanks."

I squatted next to Neely Kate's grandmother. "I'm sorry we upset you, Mrs. Rivers. Neely Kate is just desperate to get some answers."

"I hope that other woman is okay," she said.

I hesitated, assuming I must have heard her wrong. "*What* other woman?"

"When that woman left, she stopped outside the front door and took a phone call. She told the caller not to worry, that she had Jenny Lynn's gun and now she was gonna teach the other bitch a lesson she wouldn't forget for the rest of her short life."

Dizziness flooded my head. "Are you sure?"

She nodded.

"When did the woman come see you?"

"Yesterday. Yesterday afternoon."

Yesterday?

"Thank you, Mrs. Rivers," I said. Then I ran out the door to find Jed.

We had to save someone.

Chapter Thirty

Jed was standing next to the back car door, surveying the farm, when I found him. He turned to face me. "Neely Kate's lying down on the backseat."

I nodded.

He gestured toward the house. "That was a surprise."

"Which part? The gun?" I asked. "Or the fact that Kate was here digging into Neely Kate's past?"

"Both."

"Well, I'm about to add more intrigue—Mrs. Rivers said her visitor stopped by yesterday, but as she left, she took a call and told the person on the other end that she was going to teach the other bitch a lesson. Then said she was going to kill her."

He scowled. "So Neely Kate's granny suddenly got chatty, huh?"

"Not much, and I think it was unintentional. She was worried about the woman her visitor threatened."

"I think we should get you to the safe house."

"What? Why?"

"Because Kate Simmons threatened you. As crazy as she is, it's a wonder she didn't kill you in the diner and be done with it."

"I suspect she's a lot like her daddy and likes to toy with her prey. But in this instance, I think she's after Hilary."

He took a step backward. "*What?*"

"Kate practically said the same thing when she left Merilee's, but she said it specifically about Hilary. I need to call Joe." I started digging for my phone in my coat pocket, but Jed grabbed my arm.

"Whoa. What are you gonna tell him?"

"I already told him that I think his sister is after Hilary. I'll tell him I have more proof."

"Text him. You can say all of that in a text."

Good point.

I checked the screen and saw that Mason had called and left me a message. When I retrieved it, I was surprised by how relieved I was to hear his voice in my ear.

"Rose, I'm about to go into a meeting with the state police, and I don't know how long I'll be. You're onto something with Nick Thorn. He was shot in his car in a parking lot outside a bar. The police determined it was a robbery, but no one was ever caught. He was murdered two years ago, last September, so it fits with the timeline of Kate taking off. I'll keep digging, but I'm not sure what else there is to find." He paused, and his voice lowered. "If you change your mind, my offer to come stay in the courthouse still stands. Be careful, Rose."

I relayed Mason's message as I typed off a text to Joe. When I finished, I looked up at Jed. "We have to go check on Hilary."

Jed's mouth dropped open. "Have you lost your mind?"

"No. I'd call her if I could, but I don't know her number." When he didn't answer, I said, "Come on, Jed. We've still got a few hours to kill. Let me do this good deed, and maybe karma will be on our side. Besides, I suspect Neely Kate needs to eat. You two weren't gone long enough for her to get dinner and break into the office."

"She said she wasn't hungry."

"I didn't eat much while I was talking to Joe, and we need all the energy we can get to face J.R. How about we pick up some food, then stop by Hilary's?"

Rather than answer, Jed turned around and got into the car. As soon as I climbed into the front passenger seat, he pulled away from the Rivers's property.

Unbelievably, Neely Kate had fallen asleep and was stretched out on the seat. As soon as Jed got onto the highway, I asked, keeping my voice low, "Any word from Skeeter?"

He nodded. "He's scouting out the barn with a dozen men. So far nothing."

"I guess that's good, right?"

"I have a hard time believing that Simmons Sr. is gonna show up at an unfortified site. I suspect he's taking a play from our playbook."

"You think he's gonna change the meetin' spot?"

"We're positive. We also suspect he'll change the time. Anything to throw us off our game."

"Well, crap." Everything he said made sense. "How soon?"

"We're not sure, which is why I don't want to waste any time checkin' on the wicked witch of the south."

"If we don't, I'll deal with it, but I could never forgive myself if something happens to her because she wasn't warned. But how about I have a vision to see if I can figure out where we're meeting?"

"Good idea."

I put my hand on Jed's arm and closed my eyes. The vision was slow to come, and when it did, the image was in slow motion and grainy. I tried to focus on the background, but I didn't recognize where we were. It looked like a barn.

After I relayed the vision to Jed, he asked, "What does it mean?"

"I think it means things are changing and the future hasn't sorted itself out yet."

We went through the drive-through of the Chuck and Cluck because it was Neely Kate's favorite place and I was desperate for anything to make her feel better. Neely Kate's head popped up as soon as Jed pulled up to the drive-through menu board and the maniacal sound of clucking broadcasted over the speaker.

"Chuck and Cluck?" she asked in a sleepy voice. "You hate this place."

"Hate is a strong word," I said, grinning back at her. "I'll make do."

"You love me," she teased.

"You know I do."

"I hate to break up the lovefest," Jed grumbled, "but the chicken wants you to order."

True enough, there was a plastic chicken head mounted next to the menu board, and its mechanized mouth opened and closed whenever the attendant spoke over the speaker.

"Arly," the person on the speaker drawled. "Is that you messin' with me again?"

I could only imagine all the pranks the guy on the other side of the speaker had faced.

Neely Kate ordered fried chicken and mashed potatoes while Jed and I both got chicken strips and fries. When we got to the takeout window, Neely Kate squealed with delight. "He's dressed as a chicken! That's new."

Sure enough, the employee at the window was wearing a chicken costume. When he leaned out to tell us our total, he had to repeat it twice since the chicken head muffled his voice.

Jed had to practically toss the money inside the window since the chicken's hands were shaped like claws.

"Whose ridiculous idea was this?" Jed asked, getting grumpier by the minute. He glanced over his shoulder at Neely Kate. "You know this shit will kill you, don't you?"

"Ha!" Neely Kate barked. "Says the man who's about to meet a deadly killer. Might as well have fried chicken before you meet your maker."

"No one is meetin' their maker today," I said. "We're all gonna survive this and annoy the crap out of each other tomorrow."

Neely Kate laughed, but her spirits seemed to lag again as we drove across town toward Hilary's. While we ate, I filled her in on Mason's message and my worry about Hilary.

"Part of the reason I'm indulging your request is because I think the woman's perfectly safe." Jed shot me a sideways glance. "So I'm gonna park around the corner and let you two go check on her."

"I really want to argue with this plan," Neely Kate said, licking her fingers. "But I've been kind of worried since we talked to her this morning."

A ball of anxiety knotted in my stomach. My gut told me that something bad was going to happen. Maybe I could get close enough to Hilary to have a vision and make sure she was safe from Kate's clutches.

When I suggested my plan to Neely Kate, she whacked my arm. "Why haven't you been having visions today? You could have had one of my granny!"

"And what good would that do? It might work if my visions searched the past instead of telling me the future."

"You could have had visions of me or Jed or Skeeter to see if we survive the night."

I shivered. There was no way I was going down that road unless I was desperate. I had died in visions before, and while I'd changed those deaths, it was always terrifying to go through. Now I wondered if I was being selfish. But tonight felt different. Heavier. A feeling of hopelessness clung to this meeting, and the truth was that I was scared to face it head-on.

But I didn't have time to dwell on it. Jed pulled up to the curb and put the gear shift in park. I could see Hilary's house around the corner. "Why are you parking so far away?"

"I sure as hell don't want to be seen parked outside her house."

"Really?"

"Get this done so we can get out of here," Jed grumbled as he pulled out his phone. "I'm gonna check in with Skeeter." He shot me a glare. "I should let you be the one to call and tell him what you're up to."

I opened my car door. "That's my cue to leave."

He emitted a low rumble, so I clambered out of the car with Neely Kate hot on my heels. I threaded our arms as we crossed the street and tugged her close. "How are you really doin'? You've had one shock right after the other."

"I'm still processing it all, but I've decided that it's not the worst thing in the world. At least I know now." She grinned. "Can you imagine what Joe's gonna say when he finds out?"

"So you plan on tellin' him?"

She lifted her eyebrows. "I don't see any reason to keep it a secret, do you?"

I smiled. "No, after all the crap Kate's pulled, I suspect Joe's gonna be happy to have a mostly normal sister."

"*Mostly* normal?"

Hilary lived in the biggest house in town. It was a turn-of-the-century Victorian that hadn't been on the market when she'd acquired it. Rumor had it that Hilary had approached the owner and convinced him to sell.

Jed had parked close to the back of the house, but as we rounded the corner to the front, I caught sight of a dark sedan idling at the curb. It took me a second to figure out what felt off to me—the back door was open, but no interior lights were on. In fact, a man stood next to the car's open back door. A woman was scooting into the backseat, but the man gave her shoulder a push.

"Let's go!" he said, speaking none too gently.

His gaze swept over me, but Neely Kate and I had skidded to a halt and she'd tugged me deeper into the shadows of a tall oak tree at the side of the house. While he didn't seem to notice us, I got a good look at him, and it was as plain as day who he was.

"Oh, my word, Neely Kate!" I whispered as I pulled out my phone. "That's Sam Teagen!"

Teagen got in behind her, and the car sped away before he even got the door shut.

"Come on," Neely Kate said, then ran for the front door. "Don't call Joe yet."

"Why not?" I asked as I followed her, surprised she knew who I was calling. "We just saw Hilary Wilder get kidnapped by Sam Teagen. I bet you money his friend Marshal is driving."

"Let's make sure it was her."

"We're outside her house, Neely Kate. And he's getting away! We should be following them!"

"By the time we get back to Jed's car, it will be too late. We'll never catch up." She'd already climbed Hilary's front steps and now stood on the wraparound porch, knocking on the front door. The door swung in a few inches.

"Neely Kate, her door's open. I can't see Hilary doin' that."

She put her hands on her hips and sighed. "I'm afraid you're right."

"Now, I'm calling Joe."

Only Joe didn't answer, so I hung up and called 911. Unfortunately, the call went to the Henryetta police dispatcher.

"I've just witnessed a kidnapping. The man was Sam Teagen, and the woman was Hilary Wilder."

"So they knew each other, ma'am?"

"I'm not sure if they did or not. What difference does it make? I saw him stuffing her into the backseat of his car, and then he got in behind her and they drove off."

"And how could he drive off if he was in the backseat?" the dispatcher asked in a bored voice.

"He had a getaway driver."

"Uh huh . . ."

"Why aren't you taking this seriously?"

"Because you're Rose Gardner, and we have memos posted everywhere to watch out for you."

I had no idea how she knew who I was, but I had bigger things to dwell on. "What on earth does that mean?"

"It means trouble follows you wherever you go, and sure enough, you're stirrin' it up now."

"Do you think I'm lying?" I asked in disbelief. "Why would I lie?"

"That's not up to me to figure out. You just wait there. I'm sendin' Officer Ernie to talk to you."

I hung up, madder than a wet hornet. "They're sending Ernie to talk to us, and we're supposed to wait here."

"Are we really gonna do that?" she asked in disbelief, looking down the street after the car.

"Shoot, no. We need to tell Jed and Skeeter."

We hurried back to the car. Jed was on the phone when I slid into the passenger seat and Neely Kate got into the back.

Jed gave me a grim look as he hung up. "And that was the official change of plans. We have thirty minutes."

I took a slow breath to fight my sudden nausea. "Where are we going?"

His eyes narrowed. "That's the irony of it. We're goin' to the Atchison plant."

I shuddered. I hated that ruined warehouse.

He put the car into drive. "We have to meet up with Skeeter, but he's a good ten minutes south of town."

I shook my head. "Whoa. Slow down. Who did you just talk to on the phone?"

"Skeeter."

"Why didn't J.R. call me, too?"

"He didn't call you about the meeting place this afternoon, so why is this a surprise? Besides, it wasn't J.R. who called him. It was Kate."

"Kate? Why would she call Skeeter?"

Jed took off before I could get my seatbelt fastened, and I had to put my hand on the dashboard to brace myself.

"We just saw Sam Teagen stuff Hilary into the back of a car," I said. "That is too coincidental."

"Agreed. But is Kate workin' with her daddy, or is she helpin' lead us to him?"

"This is nonsense," I said, pulling out my phone. I called Skeeter and put him on speaker. "Skeeter," I said as soon as he answered. "What did Kate say?"

"She said the timetable had been altered. She told me to bring the Lady in Black and meet her at 7:45—at the Atchison plant, outside Henry Buchanan's office. I take it you know where that is?"

I cast a glance at Jed. Considering that the Atchison plant was where he'd been shot in the arm, he probably didn't have warm and fuzzy memories of the place either.

"Is she working with her dad?" I asked. "Or does she have her own dog and pony show goin' on?"

"I don't know," Skeeter said, "although it would certainly appeal to his sense of drama. What I do know is that there won't be a meeting at this barn south of town. There's no way J.R. Simmons would be stupid enough to announce the location so far ahead of time. He likes the element of surprise, and he knows any meeting we have won't end well. He's gonna stack it to his advantage."

"Well, we just saw Sam Teagen stuff Hilary Wilder into the back of a car and speed away, so I can't help thinking Hilary is part of this meeting, too."

"None of this makes sense," Skeeter said. "Why would Hilary be involved?"

"I don't know, but I have a terrible feeling about all of it."

"You need to have a vision," he said.

"I had one of Jed earlier that was fuzzy and indistinct. I couldn't tell where we were or what was goin' on. The future was uncertain."

"Well, have one of Jed now."

I knew this. I'd had dozens of them the week before, but I'd resisted them all day. I suddenly realized why I was being so resistant. I didn't want to see the future because I wasn't sure I could change it.

"Is she forcing a vision?" Skeeter asked over the speaker.

"No," Jed said, then grabbed my hand. "It's okay, Rose. Just do it. We need to know."

Taking a deep breath, I closed my eyes and focused on the meeting tonight and felt variations of darkness and cold and heat and bright lights. My vision was blurring as though I was in a sand storm, only there wasn't any sand—the vision was too obscured.

"You're caught between darkness and light."

I opened my eyes, and Jed was staring at me. "What does that mean?"

"It felt like two very different futures were at war with each other. One was dark and cold—a lot like the visions I had of Mason for a time period he would have been dead in the unaltered future, but the other was all heat and bright lights, like a fire. And I was surrounded by sand, only there wasn't any sand." I paused. "I think it was fire."

"So two choices," Skeeter said. "One choice leads to Jed's death. The other one ends in a firestorm. Which one is the path to Kate? Which one do we choose?"

And wasn't that the biggest irony of them all? I'd finally harnessed my visions to make them work for me, but when I needed them the most, they failed me.

Deep down, I'd known that the outcome of this night would ultimately rest on my shoulders, that I couldn't rely on my visions. I could only rely on me.

But I glanced over at Jed, at Neely Kate in the backseat, and then down at my phone, knowing Skeeter was there waiting for an answer.

I wasn't facing this alone. As much comfort as that gave me, maybe that was the problem.

Chapter Thirty-One

M y friends were waiting for me to answer, to decide our fate, so I finally sighed and said, "I'm gonna be honest, I don't want to go out to that place, but I still think we should meet Kate. I want to know what she's up to with Neely Kate and what she plans on doin' with that gun."

"What gun?"

Crappy doodles. I hadn't told him about our meeting with Neely Kate's grandmother. I took a minute to fill him in on everything. As I rehashed it all, I snuck glances at Neely Kate, but she remained silent, her face a blank mask.

"Well, shit," he grumbled.

"Any idea who J.R. killed with it?" I asked.

"That was twenty-five years ago. It could have been anyone."

"Jenny Lynn must have known, though, don't you think?" I asked. "Otherwise, why would she have taken it?" I paused. "Maybe it was a stab in the dark."

"She must have seen or heard something."

"Neely Kate's granny said that Allen Steyer was killed the week before Thaddeus Brooke showed up asking for the gun, and that was after Jenny Lynn told Dora she was runnin' off with the musician. What if she saw J.R. kill Allen Steyer? What if he was one of his Twelve?"

"I think you're onto something," Skeeter said. "But how would Kate know all of that?"

"Does it matter?" I asked. "Murder has no statute of limitations. J.R.'s murder weapon will be a lot more useful to us than a ledger full of twenty-five-year-old crooked deals."

"The statute of limitations is pointless since he's not goin' back to jail," Skeeter growled. "Not to mention that the chain of evidence has been destroyed."

"Maybe so, but Kate doesn't care about that, does she?" Or did she? Was she protecting him or trying to bring him down? "So we meet her?"

"Yes, but wait for me. Let me move my men into position before we strut in."

"Are you gonna be there in time?" I asked, my stomach in knots.

"She can wait," Skeeter said, then called out, "Jed."

"Yeah."

"Wait for me behind the Sinclair station."

"Got it."

We drove the rest of the way in silence. I was fretting over the unknown threats looming over us. I was sure Neely Kate was worrying about the same, not to mention dwelling on her new family tree. Jed . . . well, he was his usual stoic self.

He parked in his spot, and as soon as he stopped, I opened the car door and bolted out, needing the cold night air to help me calm down. Leaving the car running, Jed followed me.

"It's all gonna work out," he said.

I spun around to face him. He was resting his butt against the side of the car, watching me. "You don't know that. My vision told us nothing."

"Maybe we're not supposed to know. Maybe we're just supposed to prepare the best we can and let the chips fall where they may."

"And that might mean one or all of us die."

"Rose," he said softly, "sometimes you just have to accept your fate."

I shook my head. "No. I refuse to believe that. My momma used to want me to accept my fate. Do you know what that was? Working at the DMV all day, then coming home to wait on her hand and foot while everyone in town thought of me as the weird Gardner sister. I was purposeless and alone . . . and then I had the vision of myself dead. I decided I didn't want to die without *livin'* first. So I made my list, thinkin' I was on borrowed time."

A wry grin lifted his lips. "And you completed that list and a hell of a lot more things after that."

"But I'm not ready to die yet, and I'm not ready to lose anyone I care about."

"Sometimes we don't have a choice in the matter."

"Not tonight." I marched over to him and grabbed his hand, squeezing tight as I closed my eyes, focusing on what would happen during the meeting. I could see we were inside the Atchison factory, but the rest was shrouded in a thick fog.

I dropped Jed's hand. "You were in a haze."

"Still murky?"

I nodded. "But I'm pretty sure it was Atchison."

"It's a lot more than Skeeter and I would normally know. We have to be happy with it." But he couldn't look me in the eyes. His gaze darted into the trees.

"You weren't so accepting last week." In fact, they had both asked me to use my ability again and again. I put a hand on my hip and scowled. "What are you up to?"

"Why in the hell would you ask that?" he asked.

But I knew him well enough to know he wasn't telling me the entire truth. Before he realized what I was doing, I grabbed his hand and focused on his plan with Skeeter. This time the vision burst into view with surprising clarity. Skeeter stood beside me, but he pushed Vision Rose to the floor and covered her with his body as gunshots rang out. I ducked behind a metal desk, firing into a dark area full of rusted equipment. I looked down at my chest, surprised to see blood seeping through my shirt. I was shoved just as violently back to the present.

"You're gonna get shot in the chest," I said, staring into Jed's confused face.

Sadness filled his eyes. "Rose . . ."

I dropped my hold on his hand and took a step back. I had absolutely no idea how to change the outcome. There was nothing in the vision to help me steer things in a different direction. "No."

"I'm prepared to face what comes," he said.

But I wasn't. How many times had this man protected me? He was going into a situation that had nothing to do with him other than his connection to me.

I grabbed his hand again and focused on what would happen to my friends at the meeting. I was plunged into a vision and found myself lying on the floor, my chest on fire with pain. I heard a gurgling sound when I tried to breathe. Although I was behind a desk, I could see around the edge, and anger and frustration brewed at the sight in front of me.

J.R. Simmons was standing in an open space in the Atchison plant. Candles lined the room, and I saw two men lying on the floor to my left, blood pooled around them. Skeeter knelt at his feet with his hands zip-tied behind him, while Vision Rose stood in front of him with a defiant look in her eyes.

"It didn't have to be this way, Rose," J.R. purred, brandishing a gun. "If you'd only left my son alone." Then he placed the gun to Skeeter's temple as an evil grin spread across his face. "I was going to let you watch me punish Rose, but I think it will hurt her more to see this."

The gun fired, and Skeeter slumped to the ground as Vision Rose screamed.

J.R. turned his attention to Rose. "Now it's just you and me. The way it was always supposed to be."

The vision faded, and I was jerked back into the cold night air. "He wants it to be just him and me."

"What?" Jed asked in confusion.

"Nothing." I shook my head, trying not to panic. "Neely Kate wasn't there. Where was she?"

A soft smile lifted his lips, and then he said softly. "She won't be anywhere near there."

I nodded. It was better that way. Especially since she'd just found out J.R. Simmons was her father. I couldn't stomach the thought of him hurting her any more than he already had. Jenny Lynn had gone on the run to escape him, so in a roundabout way, he'd stolen Neely Kate's childhood.

"Do you have a plan for where to leave her?" I asked.

"No. We were going to play it by ear. We always suspected the location would be changed."

Looking around, I sighed. I was scared to face that man alone, but I had to try to save my friends. "This is as good a place as any."

He considered it for a moment before nodding. "Agreed."

"We're gonna have to trick her. I have an idea. Will you help me?"

"Yeah."

I opened the back door and found Neely Kate on her phone.

She glanced up. "I called Granny to make sure she's okay."

I'd wondered what she was still doing in the car. "Is she? I hate that we traumatized her."

"Witt took her back to his place, not that she's happy about that." Fear flickered in her eyes. "I've never seen her that scared before, Rose."

"I know. We're gonna put a stop to that tonight."

Tears filled her eyes. "That monster is my father."

"No. He's not. He's the pervert who took advantage of a teenage girl and happened to get her pregnant. He is not your father. But something good may have come from it."

"What on earth could that possibly be?"

I smiled. "I think you have one of the best brothers a girl could ever hope for. Once Joe knows the truth, he's liable to annoy the dickens out of you, callin' up all the time to make sure you're safe."

"What if he hates me because of it?"

"Hate *you*? Impossible. Who could hate *you*? Besides, Joe knows his father. I think he'll feel lucky to find out he's related to someone as amazing as you. Now come here." I beckoned for her to come out of the car.

She climbed out. I shut the door behind her and pulled her into a hug, hanging on a little longer than I'd intended. "I love you, Neely Kate. You're an amazing person. Don't let anyone let you think different."

She chuckled in my ear as she squeezed tight. "You sound like you're buttering me up for something."

I laughed as I let her loose. "I mean every word. I know better than to try to pull something over on you."

Jed stood to the side, looking serious.

I cast a glance inside the car, relieved to see the engine was still running—that fit with my plan.

Then I pointed behind the service station. "Would you believe I chucked a diamond bracelet in those bushes a few weeks ago?"

Neely Kate gave me a skeptical look. "Where'd you get a diamond bracelet?"

"It was a gift to the Lady in Black," I said, looking over at Jed for confirmation. "One of Skeeter's frenemies was trying to buy my good graces."

"Skeeter was none too happy about it," Jed added, playing along.

"I wore the thing," I continued, "but when I got back here and changed, I ripped it off and threw it into the bushes."

"Why on earth would you throw it away?" she asked in dismay. "We could have sold it and used the money for the landscaping business."

I shrugged. "Skeeter was there, and I was trying to prove my loyalty . . ." I lied. "But I got to thinking about how much it might be worth. While we're waiting for Skeeter, maybe we should look for it. If we can find it, we can take it to the pawn shop tomorrow." I pointed to the leafless bushes several feet from the back of the building. "I tossed it in that section. Jed, maybe you could shine your flashlight out there so that Neely Kate can look for it while I check my phone. I want to see if Mason called or left a message about his search."

Neely Kate looked suspicious, but Jed dug out his phone and turned on the flashlight to support the ruse. He gave me a slight nod when Neely Kate turned her back to us and moved deeper into the thicket.

"Are you sure?" she asked. "I don't see a thing."

"Yeah," I said, moving toward the front of the car. "But I chucked it pretty good. Maybe look a little deeper inside the thicket."

As Jed leaned over with his flashlight, I tried to inch my way to the driver's door. I didn't want Jed to catch on that I was leaving him too. My nerves felt like jumping beans, but if I acted too twitchy, I'd catch their attention sooner than I'd like.

They seemed intent in their search, so I used the opportunity to sneak into the driver's seat and shut the door carefully behind me. I'd just shifted the car into reverse when Jed caught on to my plan. He bolted for the car, but I hit the gas pedal hard enough to send it shooting out onto the empty highway. I slammed on the brakes and shoved the gear shift into drive, tearing off as Jed ran after me.

Seconds later, my phone rang. I grabbed it out of my pocket and turned on the speaker phone.

"What in the hell do you think you're doin', Rose?" Neely Kate demanded.

"Doin' what needs to be done. This is between me and J.R. Simmons. It doesn't involve you or Jed."

"Bull honkey!" she shouted. "This has just as much to do with me as it does you. He's *my* father."

"There's no need for all of us to show up to the meeting. Only me and Skeeter," I said. "So I'm goin' alone and hopin' I can get this resolved before he gets there."

"Skeeter's gonna kill you," Jed said in disgust. "You're gonna wish for J.R. to finish you off."

I released a nervous laugh as I tore down the county road. "I'll take my chances."

Jed's voice tightened. "He's gonna kill *me*."

There was a greater likelihood of that happening. "No, I'll make sure Skeeter knows I tricked you."

"I don't see that happening if you're dead," he said, still seething. "Come back here right now. You're a sitting duck without me or Skeeter."

"No. I'm gonna end this." I still had the gun in my pocket. I'd figure out a way to finish him off.

"You don't even know if J.R.'s gonna be there," Jed countered. "It could just be crazy Kate."

"No," I said quietly. "He'll be there." My vision confirmed it.

"Rose!" he shouted, sounding angrier than I would have thought possible. It sounded strange coming from the man who had dedicated himself to protecting me and who treated me with nothing but kindness and compassion. "Stop this fool nonsense right now!"

"Thanks for everything you've done, Jed," I said, tears burning my eyes. "This is me repaying you for all the times you've put yourself in danger on my account."

Before he could respond, I hung up. I was about to toss the phone to the passenger seat when I saw I had two missed texts.

You are cordially invited to The End. When? 8:00 tonight. Where? Atchison Manufacturing. Sincerely, Kate.

Seconds later, she'd sent: *Come . . . or else.*

Or else what? Was she sending me the information directly because she was worried Skeeter wouldn't do it? Or did she really not know I was the Lady in Black?

I tried to calm down and come up with a plan, but it was hard given all the unknowns. Things tended to go my way when I winged it. It was probably my best option, so I sure hoped it worked out this time.

I pulled into the parking lot with two minutes to spare. A single car was parked in the lot, and I wasn't sure whether to be worried or relieved. Had Kate and J.R. come to the plant together? Since I had no desire to walk through the equipment graveyard like I'd done the time Hattie and I met here, I searched through the glove compartment for a flashlight. Instead, I found a gun—a big shiny silver pistol that must have been Jed's backup piece. I popped open the clip of the bigger gun to verify that it was loaded. Then I got out of the car, thankful I still had my smaller gun in my coat pocket.

Taking a deep breath, I told myself to calm down. I'd been in situations just as bad as this one, and everything had turned out fine.

I tromped around the back of the building, hoping that climbing through the window would give me an element of surprise. A soft glow flickered as I approached the broken-out windows. I peered around the corner and saw Kate sitting on top of a metal desk with her back to the opposite concrete wall. She'd shoved the other desks to the side walls and covered them in lit candles. There were also candles flickering on the floor on the opposite side of the room, a hundred or more of them in all.

Just like in my vision. A chill ran down my spine. Maybe I would die, but at least I saved Jed. Now I had to figure out how to save Skeeter.

From what I could tell, she looked to be alone. That was undoubtedly a good thing, because I caught her attention before I could make my surprise entrance.

She looked up and smiled. "Rose Petal, you're the first to arrive. Come join me while we wait."

I was fairly certain I could make it back to my car before she ever caught up, but what good would that do? Besides, for all I knew, J.R. could be pulling into the lot even now.

"Expectin' other guests?" I asked, then stuck the bigger gun into the back of my jeans. Straddling the window, I climbed in.

Her grin spread. "I always did love a party, but I'm used to my guests using the front door."

"Well," I drawled, trying to decide where to stand. I really had no desire to play right into Kate's plans, which meant I was going to have stay as far away from her as possible. "I'm not sure if you noticed, but I tend to do things a little different than everyone else."

"I'll say." She sat with her denim-clad legs draped over the edge of that desk, her palms flat on the surface. I saw no evidence of a gun or any other weapon, but there was a crazed look in her eyes. She was wearing the same black, long-sleeved T-shirt as earlier, but there was a diamond ring I'd never seen before on her left ring finger.

"Who else is comin'?" I asked.

Her response was a smirk.

I took a few steps forward, trying to figure out her setup. The factory equipment—and the usual front door—was to my right. Henry Buchanan's office was to my left, but the door was closed tonight, with a path between the desks to the center of her stage. I wasn't too fond of having the window to my back, so I took a few steps toward the office wall. "What's with all the candles?

It looks like a cheesy episode of *Supernatural*. Havin' a séance?"

She propped her arms behind her and leaned back her head, laughing. "I think we should wait until later for the séance . . . to connect with the newly departed."

"Who are you planning on killin'?" I asked, deciding to take this head-on. Better to know a snippet of her plan going in, even if I was the one she planned to murder—something I highly suspected.

But where did the vision I'd just seen fit into all of this?

She leaned to the side and tried to look around me. "Where's Neely Kate?"

My back stiffened, worried about what logical jump had led her from my question to my best friend. "Neely Kate couldn't make it."

She shook her head and tsked, then grabbed her phone and started tapping on the screen. "That just won't do. I expected her to be your plus one. You two are like peanut butter and jelly."

"We don't do *everything* together."

She glanced up and grinned. "Not to worry. I'm sure she'll join us soon."

I sure hoped not. I knew Jed would call Skeeter, but would he take the time to stop and pick them up? I was hoping for Skeeter to come alone. "Stop playin' games, Kate, and just spit out what you want."

"Now, now, Rosie." She spread her hands out at her sides. "Games are what make life fun. Haven't you learned anything from my family yet?" She winked. "We're about to take this particular game to a whole new level tonight."

How much did she know about Neely Kate's parentage? Was she planning to hurt her? "What did you do with Anna and Bruce Wayne?"

Kate rolled her eyes. "Please."

I steeled my back and used my most authoritative voice. "I want to know where they are, Kate."

She shrugged. "I haven't the foggiest idea, nor do I care."

"Why did you kidnap Hilary?"

Shaking her head, she laughed. "You really are clueless, aren't you? How did you ever manage to solve all those crimes?"

A clicking sound, like heels on concrete, echoed to my right, and I backed up toward the wall with the desks, my heart beginning to race.

"Did I hear my name?" Hilary asked, emerging from an aisle of equipment. She had changed into a pair of cream-colored pants, a flowy pale-blue silky shirt, and a low pair of cream leather pumps. Her auburn hair hung loose, but the sides were pulled back with clips decorated with clear stones. She stopped just outside the opening, her gaze fixed on Kate. Surprise filled her eyes as she shifted her attention to me. "*Rose.*" She turned back to Kate. "What is *she* doing here? When I got your text, I thought this was just you and me."

"But . . ." I spat out in shock. "He put you in the car . . . I saw you get kidnapped."

Confusion washed over Hilary's face, but Kate chuckled. Then Sam Teagen moved out from behind Hilary, and I realized how wrong I'd been. My head swam as I took all the pieces I knew and tried to make them fit with this new realization.

Hilary laughed. "I don't think I've ever seen you speechless before, Rose."

"Sam Teagen . . ." I shook my head. "He works for . . . *you?*"

She walked closer to Kate's setup, staying outside the ring of candles. "You know his name? Oh, dear. That *is* unfortunate."

"Maybe I know more than Kate thinks I do." Although I worried I didn't know much at all. I was in big trouble. "Where's J.R.?"

Hilary laughed, but it sounded bitter. "If I were you, I wouldn't be in such a hurry to see him. He's not too fond of you, and trust me, that's not a situation you want to be in."

I looked over at Kate to gauge her reaction, but she kept her attention on her newest guests.

"What is all this, Kate?" I asked.

She grinned. "All part of the game, Rosalina."

"I'm not too crazy about games, so I think I'll be goin'." I took a step backward, but Kate's gaze narrowed.

"You're one of the guests of honor," Kate cooed. "We can't have you going anywhere."

Did that mean she was working with her father after all? The evidence was supporting that theory.

But before I could ponder it all, Sam Teagen started toward me. I reached to the small of my back and pulled out Jed's silver gun, which I then pointed at Teagen. "Come any closer and I'll shoot you."

He stopped and glared, his empty hand twitching at his side. The fact that he didn't have a gun drawn meant he had underestimated me. Good.

His gaze darkened. "You try to shoot me, and I'll make you suffer for these scars you put on my face." He still sported healing scratch marks on his cheek. It sure had to be tough for a guy like him to go around with claw marks marring up his good looks.

Kate released a loud sigh. "Nobody's shooting anyone . . . yet. There's plenty of time for that later. We've got too much sharing to do first."

"You said you were waiting for other guests," I said, casting a quick glance at Kate without lifting my attention from Sam Teagen. I didn't trust him for a minute, and I truly was prepared to shoot him. I'd come a long way from that scared girl who'd purposely let Daniel Crocker drag her to a private office. "Who else is coming?"

"It's a surprise party, Rose Petal," Kate said. "You'll just have to wait and be surprised."

I turned my attention to Hilary, though Sam Teagen was still in view. "Do *you* know?"

"How would I know?" Hilary asked. "I thought Kate had invited me to work out our differences. In the name of family unity."

"In a deserted warehouse?" Kate laughed, but her annoyance was clear. "You always were so gullible."

Scowling, Hilary crossed her arms, but she turned back to me. "Where's Skeeter Malcolm? I thought he was your new shadow."

"Why would she come with Malcolm?" Kate asked in confusion.

Hilary laughed. "Because Rose is the Lady in Black, of course. She's Skeeter Malcolm's little pet. He treasures her above all things."

Kate shook her head. "The Lady in Black? *Rose Gardner?*"

"Didn't you catch that she entrapped your father?"

"Yeah, but she was impersonating her."

"Keep up, Kate. Rose Gardner *is* the Lady in Black," Hilary said, her voice harsh. "She's been working with Malcolm since the auction at Thanksgiving." She rolled her eyes. "And you call *me* gullible."

"Does Joe know?" Kate asked, sounding less confident.

"Joe doesn't know a blessed thing." Hilary flipped a strand of hair over her shoulder. "He still sees her as a blushing virgin."

Kate turned livid and she jumped off the desk. "You've been making my brother look like a fool?"

Hilary took a step closer to the center of the room, walking between the candles on the floor. "What is this about, Kate? I know you have a personal vendetta against me, but why are we meeting here, and why is Rose along for the ride?"

Kate's body shivered, and then she seemed to be back in control. "We're not starting this yet."

"If you're waiting for J.R.," Hilary said, "he's not coming."

Kate's laughter had an unstable edge. "Oh, you stupid bitch. You don't know *anything*."

It was a sad day when someone looked loonier than Hilary. But then I'd totally underestimated Hilary. I'd never once suspected her of working with Sam Teagen—and the implications of that error were now becoming clear.

Common sense told me I should leave. I had a gun. I could make my escape, although I suspected Sam Teagen would have something to say about that. But as soon as that thought occurred to me, I dismissed it. I was done hiding. Last June, the old Rose had hidden naked in a linen closet, dripping wet and shaking with fear. But no more. I was done cowering. I was going to demand answers.

I gave Hilary a hard look. "You hired Sam Teagen to kidnap me. I thought it was Kate, but it was you."

Hilary didn't answer, but she didn't gloat either.

Kate burst out laughing. "You thought *I* was the one behind your kidnapping?"

I ignored her, anger igniting in my chest. Months of frustration broke loose. "I understand why you wanted me dead, but why Mason?" I asked. "He never did anything to you."

Hilary took two steps toward me, her eyes hard. "You have no idea about my past with Mason."

My heart slammed into my chest. "He told me about the way you used him to get information about his sister."

She shook her head. "No. He used me. Then he moved on to you."

I fought the urge to panic. "How did he use you?"

Her eyes glittered with excitement. "That's between me and Mason."

The woman I was facing now was a far cry from the nearly hysterical woman I'd encountered this morning.

I was stuck in a creepy abandoned factory with two crazy women and a man who looked like he wanted to rip off my head with his bare hands. I was rethinking my strategy. But it was a little late for that. "There was nothing between you. You were the one to approach him at all the social events. You were the one who got information from him that led to Savannah's death."

Hilary shook her head. "Is that what he told you?"

Kate chuckled. "You really are naïve. Are you really falling for this?"

"Then tell me your side," I coaxed. "We all know there's no way you'll let me walk out of this alive, so at least give me answers. No more secrets."

"I agree. No more secrets." A gun appeared out of the darkness of the gathered equipment, aimed at the back of Hilary's head, and Skeeter walked into the light. "So answer the lady."

If Hilary was afraid, she didn't let on. A smile lit up her eyes even though her back was still to him. "I knew you'd show up."

"And now I'm here, so someone better tell me what the hell is goin' on." He turned to Kate and gestured toward the room. "Is this your doin'?"

She sat back on the desk, her face lit up with glee. "It is."

Skeeter pointed his gun at Kate. "Then that makes you the master of ceremonies. You better start talkin'."

"I've been waiting for this night for two years, Mr. Malcolm. You can wait five minutes," Kate said. The condescension was heavy in her voice. "You never were a patient man."

Kate flicked a gaze at me. "James and I go *way* back."

"When he worked for your father."

She nodded, then turned her attention to Skeeter. "If you play this right, I'll let you make it out alive."

His shoulders stiffened. "Why?"

"Because I like you. I think we can work out some sort of arrangement." The innuendo in her voice made it clear it wasn't an above-board business deal.

Skeeter ignored her implication. "Then why'd you set this up for your daddy?"

The ring on her hand caught the light, and I said, "She set this up for her father, but not how you think, James. This is her revenge. Her revenge against her father for killing her fiancé, Nick."

Skeeter gestured toward Sam Teagen. "So what's this piece of trash doin' here?"

"He's my guest," Hilary said. Then, before I realized what she was doing, she pulled a gun out of her fancy cream-colored purse and pointed it at me. "I'm going to need Sam handy, so don't be getting any ideas about incapacitating him."

I cursed myself for having turned my attention away from her. Then again, she was pregnant. And while she was a sociopath, her baby—Joe's baby—was an innocent caught up in her madness. I wouldn't shoot her even if she attacked me, and the satisfaction on her face told me that she knew it.

"Now, *James*," she said, his given name clearly an insult on her lips. "I'm going to need you to put down the gun, or I'll be forced to kill your Lady in Black. And Rose, you need to drop yours, too." The saccharine sweetness in her voice nauseated me.

Skeeter's gaze lifted to mine, and if I hadn't known he was on my side, I would have been terrified of the rage in his eyes. He squatted and dropped his gun to the concrete floor, then rose to his full height, a good six inches above the man in front of him.

"Rose." Hilary's voice was harsh, and she looked like she was searching for an excuse to shoot me, so I dropped mine to the floor, too.

"Now kick it toward Sam."

I put a little too much effort behind it, and the gun skidded past Teagen, stopping close to Hilary.

I glanced at Skeeter and found him watching me with a mixture of anger and guilt. Since the anger wasn't directed toward me, I welcomed it, but the guilt only fueled more guilt of my own. He'd put my life before his, and now he had a gun pointed at him.

This was my fault. I should have waited for him. We could have made a plan. But I could beat myself up about it later. Right now, I needed to focus on getting us out of this. I still had a gun in my pocket.

Teagen bent to pick up Skeeter's gun, then pulled out a zip-tie from his back pocket. I watched in horror as Teagen tucked the gun into the waistband of his jeans, then bound Skeeter's hands behind his back, tugging with more force than needed.

"Got that tight enough?" Skeeter growled.

"Let me check," Teagen sneered, pulling even tighter. Then he circled around in front of Skeeter and punched him in the gut.

Skeeter bent over slightly, his jaw clenched.

"That's for killing my friends. And *this* is because I just don't like you." Teagen pulled his fist back and slammed it into Skeeter's nose.

I cried out as blood spurted down Skeeter's face, but Skeeter didn't miss a beat. He tipped his head back and dipped at the knees, then slammed his forehead into Teagen's face.

"Just wanted to add to Rose's handiwork. Not so pretty anymore," Skeeter grunted as Teagen covered his face with his hand.

I decided to take advantage of the distraction and started to lunge for the weapon sticking out of Teagen's jeans, but a bullet struck the floor in front of me, sending up sharp little shards of concrete. Startled, I jumped back and lifted my eyes to Hilary's amused face.

"I'm an excellent shot. Just ask Joe," Hilary said.

"Is Joe coming?" I asked, trying to keep the hope out of my voice.

Hilary turned to Kate. "You weren't stupid enough to invite Joe to this showdown of yours, were you?"

"I'm here." The voice came from the darkness. Joe stepped into the circle of light seconds later, still dressed in his sheriff's uniform. His face was hard as he took in the sight before him, ending with Hilary and the gun she had trained on me. His silence spoke volumes, but his hands hung at his sides, no gun in sight. In fact, his holster was empty.

"Did you come unarmed, like I insisted?" Kate asked.

He gave a curt nod, then turned his dark gaze on the mother of his baby. I could only imagine what Kate had said to get him to leave his gun at home.

Hilary turned pale. "Joe, I know this looks bad, but I can explain."

"Never feel the need to explain, Hilary," a voice I knew all too well called out from behind me.

I turned to see the object of my worst nightmare staring right at me.

It was clear from the look on his face that J.R. Simmons planned to make me beg for mercy. But the evil in his eyes assured me I'd never find it.

Chapter Thirty-Two

While J.R. climbed through the window with the assistance of a man I didn't recognize, I took a deep breath, trying to put all the pieces together in my head.

J.R. got his balance, but he seemed unsteady on his injured leg. After making sure his boss wouldn't tumble, the new guy scanned the room. A smarmy grin crossed his face when his eyes landed on Skeeter.

"The fall from grace is a bitch, isn't it, Malcolm?"

"You can't fall from the gutter, so I guess you wouldn't know," Skeeter spat out. "I see you're still in Simmons's posse of twelve pussies. I'm surprised you set foot outside of Columbia County."

The other guy looked like he was about to respond, but J.R. held up his hand.

"Enough." J.R.'s gaze turned to Joe and he blinked, the only sign that he was shocked by the presence of his son. "Joseph."

Joe's body tensed, his hands tightening into fists, but he still didn't say a word.

J.R.'s attention turned to his daughter, who now sat cross-legged on the desk, watching the goings-on with glee. "Katherine, what is the meaning of this?"

"It's a surprise, Daddy Dearest."

"I don't do surprises," he said with condescension.

Kate released a mock gasp. "Heaven forbid someone other than the great J.R. Simmons should be in charge." Then her smile widened. "There's a basket over there. Put your guns in it and gather closer."

No one made a move.

Kate leaned her head back and groaned, her hand reaching behind her to produce a gun. Before I realized what was happening, a loud pop filled the space. The man next to J.R. fell to the ground, blood seeping from his temple onto the concrete.

J.R. stumbled back a step in shock.

Panic swamped my head. I'd seen two dead men in my vision. My vision was coming true. But I didn't know what would happen to Kate, Hilary, and Joe? I hadn't seen them in the vision.

Kate's voice sounded far away as she said, "See? I'm a good shot, too, Hilmonster. We took the same shooting lessons, and if I remember correctly, I always outshot you." She paused, then said more sternly, "Now, why don't you all be good little boys and girls? Put your guns in the basket and come into the circle."

She was planning on killing someone—maybe all of us, which seemed the likeliest scenario.

I felt dangerously close to losing it, but then Joe spoke and I concentrated on his voice. "Kate, just put the gun down and let's you and me talk this out."

"Oh, we're talking, all right. *Lots* of talking, but I need you all to take your places so we can begin."

I wasn't helpless. I still had my small gun in my coat pocket. There was no way I was making the first move to *my place*. Everyone else apparently agreed with me.

Kate pointed her gun toward Sam Teagen and pulled the trigger. The man fell to the ground.

"Just to prove I mean business," she said in a bored tone. "We've eliminated the two unnecessary men in the room, and by order of importance, James Malcolm is the next most expendable person." She gave me a cold hard stare. "How much do you want him to survive this?"

I lifted my hands in the air and moved several steps closer to Kate. She pointed to a spot on the floor, marked with a duct-taped X I hadn't noticed before. There were several Xs in a semi-circle in front of Kate's desk.

"Rose," Skeeter called out. "Don't do it."

Joe gave us a questioning look, but as I moved to the spot about ten feet to Kate's right, she said, "For those of you just joining us, Rose is the Lady in Black, and Hilary hired that idiot—" she pointed at Teagen's body, "—to kidnap and kill Rose and then Mason Deveraux." She sighed. "But thankfully, he flubbed it."

"*Hilary?*" Joe choked out.

Hilary shook her head, and her eyes flooded with tears. "She's lying, Joe. Your sister was the one behind it all. She's crazy. Just look at her." She waved her hand toward Kate.

Joe's gaze swung between the two women, and it was easy to see he believed the mother of his child.

"Joe," I said, trying to keep calm. "Hilary's behind more of this than you could possibly know."

"Stop right there, Hilmonster," Kate called out, her weapon trained on Hilary. "Lose the gun and stand on your spot over here." She gestured to a taped X about ten feet to her left.

Hilary had her gun aimed at me, and the look on her face told me she fully intended to shoot me.

"Don't do it." Kate said, her voice tight. "I need her very much alive."

"Why would I care what you want?"

"Because I can shoot you in the gut and kill the baby that means more than life to you."

That was all Kate needed to say to make Hilary fall in line. Hilary's left hand instinctively covered her small belly, and she tossed her gun into the basket.

"That's good," Kate said in a soothing tone. "You look a little stressed. It's probably not good for the baby. Why don't you wait over there and try to relax?"

Hilary's heels clicked on the floor as she walked to her spot.

That left the three men in the room, all standing on the periphery.

Kate slid off the desk, pointing to an X in the middle of the marks. "This is for the guest of honor. Now who do you think belongs in *that* position?" She looked at her father and laughed. "I bet you think it's for you."

"Stop this absurdity right now, Katherine," J.R. said, sounding vicious. "If you stop, I will lessen my punishment."

"Punishment?" she cried in disbelief. "You think you can punish me anymore than you already have?"

"Is that what this is about?" he asked, hobbling toward her, obviously still in pain from the gunshot wound I gave him a week ago. "Yes, I see the ring on your finger. You are obviously still pouting."

"*Pouting?* You killed my fiancé!"

J.R. released an exasperated sigh. "He was the victim of an unfortunate robbery gone wrong, Katherine. I understand your need to lay blame, but this is unnecessary and pointless."

"And my baby?" she asked. "How do you explain that away, *Daddy*?"

Her baby? I blinked. Surely I'd heard her wrong.

J.R. bristled. "I don't know what you're talking about."

"You knew I was pregnant when I went away. You had someone watching me."

"You shared no such thing with your mother or me."

"I didn't have to," she countered. "You had access to my medical records. You had people watching me. Admit that you knew."

"Katherine," he groaned. "I really—"

She shot the ground at his feet, then screamed hysterically, "*Admit it!*"

A flicker of panic filled his eyes before his mask slipped back into place. "If it makes you feel better," he said, lifting his hands, "I knew."

Kate's eyes filled with tears. "Why? You took Nick from me. Why wasn't it enough to take him? Why did you have to steal my baby, too?"

"Katherine, I didn't—"

"*Liar!*" she shouted at the top of her voice. Then she stomped over to Hilary and grabbed her by the hair, aiming her gun at Hilary's abdomen. "Admit it."

I gasped in panic as I watched the scene unfold before me.

Joe rushed forward, terror on his face, but Kate's face hardened and he came to a stop about ten feet from them. Skeeter was still standing in the back, his hands bound behind him.

"Kate," Joe pleaded. "Stop! I know we've had our differences, but I'm begging you to stop. For me. That's my baby, too."

Kate shook her head. "This isn't your baby."

Joe's eyes widened. "What the hell are you talking about?"

Kate tightened her grip on Hilary's hair. "One thing at a time. I want our father to confess to a few things first."

Joe shot a panicked look at his father.

Kate held her father's gaze. "I killed those two men to prove I mean business," she said. "I *will* shoot her baby. You killed mine. You killed Joe's other baby. I *should* take this one from you."

J.R. held up his hand. "Kate, just calm down."

"What are you talking about?" Joe demanded. "What do you mean he took my other baby?"

He looked over at me, but Kate released a brittle laugh.

"Not her, you idiot. Savannah." She flicked him a glance. "You'll get the details, but you'll have to wait for them. I'm doing this my way." She turned her attention to J.R. "You killed Nick," Kate said in a more even tone. "When he refused to go away for a few hundred thousand dollars, you *made sure* he went away anyway. Forever. Admit it."

J.R. tensed. "He was unsuitable for you."

"Yes," Kate said. "You made that perfectly clear after I told you that we were engaged. But I want you to acknowledge that you *made sure* he went away."

"*Kate,*" J.R. growled.

Kate jerked Hilary's hair, making the redhead cry out in pain, and placed the gun directly on Hilary's stomach this time. "I will kill her baby, and then I will kill James Malcolm, then Rose, then Joe if I have to. I will kill them all until you admit the truth." She gave him a sinister grin. "And I know how much you planned to make Rose and James Malcolm pay for what they did. I will steal that pleasure from you if you don't tell me what I want to know."

Good to know she had my best interests in mind.

"What do you want me to say, Katherine?" J.R. asked, exasperated. "That I had that man killed?"

"*That man* had a name. His name was Nick. He loved me for me, not because I was a Simmons. He loved me in spite of it. You will call him by his name."

Joe's gaze shifted to me, and the misery in his eyes was nearly my undoing. He was thinking of us. Of how I had fallen in love with Joe McAllister before learning that his last name was really Simmons. His father had destroyed everything he had ever loved, so he'd been desperate to keep me away from his family.

"Fine, I had him killed," J.R. said, waving his hand dismissively. "I did it for your own good."

Joe took a step back, stunned.

"And my baby?" Kate asked evenly, as though he'd just read back her fast food order.

He shook his head. "Don't be so dramatic."

"I was in a car accident," she said, her anger rising. "Broadsided by a shiny black sedan. I was conscious until the driver came over to check on me. Then I woke up in the hospital, and they told me that my baby was gone."

"How far along were you?" I asked quietly. I was no fan of Hilary's, but I wasn't about to let Kate kill an innocent baby. I needed to distract her from her plan.

"Exactly as far along as Hilmonster is," she said, looking at me. "I told you I've been waiting two years for this. Not that it's any of your business."

"The fact that I'm here makes it my business."

"Shut up!" she shouted. "I'm talking to my father!" She turned her glare back to him. "You hired that man to hit my car. You had my baby killed. *Admit it.*"

"I swear to God I didn't hire anyone to kill your baby, Kate."

"I don't believe you!"

Kate was coming undone, and I was terrified of what she might do. "What about Savannah?" I asked J.R. "Will you admit to having her killed?"

"What are you talking about?" Joe asked.

J.R. shot me a look of annoyance. "What does it matter to you?"

"You destroyed Joe, but wasn't that the point? To keep him in line?" I asked. "To force him back into his box, so he'd finally accept his fate as the heir to your legacy?"

"She was an inconvenience."

"So you had her killed. You hired Michael Cartwright to kill her. You had the scene set up, making sure she was barely alive when Joe got there."

"*What?*" Joe demanded.

"It's true," Skeeter said from the back of the room. His nose had stopped bleeding, but his shirt and lower face were drenched in blood. "Your father couldn't let Savannah have your baby, so he had her killed to teach you a lesson."

Joe looked at Skeeter with pure hatred. "Did *you* set it up?"

Skeeter arched a brow, and Joe released an ugly laugh.

"I've been doin' my homework," Joe said. "I wanted to know why my father was so desperate to see you dead. I know you worked for him. I've put it all together. I remembered seeing you in our house when I was a kid. You were one of his elusive Twelve."

"I haven't worked for your father for five years, but once I figured out he was makin' a play for me, I started asking questions. Your father is behind Savannah Deveraux's death. And behind movin' her brother here, too."

Joe showed no emotion whatsoever as he turned to face his father. "Is it true?"

J.R. gave him a stern look. "Sometimes we are forced to do the right thing, no matter how difficult the task seems."

Joe's face turned red. *"Killing Savannah and my baby was doing the right thing?"*

"She was the wrong woman for you. The bastard would have scandalized your political aspirations—not to mention you would have felt obligated to marry her. I couldn't let that happen."

"So you had them *killed*?" Joe's gaze swung to me. "And *you* knew?"

"I just found out," I said. "Last week."

"From my father?"

I barely shook my head. "No, from James Malcolm."

"Oh, yes," Joe sneered. "Skeeter Malcolm. You two are such good friends now." He turned his contempt toward Skeeter. "You got tired of strippers, so you moved on to my old girlfriend?" he snorted. "And the D.A.'s girlfriend, too. Quite the coup for a piece of Fenton County white trash. Was this a big F-you to Fenton County law enforcement?"

"Joe!" I shouted. "What are you *doin'*?"

Joe's chest rose and fell, but he didn't argue.

"Skeeter Malcolm is *not* your enemy. *Your father* killed Savannah. He killed Kate's fiancé. Your beef is with *him*. Not Skeeter."

But my intervention only encouraged Joe to redirect his anger to me. "Did you break up with Mason so you could move on with Skeeter?"

I gaped at him.

"You're the Lady in Black. There's no way Skeeter Malcolm would work with a woman he's not sleepin' with."

A low growl rumbled in Skeeter's chest. "Shut your mouth, Joe Simmons. I've never laid a hand on her."

J.R. laughed. "But you want to. James Malcolm finally loves a woman, and the irony is he can't have her. It'll only make it that much more bittersweet when you watch me kill her."

That seemed to knock some sense into Joe. He shook his head. "Nobody's killing anyone."

"Wrong," Kate said. "So wrong." She released a sigh. "But the best part of tonight isn't here yet."

"She's not comin'," I said, my stomach twisting into knots. "Just leave her out of this."

"Who?" Joe asked.

Kate smiled. "Neely Kate—and I'd tell you why, but that would ruin the surprise."

"I'm damn fed up with surprises," Joe said.

"That's too bad," my best friend called out from the dark. "This is the best surprise of all."

Chapter Thirty-Three

N eely Kate!" I shouted. "Go! Get out of here."

"Can't," she called out, her voice echoing off the metal equipment as she lingered in the shadows. "I'm just as much a part of this as you are."

The look on Skeeter's face told me he knew she'd been waiting out there, which meant Jed was probably on the premises, too.

Joe's gaze shot from me to Kate and then to his father. "Why is Neely Kate part of this?"

"I have a story," Kate said in a singsong voice. "A true story from twenty-five years ago."

"The factory fire?" Joe asked.

"That's part of it," Kate said.

She released Hilary's hair, giving her a shove for good measure, and returned to her perch on the desk. She scanned the dark factory as she talked, continuing to shoot glances at her captive audience.

"Once upon a time," she began, "there was a king who ruled his own kingdom—and what a kingdom it was. But it wasn't enough. He wanted more, as most kings do. So he promised the lowly king of another kingdom an abundance of riches if he abdicated and became a loyal subject. The king of Fenton County—Allen Steyer—reluctantly agreed. The new king set up shop in a nearly bankrupt manufacturing plant and then manipulated and bribed his way into more riches. But when things began to go wrong, the king used the men at his disposal to threaten the owner and the bookkeeper. While the manufacturing plant owner was easily controlled, the bookkeeper was harder to keep in line." Kate gave me a wistful smile. "Like mother like daughter, they say." She gave a little shrug. "The bookkeeper kept several detailed journals filled with evidence of the king's wrongdoing, and word got back to the king that she had enough evidence to bring him down. He told the deposed king—now one of twelve knights at his twisted roundtable—to get the evidence . . . or else." She tilted her head to the side. "In the meantime, the king liked to visit his new land, especially since a pretty young peasant girl had caught his eye. The king had the knight set up a place for the king and his concubine to shack up. You see . . ." she drawled, "the king has a thing for teenagers." She winked at her father and then turned to Hilary. "But you know that from firsthand experience."

Hilary's face turned white. "What are you talking about?"

"Don't be so coy, Hil," Kate teased. "I *saw* you years ago."

Joe shook his head slightly, his eyes wide. "Saw her doing what?" he asked, fear edging his voice.

Kate pointed at him with her free hand and gave him a wicked grin. "Exactly where your mind just went."

"*You slept with my father?*"

The terrified woman I'd seen at Jonah's church this morning was back. Tears filled her eyes. "I . . ."

"Joseph, enough," his father barked. "This entire conversation—let alone situation—is preposterous."

"We'll circle back to that in a bit," Kate said, making a circular motion with her finger. "First we need to finish this story." She turned to look at Joe. "Who knew one little decision—trying to take over a manufacturing plant—could produce so many ripples?"

"How is Neely Kate part of this?" Joe asked, his voice strained.

Kate tsked. "So impatient." Then she shifted on the desk. "The king was very fond of his latest pet. He visited her often. But the pet was careless in many ways. For one thing, she was quite a nosy girl. The king had her holed up in his apartment when the knight came to bring bad news. Try as the knight might, the bookkeeper could not be swayed to hand over her evidence. The king had been having a very bad day, and while the poor girl had already taken the brunt of his frustration with both his fists and his favorite appendage, he lost his temper at the news. The king shot the knight, leaving him to die on the wool rug."

J.R.'s face had turned a pale crimson, and he looked desperate enough to physically make his daughter stop.

"The girl wisely kept her mouth shut, especially since she had recently discovered she was pregnant."

J.R.'s mouth parted, and Joe gave his head a tiny shake, blurting out, "What?"

"The peasant girl was terrified, so she stole the gun and ran away, never letting the king know about her baby. Seven months later, she gave birth to a baby girl." A mocking grin spread across Kate's face as she tilted her head toward Joe. "*Surprise. We have a half-sister.* But even more importantly—" she pointed the gun at J.R., "—we have the gun our father used to kill Allen Steyer twenty-five years ago."

"That is enough, Kate," J.R. barked, slowly losing his cool. "We are Simmonses. Simmonses stick together."

"Then Neely Kate needs to come out here and join us."

"Why?" Joe asked, but the realization grew in his eyes.

Neely Kate walked out of the darkness close to the windows, her eyes steely. "I'm not a Simmons."

"I'm sure your DNA says differently," Kate drawled. "Your mother was smart to leave. She knew our father would have killed her when he found out about the baby. No loose ends."

J.R. looked like he was close to blowing his stack. "I've heard enough, Katherine. You are done."

"I'm the one with the gun," she said waving it in his direction. "*I'm* the one who says when I'm done. You can't control me anymore."

I took a step back, bumping into a candle-covered desk.

J.R. released a low growl. "So what's your purpose with this little show? Are you trying to embarrass me? Because you're currently the embarrassment."

"Embarrass you?" she spat out. "And don't you pretend to care about me. I was nothing to you! If anything, you were so smitten with Hilary you hardly paid any attention to me. Even when we were kids."

"He wasn't smitten with me," Hilary said, looking at J.R. with tears in her eyes. "He raped me in the name of teaching me how to hold on to Joe."

The horror of it all stole my breath. I had known for some time that J.R. Simmons was an evil person, but this . . .

"My God," Joe said in an agonized voice. "Is that true?"

His father wisely kept his mouth shut.

Hilary started to cry. "I was seventeen. We were juniors. You were supposed to be in love with me, but you kept screwing other girls. He said if I learned how to please you, you'd stay with me."

Joe put a hand on his stomach, looking like he was going to vomit.

"He told me once you settled down with me, he'd leave me alone. But Roberta saw me coming out of his office that first night . . ." She wiped her face. "I went home and locked myself in my room, planning to run away Monday morning when everyone thought I was at school. It would have given me an eight-hour head start." She started to sob. "But then you came over, and you had that note from your father . . . J.R. said if I didn't cooperate, he'd accuse Roberta of stealing from the family. He threatened to have her arrested." She shook her head. "I loved her, Joe. I couldn't let him do that."

"Oh, God," Joe forced out. "We had sex that day. I thought you were a virgin . . ."

Hilary began to sob. "I was desperate to make J.R. stop. I thought he'd stop if I had sex with you. But he didn't. He didn't stop until much later."

Joe's chest rose and fell rapidly. His gaze lowered to her rounded abdomen. "Is it . . . ?"

"It's yours," she said. "I swear it. He told me I had to make you marry me. It was his idea for me to get pregnant, but he insisted the baby had to be yours."

"Are you sure?" Kate asked in an amused voice.

"Oh, my God," Hilary spat out, turning to face her. "You call me a monster, yet you're the one who's enjoying this horror show. What does that make *you*?"

"Unsatisfied."

"Maybe this will help," J.R. sneered, and the sound of gunfire burst in my ears. "Is this what you wanted, Kate?"

I dropped to a crouch—we all did—and a red stain began to blossom across Hilary's chest as she fell to the ground. I cast a glance toward Skeeter, but J.R. stood between us.

I screamed as I heard another gun shot.

Skeeter squatted and shoved his hands against the back of his legs, breaking the zip-tie. Then he ran for Neely Kate who stood a few feet from him at the edge of the equipment.

Joe leaned over Hilary's body, grabbing her wrist to feel for a pulse.

Kate sat on the desk and laughed.

But Joe ignored her and pulled out his cell phone, starting to make a call.

"Drop it," J.R. said, pointing his gun at Joe.

"What are you going to do?" Joe asked, getting to his feet, then taking a step toward him. "*Are you going to shoot me?* Go ahead and do it! You've taken everything else."

"Not yet." J.R. lunged and grabbed my arm, pulling me toward him and putting the gun to my temple.

"Call 911, Joe," I said, surprised I felt so calm. "You need to get an ambulance for Hilary."

He looked at me with a blank expression. "She's already dead."

Grief washed over me like a tidal wave, making my knees weak. He'd lost another baby. My gaze turned to Hilary, her hand covering her stomach, protecting her baby even in death. She'd never stood a chance with her upbringing and considering what J.R. had done to her . . . what he had turned her into.

J.R. didn't seem to notice the desperation around him, or perhaps he just thrived on it. "That was unfortunate, but she'd proved herself incompetent time and time again, not to mention she was warned to keep her mouth shut. Why won't people listen to me?" He looked over and realized Skeeter was gone. A wry grin lifted his lips. "Malcolm left you? That's an unexpected surprise. No matter. You'll do for now."

He placed me between himself and the dark factory as he started to limp toward the window.

"Where the hell do you think *you're* going?" Joe snarled.

"Rose and I have unfinished business," J.R. said as he continued toward the window. I let him lead me, too overwhelmed by the sight of Hilary's now mostly red shirt.

So much death. So much destruction.

Kate was not amused. She hopped off the desk. "This is *my* party, and it isn't over yet."

"That's your problem, Kate," J.R. said. "You never know when to let something go."

Joe suddenly dove for the gun I'd kicked toward Hilary. He rose to a squat, pointing the weapon at his father's head. But

J.R. viciously shoved his gun into my temple, making me cry out in pain.

"Stay back," J.R. said. "Or I'll make her suffer even more."

"Shoot him, Joe," I pleaded. "Even if you miss and hit me, I'd rather die here than let him do what he has planned."

"You're not dying tonight," Joe said. *"No one else is dying tonight."*

"Maybe one more person," Skeeter called out before I heard another gun shot.

But J.R. had already ducked behind me, and the bullet zipped over my shoulder. Before I knew it, J.R. was on the move again, tugging me toward Henry Buchanan's office. A new terror filled my head. If he got me in that room and locked the door, I knew I would wish I were dead.

I tried to kick him with my heel, but he stood far enough behind me to avoid contact. Grabbing a handful of my hair, he pulled me backward, using me as a human shield.

When he reached for the doorknob with the hand holding the gun, I decided it was time to try another escape. As if he could read my mind, he gave my hair a vicious jerk.

I tried to drop to my knees to avoid being pulled into the office, but his hold on my hair kept me upright. Once we were clear of the door, he shoved me hard into Henry Buchanan's office. He slammed the door, plunging us into darkness, and I heard the click of the lock.

How was I going to get away from this maniac? Then it hit me. I could hide in the closet to buy myself some time. I had the advantage of knowing the layout of the room, and I'd bet money that J.R. hadn't been in here for years, if ever. The factory had no electricity, so I could use the lack of lighting to my advantage. At least until he pulled out his phone and turned on the flashlight.

As quietly as possible, I groped for the closet doorknob. Within seconds, I had closed myself inside of it. With any luck, he hadn't heard me—there was enough of a racket outside the office door to cover any smaller sounds. The problem was that I didn't know how to lock the closet door from the inside.

I took a step deeper into the closet, bumping into something in front of me—something that felt like a person. Terrified, I pulled my phone out of my jeans pocket and turned on the screen to produce a low glow. I gasped when I discovered Mason bound to an office chair with duct tape, his mouth taped shut. His eyes widened when he saw me.

"Mason," I whispered in shock as I ripped the tape from his face.

"Rose, you have to get out of here," he whispered, his eyes wild. "There's a bomb."

"*What?*"

"Kate set up a bomb. It was her grand finale. Go!"

I heard J.R. cursing and metal scraping the floor in the other room, as well as the muffled shouting in the warehouse.

"I can't," I whispered, setting the phone on a shelf before squatting in front of him to work on the tape restraining his right wrist to the chair. "J.R.'s in the other room looking for me—he'll be here any second. How'd *you* get here?"

"Kate," he whispered. "I was about to head to my meeting with the state police when she called. She said that you were in trouble here at the factory and that we couldn't involve the police. She picked me up and brought me here."

Which is why I didn't see his car.

"Once we got here, I figured out you weren't here—yet. She hit me over the head in the closet, and when I woke up, she was putting the finishing touches on my duct tape. She told me that I was going to be part of the *explosive* big finale. Then she closed me in here. She has enough explosives to blow this whole place up."

Great.

The sounds in the office abruptly stopped, and my heart hurt from beating so hard.

"Rose?" J.R. called playfully on the other side of the door. "Where are you?"

I tried to work faster, but Kate had gone crazy with the duct tape. "We have to hurry." I was on the last layer. "I still have a gun in my coat—"

As if by some cosmic joke, the door opened to reveal J.R., a wicked gleam in his eyes. A light behind him produced a glow that made him look like an angel.

The angel of death.

I gave one last tug on Mason's tape, then stood and faced the monster.

"Well, isn't this a surprise? Mr. Deveraux. I planned on inviting you to my own meeting, but I had no idea you were invited to this one."

"I'm just the life of the party," Mason said dryly.

One side of J.R.'s mouth quirked up. "Not for long."

I moved to shield Mason's body, hopefully hiding the fact that his right hand was now free. "He's not part of this."

"As Kate so eloquently said about Neely Kate, Mason Deveraux is very much a part of it. But I'll deal with *you* first."

I put my hand in my coat pocket, intending to pull out my gun, but it caught on the edge of the seam. J.R. grabbed my left arm and dragged me out of the closet before I could pull it free. He spun me around and I stumbled, my right hand reaching for something to brace myself against my impending fall. But he held me upright and slapped me, and his left palm connecting with my cheek with more force than I could have expected. My body slumped as bright white lights filled my vision.

"Rose!" Mason shouted behind me. "Leave her alone, Simmons! I was the one who filed charges against you. I was the one who came up with a plan to put you away forever. If you want to punish someone, punish me."

"Not to worry," J.R. said good-naturedly. "You're next." Then he slapped me again.

I fell to the floor this time, my ears ringing. The shouting and noise on the other side of the door dimmed. Even Mason's shouting faded as J.R. hit me several more times, using his fists this time. An inky blackness hung at the end of my vision, and I knew I was about to pass out, which would mean certain death. And then he would win.

Again.

But I refused. I refused to let him hurt the people I loved. I refused to let him hurt anyone else. Ever. I never questioned if I would live. My only goal was to get the gun out of my pocket and stop him. To end this.

Only I couldn't even reach my pocket, let alone get out the gun. He was holding my right arm, using it to keep me in place as he hit me with his right fist. Then he laughed and released his hold as I fell to the floor, face-first.

I wasn't prepared for the first kick to my ribs. Nor even the second. I started to crawl toward the door, all my thoughts bent on escape.

A loud noise shook the building, and pieces of the ceiling rained down upon us. But if J.R. was worried, he didn't let it show. He acted as though he had all the time in the world. Grabbing me by the arm again, he hauled me to my feet, even though my rubbery legs refused to hold me up.

Fight, something deep within me screamed. *Fight*.

I clung to it.

He released my arm and grabbed my hair to hold me in place, leaning his face so close to mine I worried he was going to kiss me. Instead, he laughed. "Not so pretty now. And not so tough. You're all talk, Rose Gardner, but don't feel too badly. Most people are."

My anger exploded.

I spat blood and saliva in his face, and then I grabbed his arm holding my hair as I kneed him in the thigh where I'd shot him the week before.

He shouted and released me, stumbling backward and landing on the floor in front of the office door. He clutched his leg, cursing.

With my escape blocked, I tried to reach for the gun, but my hand was too shaky to get the gun out of my pocket. I scrambled into the closet, praying that Mason was close to getting himself loose from the chair and could help.

Horror filled his eyes when he saw me. I could only imagine what I looked like.

"Oh, my God. *Rose.*"

I shook my head, which felt like it had been driven through with a spike. My intention was to help him get his legs free now that both his hands were unbound, but nausea washed over me and I threw up.

"Rose!" Mason shouted in warning, so I wasn't surprised when J.R. grabbed the back of my coat and started to pull me backward. My shirt slid up as I scooted across the floor.

Smoke filled my nose, and I looked back to see white wisps of smoke floating in under the door. If J.R. didn't kill me, the fire would.

I made a last-ditch effort to get my hand into my pocket. I made it this time, but getting the gun out took more coordination than I currently possessed.

J.R. rolled me over onto my back, pure happiness shining in his eyes. "I knew you'd be a fighter."

I heard gunshots on the other side of the door, but while a distant part of my mind wondered if Kate had shot someone else, I couldn't think about that right now. My mind was a jumble of thoughts I could barely put together. I had to accept that the gun wasn't coming out of my pocket. But that didn't mean I couldn't shoot him through my coat.

"You won't win this time," I said, hoping he understood the words in spite of my swollen lips. I started to get up but couldn't find the energy. "I'm stopping you, J.R. You won't hurt anyone ever again."

"Those are big words for someone who's about to die."

"If you're gonna finish me off, do it with your bare hands. I don't think you have it in you."

He grabbed the front of my coat and lifted me to my feet, shoving my back to the wall. I let out a grunt as I hit, just before his hand tightened around my throat.

My hand was still in my pocket, but my mind was already addled, and the lack of oxygen wasn't helping. I wasn't sure where the tip of the gun was pointed. For all I knew, it was aimed at my feet. But if I didn't shoot soon, I'd pass out from a lack of oxygen.

I twisted my wrist and angled it upward, hoping I wasn't pointing it at my own head. Just as my vision started to fade, I squeezed the trigger, thankful I didn't feel the sting of a bullet— but J.R.'s grip didn't loosen.

More gunshots rang out in the factory, sounding closer than before. I squeezed the trigger again just as the door burst open.

Smoke billowed in from the outer room, and a dark figure entered with it, but I couldn't see a face. Then again, I couldn't see much of anything anyway.

More gunshots filled the room, which surprised me because I was pretty sure I hadn't pulled the trigger of my gun.

Then Mason burst from the closet, tackling J.R. to the ground. Mason stayed down with him, repeatedly punching him as I slid to the floor.

"Deveraux, we have to go," Skeeter shouted above a roar. "This whole place is going up." He was next to me in seconds, looking me over. "I'm going to get you out of here."

I nodded, starting to sob.

"Deveraux!" Skeeter shouted, about to scoop me into his arms.

Mason climbed to his feet, but when he leaned over to haul J.R. up, another gunshot rang out. Mason's body slumped sideways and he fell to the floor as J.R. climbed to his feet, holding his gun. His smile was wobbly as he took a step backward.

"*Mason!*" I screamed.

Skeeter pushed me down and then stood, shielding me with his body as best he could, his gun trained on his old mentor. But there was no way to shield every part of me. I was a sitting duck.

"It's over, J.R.," Skeeter said. "Just give it up."

"I taught you better than that, boy," J.R. sneered, pointing his gun in my direction. "I taught you to never give up."

"You taught me a lot of things that I should have never listened to, but I'm tellin' you now. Give it up. You'll never get out of here alive."

"You'll make sure of that, won't you?" J.R. taunted, then coughed.

"I think we can reach some sort of compromise. A trade."

Mason was still lying on the floor, not moving. I swallowed my rising terror and the urge to crawl over to him. To do so would compromise Skeeter's safety as well as Mason's. I had to wait this out.

"What kind of trade?" J.R. coughed again and placed his hand to his chest, which I realized was covered in blood. His? Mason's? Both?

"I'll let you walk out of here without any further injuries if you agree to leave without hurting anyone else."

J.R. laughed. "You think I'm going to trust you?"

Skeeter rose to his full height. "I give you my word."

"Your *word*?" J.R. shook his head in contempt. "Since when did James Malcolm give his *word*?"

Skeeter remained still. "I've changed, Simmons."

"You've gotten soft."

"No, I've found something worth fighting for."

"Her?" J.R. scoffed. "Why is she so special?"

"She's taught me that life is meaningless without people to share it with."

J.R. laughed, then began to cough. "Fine. Be a pansy. The old James Malcolm would have shot me already, to hell with everyone else. I'm glad you don't work for me. I can't stomach the sight of you."

Skeeter barely flinched, the only visible sign that J.R. had gotten to him.

J.R. took a step back. "If that's the way you want it, I'll back out of here and leave you be, but if you follow"—he waved his gun between us — "I'll hunt you both down and make you wish I'd killed you this time."

Skeeter's body tensed, but he nodded. "I can live with that."

"I can't," Joe said out of nowhere, his body filling the doorway.

A gunshot went off and J.R. fell to the floor in a heap. Joe stomped over and stood over his father's body, then pulled the trigger one more time.

"Simmons!" Skeeter shouted. "Deveraux's been shot!"

Both men knelt beside Mason's unmoving body, and I felt my consciousness slipping away.

No!

I had to make sure Mason was okay. But my eyes burned and my chest felt tight. As much as I tried, I could barely keep my eyes open, even when Joe picked me up, cradling me to his chest as he strode through the smoke-filled building. A section of roof over the factory equipment collapsed with a loud crash, and the last thing I remembered was the cold night air as Joe passed me off to someone else.

Chapter Thirty-Four

I woke up to an irritating, continuous beeping noise. My eyes were too heavy to open, so I blindly reached to turn off my alarm, but something tugged on my hand. Terror sent my heart racing, making the beeping noise increase.

J.R. had caught me.

I bolted upright, gasping in fear, but confusion settled in as I took in my surroundings and registered the shooting pain in my side. I was in a hospital room. There was an IV in my arm, and I could feel something wrapped tight around my chest under the hospital gown I was wearing.

"You're okay," Neely Kate said in a soothing voice, lightly stroking my arm. "You're safe."

I turned to look at her, starting to cry even though I wasn't sure why. "What happened?"

"Joe and Skeeter got you out just in time. The building collapsed seconds later." Tears filled her eyes. "I've never been so scared in my life."

I tried to shake my head, but pain shot through my skull. I pressed my fingers to my temple, trying to ease the ache as well as shake my memories loose. "I'm forgetting something. Something important."

Worry filled her eyes. "You have a bad concussion, Rose. The doctor said memory loss is normal. It should all come back."

"No. There's something else. Something I need to remember."

She gently pushed me back to the bed. "You *need* to lie still. You have broken ribs and a concussion. You *need* to rest."

"Violet!" I cried out, sitting up again and gasping from multiple sources of agony. "She was leaving today! Is it today?"

A soft smile spread across her face. "Yes, it's the morning that Violet is leaving, but she hasn't left yet. She's with your Aunt Bessie on her farm in Lafayette County. Joe said he suspected something big was happening last night, so he moved Violet and the kids to your aunt's farm." She pushed me back again. "*Now lie down.*"

The nurse came in to check my vital signs and my IV, then she unhooked my heart monitor now that I was awake.

When she opened the door to leave, Jed walked in. There was a scowl on his face, but it vanished as soon as he saw me sitting up in bed. "She's awake."

"And stubborn and uncooperative," Neely Kate said, pushing me back again.

"So she's completely back to her old self?" he teased.

"Very funny," I grumbled.

He moved to the other side of my bed, looking me over. "You scared the shit out of us, Rose."

"She doesn't remember everything," Neely Kate said softly, looking into his face. "She's forgotten what happened at the end."

They looked at each other for a quick moment, but that glance conveyed some secret message.

"What's goin' on?" I asked, getting suspicious.

"Rose, you need to get your rest."

"I've been resting. What time is?" I looked around for a clock, gasping when I saw the time. "*Ten in the morning?* Apparently I've gotten a *lot* of rest." Still, I couldn't ignore the fact that they were hiding something from me. "Where's James?"

"Why do you call him that?" Neely Kate asked in a blatant attempt to change the subject.

"Because it's his name. Now where is he?"

Jed shifted his weight. "No one's been allowed to call him that since we were kids. With the exception of J.R. Simmons."

"Yeah, and I know why, which is exactly the reason I use his given name." I grabbed a handful of Jed's shirt and pulled him closer. "Now where is he?"

Jed gently unfurled my fingers, then fanned his hand in front of his face. "You know I'm fond of you, Rose, but that has got to be the rankest breath I have ever smelled."

"Where is he?" I asked again, my anxiety rising.

"Rose, calm down," Neely Kate said softly. "He's giving his statement to the state police. Backing up Joe's story."

"What story?"

They exchanged looks again.

"Where's Joe?"

"He's dealin' with his crazy-ass sister," Neely Kate grinned. "Kate's just gonna make him appreciate me all the more."

I closed my eyes, trying to remember what happened the night before. "Kate . . . she shot two men."

"Yes." Her voice was so quiet I could barely hear her.

What were they keeping from me? Now I really needed to remember. Another image hit me.

"Hilary." My eyes flew open in a panic as I searched Neely Kate's face. "She's dead."

She nodded.

"Joe? Is he okay?"

Neely Kate paused. "He's a mess, but he's holding it together. At least for now."

I could only imagine the pain he was going through. Tears filled my eyes.

"What about James?" I asked. She'd said he was giving his statement to the state police. That was two encounters with the law in the past two weeks. With his record, that couldn't look good.

"Skeeter's fine. He's not in trouble. He's merely giving his statement."

I searched my exhausted and slow-to-react brain, trying to remember who else had been there the night before. "J.R.? What happened to him?"

They both tensed.

"He was shot," Jed said. "By Joe."

"Is he in the hospital?"

"No," Neely Kate said. "He's in the morgue."

Maybe it was wrong to feel this relieved by someone's death, but J.R. Simmons had been an evil man through and through. I doubted anyone would mourn him.

"Hey," I said, suddenly remembering Kate's retelling of J.R.'s involvement in Fenton County. "How did Kate know all those things about the past?"

"She found my mother," Neely Kate said. "And she threatened to hurt me if my mother didn't confess everything."

"So she did?"

"Yeah."

I knew my best friend had to have mixed emotions about that. Her mother had abandoned her when she was twelve, and she hadn't seen her since. She'd never come out and said the actual words, but I knew Neely Kate questioned if Jenny Lynn loved her. This was pretty compelling evidence.

"Momma told Kate that she'd left the gun with Granny."

I let that soak in for a moment. "Who were Sam Teagen and his friend really working for?"

"Don't you want to rest?"

"No. I want you to answer the question."

"Kate says that Hilary was the one spying on you and Mason," Neely Kate said. "She found that stack of paperwork when she dropped in on Hilary one day to annoy her. So she snuck in a few days later and stole it all. After you told Joe about it, Kate moved it up to the shed. Teagen saw her do it, so he got a locksmith friend to make him a key. Marshal was arrested outside the warehouse, and he's confirmed Kate's story. He said they'd sneak into her apartment and the shed every few days to see if she'd found something new. That's how they discovered Anna. Kate had searched her out, looking for answers."

"Oh!" I gasped. "Bruce Wayne and Anna!"

"Were tied up in Hilary's house. They were about to warn Joe, so she had Teagen stop them."

"They're okay?"

She nodded. "They're fine. I promise."

"Why was Anna here?"

"Anna had no idea why her grandmother left, but Kate's visit made her realize there was more to it than she knew. So she moved to Henryetta, hoping to get answers. She knew Joe was part owner of the nursery, so she asked for a job with the goal of getting close to him and discovering the truth."

"So why did she hate me?"

"She didn't hate you. She was scared to death of you. She knew you had visions, and she was worried you'd figure out what she was doing here."

I wasn't sure I bought that, but I didn't feel up to arguing the point.

"Was Kate pregnant? Did her baby really die?"

"Yeah, and even though J.R. said he had nothing to do with the accident, Joe says it's pretty fishy."

"So what happens to her now?"

"She obviously has mental health issues, so they've put her in the psych ward for an evaluation."

"I'm still forgetting something . . ." I squeezed my eyes tight. "What am I forgetting?" And then it all rushed back and my chest tightened, sending a shooting pain through my side. "*Mason* . . . is he. . . ?"

Neely Kate grabbed my hand and squeezed so tight I worried she'd crush my bones. "No. He's alive, but he's hurt bad."

I sucked in a breath and nodded slightly. I needed to keep control until I knew all the facts.

"J.R. shot him in the liver. Up close with a powerful gun. It did a lot of damage. Mason was in the ICU after surgery, but he started bleeding again, so they took him back. The doctors were telling Maeve to prepare herself for the worst."

"Maeve!" I gasped, sitting up again. "She's all alone!"

"No, Rose. She has so many people who love her. You wouldn't believe how many of them are with her now."

I lay back on the pillow, tears streaking down my face. "It's my fault."

"You really *are* a narcissist," Carter Hale said from the doorway. "Takin' ownership of the terrors created by a maniac."

Carter turned to Jed. "Skeeter's done with his questioning, and the state police sent him home with the warning that they are watchin' him extra closely now. Do your best to keep him on the straight and narrow." He paused and a cocky grin lit up his face. "Or at least cover your tracks really well."

Jed nodded, but he cracked a grin, too.

Carter turned to Neely Kate. "As for your wayward husband, there's still no sign of him. They caught Al Moberly, the guy he worked with at the garage, and he swears he has no idea where Ronnie is. The rumor mill says he left town, but there's no word as to where. I've got another guy workin' on it. Hopefully he'll have better results than the first one." He winked at me.

Neely Kate didn't seem to notice. "Thanks."

"As for you, Ms. Gardner. You are free and clear, with no threats hangin' over your head . . . for now. But you know how to reach me should the need arise. Which I am positive it will."

"I'll program your cell number into my phone."

He grinned. "No need. Just use my bat signal."

Neely Kate rolled her eyes and pushed him out the door, but she didn't come back in right away.

"How long has Mason been in surgery?" I asked Jed.

He looked into my eyes. "Several hours. It doesn't look good."

I told myself not to cry. No use borrowing trouble until it came calling, but my eyes refused to listen.

Neely Kate came back moments later and fussed over me, calling the nurse to change my IV bag so I didn't get dehydrated.

Jed stayed with us, but it took Neely Kate some convincing to get him to sit inside my room instead of standing guard outside the door. At least he could watch the *Price Is Right* instead of staring at the wall. Then they got into a semi-argument over the price of a can of pork and beans.

And I still waited for word on Mason.

A half hour later, Neely Kate and Jed were on their second episode, bickering over the price of a ski boat in the showcase.

I couldn't take it anymore. "I'm going to check on Maeve."

"You can't," Neely Kate protested.

"Watch me." I slid my feet over the side of the bed and nearly fell when my legs turned to rubber and the room swam. I fought a round of nausea.

Neely Kate tried to push me back into bed, but when she realized I was so intent on doing this that I'd crawl if need be, she insisted that I at least ride in a wheelchair. I refused. I didn't want Maeve to see me acting like an invalid because of a bunch of scrapes and bruises. Not while her only living child was in surgery.

Neely Kate grabbed another hospital gown to use as a robe so my booty wasn't flashing the world, and the three of us slowly hobbled down the hall and up one floor by the elevator to the surgery waiting room. Everything was spinning and I felt close to throwing up, so I clutched my IV pole for dear life. Neely Kate held onto my left arm, and Jed gripped my right elbow. He took most of my weight, keeping me upright and on course until we reached the entrance to the waiting room.

I stopped and gasped.

The room was overflowing. Jonah and Jessica, Bruce Wayne and Anna, Miss Mildred, and at least twenty other people sat around Maeve like she was their queen.

"You're almost there," Neely Kate said, giving me a little push. "I'm sure someone will give up their seat for you."

"I can't," I whispered, realizing what a bad idea this was. "I can't face her. What if she hates me? I don't think I can stand it."

"Why would she hate you?" Neely Kate asked in disbelief.

"Because I did this to her son." Despite what Carter had said to me, I knew it was true. Someone else might have pulled the trigger, but Mason would never have been there if not for me.

"No. *J.R.* did this to her son," Neely Kate insisted.

Deep in my heart, I knew Maeve would never blame me. It was my own guilt holding me back.

I was about to turn around and leave, but Maeve glanced up and noticed me. She slowly got to her feet, and the people around her parted, making a path. I remained frozen in place, scared to death of how she'd react.

When she stopped in front of me, she gently cupped my neck.

"Thank God you're okay," she said.

"Mason . . ." My voice broke off into tears.

"He's still in surgery. We're waiting."

I nodded, which sent a new wave of pain through my head and a tsunami of nausea through my gut.

"No offense, my dear, but you look terrible," she said. Though her eyes were shiny with tears, she was grinning.

Most of the people in the waiting room were openly gawking at me, and it occurred to me that my face was undoubtedly a mess. Neely Kate had moved in front of any reflective surfaces during our ten-minute trek, so I had no idea what I looked like.

"Come sit down," Maeve said, taking my hand.

"I can't," I said. "It's not right. It's my fault he's in there."

"No." Her eyes turned stormy. "He's in there because a very bad man shot him." She took a breath. "That lovely Mr. Malcolm came to see me. He told me how Mason attacked J.R. Simmons to save you. Joe told me that Mr. Malcolm was the man who carried Mason out of the building before it collapsed." She looked deep into my eyes. "You are not to blame."

Skeeter had saved Mason without being coerced. He really had changed.

I looked at Maeve and considered forcing a vision to see if Mason would survive, but I was too chicken to see the future. If I saw his death, I'd have no idea how to change it. Maybe Jed was right. Maybe sometimes you just needed to accept fate.

A murmur swept through the group as a man in surgical scrubs appeared at the opposite end of the room.

My heart stuttered with fear. I gave Maeve a tiny push. "Go. It will take me forever to get over there. I'll catch up."

The older woman looked torn, but she crossed the room toward the doctor. Jonah met her halfway. The doctor talked to her for a few seconds before Maeve's legs buckled. Jonah and the doctor led her to a chair someone had vacated.

I felt lightheaded, but I stayed on my feet. I had to know.

I had to hear the words.

But then Jonah stood and looked around the room. "He's okay. He's going to be okay."

That was all I needed to hear.

Everything went black and the next thing I knew, I was back in my bed, Neely Kate hovering over me like a momma duck.

"I'm fine, Neely Kate."

"You just passed out for fifteen minutes. You are *not* fine." Fear filled her eyes.

I grabbed her hand and stroked her knuckles and stared into her face. "I'm not goin' anywhere."

"Who said you were?"

"You're stuck with me for a good fifty years."

"Fifty?" she scoffed. "I was thinking more like seventy years. We'll be past ninety, wearing those purple dresses and red hats." Then she scrunched up her nose. "Although I look terrible in purple. It makes me look washed out."

I grinned. "Then we'll start our own red hat club. We can wear pink dresses. You look great in pink."

"I do," she said. "It makes my skin glow."

My smile fell. Seeing Maeve's terrified face had taken a lot out of me. "I want to see Mason."

Neely Kate turned serious. "He's still in ICU, but Maeve said they expect him to be moved to a regular room tomorrow." She paused. "You'll still be here. After your faintin' episode, they want to keep you another night for observation."

Violet came to see me in the early afternoon, holding an envelope. Neely Kate stood to leave, declaring she was going to grab some lunch.

I'd been dozing, but I forced myself awake, a task more difficult than it should have been. "I'm sorry I didn't come to see you this morning."

Violet laughed despite the tears in her eyes. "You have an excuse this time. Besides, I wasn't even home. I just got back into town."

"What's in the envelope?"

"Your test results."

I sucked in a breath. "Am I a match?"

"I don't know. I didn't open it. Technically, they're your results. You're supposed to be the one to open them."

I took the envelope, looking at the seal. "You didn't peek."

"No."

I grinned. "Wonders never cease." The old Violet wouldn't have hesitated to check it out.

"I was too scared."

I chuckled, then winced as pain shot through my head. So maybe she hadn't completely changed, and I was okay with that.

"Will your face scar?" Violet asked.

I gingerly touched a swollen cheek. "Neely Kate says they took X-rays while I was out and nothing's broken. It's just swelling. They told her it will go down."

She grabbed my hand, looking serious. "I just want you to know that no matter what the results say, you're still my sister. And I will love you even if you look like Quasimodo. I might even allow myself to be seen in public with you every once in a while." Then she cracked a grin. "But only at Walmart. Or the Chuck and Cluck. And only after dark."

I burst out laughing, then instantly regretted it. I closed my eyes and waited for the room to stop spinning. "Why, Violet Beauregard, you just made a joke."

"A bad one, but I'm trying."

I cracked my eyes open.

"Life's too short to waste it," she said. "I know you learned that lesson last June." She grinned. "But we both know I'm slow to catch on."

I handed the envelope back to her. "Open it. I can't read anything with my double vision. You read it and tell me what it says."

"Are you sure?"

"Yeah."

I tried to watch her, but I was getting nauseated from the effort of keeping an eye on the both of her. I closed my eyes for a moment to let them rest, then forced them open when I heard her gasp.

"What?" I asked, watching her through cracked eyelids. "What does it say?"

Tears streamed down her face. "We're sisters."

"I know that already," I said impatiently. "I want to know if we're a match."

She nodded, her chin quivering. "Yes. We're a match. It's truly a miracle."

"Oh, thank God," I said, dangerously close to tears again. "When can I donate?"

"Obviously not now. Even if you *were* ready," she said. "I need to go through several rounds of chemo and radiation. You can donate once they've killed everything off."

I wished she hadn't used the words *killed off*, but I focused on the positive. "So a few months?"

She nodded.

"I'll be waiting."

My eyes drifted shut again, but I heard Violet whisper in my ear, "I love you, Rose."

The sun was setting when I woke up next. Skeeter was sitting in the chair beside my bed, balancing his laptop on his leg. He glanced up, his eyes softening when he saw me staring back.

"Hey," he said, closing the lid and setting his computer on the nightstand as he stood.

"Hey, yourself," I said groggily. "You look all legit with your laptop."

He chuckled. "I don't keep my books in old ledgers you know."

"What about spiral notebooks?" I asked.

"Try QuickBooks."

"Hey, me too," I said, forcing my eyes to stay open. "Did you get in trouble with the state police?" While Carter has assured me that wasn't the case, I wanted to hear it from Skeeter himself.

"I'm just fine," he said softly. "Don't you be worryin' about me."

"Carter said they're gonna be watchin' you."

"Which was part of the reason I was on my laptop. I already told you the above-board businesses have been outperforming the under-the-table ones, especially with all the turmoil the last few months. Jed and I are going to make a bigger push on the ones approved by Uncle Sam."

"So you'd give up bein' king?"

"No." He paused. "Remember when I told you someone has to be in charge, and I'm a better alternative than a lot of men? I still believe that to be true. Things are too shaky for me to just abdicate. So I'll do as much as I can legit and work on keepin' the peace in the underworld."

"Sounds like you're doin' something selfless, James Malcolm," I teased.

"God, no," he said in disgust. "Say that in public, and I'll call you a dirty liar."

"I suppose I owe you another six months," I said, turning serious. "For savin' Mason's life."

He lifted a shoulder and grimaced. "That was a freebie."

"You were right," I said, fighting to keep my eyes open. "When you told J.R. you had changed. You have. You care about people."

He leaned over and tenderly kissed a spot on my forehead. "That was all you, Rose."

I grinned. "I might have pointed a thing or two out to you, but the rest was all you."

He quickly changed the subject, then called Jed to bring us hamburgers and fries. Jed and Neely Kate ate with us, and I managed to keep down a few fries.

The room was dark when I awoke, but Jonah was dozing in the chair beside me. A tablet and his bible sat on the nightstand—he'd clearing been working on his sermon.

I watched him sleep for a few minutes, not wanting to disturb him, but once again, I realized how lucky I was to be blessed. My entire life, I'd struggled with being alone. Now my cup overflowed with friends.

I fell back asleep, surprised to find myself alone when I woke up again. To my surprise, I was also hungry. Sunlight streamed in through the window. I pushed the button to call for the nurse.

When Neely Kate showed up, she was happy to see the nurse had removed my IV and that I'd had few bites of toast and Jell-O.

"She said I could go home in a few hours. After the doctor makes rounds."

"That's good news," she said. "Muffy is stayin' with your brother-in-law. We can pick her up on the way."

"I want to see Mason."

Neely Kate studied me for a moment, then nodded. "Fine, but you have to ride in a wheelchair this time. Jed's not here to carry you back."

My head felt better, but I nodded in acceptance. I wasn't sure how strong I'd be coming back. I had a feeling the guilt from seeing him would tear me apart.

She procured a chair, then pushed me toward the elevator, chattering on and on like a magpie. I didn't pay attention to a word she said, but I was grateful to her nonetheless. The silence would have strained us both.

Once we reached Mason's room—thankfully a regular room—Neely Kate pushed my chair aside and knocked on the door. Maeve answered, looking exhausted and thinner than I'd ever seen her.

"Rose," she said, smiling. "You are just what the doctor ordered. Mason's been asking about you nonstop. I wouldn't have put it past him to crawl down the hall to see you. But it felt wrong to ask you to come."

"Rose has been the same way," Neely Kate groaned. "I had to force her to use a wheelchair to come down here."

"How's he doin'?" I asked, twisting my hands in my lap.

Maeve's smile fell. "He's sleeping right now. He's been in a lot of pain, and his spirits are low, but I think you'll be a good cure for that."

I nodded. I hoped so.

Neely Kate pushed me into the room and next to his bed. He was connected to various tubes and monitors, and like Maeve had said, he was sleeping.

Tears filled my eyes as I took in his pale face. He'd gotten shot because of me.

But then his eyes fluttered open. He smiled when he saw me, and some of my worries faded.

Neely Kate leaned toward my ear. "Maeve and I are going to get a cup of coffee. Press the call button if you need a nurse."

"Okay."

As soon as they left the room, I stood, pushing the wheelchair a few feet away.

"Rose," he said, sounding hoarse. "You shouldn't—"

"Hush," I said, taking his hand in mine. "I'm only in that thing because it was the easiest way to get Neely Kate on board with comin' to see you."

He looked up at me, worry in his eyes. "You're okay?"

"I'm fine. A concussion and some broken ribs. I'll survive."

"Your face . . ."

I grimaced, then flinched from the pain. "Everyone keeps telling me how bad it looks, but Neely Kate has shrouded the mirror. She even makes me eat my Jell-O with a plastic spoon so I didn't accidently see myself."

He squeezed my hand. "You're beautiful."

My heart melted. I loved this man something fierce, but I couldn't ignore my unsettled feeling. "You saved me, Mason. And then you almost died. Because of me."

"Sweetheart," he said, searching my face. "I love you. I would do anything to protect you."

I nodded, tears filling my eyes. "Me too."

He smiled. "I know. You've proved that time and time again. Only, I was too stupid to acknowledge it."

"Mason, no."

"Rose." He waited. "In some ways, I've treated you no better than Joe did."

"That's not true!"

"It is. We both know it's true." He paused. "I've never known anyone like you."

I cringed. "I think that was a compliment."

He chuckled, then tensed with pain. "The highest of compliments." He looked down at our clasped hands and stroked the back of my knuckles with his thumb. "Sometimes I forget how young you are."

My chest constricted, sending pain through my broken ribs. "What does that mean?" I asked, my voice sounding strangled. "I'm twenty-five years old, Mason. I'm hardly a child."

His gaze lifted to mine. "But you were until last year when your mother died. You'd lived such a sheltered life. And then, like a butterfly, you were set free." His eyes glistened. "But Joe held you back. We both know it, and I think Joe knows it, too, when he lets himself acknowledge it."

I shook my head, ignoring the pain that shot through it. "What are you saying, Mason?"

"I'm saying you've only really been free for eight months, and during that time you've been in two serious relationships. You've never had the chance to find out who you *really* are."

I started to cry. "That's the biggest load of dog crap I've ever heard, Mason Deveraux. I know exactly who I am."

"I think I've known it for a month or so, maybe even since our pregnancy scare. I would have married you in a heartbeat. I'd marry you right now without a single regret. But I never stopped to ask myself if *you* were ready."

"Then why don't you ask me, Mason?" I said, getting angry. "I love you—" My voice broke. "I risked everything to save you. How can you doubt me?"

"Oh, Rose. Sweetheart." He lifted his hand to the back of my head. "I have never once doubted that you love me. When you love, you love with your whole heart. You glow with it. I know how blessed I am to have that."

"Then what are you saying?"

"I'm saying I'm holding you back."

"No."

"*Yes.* Tell me the truth. Over the last two days, how many times have you thought of me or wanted to talk to me?"

I sucked in a breath, sending daggers into my side. "That's not fair."

"No, it's not. I haven't been fair to you," he said. "I'm thirty-three years old. I've had my fun, but now I'm ready to settle down. I'm ready for a family."

"And so am I."

He shook his head. "*No*, you're just starting to live your life. You need to experience it before you can settle down. You may be twenty-five, but you haven't had a chance to experience a full life like most twenty-five-year-olds have. I don't want to steal that from you. I don't want you to resent me for it later."

"How can you say that?"

"You found it liberating to do what you needed to do without checking in with me," he said softly. "Look deep inside and tell me I'm wrong."

I didn't have to look too deep.

"I think I fully realized it yesterday, as I worried myself sick over you. When I saw you in the stairwell, I knew you didn't need me like I need you."

My chest hurt. "That's not fair, Mason."

"It's not a criticism of you," he said softly. "It's only a sign that you're not ready. You still have living to do." When I didn't answer, he said, "When you broke up with me, I panicked. It made me realize something. Besides my job, I've made you my whole world, but you have so much more."

A lump filled my throat as tears rolled down my face.

"I realize I probably need more in my life, too."

"You're leaving me," I choked out. "Because of the Lady in Black. Because of my association with Skeeter."

"No, but it brings up a good point. Jed Carlisle is your friend"—he squeezed my hand when I started to protest—"I know there's nothing between you. He cares for you as a friend. But we both know that Jed—*and* Skeeter—have a reputation. A reputation that could hurt me with your association with them."

"You want me to not be friends with them?"

"No, Rose. The opposite. You have no idea how relieved I've been knowing Jed was watching over you when I wasn't there. That he shows up as your bodyguard when you put yourself into dangerous situations." He gave me a sad smile. "And yes, you *will* find yourself in one again. You can't help it. They find you. But I want to know you're as protected as possible. And that means having Jed Carlisle there to watch over you."

"And Skeeter."

His eyes darkened. "And Skeeter Malcolm."

"There's nothing between us, Mason. I would *never* cheat on you."

"Sweetheart, you are the *last* person I would think capable of cheating."

"Then what?" I asked.

"He loves you, Rose. You have to know that."

"He's never made an advance."

A wry smile lifted his mouth. "Which only proves my point." He shook his head. "I'm off track here. The point is they are your friends—*loyal friends*—who could hurt my reputation and career if it became known that you're friends with them. And you're right, I love what I do. I love seeking justice . . . on the right side of the law. I'm not ready to give it up. Your friendships could end my career."

"You want me to choose."

"No. I don't want you to be forced to choose at all. I'm choosing for both of us. I'm making the choice to end us before we hate each other for things we're not ready to change."

"You're breaking up with me," I said in disbelief. How was this happening? But I had to acknowledge that he was saying everything Neely Kate, and Jonah had already said. He was confirming things I'd told myself. Deep in my gut, I knew he was right, but my heart refused to accept this. Why couldn't love be enough?

Tears filled his eyes. "My hope is that I can give you time. Time to live your life without having to answer to someone else. And my hope—" His voice broke. "My hope is that someday you'll still want me. That this isn't goodbye forever. I'm fully aware that you might end up with someone else, but it's a risk I need to take."

"I love you, Mason. I don't want to be with someone else. I don't want this to be the end of us." But he was right. His life and mine were at odds that could destroy his career.

He pulled my lips to his and gave me a gentle kiss. "I'm not calling it an end. I'm hoping it's an interlude. I still want to spend the rest of my life with you, Rose. We love each other so much, but sometimes love just isn't enough." A sad smile covered his face. "Maybe it's a matter of timing. When you're ready to settle down, maybe I'll be ready to give up working as a district attorney and have more time for you and a family. Maybe we'll work then."

He loved me. There had to be a way to work this out.

"But we can't stay away from each other. This will never work," I said softly. "The other day was proof of that. I broke up with you, but we couldn't stay away." Would my inability to stay away from Mason destroy him? Would he hate me for it? I couldn't bear the thought of that either.

"I know. Which is why I called the attorney general after I left you in the stairwell and accepted the job he'd offered me in Little Rock."

I took a step backward, bumping into a chair. "You did *what*? Without talking to me first?"

He looked heartbroken. "I knew I needed to give us space."

"When?" I choked out.

"I was supposed to start at the first of the month, but losing half my liver has put a damper on that." He grimaced. "I'll go as soon as I can make it happen. But I have a favor to ask of you, even though I have no right."

I nodded, trying to hold by my tears. While I knew this was probably the right decision, my heart was being ripped apart. "What?"

"Will you look out for my mother? She loves it here, and she's made so many friends. But sometimes she gives too much. Just make sure she takes care of herself."

"Of course. I love Maeve."

"She loves you, too."

We were silent for an unbearable moment.

"So that's it?" I asked, crying again. "I'm supposed to just walk out and say goodbye?" How did I walk away from the man I'd planned to spend the rest of my life with?

"Not goodbye, Rose. I hope it's not goodbye."

I wanted to hate him for breaking my heart. But there was no denying the truth in what he was saying. I *had* felt free over the last week. I *would* destroy his career. We would resent each other.

I would rather let us go now while we still loved each other than later, when we would surely be at odds and be filled with hate and resentment.

Because I loved him. I loved him more than I'd ever loved anyone before. But he was right.

Sometimes love wasn't enough.

No.

That wasn't true. Love *was* enough.

Sometimes it was the only thing that gave us the strength to do what needed to be done.

Chapter Thirty-Five

I sat on the front porch of my farmhouse, covered in a thick blanket while I watched Muffy play in the yard. I was making a slower recovery than the doctor had expected, so he still hadn't cleared me to go back to work, even after a couple of weeks. I didn't tell him that he didn't have a medicine to cure my true ailment.

I knew from experience that only time could heal a broken heart.

Mason had been released from the hospital a few days before. I hadn't told anyone about our official breakup—and I was pretty sure he hadn't talked about it either—but we'd been apart for a week before the factory fire, so no one really asked.

But Neely Kate knew without me even telling her.

The front door opened, and Neely Kate walked onto the porch. Plopping down in the chair beside me, she said, "It's supposed to warm up tomorrow."

"Really?" I asked.

"Maybe we can go to the Tibeau job site and you can tell me what to do. It's a small one. I think I can handle it." She looked over and grinned. "You can bring a chair and look like the queen of Henryetta bossin' your subjects around. I'll even get you a tiara."

I chuckled. "You hate people bossin' you around."

"I might make an exception in this one instance." She stood and pulled me to my feet. "Enough mopin'. We're having a girls' night out. Dressin' up and everything."

I laughed. "You just want to have a reason to wear that new dress you ordered online."

She propped a hand on her hip. "And what's wrong with that?"

I instinctively touched my face. The swelling had gone down, but bruises still lingered. Neely Kate had experimented on me with makeup the day before and declared me ready for public. "Nothing. Just making an observation."

"Come on. I'll do your hair."

I wasn't sure whether to be excited or scared. The last time she'd fixed my hair, it ended up looking like a family of robins had made it their home.

But an hour later, Neely Kate and I were dressed to the nines—wearing dresses and heels, with makeup and styled hair that I'd approved. We walked into Jaspers and were led to a table for two.

Over the course of our dinner, I felt my heart begin to lighten a bit. That heavy gray cloud began to lift.

We were eating dessert when Neely Kate's eyebrows lifted. "That's Martha Peabody."

"Oh?"

The small forty-something woman looked to be on her way to the restroom, but Neely Kate motioned her over. Martha changed course and sat down in the chair between us.

"Hey, Neely Kate," she said, looking us over. "Don't you two look nice tonight!"

I smiled.

"I heard about Gunther," Neely Kate said, uncharacteristically ignoring the compliment. She usually milked them for all they were worth or at the very least acknowledged them. "Have you found out where he went?"

"No, but he's been gone a week now. He just up and disappeared."

My ears perked up. "Did you call the police?"

"Of course I called the police, but that Officer Ernie is a buffoon. He refuses to do a thing."

"Has Gunther run off before?" I asked, irritated by this evidence of the continued incompetence of the Henryetta Police Department.

Martha laughed. "I should hope not. Gunther doesn't have legs."

"He's a double amputee?" I asked in confusion.

Martha laughed. "No, he's a garden gnome. But he's very special. I won him as the prize of a gardening contest two years ago. You know, my neighbor Trinnie has been so jealous of me winning him. I'm certain she had something to do with it."

"Sounds like you could use some help recovering Gunther," Neely Kate said to Martha, though she gazed at me pointedly. "I'm surprised you haven't gotten more tips with the *five-hundred-dollar* reward."

My eyes widened. That could help pay the upcoming rent. The business was still cash poor, and things were tighter than ever now that Mason no longer lived with me and helping with the bills.

Five hundred dollars . . .

Neely Kate shot me a grin. "Martha, you don't just need tips. You need someone to do a proper investigation."

"Where on earth would I find someone like that?"

"I bet we could help you. Right, Rose?"

What was Neely Kate thinking? Sure, we'd solved some mysteries before, but truth be told, I'd stumbled into most of them. This would be our first *case*.

It was on the tip of my tongue to say no. I still wasn't feeling one hundred percent, and despite our previous success rate, I wasn't so sure we could help this woman.

But I couldn't deny the excitement bubbling up in my chest, the anticipation of looking for clues. If we were going to start taking cases like Neely Kate really wanted, it would probably be good to start off small.

"Martha?" a woman called from the bar. "Are you coming?"

"I'll be right there." Martha gave me an apologetic smile. "Sorry about that. The girls in probate always come here on Thursday nights for margarita night."

I cocked my head, starting to smell a rat. "And Neely Kate knows about this?"

"Of course," Martha said. "She's the one who started the whole thing a few years back." She patted Neely Kate's arm. "You should start coming again. We don't care if you don't work at the courthouse anymore."

Neely Kate had set up this entire *accidental* encounter—not that it surprised me.

"I'll see what I'm doin' next week," Neely Kate said, then leaned forward. "Now about Gunther . . ."

Martha turned to me. "Do you think you really might be able to get Gunther back?"

I wiped a tear from the corner of my eye. Maybe I could do this. Maybe I could be okay.

It would start with finding a garden gnome. All I had to do was say yes.

"Rose?" Neely Kate prodded.

I turned to Martha and smiled. "Now what can you tell us about the day Gunther disappeared?"

Family Jewels (Rose Gardner Investigations #1)
November 29. 2016
Read the first chapter now—after my letter.

Letter to my Readers,

I hadn't planned to write acknowledgments for this book—I haven't with my past several books—but this book seems to monumental to let slip by.

This series was born in the Lee's Summit, Missouri DMV back in June 2010. Had I known then how many people would read and love the Rose Gardner Mystery series, I probably would have fainted dead away like Rose did in the first chapter of *Twenty-Eight*. (Okay, not really, but I probably would have stumbled a bit.) I'm always astounded that NO ONE in the traditional publishing world wanted that first book. But my beta reads LOVED Rose, so I took a chance and self-published *Twenty-Eight and a Half Wishes* in July 2011.

I'm sure most readers don't know that I almost gave up on this series. I released *Thirty and a Half Excuses* in September 2013 with lackluster sales. As an indie publisher, I had to look at the hard facts—my urban fantasy series was selling better. I either needed to figure out how to find more readers or focus on urban fantasy. The series had fantastic reviews, which told me the issue was discoverability. Readers just needed to find her.

I'm so happy I didn't give up.

This series has always had the support of Trisha Leigh/Lyla Payne. We've been critique partners and best friends since 2010, after we "met" on Twitter. She critiqued the first book and has helped me brainstorm that book as well as the rest. When I finished the revision of this book—which I finished at Starbucks—I texted her that I had to leave because I couldn't stop tearing up. She called me as I drove home, consoling my broken heart, as I literally broke down and cried.

Not only did Rose lose the love of her life, but I felt like I'd lost mine too.

I went home and emailed Angela Polidoro, my developmental editor, who has edited the series since *Thirty and a Half Excuses*. I told her I wasn't sure if it was my emotions speaking, but I had to wonder if I should end the series with this book. The ending seemed TOO perfect. Maybe I needed to let love make me strong enough to let Rose go.

Angela's answer: "Rose's story isn't over yet."

Have I mentioned how much I love Angela?

So I gave myself a day and the next two titles for the new series, as well as a plot for *Family Jewels* popped into my head. (I hope you read the first chapter.) After I grieved (that seems the best description of how I felt) I was ready to consider the new series.

I hope you'll consider it too.

But if you don't, I understand. I hope you've enjoyed the journey as much as I have. I realize that there are more than three million eBooks available to read, and yet you chose mine. That is NEVER lost on me.

Thank you for inviting me into your eReaders, into your lives, and hopefully into your hearts.

Family Jewels

Chapter One

The dark clouds on the horizon were my first clue it was going to be a bad day.

June thunderstorms were a common occurrence in southern Arkansas, and truth be told, we needed the rain. But I also needed to get six azalea bushes into the ground by five p.m., or I was not only going to lose the cost of the bushes but the labor too.

"You think we're gonna get it done?" Neely Kate, my best friend, roommate, and co-worker asked as she cast a nervous glance to the west.

"If we don't, Mr. Hodges is gonna throw a conniption."

"Thank you, Marci," Neely Kate grumbled about our ex-employee as she dug her shovel deeper into the dirt.

Business was booming at RBW Landscaping, enough so that my business partner, Bruce Wayne Decker, and I had been forced to hire several new employees. One of them, Neely Kate's cousin, Marci, had been tasked with staying in the office to talk to the clients. Her first—and last—day had been yesterday, and the amount of damage she'd done was impressive. Without any prompting, she'd told Mr. Hodges he'd get a one hundred percent refund if we didn't have his bushes planted before five today. Apparently Marci was obsessed with *Plant or Die*, a new reality TV show in which landscapers had twenty-four hours to complete their project or be eliminated. She'd hoped to get on the show by making a series of outrageous self-imposed gardening challenges on camera. Or so she'd explained to us.

"What in tarnation are you talkin' about?" Neely Kate had asked her cousin in horror.

"I *really* need that five thousand dollars prize money," Marci had said. "I want to go to beauty school, and I need the money for my tuition."

"Five thousand dollars?" I'd asked, suddenly wondering how we could get an audition for real.

Marci's eyes had widened as she turned to her cousin. "*Of course* I was gonna share the money with you and Rowena."

"Rose," Neely Kate said.

Shaking her head, Marci said, "No. Azalea bushes. Not roses."

Neely Kate looked like she was about to say something, then closed her mouth.

Marci took that as encouragement. "I only need thirty-five hundred dollars. You two can split the left over three thousand."

"Fifteen hundred," Neely Kate said, looking like she wanted to strangle her cousin.

Marci's eyes squinted in concentration. "No...I'm pretty sure the lady said the tuition was thirty-five hundred."

"*Marci.*" Neely Kate groaned. "Five thousand minus thirty-five hundred is only fifteen hundred. Not three thousand."

Marci looked confused. "Are you sure?" Then she waved her hand. "What am I askin'? You were the math genius in the family, with your D-minus in Algebra and all."

Neely Kate ignored the compliment to her math skills. "And you think it's fair that you should get the majority of the money from the show? On your first day?"

Marci blinked, the expression on her face showing just how ridiculous she considered Neely Kate's question. "Well, yeah... I really *need* it. And besides, I'm the one who's auditioning."

"How on earth do you figure that?" Neely Kate shouted. "Where are the cameras, for Pete's sake?"

Marci pointed up at the ceiling. "Up there."

I glanced up just as Neely Kate groaned.

"*Marci*," Neely Kate forced through gritted teeth. "That's a sprinkler head."

"Oh." She laughed. "Silly me."

The very next thing Neely Kate had done was fire her.

In the end it didn't matter why the promise to plant the azaleas had been made, all that mattered was that we were going to live up to it. Bruce Wayne had his own planting crew of two men and they were working on a tight deadline at a commercial office site. He couldn't afford to send anyone over to help, so Neely Kate and I had put our design and estimate jobs on hold to get this project done up close and personal.

And now Mother Nature was conspiring against us.

"We can do it, Rose," Neely Kate said with her characteristic optimism and perkiness. "Besides, what's a little rain? We won't melt."

As if to taunt us, a large bolt of lightning filled the sky and thunder shook the ground just as rain started to fall in fat drops.

Resisting the urge to groan, I moved the bushes closer to the fifty-year-old house and laid a bag of our premixed fertilizer/potting soil in front of the containers to keep them from blowing away. Neely Kate quickly began to help. We finished arranging them just as another bolt of lightning struck, the thunderous boom sooner than the last one.

"That was too close," I said. "Let's go."

We put the shovels into the back of my RBW Landscaping truck, then climbed into the pickup, shivering in our semi-drenched clothes.

"We're not givin' up, are we?" Neely Kate asked, incredulous. But her tone also held a hint of guilt. She was the one who'd insisted on hiring Marci despite the foreboding fact that the girl couldn't fill in the address of the house where she'd lived for the last eighteen years with her parents on her job application. Not to mention the way she'd filled in the "Date of last job" blank with "last night with Bobby Hixler," mistaking the word "job" for something else entirely.

Being the bigger person, I'd held back my told-you-sos.

I was polishing those up for when I might need them later.

"Of course we're not giving up." I turned the key and the truck engine started, hitting us with a blast of cold air that made me shiver.

Neely Kate fumbled with the air conditioning knobs to turn off the air as I pulled away from the curb.

"We can come back when it blows over," Neely Kate said. She flipped down the visor and looked in the mirror as she took her long blonde hair out of the messy bun she'd put it up in before we started digging. She gave it a fluff, then ran a finger under her eye to wipe away a mascara smudge. While Neely Kate had learned a lot about the landscaping business since I'd hired her at the first of the year, digging in the dirt was one of the few jobs she detested and avoided at all costs. "There's a reason I moved away from a farm, Rose," she'd say, wrinkling her nose. "To get away from dirt and cow manure."

I sighed. "Let's get some coffee and look at how we can shuffle our schedule around and still get everything done. We're also supposed to plant those begonias and then get an estimate to the Hendersons by five." *Thank you, Marci.*

Neely Kate snatched her pink sparkly purse from the floor board, then removed a tube of concealer and placed dots under her eyes. "You want to go by the office?"

"Yeah. But I want to check on Muffy first."

"Afterward, why don't we stop by the new coffee shop? I hear it makes a great white mocha."

I wasn't sure a town the size of Henryetta could accommodate two coffee shops, but so far The Daily Grind had attracted a flock of courthouse employees and city police, as well as foot traffic from the downtown shoppers and store owners. It helped that they carried pastries from Dena's Bakery, the best thing to hit Henryetta in five years. Besides, The Daily Grind's competition was on the edge of town, close to a newer neighborhood and a condo complex. Those residents tended to avoid downtown anyway.

I parked in front of our office and grabbed an umbrella from under my seat.

She held out the lip gloss. "Here. You need this."

I gave her a hard look. "Why would I put on lip gloss to get coffee?"

Neely Kate groaned. "Rose..." She dragged my name out like it pained her to do so. "You'll never find a man if you don't start putting more effort into your appearance."

I laughed. "You think lip gloss is going to make me look better?" I knew what I looked like—no makeup, muddy jeans, my dark hair up in a ponytail. "And besides, it's ridiculous to put on makeup when I'll just sweat it off in ten minutes."

I could see my dog Muffy in the window jumping up on the glass in her excitement. She weighed about eight pounds, but that didn't stop her from trying to break through. I hated leaving her alone out at my farm, so I brought her to work most days and even to job sites. Neely Kate and Bruce Wayne had dubbed Muffy RBW Landscaping's mascot, and lately, Neely Kate had begun shopping for dog costumes online. She was wearing one now—something that made her look like she'd been attacked by a giant white daisy. That alone could have been the reason she looked so frantic. Or maybe she was freaked out by the storm, the reason I'd left her behind.

But one look inside the window told me the real source of her distress.

"Neely Kate, I thought you fired Marci."

"What are you talkin' about?" she asked, digging in her purse. "I did."

"Then what is she doing in our office?"

"What?" Neely Kate screeched, leaning forward to peer inside the windows. "I fired her. You heard me."

"Well, she's in there now. Let's go find out why," I said as I hopped out of the truck.

Neely Kate followed me. I opened the previously locked office door, and Neely Kate slammed into my back when I came to an abrupt halt.

Muffy stood on her back legs and her front paws scratched frantically at my legs.

I gasped as I bent down to scoop her up. "What in the Sam Hill…"

Files and papers were scattered everywhere—the floors, the chairs, and the desks. Not one inch had been left uncovered. And in the middle of the chaos stood a woman with long blonde hair, cut-off jeans shorts, and a lavender-colored tank top.

She spun around to face us and a frown tugged on her lips. "You just ruined the surprise."

"That a tornado came through?" I asked in dismay.

She laughed. "Don't be silly, Rowena. I'm redoing your filing system."

"But Neely Kate *fired* you," I said.

She waved her hand and rolled her eyes. "She was always such a kidder."

"I wasn't kidding!" Neely Kate's voice rose as she stepped around me. Her foot slipped on a folder, and I grabbed her arm to keep her from falling on her booty. "What else did you do?" Neely Kate asked.

Marci put a hand on her hips and gave us an impressive pout. "I was only trying to help."

"I told you that you are not auditioning for *Plant or Die*!"

Marci lifted her chin and gave Neely Kate a defiant look. "That wasn't it. It was something else entirely."

"What was it?"

"It's something you love to do anyway," Marci said with attitude. "You've said so a million times."

Neely Kate put her hands on her hips. "What TV show did you think you were on this time?"

"Not me," she said. "You." Then she pointed to me. "And Rowena."

"Her name is Rose!" Neely Kate shouted. "Who doesn't get their own boss's name right?"

"Are you sure it's Rose?" Marci asked, giving me the once over.

"Yeah," Neely Kate said. "I think I'd know since she's my best friend. Now, what did you promise?"

"That poor man needed help. He was desperate."

"What man?" Neely Kate asked.

"Radcliffe Dyer. His grandmother's jewelry is missing."

A shiver ran down my spine, but Neely Kate perked up. "Why did he come by here?"

"He heard that you and Rowena were good at finding things."

"Rose," I said with a sigh.

Marci shook her head. "He's not looking for roses. It was jewelry."

Tipping her head back, Neely Kate released a loud groan. "What did he say, Marci?"

"He said 'I need to talk to the two girls who work here,' and I said, 'Well, you're lookin' at one of 'em.'"

I gave Neely Kate an exasperated look. Had we really let this girl represent our business for ten hours?

"Why did he want the two girls who worked here?" Neely Kate asked.

"He said—" Marci's voice lowered into a deep bass "—'I need them girls to find my grandmammie's jewelry for me. My ex-wife has something to do with 'em going missing and I want to get to the bottom of it.'"

Neely Kate put a hand on her hip again and waited. When Marci didn't continue, she asked, "What else did he say?"

"He said—" she lowered her voice again "—'Sorry to hear about your yellow dress. When do you think they'll be back?'"

Neely Kate turned back to me. "She obviously left out what she said to him, but I'm scared to ask what it was."

"Agreed."

Neely Kate turned back to her. "What did he say when you told him when we'd be back?"

"Oh, I told him I had no idea when that would be. So he gave me his number..." She spun in a circle, scanning the room. "Now where did I put it...?"

"Never mind," Neely Kate said. "I know where to find Raddy. Now tell me why all those files are spread everywhere."

"Oh!" Marci said, clapping her hands. "I was reorganizing your filing system."

"By spreading them out on every horizontal surface?" Neely Kate demanded.

"I just set out the files," she said defensively, then waved to Muffy. "That overgrown daisy was the one to mess 'em all up."

Muffy let out a low growl. I stroked her head to quiet her.

Neely Kate shook her head. "You were fired, Marci. *Fired.* I fired you *yesterday.* Now get your purse and get out of here. Now!"

Marcie looked offended. "Does that mean I'm not getting my thirty-five hundred dollars?"

"You'll be damn lucky to get the seventy dollars we owe you for yesterday." When Marci started to protest, Neely Kate held up her hand. "And if you think we're paying you for creatin' this mess today you're plum crazy. Now get out of here!"

Marci grabbed her purse and marched the walk of shame to the front door, nearly slipping a couple of times. When she passed us, she held up her head and kept her eyes on the door like she was Anne Boleyn marching to her beheading.

When the door closed, Neely Kate said, "Rose... I had no idea."

Looking at the mess made me exhausted, and we hadn't even started to clean it up yet. "We don't have time to pick this up, but we can't leave it like this either." I set Muffy down, then grabbed my phone out of my pocket and called the nursery I co-owned with my sister. Violet was in Texas, recovering from her bone marrow transplant, but we'd found the perfect person to fill in until she came back. Maeve Deveraux answered on the third ring.

"Gardner Sisters Nursery, Maeve speaking. How can I help you?"

Hearing her cheery voice helped ease some of the tension in my back. "Maeve, I was wondering if I could borrow Anna for a bit. Are you too busy to turn her loose?"

"Of course I can spare her, Rose. But she's really not dressed to be digging."

"I actually need her in the office." Then I filled her in on the details.

"Oh, dear. I'll send her over right away." Then she paused and lowered her voice. "I haven't talked to you in over a week. How are you doing?"

"I'm great. Good." And I was. Mostly. My ex-boyfriend Mason—Maeve's son—and I had broken up four months ago, and he'd moved back to Little Rock. My heart had been broken, but I'd moved on. Mostly. Even if I still refused to consider dating anyone, much to Neely Kate's dismay. "How about you?"

It was no secret Maeve had moved from Little Rock to tiny Henryetta to be closer to her only living child. She'd been lonely and eager to feel wanted and needed again. But she'd found a place for herself here, and despite Mason's decision to leave, she'd stayed. Still, I knew she missed her son something fierce.

I'd kept my distance, mostly out of guilt. I couldn't help wondering if she secretly blamed me for him leaving.

"Good. I'm excited about Violet coming back." But I heard the wistful tone in her voice.

While her position had only been temporary, she'd been working full-time for the past four months and seemed to love every minute of it. "You know, Violet won't be back to one hundred percent," I said. "It occurs to me that we'll still need help. Would you be willing to stay on part-time?"

"Of course. I'd love to."

It warmed my heart to make her happy. Maeve had been like the mother I'd always wanted. I missed her. "Well, then that's settled. You're an official permanent employee at Gardner Sisters Nursery."

"I'll send Anna right over. And Rose...thank you."

"No, thank *you*. I have no idea what we would have done without you these last four months." I hung up and stuffed my phone back into my pocket. "Anna's on her way."

"Well, now that this is taken care of..." Neely Kate said, brushing off her hands. "Let's go talk to Raddy Dyer."

I held up my hand, blocking the exit. "Hold up. We're not going anywhere just yet."

"But Anna's coming to clean up, which means we can go."

I narrowed my eyes.

"I'm really sorry about Marci," Neely Kate said with a sigh.

"Everyone deserves a chance. I'm sorry if you're in trouble with your aunt for firing her." It was hard to hold this against my best friend. I'd met her aunt. I probably would have hired Marci too.

She waved it off. "I might get stuck with the burnt ends of Aunt Jackie's raccoon roast next Christmas, but I'll manage."

I almost blurted out, *raccoon roast?* but I wisely kept my mouth shut. Neely Kate's family was one of a kind.

She shuffled her feet and shifted her weight before giving me a hopeful look. "I checked the weather on my phone, and it looks like the rain won't clear off until this afternoon…which means we have some time to talk to Raddy Dyer."

And there it was.

I sighed. "Neely Kate—"

"Now, before you say no, let me plead my case."

"Funny choice of words," I said, crossing my arms over my chest. "I'm listening."

Excitement filled her eyes. "You and I have solved cases before—" I started to protest, but she held up her hand, "—let me finish."

"Okay."

"I know we accidentally stumbled into some bigger things last fall and winter, but we got out of all of them, right?"

Stumbled into some bigger things was an understatement. But she was right. We'd uncovered who had been behind my kidnapping attempt, what had happened to her missing cousin, and who had tried to steal the throne of the king of Fenton County's underworld. And every single instance had been dangerous. After last February, I'd vowed to leave danger behind and live a quiet life.

Only Neely Kate was bound and determined to make me live boldly.

"Neely Kate…"

She held up her hands. "You said you'd listen." When I didn't answer, she lifted her eyebrows. "Over the last four months, we've solved some mysteries that had nothin' to do with us. Not to mention they were completely harmless."

"We found a missing garden gnome, a lost dog, and figured out a dispute between two neighbors." And I couldn't deny I'd loved every minute of it.

"So why won't you consider this?" she asked in frustration.

"This is different. From what Marci said, this man thinks his ex-wife is holding his grandmother's jewelry hostage. It's not a mystery. It's a hostage negotiation. You should tell Carter Hale," I said, referring to our defense attorney friend. "It seems more like a situation for a law shark, not two landscapers."

"We're not just two landscapers. We've solved mysteries before. You've worked with the crime lord of Fenton County, for Pete's sake. Missing jewelry should be a piece of cake."

"Neely Kate…"

"Let's just talk to the guy, okay?" she asked, hope filling her eyes. "We can find out what he wants."

"He wants us to get his jewelry back. His ex-wife has it. Where's the investigation? Maybe he expects us to beat the jewelry out of her with our shovels."

"Please?" She gave me a pout, then her eyes widened. "If it makes you feel better, you can have a vision. See how the meeting goes."

She had to be really desperate to ask me that. I was capable of seeing visions, images of the future through another person's eyes when I touched them, but after everything that had happened four months ago, I avoided having them whenever possible. But now that I wasn't "forcing" them as I'd begun to do last winter, they were spontaneous again—coming out of nowhere. Seeing as how blurting out whatever I saw was part of my gift, it often put me in embarrassing situations.

Still, I had no desire to force one now.

I groaned. "Fine." When she started to get excited, I held up my hands. "We'll talk to him. *That's all*. Then you and I will talk about it and decide where to go from there."

Her head bobbed as she nodded. "Sure. Of course."

I'd seen that look before. I suspected she'd already texted Raddy Dyer and accepted the case.

My phone began to ring and I pulled it from my jeans pocket, surprised to see the initials SM—Skeeter Malcolm—on my screen. I shot Neely Kate a glance before I answered.

"James, I haven't heard from you in a while." Several weeks, to be exact.

"Lady," he said, his voice tight. "We've got a problem.

About the Author

N *ew York Times* and *USA Today* bestselling author
Denise Grover Swank was born in Kansas City, Missouri
and lived in the area until she was nineteen. Then she
became a nomadic gypsy, living in five cities, four states and ten
houses over the course of ten years before she moved back to her
roots. She speaks English and smattering of Spanish and Chinese
which she learned through an intensive Nick Jr. immersion
period. Her hobbies include witty Facebook comments (in her own
mind) and dancing in her kitchen with her children. (Quite badly if
you believe her offspring.) Hidden talents include the gift of
justification and the ability to drink massive amounts of caffeine and
still fall asleep within two minutes. Her lack of the sense of smell
allows her to perform many unspeakable tasks. She has six children
and hasn't lost her sanity. Or so she leads you to believe.

You can find out more about Denise and her other books at
www.denisegroverswank.com

Don't miss out on Denise's newest releases! Join her mailing
list: http://denisegroverswank.com/mailing-list/

CPSIA information can be obtained
at www.ICGtesting.com
Printed in the USA
LVOW01s1919220616
493671LV00020B/1096/P